Rock 'n' Roll Heretic

Rock 'n' Roll Heretic

The Life and Times of Rory Tharpe

A Novel

Sikivu Hutchinson

INFIDEL BOOKS
Los Angeles, CA

Published 2021 by Infidel Books

ISBN: 978-0-578-85236-2
Library of Congress 202-19-02411

Cover design by Alan Bell

Contents

Part One

HEAVY METAL

Highway 17

COLD, DANK, AND BURIED to hell with slanting rain was the forecast they'd heard on all the news stations that afternoon. The coach bus rutted forward, sagged backward, helplessly mired in the sinkhole rot of Highway 17, bracing itself for more jackhammer tears of the apocalypse.

Rory cursed out a prayer then restrained herself.

"Dammit, get the defroster on," she said to Mick, the driver.

"Sure thing, chief. Anything else you need?"

"Coffee. Lots."

He rustled out a thermos from his pocket and gave it to her.

She swigged, grimacing. "Black sewer water. I can't drink this crap straight up."

"Non-negotiable."

"Fuck me."

The gig was two hours away. A special nine at night consolation slot dredged up for them in limp hocus pocus by their manager Russ, a guttersnipe who could spin a dried-up cotton ball into a buck. They'd be the back-up band for a beer jingle produced by Harlan Carruthers; sloth-eyed, maggot white, ever ready with a court jester grin, lugging around a 24-7 mini dental kit for his oral afflictions.

"Always dug your stuff, Rory. All those funky licks of yours," Harlan said when they were negotiating. "But, like, I got zero musical ear on my own, man. I could only do the simplest Chopsticks kinda shit on the piano."

"How much, Harlan?" she asked.

He twisted his mouth, a yellow fang peeking from between his pimpled lips. "Five-hundred all cash."

"What—"

"Five-fifty then… I gotta get this thing in the can, Rory. You all are my last hope."

"Six-hundred."

"Five-seventy-five."

"Grand larceny."

"That's the best I can do, Rory. The skinflints are riding me, squeezing me for every penny I got for the recording time at this fucking shit-can studio. Promise though, once I get this together, there'll be plenty more sessions where this came from. Swear on a stack of Gideons."

That's how she'd negotiated up from a little more than chicken feed. After the gas costs for the bus, after the 2-for-1 blue plate special botulism they ate every night, after the group smokes and the medicinal stash of booze they'd put in the trunk, after the last dregs of the fee had been divvied up among the band, it would come out to a grand total of $54.60 for her.

At the wheel, staring into the gray muck of the evening, Mick muttered through his usual litany. "Wish I'd learned to play properly, read music, practiced and shit, gotten beyond the washed-up-never-was bass guitarist with the busted hand."

Piddling gigs stretched from week to week, never ending. Checks dribbled in. Bill payments rocketed out. And how was she supposed to weather all of it; stay awake, stay present, keep on her feet, beat back the round midnight demons running scrimmage in her head and balance the "company" budget? Make sure all the scamps on the bus, all the men who depended on her were warm, washed, fed, and at their fighting weight for the next bout?

"Shut the fuck up, Mick. Christ."

"Taking his name in vain again?" Butch, the band's keyboardist, sat up from his seat in the second row, blinking blearily through itchy contacts, blowing hot air into his hands, a dented harmonica swinging from his speckled neck. "Mick's gone and stole my fucking glasses. He don't want me to see how bad it is out there."

"Won't make it to the studio by nine," Rory said.

"If it stops pissing buckets we will," Mick replied.

Butch rubbed the harmonica on the front of his shirt. "From your lips to God's ear."

Mick scowled, eyeing the desolate trickle of cars on the opposite side of the highway. "This front's supposed to move outta here in a minute."

Butch leaned over to Rory. "I hear Harlan's paying us less than shit."

"It ain't the pay, it's the exposure."

"A few chords selling rotgut? Come on, Rory."

"Brand's big in the Midwest."

"What do we need those knuckle draggers for? I'm sick of playing pissy little holes in the wall."

"Oh gee, it's the top of the hour, Butch must be on his soap box again," Mick said.

"Keep your eyes on the road and your hands upon the wheel and just get us the fuck out of here, brother."

Mick grunted. "Not your brother, hambone, least not tonight."

The three of them stared out the windshield into the wet dark. A truck struggled into view, all white light and mud flaps, a child waving at them from the gloom of the bed. Mick perked up. "Damn, what's that kid doing out in the back like that in this kind of weather?"

They watched as the truck zigzagged, maneuvering around the hub-cap-size craters in the sodden blacktop, the sky above splitting down the middle, venting righteous bile. Rory hated rain, but had always liked the smell, basked in the clouds' coy presentiment when she was a kid learning Godzilla chords loop de loop up the neck of her first guitar, deeded to her by her grandmother. The smell of rain took her by the hand to the first time she played hard; getting her calluses, making the strings obey, doing crazy quilt pickings in REM sleep.

The truck dipped, then hydroplaned, smashing through an exit sign. Rory hopped up from her seat. She signaled Butch to stop. He clunked to the side of the road, opening the door. Rory ran into the rain, the two men tumbling out behind her.

Steam rose from the truck's hood. The driver sprawled in the front seat, his head a corona of blood blooming against the steering wheel. Butch rattled the door. "It's too busted to open," he said. He rapped on the window as Rory searched the empty truck bed then went over to the passenger's side.

"Where's the kid?"

She scanned the shoulder of the road, peering around the guardrail where the truck had crashed, the embankment below a mess of shredded tires from semis, fast food wrappers, ratty clothes, melted construction cones from a long-ago fire that had blackened the underbrush into the maw of Jupiter. Thurston, her drummer, ran out to them with a flashlight, the faded red lips of a Stones t-shirt pouting out from his scrawny white torso.

"Take this." He handed the flashlight to Rory, shaking his head at the damage to the truck. "Detroit's finest. One step below junk."

"Come on, help me!" Rory yelled. They stepped over the guardrail as Butch and Mick opened the passenger door to the truck, calling out to the injured man.

The child was twisted up under a tarp from the truck, blinking out of mud-encrusted eyes.

Thurston reached his hand out. "You ok, little man? We're gonna get you out of there."

"I'm not a man," the child croaked.

"Whatever, let's just get you out of there."

They lifted the child up from the tarp. "What's your name?" Mick asked.

"Sid."

He gestured to the truck. "That your father in there?"

"Uncle."

They helped Sid over to the truck as Mick clambered into the front seat, cringing at the blood. He shook his head at Rory. "Looks like he's fading fast."

"Christ, how're we gonna get an ambulance out into this mess and get to the session on time?"

"Can't."

Thurston bowed his head, closing his eyes in prayer. "Motherfucking Jesus, do something."

Butch grit his teeth. "The man's dying, that ain't gonna do shit. We've got to get this rattletrap piece of shit out of here, get to a phone booth or a hospital or something."

Thurston sneered at him. "What do you suggest we do, levitate it?"

Butch put his hand up to silence him. Thurston was a dumb bunny white trash runt as far as he was concerned. Never voted, never talked politics, never took his stoner beak out of his drum kit long enough to dabble in the outside world. Gorged on foot fetish porn behind the bus every time they did a pit stop, jack o' lantern hair standing straight on end as he came.

Sid watched the smashed truck impassively. Rory surveyed the child's thin, shivering body, hair kinked in dark tendrils around her closed face, a look like Rory's own, snaking back forty years ago when the world had begun to reveal itself to her, the grinning skull beneath the skin.

"Screw it," the child rasped.

"What?" Butch asked.

"Screw prayer," she said.

Rory stiffened, guiding the girl and Butch away from the wreckage. "Take her back to the bus."

Sid shook her head. "No."

"You can't stay here. You'll catch your death of cold."

"What's gonna happen to my uncle?"

"We're going to try and get him an ambulance."

They walked along the shoulder, back toward the bus. Headlights flickered from the north, washing over them. Rory waved her hands at the oncoming car. It hurtled past. "Mick, get your ass over here, next car comes by we need you to flag it down!" she yelled.

"Why him?" Sid asked.

"'Cause he's white."

Mick nodded, accepting his call of duty. "C'mon motherfuckers," he muttered into the wind, willing another car to appear on the horizon.

Rory headed back to the truck where Butch was watching over the uncle. "He's fading," Butch said. The man gurgled, lanky body crushed like an accordion, fingers bunching up around a wrapper congealed with cheese, the crumbly dust of a Jack n' the Box hamburger smeared on the seat.

Sid edged closer, eyes blank, bottomless. "Is he gonna die?"

"Hope not, sweetheart," Thurston said. "We're gonna try and do everything we can."

Headlights swept over them. Rory snapped her fingers. "Jackpot. Work your magic, Mick."

Mick waved his arms over his head at the oncoming car, a two-tone Cadillac Fleetwood, nicked hood ornament nursing the soggy remains of pink "Just Married" confetti.

A white woman wearing a cowboy hat leaned out of the window, wiping drizzle from her face. "Whoa, what the hell's going on?" She paused, squinting up at Rory. "Holy shit. You, you're that guitar lady, right? Starts with an R, right?" She squinted again, trying to remember the rest.

"Maybe," Rory said.

Starting out, the C chord is the Mississippi River and its tributaries all rolled up into one. A rough ride, but sweet if you do it just right, catch it at a decent hour, without the bend of rush hour traffic. This is what the fret vet sharecroppers told her she could do real good as a four-year-old finding her way around the guitar neck in Cotton Plant, Arkansas. Good as Looney Tunes' dynamite crackling under Wile E. Coyote's butt. Good as ice down your back on a 105-degree summer afternoon. Good as a balcony church pew battling the sleep of the dead during a boring as shit sermon.

But first, 1945.

Women dragged together in mopey two-steps at the Savoy, zeroing in on the men gathering on the sidelines to watch, swirling vodka in their shot glasses, fingers stiff from the New York cold. Rory hopped around onstage, trying to keep warm, ice blasts blowing through the door as soldiers dribbled in, tired eyes popping from the smoke and the dark. There were three women for every male. The soldiers reveled in the attention, young chests swimming with fresh stripes.

We made it out alive from Europe's carnage, double triple dare you America the Beautiful to try and beat us down.

The Savoy was the only club Rory and the band were booked at that week; pell mell days on two hours sleep and snatched rehearsal time as riots rocked upper Manhattan after a Negro man had been shot by the police. Her first time being in Harlem at the top of the bill and what the fuck did they have to go and riot for? Rory thought. The tenement walk-up her sometime agent Columbus had arranged for her to stay in was on a block that had been shut down by the police. Now she would have to kill time flopping on the city bus.

It was during these moments that her mother liked to visit her, staggering in on the Sherman-tank church heels she'd refitted with plywood soles, a wraith imitating a good, god-fearing woman when nobody was watching. Prophetess Katy, they'd called her. Or so she made them call her. *'Cause I'm just as much an oracle as any goddamned bootleg divinity school Negro,* Katy proclaimed, on her fifth shot of Jack Daniels, smacking her lips at the sorry spectacle of Rory shoehorned in the back seat of the bus, nursing the blisters on her fingers.

"Let me see," Katy said, grabbing Rory's left hand, putting it in her mouth to soothe it like she had done when Rory was just starting to learn scales. "Mother's spit has special properties. Healing agents. Medicinal gold. They'd bottle this shit and farm it out to all the doctors if they could. Don't think I'm telling the truth? Well, it brought you back from the dead, Missy."

"Mama."

"C'mon now, Boo, you know it feels good."

"Mama."

"Quit squirming. They pay you yet?"

"No, I get it after the gig."

"What did I tell you about that? Half before, half after. Cold cash. Those bastards'll try and con you right out of a nickel's pay if you let 'em."

"Right."

"Listen to me, dammit. Don't let them get over on you and catch you sleepin'. You not hungry enough, then someone else will be, that's for damn sure."

Death had emboldened Prophetess Katy.

"Stay off the sauce, baby. I know you been hitting it hard lately."

"Mama."

Katy screwed up her mouth, brushing Rory's cheek, then took her arm, holding her firm in the skeletal grip of bath time, their once-a-week evening ritual from age five to fifteen, before they went on the road permanently, and a tub became an ancient, arcane luxury.

"Steady baby, steady," Katy said.

"Mama."

"This'll rejuvenate you."

"Mama. Somebody will see."

"How can anybody see something that's all in your head, Boo?"

The paramedics scraped Sid's uncle's body off the front seat of the truck and gave him CPR. They took his vital signs. He gasped and sputtered back to semi-consciousness, moaning about chocolate waffles. The rain had stopped. Sid blinked out from under her hood, watching the scene in wet defiance.

"I don't want to go back with him."

"What?" Rory checked her watch, impatient. No way they'd be on time for the gig.

"I'm not going back with him."

"What about your home, your parents?"

"I don't have any."

Mick opened his mouth to interject. The paramedics thrust a clipboard in front of him. "We need a signature from you, sir."

Mick looked at Rory. "Actually, she's my boss. You need anything official get it from her."

Rory took the clipboard, nodding toward the busted-up Uncle. "Where're you taking him?"

"San Jose."

Thurston shook his head. "The bill on that is gonna be crazy expensive."

The paramedic shut the door of the ambulance. The driver looked through Rory, smudged glass eyes fixing on a fat dark cloud crackling toward them.

"Police'll be here in a sec. This girl in the truck at the time of the accident?"

"Yeah."

"We'll need to examine her for injuries."

"No!" Sid yelled.

"Required under state law."

The paramedic put his hand on Sid's shoulder. She wrenched away.

"Look, they just need to check you out to make sure you don't have any internal injuries or anything," Rory said.

"I'm not fucking going! There's nothing wrong with me."

The driver recoiled. "Well, don't you have a nasty little mouth on you. We'll let you deal with the police then."

Sid stared at the back of the driver's head as he walked off. "They can't force me to go."

"No, but the cops can, and you can't stay here in the middle of nowhere."

Sirens wailed in the distance. A police car rolled up and two officers jumped out, eyeing the group with droopy disdain.

"Evening, folks. We're going to need some statements about this accident." The lead white officer looked from Mick to Thurston, making eye contact with Mick, quickly assessing the pecking order of each fellow Caucasoid based on degrees of facial hair and general dishevelment, reflexively casting Rory, the Negro, Butch, the Asian, into the dung heap of his brain. Rory stood to the side with her arms crossed, too hopped up by the time the whole thing was eating up to say shit about the slight.

"Interesting that out of all of us he's the only ex-jailbird," she muttered to Butch.

Butch chortled. "Criminals… takes one to know one."

The white cop paused and glared at them over the rims of his eyeglasses. "You say something, Bruce Lee?"

"My name's Butch."

The white cop stepped forward. "Approximately how fast would you say the vehicle was going before it crashed, *Butch?*"

"No idea."

"That so? Thought you folks were human calculators."

"Naw, only calculations I know for sure is the exact cranial capacity of modern whites versus Neanderthals. Want to hear it?"

The white cop gave him a long, hard look. He waved a gnat away from his face. "Fucking vermin," he said, keeping his eyes on Butch. "Paramedics will do a toxicology test on him, make sure no drugs or alcohol were involved." He turned back to Mick. "The girl here was the only one in the truck?"

"Yeah, far as we could see. We were driving and saw when the man went out of control."

The cop nodded at Sid. "What's your name, sweetheart?"

Sid was silent, nostrils flaring instinctively in ripe disgust at the white man's octopus descent. She wanted to run, to hide, to melt into the tiny space of superhero invisibleness she'd created for herself with every rout or humiliation in the Promised Land.

"Her name's Sid," Rory said.

"Last name?"

"Hastings," Sid croaked.

"Parents?"

"They're dead."

The white cop's voice softened a hair. "How'd they die, honey?"

"I don't know."

He paused. "I lost my folks when I was kid."

The group shifted, waiting for the next round of questioning.

"Shit, was probably a blessing in a way. Toughened me up to the realities of things. You'll have to come with us. We'll notify next of kin."

"No," Sid said.

The other officer chimed in. "That's just the shock of the accident speaking. "

"There's got to be someone we can notify. Auntie, grandma, somebody?"

She shook her head. The officer moved toward her. "It's not a request young lady, it's a demand."

Rory stepped between them. "Look… come on… she's traumatized. Can you give us a moment?"

He backed off slowly, keeping his hooded bat cave eyes on them. Rory took Sid aside. "Listen to me. You can't fuck, I mean, screw around with these people. They don't give a shit about some little colored girl stuck out in the boondocks, and if you don't cooperate they'll bury you."

Sid hunched down deeper into her clothes, biting her cracked lip bloody. "It's black, not colored."

"Black, colored, Negro," Rory hissed, taken aback. "Don't make a damn's worth of difference, they'll bury you."

A police tow truck rumbled up. The driver banked his wheels and slid out, surveying the damage to the smashed pickup through a haze of cigar smoke and ginger-colored eyebrows.

He nodded to the empty driver's seat. "They scrape this boy out in one piece?"

"Far as I know. Probably high as a kite, given the damage. Lucky no other vehicles were involved. We're 'bout to roll, though. I got two hours left on my shift. Overtime's good but not that good." He paused, looking at Sid. "C'mon, little Miss."

Sid jerked away from his grasp. She bolted around the police car, out to the dark tangle of open fields.

"Son of a bitch," the white cop spat, hitching up his pants as he pulled a flashlight from his pocket. The light swept over the expanse of open field, catching emptiness, the girl seemingly vaporized, slurped up by the sky.

He opened the squad car and yanked out the mouthpiece on the police radio. "Base, we got a problem down here with a witness gone AWOL."

Mick walked over to Rory. "What are we going to do?"

"Leave."

"What?"

"If we're not at the studio by nine we lose five-hundred bucks. You got money to make up that hole?"

The officers crept tentatively out into the darkness, waving their flashlights.

"Tiny thing like that, they ain't gonna find her," Thurston said.

The police searched for fifteen minutes, cursing volumes between them as the police radio squawked out conquests and prospects, street addresses for burglaries, car jackings, panty jokes, predictions on the upcoming primary elections, wisecracks distorted through mouthfuls of food and background station buzz.

The men clambered back to the squad car empty handed, panting from the exertion.

"We free to go?" Rory asked.

"Motherfucker," the white cop scowled at her, disgust bugging his bloodshot eyes.

"Come on," she said, motioning for everyone to get back on the bus. Rainwater trickled down the aisle from a leak in the roof as they trundled up the stairs. Mick slid into the driver's seat. The cop huddled with the tow truck driver, a report of an itchy trigger police homicide, with a suspect reaching for a gun, ricocheting behind them. Mick turned on the engine, maneuvering away from the shoulder, wondering a little about Rory's bluntness, her haste to take off while the girl was still out there bumping around alone in the wilds with the pigs on her heels.

Rory grabbed her guitar from the front seat and hunkered down in the back row, doing scales. It had always been a signal that she didn't want to be bothered with any of them. Doing scales like a speed jonesing robot was a temporary beachhead from the storm of whatever was going on around her. A waystation blocking out their odors, their noise, their drama, their infernal, forever in her ear nearness.

With each waking hour, Rory rued the day she'd rescued the three of them from the nine to five. The middling minimum wage club gigs, the studio jingle sessions, and the opening act touring grinds were just delaying their inevitable return to civilian life.

Mick swung out onto the highway. Thurston teetered up to him, examining a can of Spam like an Olduvai Gorge artifact.

"Look what I found stashed away in the cooler. Rory's been holding out on us. Hungry?"

Mick ignored him.

"Fried up Hawaiian style with sautéed onions this stuff's a delicacy."

"Get that crap out of my face."

"This is the only protein you're going to get in a few hours, brother. Don't knock it until you've tried it."

"Stuff's inedible."

"It's God sent. What Jesus would've ate if he'd chosen the menu at the Last Supper."

"No thanks."

Thurston leaned into Mick. "She sulking 'cause of the detour or because of the kid?"

"The detour."

"She give a damn about the kid?"

"Ask her. I'm not a fucking mind reader."

"Naw, that's for sure. Otherwise, you would've known about the weed-spiked Spam."

"That supposed to entice me?"

"I can dream, can't I?"

Thurston batted his eyes, blue strobes of desperation dulled by a week on the road.

Mick hesitated, then waved him off. Thurston was an idle flirt, a lazy tease, a bored lizard. Not his type, no way, no how. Even if he had been, even Mick was halfway tempted, even, even, even. The creeping gut of his own middle age stopped him cold, making him self-conscious, doubting. Truth was, his taste for wrecked men, mirror images of himself, had been off for a while. Every time he thought about fucking, his desire wilted into the weeds. Evaporated in the after-midnight ditch when his arthritis flared up and he'd collapsed in an inanimate lump on the motel bed in the room Rory had paid for.

Mick was beholden to Rory. Kept the Scotch, the aspirin, the laxatives, the rubbing alcohol, and petroleum jelly for her raw fingers after sessions when she imploded from exhaustion. Unlike the others on the middling circuit of traveling musicians living paycheck to paycheck, she'd mostly steered clear of uppers, downers, acid, blow. When disco hit, many of the live gigs evaporated. The airwaves burst with synthesized candy asses, schmaltz operas composed through snorts of coke, and a wank at a urinal. Rory's sound was too hard charging, too primitive to survive under the glossy roar of disco. The band hadn't seen it coming, hadn't been prepared, the white boy arena rock fizzling, leaving them with a patchwork quilt of work as Rory tried to eke out original songs, her ear gone to tin, the writing dogged, stalled by the old complaints that she wasn't hallowed enough, had turned her back on Jesus.

Rory often recalled how she'd started off playing guitar in church with her mother, on an organ in Cotton Plant, Arkansas. *Mama had me at the end of the Great War, a year before the Red Summer riots tore up the big cities. Spent grade school banging frets as the novelty act in a choir that didn't know what to do with me after I done mopped the floor with Bethany Baptist's best lead guitarist. Boy was a hog farmer fifteen and change, older than me. Thought he was gonna be the big shit in the Memphis clubs, and here's this nappy-headed butterball girl showing him up.*

Rory doled out different versions of her childhood in the wee hours when she and Mick were the only ones awake on the bus and they huddled together, fantasizing about big things, snug as conjoined vipers in a rug. The white queer sometime glue sniffer, sometime bass player from Astoria, Queens whom she'd picked up on a New York subway train. The map reader and scheduler, bad with numbers, good with common sense and chocolate, Mars bars stashed under the driver's seat for a quick late morning fix. In his head, he nicknamed her Flame Fingers, a thief stealing the thunder of cocky men guitarists. In his head, they were the stuff of legends, a force field, an inner sanctum, the last outpost of purity and shelter from all the fucked up contaminants of the music industry, the outside world, the gnashing fangs of wasted time. In his head, all their years of road dogging together were bookended by assassinations and botched assassinations—JFK to MLK to Malcolm X to Gerald Ford—a thrum of death and dying uniting them In A Gadda da Vida.

The highway pulsed with crawling semis, white tops glittering maggoty in the dark, drivers fighting to stay awake. Mick maneuvered around them, keeping slightly over the speed limit, trying to make up the hour they'd lost, eyes out for the highway patrol.

"I'm beat," Thurston whined from the back.

Rory kept her eyes on the road, bracing for more complaints. "You got a couple hours to get some sleep. Once we get there we're on."

Butch stirred from the middle of the bus, still pissed about the white cop. "We can't carry your sorry ass anymore, Thurston. Your timing's off, your sound's crap."

"Quit with the firing squad," Rory barked.

Mick turned on the radio for a diversion. A caterwaul blasted from the speakers, the mating call of a hundred stampeding wildebeests.

"Aw shit," Thurston said. "Jude Justis, number one scream queen." He turned to Mick, hand on hip. "What's less appetizing than Spam, Daddy O?"

Mick snorted. "That's her new single. Another Odetta rip off, Greenville, circa 1930."

"Tired junkie's raking it in as usual. Suckers can't get enough of her shaking her white trash ass, bastardizing our shit," Butch said.

Thurston did a double take, scraping the bottom of the Spam can with his long sloth fingers.

"Ours? Who died and made you Black?"

Rory ignored the dig at Butch and the chance to play referee. "Jude's middle class. Parents are knee deep in Galveston oil."

"Whatever. White trash is a figure of speech," Butch said.

Thurston slurped at the can. "Don't see her riding in a beat-up bus with no air conditioning."

The bus was a rattletrap with nearly 200,000 miles on it. All of Mick's grease monkeying power wouldn't be able to revive it the next time it blowed. Rory had gotten it in the late fifties, a rolling refuge from the few fleabag Jim Crow motels that Negroes could stay in when they were out on tour. In the early days, before she hired Mick, Katy or her backup singer Marie would scour the Green Book in advance for places where they could stay. The Green Book was the Negro Bible for interstate accommodations. Then Marie got bit by a rat in a joint that was more outhouse than motel. After that, they slept on the bus, occasionally tapping into an informal network of local homeowners who thought Rory walked on water.

There were fewer of them now. The fawning white boy barnacles with a thousand questions for their college term papers on the origin of rock; the Jude Justis wannabes flipping their grimy hair in the wind as they offered their elbows, cheeks, and shoulders for her to autograph. Sometime in the mid-seventies, the black audience had bottomed out and just the white bush leaguers remained, always curious, always hungry, always roving… sabertooths licking the veldt clean.

Rory leaned into Mick, noting the march of bushy gray hairs at his neck, the unassailable evidence of his, of their, mortality. The luxury of how he could let himself go swaggeringly to shit while she had to be careful not to play the old lady beating the crooked axe on stage.

"You gotta pump it up, otherwise we're fucked," she commanded, swiveling around to face Thurston and Butch. "Do all your pissing now, we're not stopping."

Nobody would hire Mick for a day job, so he toiled for her in neo-indentured servitude, owing thousands of dollars from the sludge of klepto-fueled bouts in jail and compulsive gambling—cards, dice, coin tosses, number guesses, greyhound races, and on and on—the tiniest niggling schemes of calculated chance getting him hard.

Damn lucky you're white, Rory always told him.

Why do you keep me around? he always asked.

Because you could pop a wheelie on a bus at eighty miles an hour in a snowstorm.

They'd been driving for thirty minutes when she thought she heard a tapping sound somewhere on the bus.

"What's that?"

"Dunno."

"If it's mechanical and we need to put this motherfucker in the shop, we're screwed."

"I'll stop."

Mick waited until they came to a turnout, then stopped the bus, listening. Butch had fallen asleep. Thurston was playing Solitaire. Mick and Rory got out to check. A busted call box sat to their right, mocking. Mick looked under the hood again, then stood back, trying to sort out the stray noise they'd heard from the lethargic whir of twin campers with Louisiana plates plodding in the slow lane. He closed the hood and walked around the cab. Thurston popped his head out.

"Sounds like it's coming from inside, under where the luggage is."

They hadn't used that compartment in ages; mostly piling their junk in the empty seats in the back. Mick opened the compartment door. He poked behind a case with a broomstick and saw something skitter to the back.

"What the fuck? Thurston, gimme a flashlight."

He waved the flashlight over the compartment. Sid's head popped up in the dark corner.

"How did you get in here?"

"Don't be mad at me."

Mick grunted and helped her out.

"Son of a bitch."

"We have to get her back," Rory snapped.

Mick hesitated. "You sure?"

"It's kidnapping, Mick, evading, something. Cops probably got a tail on us now."

Thurston bristled. "Pigs'll make up some shit out of thin air."

Sid eased out of the compartment, getting her bearings, the ragged, strange faces of the white men, the judgmental scowl of the black woman zooming out at her, a sour taste of home. She ran, barreling past Mick, dodging Thurston, a baby junior varsity Harriet Tubman faking out the slavers, Mary Poppins' umbrella foisting her up up at long last to the waiting stars. But fuck, she hadn't even gotten a centimeter off the ground when Rory wrestled her down, folding her into her arms just tight enough to hold her, just loose enough for her to breathe, the spit of fear a cyclone in her throat.

"Easy, easy," Rory whispered, rough hand closing tightly under Sid's ribcage. "Stop it, goddammit. I won't bite. Not yet. Not if you cooperate."

Sid went limp, the woman's voice echoing in her ear, underwater burble from a shipwreck.

Mick caught up to them, drained. "What are we going to do about this?"

"Get to a gas station so we can call the police," Butch said.

Rory shook her head. "That puts us behind on the session. Every half hour we're late I gotta pay for and y'all know I don't have that kind of money to burn."

"Well what are we going to do? You're right about the cops, but we can't just leave her out here."

"No one's talking about doing that, Butch, but we can't stop this thing again, hear? Everybody get back on, I'll call the cops when we get to the studio."

Night Music

SID WAS SHORT for Sidra. Curator of girl group grunts, oohs, aahs, hand on hip chastisements, dagger in the back flattery, any cornpone melody she could squeeze out of her smidgeon of a transistor radio before the batteries died, and, splat, fade to black. Her genetic parents, from Little Rock, Arkansas, were barely out of their teens when they had her. Joined an End Times cult to spite their high rolling parents. Camped out in the Texas desert's armpit heat where the insurgents had taken up residence, a nose to the grindstone crew of all races and ages counting down to the apocalypse.

Some left before the slaughter inside the cult. A group of them, hobbled by stomach flu, were transported to safety by truck, their intestines in their laps, babbling in pain, the slick river of endless night taunting them, no rich parents to wire them money for plane tickets back home to mommy like the white golden girls in the group. For a week, the slaughter was the headline in all the American papers. The Associated Press, the Posts, the Times, the Intelligencers, Chronicles, Gazettes, Heralds, and Bees; the early morning teaser for all the scrappy, funky little tucked away radio stations rolling tumbleweed thick through the belly of the South and Midwest.

For a while, Sid believed she'd dreamt or misremembered all of it. The knives at the babies' throats, the slow-mo swirl of GI Joes storming the compound, the reporters sticking their mics in the faces of the white golden girls, coaxing brand new salacious details of the slaughter with each telling. She convinced herself that it was the detritus of some other crazy girl. Semi-orphaned, awash in gibberish in a place she'd learned about only a week before she'd been forced to move; gathering up her toys, clothes, her igneous rock collection and being stuffed on a steamy charter bus with the rest of the urban refugees, or so Genetic called them.

Genetic used to sneak and listen to Jude Justis, the white lady blues rock singer. Rip her throat out with the guttural bog bottom melodies that she'd spewed all over Top 40. She was the ripe con that made whities all across America feel like they were down, dirty, and fucking in savage land. As if they'd been transported to a place beyond the pale of reason, good breeding, and constraint. *They think they know us better than ourselves*, Genetic said. But still, she hummed Jude's multi-platinum hoodoo jingles under her breath, couldn't help herself, couldn't police its infernal cocaine fix catchiness, couldn't stop its blasting every damn where that slick summer of death. Music was a sandbar that she crept onto when she was feeling tense, dislocated, wrung inside out. *Get out of my goddamn head, ofay!* She raged into the darkness, on the rare occasions Sid was allowed to stay with her.

That sticky beetle-infested summer in the desert, Sid had borrowed someone else's body. Allowed the physical Sid, the flesh and blood vessel, to go back to the boiling sun of Little Rock, to her room overlooking the city bus yard, to her friend Marcel, who was going to be the second Black woman to orbit the moon in 1990, following her lead. Sid drifted through the desert, to the Gulf of Mexico, across the Atlantic on butterfly wings. The borrowed body, the decoy, a shell on the cot in the cabin she shared with ten other people, the body unflinching from her uncle's hands on her under the covers, the body's ears gone deaf to his shriveled panting moan as he came, the body's phantom skin insensate to the crocodile tears he always shed afterwards… in weak penance for what he'd done.

Why ask for forgiveness when there is no god.

Reports of My Demise

THE BUS WAS MAKING good time now. The five of them marooned in silence. Rory went over bills, her mind racing between figures and how to deal with the girl. Mick kept track of the exits. Thurston started back up on Solitaire. Butch thumbed through a spy thriller, wishing there were pictures, a diversion to relieve his aching head. Sid pretended to be asleep, her pocketknife at the ready just in case.

When they pulled into the lot of the recording studio, it was 9:30 p.m. The residue of the night's calamity washed over them. Rory jumped out to alert the session manager.

"Rehearsing this late is inhumane," Thurston whined as she barged into the building.

Butch rolled his eyes. "You just make sure you piss all the weed and smack out of your gut before we step in that room."

Mick jumped out and unloaded the instruments. Rory came back out and checked on Sid. She would be ok staying on the locked bus while they rehearsed, then she would call the cops and explain.

Inside the recording studio, Leviticus Jenson was parked at his desk slurping a bowl of cornflakes, a bottomless pit disguised as a human, duck sauce encrusted invoices teetering in mountainous piles at his elbows. Levi, as associates called him, ran a string of recording studios up the 101 freeway and didn't like to be kept waiting, the flickering flame of his ambition to be a side player on congas at stake with every minute some deadbeat band was tardy or went overtime.

"Rory, baby, ya'll better get your asses in here quick," he said, wiping milk off his chin as the band clambered in.

"We know, we know. Had a slight delay coming in."

"You gotta hit it. I have another group due in three hours. Deep Purple cover band trying to go legit."

Butch slapped Levi's outstretched high-five. "Legit and 'Deep Purple cover band's' an oxymoron."

"Three chord wonders," Thurston said.

Rory took off her shades and stifled a yawn. "We'll be out of here by twelve. Russ call?"

"Naw."

Rory hesitated, glancing at her watch as Mick groaned in irritation and shoved the equipment into the studio's live room. Russ was supposed to have called to confirm a gig in Fairfield, Connecticut. A four nighter he'd promised could pipeline them to a Manhattan show opening for the Stones. Russ' promises riled Mick, got him plotting a grisly end to the man and the way he strung Rory along with fairytale gigs.

He took out her guitar and handed it to her, sulking.

"Don't start," she said, cuffing him gently on the cheek.

They started tuning. Thurston drooped over his cymbals, trying not to look checked out, ignoring the mournful piano pings Butch always did to start them out. Rory tuned methodically, bending the strings until they obeyed, skirting perfect pitch, scratching out zigzags and chromatic quirks.

"Sounds good to me, let's go," Levi barked from the control booth. The phone rang. Levi held up his finger to halt, answering the phone with a snarl. "It's Sugar Daddy," he said to Rory.

Rory went to the wall phone in the hallway and picked up the receiver. A racetrack announcer's voice bleated in the background on the other end.

"What you got, Russ?"

There was a pause. "Aw shit, this horse is hotter than the fourth of July."

"We got the gig or not?"

"Christ almighty, this baby's gonna make me double!"

"Russ, we're in the middle of doing the beer thing. We got Fairfield or not?"

"You know, I woke up this morning thinking about Boise."

"What the fuck—"

"Any of your boys know bluegrass fiddle?"

"Who'd you give Fairfield to?"

"Lot of respect for you, R. Manager at the The Roost knows your gospel stuff inside and out, why—"

"Who, Russ? Who'd you give it to?"

"Angel."

"Jude Justis' little backwoods fuckee."

"I don't know anything about that."

"The hell you don't. You're still kissing her ass, Russ. What do I pay you for?"

"You're paranoid."

"You're screwing her, aren't you?"

"You know I don't do white and scraggly."

"Well I know Jude doesn't make such fine distinctions."

"Look... it's out of my hands. The bookers want tits, flash..."

"Save it."

He sighed. The announcer reeled off the names of the horses in the next race. Russ softened his voice, coaxing. "Can we make Boise work, Sister? It's two weeks, a long haul, but the club manager is a monster fan of 'Didn't it Rain', the classics, knows your whole catalog backwards, forwards, in his sleep. Heard they've got something of a Rory Tharpe renaissance out there."

Rory hesitated, pressing the phone to her temple, her gut seizing up from the soda and Rolaids she'd downed for dinner. Levi came out into the hall, frowning, tapping his watch.

"Go on, book it," she said, conceding. The starting bell for the race blasted on the other end. She hung up the phone before Russ had a chance to respond with more sweet talk. She hated it when he called her Sister, the old Pentecostal stage name clinking rustily in his mouth and the mouths of the thrift store scavengers who thought they knew all there was to know about her for the price of a '78 collector's item record.

Reports of my demise aren't greatly exaggerated, she thought. She was fucking drowning. Her lungs, a bucket of saltwater pus. In the nautilus shell of Rory's inner ear, Katy croaked out Auld Lang Syne. New Year's Eve, 1946. The world and its possibilities, bright, burning, at War's end. Katy had dragged her to another tent revival at the crack of dawn. They were second on the bill before the handkerchief head pastor staggered onto the stage, whooping, hollering, sassing the narcoleptic rubber plant workers awake with his moonshine drawl. At the piano, Katy's hands started shaking. She played fast to cover it up, hiccupping a nervous laugh into the mic she was hogging from Rory. *Just remember they ponied up fifty cents of their hard-earned money to see me, baby girl, me, me, me.*

"We ready?" Levi asked, pacing, pungent, wrist like a bullwhip.

Rory went back into the studio. Butch slid into the piano seat, scrutinizing the session players for signs of life behind nicotine-glazed eyes. The last ones they had worked with were robots. Shut on and off when they broke for lunch, slurping down the saltines and chocolate milk they got from the strip mall liquor store.

Ever since Rory's bass player split over money, the group had relied on temps and session players. On recordings, Rory liked sheer compliance, no frills competency, boys who could be upright rhythm fiends to her melodic strut and preen; the showy tangents that had had every feckless white boy lead guitar player coming, stealing from her, armed with ten shovels.

Shit, I never knew there were so many piss poor bassists within a one-thousand-mile radius, she scoffed, eating the criminally bad ones for breakfast. It was during their first car insurance jingle for a company out of Buffalo, that Cardinal Jefferson walked in and killed it, not batting an eye. Card, as he liked to be called, was a refugee from Motown and Kansas City blues bands that worked the house party circuit. He'd been mired, for most of his adult life, in the backwater of IOUs, maybes, bankruptcies and diminishing returns in the speakeasy market, though he'd always nursed a secret classical jones, joking bitterly about being rejected by the local philharmonic while the white boys, straight out of junior college, got plucked fresh from the tree.

Mitch distributed the sheet music and they started, Card moving effortlessly through the plodding chord progression.

"You play that bass like lead guitar, Card," Rory said.

"Good bass always leads, the guitar just don't know it most of the time."

Rory laughed, morbid thoughts of the lesser gig in Boise draining away for a moment. Once she got Card taken care of, she would deal with the girl. "Ever consider leaving Kansas City?"

"There aren't enough hours in the day when I'm not thinking about it."

"We have a few Northwest gigs coming up, interested?"

"What's the pay?"

"Negotiable with transportation."

"I need more specifics."

"You got a life out there in KC?"

"A middling one."

"Wife, kids?"

"Yup. All that."

"Condolences."

He nodded, cupping his hand protectively under the neck of his bass.

"Hundred a week, you cover your own expenses."

"What about Gidget here?"

"Who?"

He motioned to his bass. "Gidget, meet skinflint."

She pursed her lips. "Repairs and strings are your responsibility."

"You kin to Howard Hughes?"

"No, otherwise I'd ask you to work for free."

"Woman, that's less than dead."

He was roadkill cocky like most of them. Even the passable ones thought their shit didn't stink, building their own legends out of tinker toys. The good ones glowed like made mafia men. The great ones thought they walked on water, crapped solid gold, droves of women trailing strategically in their wake.

The lazy cultish hunger of the Top 40 hit-fickle-herd repelled her. Would that she had a few hundred men to fuck, diddle and dispose of without judgment like them. Would that her threshold for boredom was higher. Would that she could navigate the wilds of indiscriminate flesh, of aching, want, and abandon without a second thought.

They broke for a ten-minute pee break. The room got warmer with every muddled take. Levi blasted the fan and passed around ice, retreating to talk with his lover on the phone by the main console.

If Rory hired Card, they would all have to tighten their belts. Stretch the royalty checks that dribbled in from her gospel and R&B recordings, tap another hundred from the small inheritance she'd received from selling the acre of land Katy had owned in Cotton Plant. It was castaway land, rocky, rough, good for nothing except star gazing on a winter night, or so some thought. The church pastor had wanted to use it to build an extension of the sanctuary, a reserve for pilgrims from around the world. Katy had stood between him and his ambition. Ornery, disreputable, traveling all the time, packing Rory up at a moment's notice to play in any grimy hole that would pay them. Couldn't stand still long enough to attend a board meeting of the church elders, the whole thieving lot of them licking their chops at the thought of buying her out. She had become land obsessed, talked about her family having had a compound down on the coast of California. A resort for Negroes before it had become a colony of white surfers. *Your inheritance is more than this boondocks heap of Arkansas dust*, she'd said.

In death, her meddling and second guessing had become more cutthroat, desperate, a hobgoblin of her brief, unhappy stint as a second string organist clawing to the top of the Negro tent revival hierarchy, pulling every slapdash gimmick and flourish she could muster out of her hat to keep the holy rollers sated.

Mick knocked Rory out of her brooding. "What were you talking to Card about?"

"Touring with us."

"Butch'll love that. Thinks Card's an asshole."

"Butch is just gonna have to get over himself."

"The numbers make sense?"

"Yeah. Russ called about a few new gigs."

She paused, glancing over at Butch. He sat at the piano, thumbing through his bankbook, purposely keeping Card and the rest of the session players at a distance. She didn't want to mention Boise to him and Mick yet, fearing backlash about the comedown of trekking into the Northwestern wilds without a plan B.

"What's happening with the East Coast thing?"

"Nothing. Russ gave it to Angel Hererra."

"For all that mugging and pop shit she does?"

"Teacher's pets."

Mick shook his head, enraged, cattle-prod blue eyes jolted fully awake. "Let me guess, as a 'consolation prize' he got us something in Podunk."

"Boise."

Card walked past. "They still lynch black folks up there?"

The door to the studio office opened. Sid poked her head in. Levi swiveled around from his phone call.

"Can I help you?"

"I'm looking for the lady, the guitar player."

"Rory? She's back through there, but we're starting a recording session up again in two minutes."

Sid ignored him and started walking through the hallway, Levi on her heels.

"Hey, you can't go back there!"

She wriggled past the musicians as they came back from the break to the live room, the walls oozing with their slurred chatter and cigarette smoke, their antsy yen to get it over and done with. They would go back to their day jobs further up North, in Oakland, Richmond, San Francisco, Vallejo; bank security guard, waiter, gas company meter reader dodging Dobermans in white ladies' freshly mown backyards. Overhead, black silkscreen nudes gazed blearily down on her, sandwiched between two platinum records, dust congealed, hanging crooked, braced for one fatal breath to knock them off.

Napping on the bus, Sid had awakened with the feeling of being entombed, the random personal effects of Rory and company staring at her in silent rebuke, Egyptian sarcophagus items for the afterlife. She peeked into the window of the live room and there was Rory, bags under her eyes, the pin curls of the night before tucked into a silk scarf with constellations stitched into the fabric.

"Girl's here," Butch said, nodding to the window.

"Who's that?" Card asked.

"A stray," Thurston said. "Picked her up back near Santa Clara."

Levi barged into the room. "We can't have her in here. This ain't no day care. Police already think I'm running a front for smack dealers. All I need is to get busted and shut down."

Rory paused, irritated, gesturing for Sid to come in. Sid sidled through the door, wide-eyed at the sight of Rory with the guitar.

"What happened on the bus?" she asked the girl.

"Nothing, just didn't want to be in there anymore."

"Well, you can't stay here. We'll just be another hour."

"I'm not going back on there."

"Look, we're working. We won't be long, then we're hitting the road. Get you back to your people."

"Told you I don't have any. I want to stay and watch."

Rory hesitated. The whole band had finally clanked in and assembled, waiting for her to give the signal. Butch sat erect and ready at the piano, Thurston did karate chops in the air with his drumsticks, the for-hire saxophone player who schlepped around the state earning a living on sexy wine, dine, and fuck jingles, wiped his mouthpiece compulsively while Card surveyed the room from behind his lemon tinted aviator shades.

"Aww, c'mon, let her stay, Levi," Card said. "Kid might learn something."

Levi rolled his eyes. "If I get busted, I'm docking you."

"You ain't docking nobody, motherfucker. If this little girl looked like Shirley Temple you'd be making space for her."

"What's that supposed to mean?"

"You touch her, you get a foot in your ass, hear?" He took off his shades, making his point with a lopsided, silver-toothed half grin that captivated Sid as she watched over her shoulder. His long lankiness was too much for the studio's grimy decrepitude.

Levi squinted at him long and hard, his neck vanishing into the collar of the soiled rayon dress shirt he'd slept in for two days. "Look, don't threaten me, turd brain. You only here because of your rep with Motown and because she requested you… The kid can stay this time, but y'all are out at twelve sharp."

Sid plopped on a stool across from Rory. They started the first few bars, a deep rich swirl driven by Rory's scratchy chords. Sid had picked up a guitar once, more interested really in taking it apart to see what was hidden inside than in playing it, bashing the tubby body with a hammer and looking inside for stowaways, the gremlin whisperers who made it wail like a cartoon cat sprung six feet off the ground.

Rory held up her hand in disgust. "Stop rushing, damn it," she said to the men. "Thurston, the extra fills are too loud, too fast. This ain't Wipeout. Ya'll are knocking through this thing when the pace should be 4/4."

Thurston got up from his drum stool, teeth bared. "That's a sure way to put whoever the fuck is watching this thing on the tube asleep."

"It's a beer jingle," Mick said. "Corporate wants it mellow."

"What they know about how to play music? This time signature sucks dick."

Rory smoothed down her guitar strap, determined to stem the outbursts, Thurston's stoner gaze dull and manic at the same time. "Harlan's cutting the check, so he can have any time signature he wants. Just get it right, otherwise I'm out of pocket for the extra time up in here."

Card reared up, indignant. "You stop bitchin' we will."

"Well, this 'bitch' is getting your ass paid this week. That's one less day busting suds at the car wash."

Card smirked in spite of himself.

"Don't work at no car wash, Sister Tharpe. Matter of fact, I just started dental school last week."

"Good, if we can get you to do 4/4 and slow it down on the bridge you got your first customers when you open your practice."

"Yes ma'am. I'll hold you to that."

They went through four more takes. Outside, the Deep Purple cover band, who had the next rehearsal slot, filed into the waiting room in an explosion of Clairol iceberg blond-on-black roots, Norse god parachute pants billowing over Santa Claus sleigh boots with furry tassels.

Thurston eyed them, whistling. "A little early to be in costume, boys?"

The keyboardist shrugged, brushing wilted bangs from dandruff speckled eyebrows. "We got a gig right after this. Sixties rockabilly revue in Oakland then we hit Colorado, Ohio, Pennsylvania, upstate New York." He cracked his knuckles, gloating. "Just got an invite to the Valhalla festival."

"What's that?" Butch asked.

"Jude Justis' confab. Word is, there'll be a little comeback action from the Airplane. Jagger and Keith might even show up. Which means all the pussy and filet mignon you can eat."

Butch snorted. "Not for the rabble on the undercard, you dumb fuck. You'll be lucky to do your tuning in the john."

"Fuck if I care, just so long as Russ gets our loot on time."

Mick paused, calculating the fallout from another booking lost, trying not to look at Rory. "Russ booked you in that?"

"Yep. We signed with him last month. Dude's almost earning his keep so far. Old fart wanted to clip us for 60% but Sylvester here put him in his place," he nodded at his shaggy cohort, thumping him on the knee. "Einstein double majored in accounting and forensic psychology at City College."

Rory folded her arms. Mick had started packing up the instruments, a greasy catfish bag balanced on top of Rory's guitar case. "Quite sure Jude's getting a piece of the action," she said, snatching at the bag and taking a piece of fish. "Right? You don't get on JJ's payroll without a little quid pro quo."

Thurston let out a loud whoop. "Pay to play! Aw, that's hilarious. She's gonna make you a backdoor man yet, Murray—"

"Thurston!" Mick snarled.

"Well, it's fucking true, all she wants is lackeys that are gonna prop her up and suck her off."

"While she's stealing from every Black person on the planet," Rory added. Sid trailed behind her, curious about the roomful of strange bloated white men parading their flat butts in tight pants. They copped hard, serious attitude, eyeing Rory sideways with conflicted awe as they flipped through the coffee-stained *People* magazines piled up on the reception table. "We're gonna have to wash your mouth out with Castor Oil, Thurston. Keep it clean around the kid here."

"I've heard that stuff before," Sid said quietly.

Mick took Rory aside. "Did you call the police yet?"

"No."

"Rory, what the fuck—"

"In case you haven't been paying attention I've been busy."

"The longer you wait, the more suspicion it raises."

"Don't you fucking think I know that? If the girl gets wind of it she'll bolt again."

It was after eleven when they wrapped. The other band shuffled into the live room and the isolation booths, spreading out their effects, burrowing in like Rory and her men had never been there.

How did bottom feeders like them get signed by Russ? she wondered, staring into the hard-bitten tundra of their faces, cringing at their rote play, their sludgy familiarity with one another, the twist of their bodies signaling primordial ease, an inborn lack of self-consciousness. In a split second, she envied them, holding it rough and wriggling on her tongue, envied them, repelled at the same time, her stomach churning from the long night and the prospect of the ride to Boise.

Levi handed Rory a clipboard with a copy of the recording contract on it. "Need your initials to close this out. I should have this thing turned around and spruced up in a few weeks. Russ'll let you know when it's ready to drop."

"Just make sure my solo doesn't get lopped off on the final cut when the ad runs."

Levi grunted, taking the clipboard back. "You know that's above my pay grade, Lassie. Whatever corporate wants, corporate gets. As always, though, I'll aim for structural integrity."

Full Tilt Flotsam, 1978-1928

YA'LL KNOW ABOUT that rumor that King special requested me to march with him in Chicago during the sanitation workers' thing. His people told me he wanted me front row and center, the cherry on top of it all, but I deferred big time. Would only do it if I could be incognito, dark shades, wig and everything, like the Southern church ladies we saw primping and preening in their car mirrors Sunday mornings at the First Baptist Holy Word in Port Arthur. I could never stomach that pristine, angels and trumpets on high shit. If I was going to sit up in church for umpteen hours, the shit would have to make me weep. Anyways, they got Dr. King a few weeks later. Tried to pin it on that white trash motha fucka Ray. I wasn't buying it. Throw a rock anywhere south of the Mason Dixon and you'd hit a dumb don't-know-his-head-from-a-hole in-the-ground cracker like that. Shit, I had kissing cousins that were smarter, sharper. Naw, this had the dirty fingerprints of the feds all over it.

But who was listening to me? At least not then, and not on that.

In '63, I did every little mangy club in the Florida panhandle, then made my way back west to Texas. Played behind cages in the honky tonks. Played between banjo sets and bump 'n' grinds in the titty bars. Dead last and a laughingstock in every pissy little singing competition I entered. Tried my hand at guitar and picked till these stumpy good for nothing fingers bled.

So don't talk to me about no fucking dues paying. Jesus saw it all. He's my one and only witness. People asking me to document what I did can go to hell with Ray and Lee Harvey Oswald. Heaven is for the birds, but hell is real.

The buckets were lined up on each side of the church to catch the leaks when the raindrops hit. It sounded like the street musicians Rory had seen in Memphis, plinking at water glasses with little spoons. Some of the women carried umbrellas or slapped newspapers onto the tops of their ornate hats, not sure where the next eruption would hit. *God has a plan*, Sister Bethune said, the congregation nodding sodden heads. Rory wondered whether the plan was to see them all get pneumonia while the white church on Charles Street got a city grant for a new roof.

Sister Bethune was the de facto leader of Galilee Mission. Could roar and purr in one sentence, weaving biblical and topical, keeping the children awake and on the edge of their seats despite fourteen hours of sharecropping the day before. Rory, because of her music, stood apart from her peers, freed from the backbreaking work in the fields… traveling to a string of small town revivals with Katy, while the others busted their asses in indentured servitude.

"It's umpteen years after Emancipation and look at us now. Still staring up at massa's boot and licking the heel for nourishment. That ain't and won't never be for you," Katy said.

"But mama, they hate me. Cut their eyes. Talk about me behind my back. Think I think I'm better than them."

"They ain't far from right. None of them got the blessing that you do. God give you a gift like this you damn well better not squander it."

Galilee's choir had a rep for mixing it up, divinely inspired to crush all competitors, using oboes, trumpets, harps and even a glockenspiel when the manic choir director could get his hands on one from the white marching band at Little Rock High school. Rory became the choir's star attraction and curiosity. On Sundays, she practiced as soon as she woke up until second service, sometimes accompanied by Katy, sometimes running through chords under her watchful eye. During second and third service, the choir could swing unhindered by the piety of the holy rollers who saw her guitar licks as dirty, godless, unladylike. *Katy you raisin' a hellion and a heathen, best to put her on piano and have her learn up under you*, Bethune said at first. Then, a reporter from the Cotton Plant Bee got wind of the five-year-old girl who could play like Charley Patton riding lightening and Sister Bethune came grudgingly around, sniffing out an opportunity for the church to boost its fickle membership.

"You teach her how to sing like the rest of our Sunday school angels. She be ok, sis Katy."

That was the tried-and-true path, to have a voice that could soar up over the rafters and greet Peter and Paul at the pearly gates. Black girls who could sing had a chance at going somewhere, past the drudge and drear of the fields, past their own four walls and that of Miss Ann's house. They could move past the known world for women in the Galilee church, their dreams of mutiny and escape ground down in the raw, dark earth of the blip on a screen town with only one schoolroom for Colored children.

Gazing into the sky, the stars asked her to be an astronomer, to take a chance on us, they purred. The sky's blue black liquid mystery was all hers, the one thing she could claim, lying on top of the covers in the bed she shared with her mother, as she fought with phantom bill collectors in her sleep after the day's shift picking cotton. She wanted to play with the other kids, to at least share in their mischief, their frolics, their end of the week revelry, but Katy would never let her go near them in the fields. Tearing apart cotton bolls would ruin her hands, wreck her exquisite fingerings.

"Don't get to longing for common things," she said, washing the bloody nubs of Rory's fingers after an hour's practice, the calluses roughening, growing into a force all their own. "The grass ain't greener over there with the rest of 'em. You can get a whiff of them and what they do in school."

At school, she faded behind the boisterous wrangling of the older girls. Everybody crammed disagreeably into one room, a hurly burly of ages, dispositions, damnable quirks. Everyone knew how to read each other, except for her, always bringing up the rear in tag and kickball. Everyone knew the tired score. The tyrants to avoid or suck up to. The pushovers to needle, exploit. She envied their unspoken intimacy. The pencils they shared and sharpened for each other, the synchronized eye rolls behind the back of the teacher, the elaborate favor currying done just for the benefit of her secret crush—Divinity Mason Mulvaney; a tall, curtain rod legged twelve-year-old charlatan in purple knee socks, proud to be stamped with an Irish surname by the slave master way back in the mists of time. Divinity wielded her shrunken inheritance like a club. But when talent show time rolled around, her imperial sway was no match for the attention Rory got for playing the guitar.

Rory's time in school was limited by Katy's wanderlust, a desire which deepened with the congregation's disdain for her; the uppity harlot who'd had the out of wedlock birth and gave no shits about it. She was the only single mother in the church. A natural target for sanctimony. Sister Bethune's exhibit A for sin and transgression when the money slowed to a trickle and she needed a bogeywoman to get the coin purses out again. Keep your legs closed until you get a man and nail him down, she thundered. Carnal knowledge is the worst kind of wisdom.

The girls from school scrambled to show how righteous they were. Sister Bethune's little posse riding in to shame the besmirched. This one's skirt was too far above her knee. That one's underarms stunk of cow must. Floozy over there let a boy feel her up in the outhouse underneath her panties. Then the rumor that Rory let herself be finger fucked by one of the older boys in exchange for a guitar pick. No surprise, they said, 'cause she had no home training, no common sense, no real mama to show her right from wrong. When they pulled her into the headmaster's office to account for her shameful behavior, one of the posse was there as a witness, sticking her tongue out at Katy behind the headmaster's head.

"If Miss Katy don't whip your treacherous behind, Sister will get to you later," he said.

Rory sat with her head down, veering between stupefaction and rage, wanting to rip his beady brown eyes out and feed them one by one to the yapping rat dog that was the headmaster's constant companion.

"I don't beat my baby for nothing," Katy lied. "Especially when it's her who's been wronged."

"Well, show her some discipline, then," he said.

"And the little savage that did this to her?"

"Tanned his behind before lunch. One step ahead of you. You take care of that girl before she gets knocked up and gives you another illegitimate mouth to feed."

Later, at home, they spent hours in silence. Katy washing clothes, scrubbing floors, dusting to gleaming every undiscovered corner of the two-room house they rented from one of the church elders. Rory tried to do her arithmetic homework, afraid of the questions in Katy's eyes. She had not looked in her direction since they'd come back from the school, the avoidance worse than the brewing confrontation.

"Mama," Rory said.

"Don't say a word. This place is a goddamn cyclone."

"Can you check this?" she asked, holding out her homework paper.

Katy squinted at the mass of chicken scratch. "Go get me the kerosene lamp."

Rory brought it to her. Katy snatched it out of her hand. "Stop that slouching. You gotta keep your posture up or you won't be able to play properly." She scanned the paper. "Clean this mess up before you turn it in. Number ten should be subtracted not added."

She dropped the paper on Rory's lap and picked up a broom. "You know I can't abide by no sloppy half-assed work. I always did just fine in numbers the few years I was in school. You gotta have a head for them if you're going to make it on your own."

She paused, her breath coming quiet as she swept around Rory's bare feet.

"Why did you let that heathen touch you, baby?"

"I didn't let him, mama."

She swept around Rory's ankles. "Didn't give him the eye?"

"No, mama."

"You didn't eat all your supper."

"Not hungry."

"I don't have money to waste on you not eating."

Rory looked down at the paper. A fly buzzed around the unfinished plate of ox tails on the counter, the smell making her gag.

"You let him pull your dress up."

"No, mama."

She put the broom handle on the ground, spreading Rory's big toe with it.

"Jesus will strike you down, baby."

Rory looked at her sloppy homework, fives merging into sixes, sevens nuzzling eights, a tornado gathering at the center of the paper. She shook her head. Katy nudged the broom handle into her daughter's skin, pressing, probing, spreading the big toe wider.

"Don't lie to me. I can't defend you if it came out that you gave him the eye, hear?"

Rory grasped the edge of the chair. The tornado bounced off the page, blowing over her eyes, suctioning up the tears that were threatening to spill, betray her. Katy probed more firmly, the toe crumpling, giving.

"Jesus knows if you're lying."

"I'm not," Rory whispered. The girls from school loomed up, perched on her mother's shoulders, baby scarecrows reveling in their moment of tribunal.

Katy lifted the broom handle, inspecting the tip as she brought it to Rory's chin and lifted it up, soft as milk.

She waited. The familiar clang from the cow slaughterhouse sounded, signaling the end of the evening shift, the ghost march of men going back home, stuporous from the grind, painting blood castles in the air with stained fingertips.

"I intend to have the headmaster fired, then."

Rory took a breath, waited. The girls batted their eyes at her, cawing. "What he gon' do for a job?"

"Hell if I know. That ain't our concern. Probably go back to picking cotton with the rest of the niggers." Katy walked over to the kitchen counter and picked up an ox tail, cleaning it to the bone. "Once you finish your schoolwork, you get on them scales," she said, digging into her apron pocket. She handed Rory a guitar pick. "Soon as I heard you was letting that nasty boy stick his finger up you for a pick, I knew it had to be a lie."

The sign said four hundred miles to Boise, Idaho. She girded herself, took a drink of Vodka, looked around to see who was awake. The boys were knocked out. Sid had crawled into the backseat, snoring under Rory's overcoat.

The cops would come pick her up at a gas station off route 45. Rory had snuck out and called the police at a pay phone by the studio. Waited on hold for twenty minutes, got routed through three different operators to explain the situation, trying to stay calm, cool, collected. Stressed to the gum smacking white woman lieutenant on the other line that the girl was a flight risk. That she'd been traumatized by the crash and had stowed away on the bus out of fear. Did her best firm, but bourgeois, Negress imitation to get the violins going, even though she had as much faith in pigs as she had in God.

After years of being on the road, touring with her mother and the known universe, Rory had stopped checking miles on highway signs. In these Podunk nooks and crannies, she could smell the hair trigger sullenness, the boozy, clawing nicotine cloud despair of the audience before she even stepped on stage, single out the cesspit desperation of the last-chance-for-a-Saturday-night fuck nail biters. All of the second, third, fourth cousins once removed from the manager, the bartender, the janitor who'd coaxed them to come in before last call. She could spot the townies searching for a cozy place to settle in and get intimately shit-faced with their Jack Daniels. Looking past them, she could always find a woman to flirt with in her head; a random face to fixate on, to power her through even if the crowd was gruff, listless, evil. Katy had taught her to find a sweet spot of Zen and stick with it; otherwise, she'd go crazy fixating on what devilment the third row was hatching for her.

There was a gnawing unrest that crept in between gigs. A dingy coda when the band shape shifted and went back to their lives in shared apartments mired in two months back rent, dirty sheets alive with the residue of old trysts, one night stand phantoms strangling them in their sleep. Rory could never sleep more than four hours without jolting awake, expecting a visit from Katy. Could never settle into the bland set of rooms she'd leased in Baltimore, forever aiming to nestle in, do quotidian things like grow flowers, snoop on her neighbors, laze on the porch in the sun, watching the cream of the Negro middle class roll by in a flurry of ambition. She had sold her first house in the late sixties, when riots convulsed D.C. after Dr. King's assassination. She'd watched stores burn to the ground on the big new color TV she bought with her Memphis Soul Revue money. In the midst of death and chaos, it had been one of her best years financially. The Revue was a seven-city tour that dragged through the winter and spring but kept her and her backup singers in Italian shoes, tailored suit dresses, and the stacked to the heavens hairdos she dyed beet red to keep tongues clacking and ticket sales flowing. For one set, she dueled with Joe Tex and Wilson Pickett, scatting nimbly up and down the neck of her guitar to show who was boss. Better than fuck-ing, better than the womb-kissed tranquility of a soft bed after twelve hours on her feet. Better than a hundred things she could name but the smell of Marie's neck after she'd washed, pressed and pin curled her hair with that heavenly dab of water and Dixie Peach.

Under the forward churn of the bus, she tried to keep thoughts of Marie at bay; squashed, an ant between her fingers. It was in idle, frittered away moments that she wished she could get back from the Fates that Marie dribbled down on her in pieces. The way she laughed in half-snort. The way she whistled, winked at Rory, cooing, "hey sexy", mock-serious during her solos, keeping her going with wisecracks about the opening band's body odor, their prima donna demands for foot rubs, weed, or pigs in a blanket for dinner. Back then, when Rory was headlining four out of the five shows she booked, she could pick who opened for her. Russ would compile a short list and a long list, and she and Marie would rank the contestants on chops, looks, manners, charm, fuckability, and who seemed closer to Jesus.

The night Dr. King was killed, they'd been deciding between an Alabama R&B group and a rockabilly outfit from Scotland, dancing buzzed to *Hurdy Gurdy Man* in the living room, kids playing stickball in the street outside the house. The first scream of grief was a gut punch. Then, the neighborhood emptied out onto the lawns, driveways, sidewalks in blind cacophony. The kids going silent amidst the disbelieving wails, mounting rage, a dark pit of sorrow opening up before them. Every radio on the block on and synchronized.

Marie slumped onto the floor, gripping her brown nylons in knots like they were the only things that could keep her in one piece. "Motherfuckers, they got him," she moaned. "Dirty Klan motherfuckers took him out. I knew he wouldn't be able to go back down there without getting killed."

"Shit," Rory whispered, immobilized on the plastic slipcovered couch that had barely seen action since she'd gone on tour.

"Screw those bagpipe playing motherfuckers, we going Black all the way with this next one."

"They don't play bagpipes girl, they're more like, uh, Carl Perkins."

"Well, they white and the other group is black and I know they ain't gonna ride our backs to an American audience while Dr. King is lying dead in Memphis."

Marie had more savvy for sniffing out band strategy and compatibility. That was how Rory hooked up with Butch, blues improv plinker extraordinaire. Always had a raised eyebrow, surveying life with crotchety, salty Baby Ruth bar disdain. Marie spotted him when they were doing a one-off in Newark. He was seesawing between cajoling and banging on his piano, a flash of kinetic brilliance among a group of milquetoast dead-enders that would've played for a dime bag. She stole him right from under the nose of the band's pothead front man. Dug his directness instantly. Tall, rat's ass thin, chain smoking nasty clove cigarettes, his wavy black hair teased into a ponytail streaked with gray. Maybe if she and Marie had been curious and he'd had more meat on his bones they would have done him. She hadn't been thinking about adding a piano to the mix but Butch was a good stopgap for not having a bass player.

After eight years together, they were going to be the toast of Boise for two weeks.

The first one to break Rory's reverie was Thurston. "It's an armpit for sure. But my motto is, better to be like a shark and keep moving, than to sit around with your thumb up your ass rotting at home," Thurston said, when she told them about the Idaho gig.

"You got that cliché down cold," Butch said.

Rory stared ahead. "Right now, this and the beer commercial are all that's keeping us out of the unemployment line."

"And this is the absolute best Russ can do? What about the New York tour?"

"Not an option. Jude's got him by the dick."

"Managers," Thurston sneered. "Can't live with 'em, can't shoot 'em."

Mick lowered his voice, addressing Rory in the rearview mirror. "What are you going to do about the kid?"

"I made the call back at the studio."

"Ok, so what's the plan?"

"We discussed a designated drop off spot thirty minutes from here."

"Nice of you to tell me."

"Stop riding me on this."

"Not riding you, just want to know what you got in mind."

"I got getting rid of the issue in mind."

"That's harsh."

"What's your alternative?"

"Don't have one. Just keep me informed."

In the midsection of the bus, Thurston lurched forward to Butch with a pack of playing cards. He plucked an ace from the pack. "Can I tempt you maestro? We got another three hours of scintillating butt ugly California scenery."

"Learn how to count first."

"So, should I deal you in?"

"I don't exploit little chickies. Mick might go easy on your ass, but I won't…"

"I'm quaking Butchy. You can barely get it up for Go Fish, bush league motherfucker."

Butch swung into the aisle, rolling his spy thriller up in his hand like a newspaper. "I've had enough of you," he said, jabbing the book at Thurston. Thurston dodged, laughing. Butch lost his balance, sprawling on the floor.

Thurston got up and extended his hand. "C'mon, mate. No hard feelings."

Butch ignored him, staggering up on his own. Flat lands, empty billboards, vacant lots, pawnshops, churches with forlorn welcome signs floated past. "Lord, gimme strength," he said. "Looks like this is just the right place to find Thurston a good local Christian girl to inbreed with."

"My head's killing me," Rory barked at them. "Whatever you people do, leave the bitchin' and moanin' offstage tomorrow."

Butch sat down. "Sure, Rory. We know this crap Russ is pulling is wrong. Way wrong."

"Fucker's made a good living off your whole catalogue," Thurston said.

"He's no different from the rest of the fair-weather white boys. I'd say he's doing pretty good for only having a seventh-grade education."

"Why do you stay with him?"

"Shut the fuck up, Thurston," Butch said.

"Nobody's beating down the door to represent me. You know that."

The men fell silent. Butch shot Thurston a look, daring him to say something. Mick turned on the news. More rain was forecast. Protestors shadowed Carter at campaign stops. A serial killer was freshly executed in Texas. The stock market dipped. Food poisoning rocked two Midwestern Catholic school cafeterias. A fifteen-hour search and rescue had been launched for a white girl who'd fallen down a West Virginia well. Through it all, was the steady bleat of Jude Justis, rocketing up the charts.

Rory gestured to an Esso station on the horizon. "Turn off here." The squad cars were already there when they pulled off the exit. Two cars blocked the first gas pumps, a line of cars snaking out from the open ones. Her heart pounded, watching the officers get out of the car, their bodies, uniforms, and badges framed bulkily against the slate evening sky. Mick maneuvered the bus into a corner, killing the engine. The waiting drivers cranked up their radios, shifting impatiently, counting the minutes it took for each car to gas up and get going.

Rory got out of the bus, Mick on her heels. The officers plodded toward them, the eyes of everyone at the gas station following along. The first one smiled topsy-turvy at Rory, cocking his head in the direction of the bus.

"That's a pretty big rig. You drive that cross country?"

"Yes," Rory said.

"Don't envy you on the gas mileage. Where's the girl?"

"On the bus, asleep."

He paused, eyeing Mick. "You part of the traveling circus too?"

"My name's Mick."

"Mick, what's your occupation?"

"Roadie. Why's that relevant?"

"You don't ask the questions, we do. Any other adults on the bus, Ma'am? If so, we need them to exit the vehicle."

Rory frowned. "The officer I spoke to said this would be quick."

"I need everybody off that bus, or do you want us to get 'em off for you?"

"Take it easy on the girl."

The officer repeated his command, voice rising. The gas station quieted. Pumps clicking on and off, radio volumes lowered, heads craning out of windows, cigarettes stamped busily under shoe heels, the American guzzler mob lingering just a little longer to see what happened next.

Rory got on the bus. "Butch, Thurston. Come on off. Cops want to see you."

"What's going on?"

"Come on."

The two men shuffled off groggily as the officers brushed past them and onto the bus.

Rory whirled around. "What the fuck?"

"Ma'am, we're going to need you to get off while we search this vehicle."

"I thought we were just dropping off the girl, no one said anything about a search."

"We have the right to execute a search if we think there's been illegal activity."

"What illegal activity are you talking about?"

"Need you off the vehicle, Ma'am."

"Rory, just do what he says!" Mick yelled.

Sid rose up from the back seat, wide-eyed, bundled in Rory's jacket. "Can I take her off before you start the search?" Rory asked.

The officer nodded. Sid filed past him, grabbing at the bottom of Rory's shirt for support. A crowd had begun to gather around the pumps. Traveling vacuum cleaner salesmen, families stuffed into musty camper vans, stretching their legs, day laborers slurping cokes joking, relishing the end of the work day.

Rory cursed herself for waiting, for dragging the whole thing out. She should've ditched the girl at the beginning. Should've listened to Katy, paid attention to the back of her mind thrum of second and third thoughts that dogged her every waking moment. Even though she'd spent most of her life onstage, the gaze of the crowd milling about unsettled her, her next to empty stomach churning again with the bile of cowardice.

The girl hadn't suffered any injuries after the crash. Not a scratch, bruise or blemish. As they got off the bus, a third squad car drove up, squawking for the bystanders to move. A white female officer jumped out, followed by a black woman, stately, polka dot gloves on her long, tapered hands.

"Afternoon. Miss Tharpe?"

"Yes."

"I'm officer Braden and this is Mrs. Lanneville, legal guardian of the minor you've been driving around on your bus."

"I told the operator that she snuck back on the bus."

"We'll get all that sorted out once we have an opportunity to interview the girl," the policewoman snapped.

Mrs. Lanneville tugged on the polka dot gloves, opening her arms stiffly to embrace Sid. Sid let the woman handle her, the hug devolving into a clinical back pat. "Thank you for looking after her," she said to Rory in tinkling tones. "Especially given the circumstances of her uncle passing away yesterday."

"Uncle died?"

"Yes, sweetie. I just came from the hospital." The woman tinkled to a high C, showily aggrieved, lingering too long on the endearment. Sid looked through her in dull recollection. She had been one of the budding youth ministers at the church. A lemon-skinned, former file clerk with dewy pressed hair like her mother's. One of her many sisters, she was told. Vaporous and always borrowing money before they moved to the colony and Jesus smiled on her.

The other officers questioned Butch, Thurston and Mick as the first officer continued to search the bus. If he found the weed they'd be busted, set back for at least another few days while Russ scraped up money for bail and a lawyer.

"I'm glad he's dead," Sid said quietly, the grind of a semi turning in the driveway swiping up her last word.

Lanneville looked at her hard, pained, then dull, the light seeping from her eyes. "Now, sweetie, Sidra, you don't mean that, do you?"

The officer emerged from the bus emptyhanded.

"Miracle they didn't find that shit," Mick muttered, walking toward Rory, the first to be liberated from the interrogation. "Thurston probably stuffed it in his crack."

The officers huddled over their walkie-talkies. Lanneville gripped Sid by the shoulder. She wriggled away, kicking at the gravel under her feet. The woman turned back to Rory. "Like I said, I appreciate you keeping an eye on her. This one can be a handful. Girl, looks like you need a good hosing down too."

"I'm not a dog," Sid said.

Lanneville looked up at the sky. "Come on now. We have a long drive back to Oakland. Don't want to get caught in any more of this rain."

"Yeah, and it's gonna get nasty," the white female officer said. She gave them a final onceover, nodding at Rory. "Looks like your tags are about to expire soon. Should check on that. Wouldn't want to get pulled over again."

A radio call came in, sending the officers scuttling to their car. They peeled off onto the highway in a plume of dust and grit in pursuit of their next prey. Activity resumed around the gas pumps.

Lanneville dug in her purse. "Jesus. Can you wait here while I get some cigarettes?"

She strode across the parking lot to the line for the cashier. Rory signaled for the men to board the bus, antsy to get back on the road, on the schedule, on the clock… craving deep dead to the world sleep in a regular bed, even if it was at one of the shitty motels Russ had booked for them.

Sid walked over to a nickel-a-ride toy train by the bathroom. Three towheaded white kids bobbed up and down on it, blissed out, whining for another whirl when it ended. Lanneville nodded admiringly at them, unfolding a one-dollar bill into the hand of the cashier, counting her change.

She tossed Sid some coins as the white kids tumbled out of the train, clustering at the heels of their father, who was licking a Popsicle. "Here, take a ride, then we'll get going," she said.

Sid put the nickel in and got on.

"You're too big," one of the white kids chided.

"Fuck you."

The kid screamed that she'd said a bad word. The father huffed over to Sid, red-faced, licking Popsicle juice off his hands.

Across the parking lot on the bus, Mick settled down into the driver's seat. "Still say we dodged a bullet on that cop search. You can cough the stash up now, Thurston."

Rory checked the road map for the route to Boise, looking for a shortcut in the arid twists and turns of the Interstate 95. She glanced back at Sid. A small hubbub of finger pointing whites surrounded her. Rory ran out of the bus.

"What's going on here?"

The father lurched forward. "This kid has a damn foul mouth and she tried to push my boy off the train!"

Sid remained in the train seat, stock still, arms folded, not giving the twisted white faces an inch. Rory pushed into the middle of them, kneeling in front of Sid. "Where's your guardian?"

"You mean that tall black lady?" A white man in a grubby tank top showing his nipples said. "She took off a few minutes ago."

"Took off?"

"Yep, vamoosed."

"Fuck me," Rory whispered. She pulled Sid off the train. "Come on."

You Can't Always Get What You Want

THEY PULLED UP TO the Haven Motel in Boise, the two-star dump Russ had booked them into, its baby blue walls festooned with sagging Christmas lights, plastic reindeer, Santas gazing dejectedly at the straggle of old cars and trailers parked in the lot.

Butch rubbed his elbow, warily taking in the dilapidation. "This it?"

"Yep, home for the next few weeks," Rory grunted.

At the Podunk white motels, she would let Mick be the advance guard when they went to check-in. The rare times they were booked in the ritzy white ones, she would sweep in wearing her chinchilla fur and shades, get mistaken for Mahalia or Aretha, sop up a little of the deference from the seasoned white counter staff who could hum some authentic Negro spirituals, and corner her in the lobby later to autograph their mint condition copies of "This Little Light of Mine".

When they walked into the office, the woman at the counter barely budged from her desk, riveted to the final moments of a quiz show on TV. "Duck sauce, you dumb fuck!" she yelled at the set. "There's soy sauce, then there's duck sauce. Two totally different things. Sheesh!"

"Evening," Mick said.

She looked everyone up and down disinterestedly. "Yes?"

"We're checking in."

She flipped through the half empty appointment book, one eye on the TV, whirring to the beat of a beer jingle. "Three rooms under the name Rory Tharpe? That you?"

"That's me," Rory said, taking a pen on the desk to sign the room confirmation slip. "Know where we can get some decent food?"

"You can try the diner over there. It won't poison you too bad. Closes at nine so the church folks can have a place to eat when they get out of prayer meetings. Ornery gal who owns it makes a stew that'll knock you awake, even tries her hand at fry bread with Crisco. Does a semi ok job for a white chick."

She narrowed her eyes as Mick returned with Rory's guitars. "You all playing one of the clubs in town?"

"The Roost, heard of it?" Butch said sarcastically.

"It's a few inches short of being a dive."

"Story of my life."

"Good acoustics though, or so they tell me. Haven't been in ages. Mostly central casting good ol' boys. Me, I'm partial to the crusty must-ies. Roy Orbison's 'Only the Lonely', Buddy Holly doing Peggy Sue. Richie Valens, Big Bopper. The plane crash dudes, that's me."

Butch plopped down in the only chair in the office. "Last I checked, Roy was still alive."

"'Scuse me, I meant Otis. Shit, pardon my French for confusing pas-ty-face with Otis."

She opened a box on the counter and dug out three keys. "TV is on the blink in one of those rooms. Repair guy will be out at the end of the week. I can you give a discount coupon for the prime rib."

"Sure, Thurston here will eat any piece of red meat you put in front of him." Rory took the keys and handed them to Mick. "Put my instruments in my room and get the heat going in there, would you?"

Mick gathered up the guitars and headed outside. Thurston followed, grumbling about sharing a room with Butch.

The woman watched them leave, shaking her head. "Like babies, huh? You travel cross-country in that hunk of junk with them? Must get stir crazy."

Rory chuckled, the woman looking at her hard, leaning on her ashy elbows as she rearranged the bills on the counter. "Don't mind my asking, where'd you get all those white boys?"

"There're only two of them."

"More than one seems like a whole bunch to me. The way they suck up space."

"Known Mick, the husky one, for twenty years or so. Thurston about five. They know their shit."

"I assumed so. Why else would you keep them around?" She sized Rory up, a sly flicker of curious interest in her dark eyes, the lids tattooed with flecks of powder blue shadow. The quiz show had resumed and the lantern-jawed host read ponderously from his question card as the three contestants wet their lips and adjusted their thinking caps. "I could cream all them suckers. Shit's easy. I've applied a million times, always get the same form letter. Probably don't want any Indians messing up the snowstorm. If we started winning it'd fuck with their ratings. Like that Jewish boy they fucked on that quiz show in the fifties and replaced with the cheating WASP. Ratings is big business."

"Indeed."

"I gave you a room with a view of the mountains. Bitterroots. Nothing like 'em. When it's clear out, they'll knock your socks off. Your ofays are facing the gas station."

"Thanks. We'll check out that place you recommended… what's your name?"

"Cruz," she said, wiping her hand on her jeans then extending it to Rory. "Good to meet you."

Rory went out into the parking lot. Sid was standing in the door of the bus, clutching the flannel blanket Thurston had surrendered to her because of his night sweats. After Sid had been deserted by Lanneville she'd pleaded for Rory to take her with them. Every time Rory called the police station from the rest stops, she was put on hold. The hours grinding down for when they needed to be in Boise. The specter of more money lost. She toyed with taking her to the Highway Patrol, finding a shelter, ditching her at a rest stop; every scenario more desperate as they approached the California-Nevada border, steaming north on the 95 to Idaho.

"Don't make me go back there," Sid said.

"Even though she dumped you, that lady was kin to you, right? The police'll find her, make her do right."

"Kin don't do what she did."

"Yeah, maybe."

"You got any kids?"

"No."

"When I grow up, I don't want any either."

"Smart."

"Can I see one of your records?"

Rory thought of Marie. The moon wincing down at her, tucked away in her own patch of the world. The day-to-day of holding down a relationship had dogged them. Dealing with the secrecy, the hound dog of keeping up appearances amidst the chatter of neighbors, studio musicians, the women in her family with their knives out for their nasty ways. She could've held on if the money hadn't evaporated. If the attacks about their commercial viability hadn't begun with a vengeance. If Marie hadn't blamed her for the record label's final betrayal, dumping them after their second record stalled.

"Sure," she said. "I have a cassette tape. Wanna listen?" She took out a player from her duffel bag and switched it on to a jaunty duet that she'd recorded with Marie. Sid listened, curious, intent.

"Did you use to be on TV?"

"Yeah, on variety shows and gospel hours. Did some concerts overseas that got filmed."

"That lady's voice is nice."

"She's one of the best."

"You sing ok too. Sorta like how we sang in church," her voice trailed off, tentative again.

"The church you were in before the crash?"

"Yeah."

Rory turned the tape off. "I've got to get ready for the show."

"They gonna give you a record deal?"

"Nobody'll just up and give me a record deal."

"Why not? Aren't you good enough? How come your stuff's not on the radio like Parliament-Funkadelic? They got this new song about this no-swimming, big nose man that sounds like a nursery rhyme. I almost got the words right—"

"They play a lot of trash on the radio… We have to find your other kinfolk."

"I told you, they don't want me."

"They're assholes then."

"Where are we?"

"A place called Boise, in Idaho. They teach you state capitals in school?"

"Yeah, at the church school," she said, rattling names off proudly. "Little Rock. Austin, Oklahoma City, Baton Rouge, Nashville." She rubbed her eyes, letting out a wet burp. "Can you show me how to play like you?"

"Impressive. What you know about Little Rock?"

Cruz walked past Rory and Sid. "You having an extra guest in your room?" she asked, eyeing Sid.

"Yeah. You going to charge us?"

"Naw. Only pets and deadbeat men are extra. And I'm assuming she ain't the former or the latter."

It was not her, she was sure, but a child, an urchin, a dumpling with a heartbeat playing dress up in a white sheet poked with holes for air, beckoning from the night sky. Casper. A Grand Dragon. An interrogator asking, what if she'd died at twelve. What if she had never known Marie, or sweet potato pie with ice cream, or the year 1978, lodged in the belly of a near broken down tour bus.

Had she died at twelve and didn't know it? The ghost cobbling a made-up adult life from carrion.

She only had these reoccurring dreams while on the road. Dreaming that they were driving when they were standing still. The bump of the wheels stuttering along, making them land like lizard brain terrorists stalking behind her eyes. She was certain it was because she hadn't resolved to do something about the girl. And now she was being punished.

Every time the phone rang, she fantasized it was the aunt or the police. Charging her with being a molester, a kidnapper with infants' skin under her fingernails. In the maw of sleep, she heard sirens, mayhem, as their bus crashed into Cruz's motel, and the girl crawled out of the wreck alive, jeering at Rory's weakness.

When Sid woke up from a nap that evening, Rory was sitting on the edge of the bed in her slip and socks, combing through receipts, the news playing on the TV in jumpy black and white. A missing white baby swaddled in a yellow receiving blanket had the entire Eastern seaboard mobilized and alert, torches, lanterns burning bright in dark forests, hamlets convulsed in mourning and clenched teeth purpose as the county sheriff held forth to the international press corps.

She looked over at Sid. "Go back to sleep."

"Can't."

"Try. You'll be bombed in the morning."

The phone rang. Rory tensed up. There was silence on the other end of the line, then a click.

"Can I go with you?"

"No."

"I... I don't want to stay here by myself."

Rory put on her boots, looking at the phone, the TV screen. Vertigo gripped her suddenly, as though the white people would flood the room, burn through their search and rescue, root around for the little white child under the bed, scoop up Sid as incriminating evidence of a lesser variety.

Sid watched the white people hold forth on TV, muted. "I hope she's dead," she said.

The phone rang again. Rory picked it up then slammed it down. Silence, another click. She looked at the girl, bony and dwarfed inside the oversized sweatshirt she was wearing the first day they found her on the highway. "She probably is dead," she said. "C'mon, wash yourself up. Go pee. Toilets at this dive bar are gonna be filthy."

The Negro thrill chills got them twisting out of their seats. A mass of breakneck, throbbing at 78 rpm speed insatiable whiteness. One day before the election, and Nixon and JFK were neck and greasy neck. The aging bobby soxers from the tri-state area were mobbing the dance floor, martinis in hand, belching out stock tips and babysitters' names and Christmas vacation plans in thuggish force. The whole of the country drunk with unease. It was a rare rock appearance for Rory and Katy. Side by side, playing that running-with-the-devil music, as if no shit had ever happened to separate them. Jamming; here loose, here tight, here tender; as if Rory hadn't up and married that crum bum couldn't-tell-his-head-from-a-hole-in-the-ground Eamon Temple just to have a beard, a straight man to make nice for the record company. As if crown jewel

Negress musicians like Ma and Bessie hadn't been doing that rent-a-dick camouflage shit since time immemorial just to have a fighting chance. As if Katy hadn't had to suffer the indignity of overhearing them fucking... an all business quickie Rory initiated in the bus bathroom when Katy was supposed to be asleep.

Eamon had claimed to have connections in the music industry. A great uncle on his white side was married to a second cousin of the Chess brothers. Chess had signed Muddy Waters and Etta James. Had gotten their music into every little foul cranny of Main Street, stitching it into the backbeat at bus stations, Laundromats, cafeterias, car shows, debutante balls when them savage ofay queens kicked off their pink pumps and got down and dirty. But them creaky old Chicago Jews probably wouldn't know that shiny-haired, pink-skinned nigger Eamon from a Pullman porter serving their egg creams, Katy said. And if they did, we'd just get ripped off twice. Once by them, second time by him.

Word from the Black musicians on the circuit was that the Chess' were doing pay to play with radio stations to get their records on air. Rory didn't like all that under the table mess, but the industry reeked of it. Eamon swooped in, claiming to know how to work the dee jays without payola. So greasy he blinded you, Katy said in disgust. A plaything Rory'd get bored of in short order. He'd been a few steps up from a groupie, fancied himself an entrepreneur, a race man with an eye for turning a creative profit in so-called up and coming industries, he told people, doling out homemade business cards to anyone he thought might be useful.

He'd been hovering outside in the alley, smoking after a crappy show she did in Montgomery, Alabama. Her stomach aflame from downing two packs of antacids onstage, the backing band muddling through the set like they were working a teeny bopper birthday party.

"You know, I dabbled a little in that once upon a time," he said, pointing to her guitar as she cussed out the drummer and the bassist in her head, a fart bubble making its way torturously up from her gut.

She looked at him, stepping back, taking him in, a fireball of solicitousness with pitch black hair in a scalpel cut side part. "Do I know you?"

"No, but I'm hoping we can change that sad state of affairs, Miss Tharpe. Would you have a drink with me tonight?"

"I only drink on weekends."

"Well let's pretend its Saturday, baby, and the next morning we'll be in the front row at church, I promise."

"We'll keep it at one round. And I don't do church in strange cities."

"Well, if that works for you, it works for me. You call Montgomery strange, girl? This about the least strange place on the planet."

"Yes, and I'm not your girl or your baby. I'm also not partial to men with limited vocabularies. Puts me right to sleep."

He ran his hand through his hair, pinching away the dots of black dye that came off on his fingertips. "We wouldn't want that now."

The drink went down easy, and she laughed, unburdened, amused by how quickly he was able to knock back his liquor and maintain a steady stream of stories about his past in Indianapolis; the fortune in rare mint condition records he owned, the time he got out of being called up for the war because of the rumors he was fruity, caught parading around in his big sister's drawers.

"Been getting that shit all my life, because I was yellow."

"And a man."

He nodded. "Fuck that."

"I'll see if I can work up a few crocodile tears for you."

Under the table, she put her hand on his calf, sliding it up his leg through the soft crinkle of his suit to the hinge of his knee.

He smiled and kept drinking. Pool balls crashed together in the room next door. A dishrag of a man bleated to Big Mama's "Hound Dog" on the jukebox. Rory probed, resting her hand on a patch of scars. Eamon flinched, then relaxed, watching her.

"Don't," he said.

"Still hurt?"

"Naw."

She rested her hand between his legs, probing the groove of his slacks, the doleful hang of cheap fabric, erratically dry-cleaned, well-traveled, pulsing with secrets. He shifted, waving off the waitress who stopped to clear their glasses, her lip curling in disdain at the scene unfolding under the dingy tablecloth.

"This ain't no whorehouse," she hissed.

Rory drained her glass. "And he ain't no whore. Why don't you get on, mind your own fucking business?" She put down a five-dollar bill.

The waitress cut her eyes at them, snatching up the glasses and the money. The dishrag man let out a whoop from the jukebox. "Damn, if I had the money Elvis Presley stole from Big Mama you wouldn't have to work graveyard, gal." He leaned over, swatting at the waitress. She ducked away from him, raining a spout of gin into his pasty concave face.

Rory leaned into Eamon. "Who would you vote for if you could?"

"None of them bastards. Naw, I take that back, maybe that side of his mouth talking rich boy with the big teeth, big hair. The one the white girls think is so pretty. Blind ones, that is."

"Ya'll pretty ones gotta stick together."

"That's right."

"Well, fortunately we're registered in California."

"Oh? They let spooks vote out there?"

"*Negroes.* My mother's people have property out in Los Angeles."

"Never been much past the Mason Dixon. Hear it's beautiful, though."

He paused, drawing her closer to him. His breath coming moist on her cheek in licorice-like tendrils, heart beating desperate, tiny castanets inside his chest that she wanted to reach in, grab, squeeze, lift up to the light, juice dribbling on her fingers. Instead, she put her hand on his crotch and rubbed, gazing into the blighted moons of his eyes.

"You wanna take me there..." he said.

They did an inaugural twenty-four-hour presidential election fuck, then emerged, limping to their separate corners of Rory's motel room, the world outside the window surging with the promise of the new regime, the savior who'd pissed on Rev. King when he was in jail.

They married after a month of circling each other, morbidly curious. Before the deal was sealed he popped up unexpectedly during her most obscure appearances, brandishing flowers, dead on arrival jokes and a downturned hedgehog's grin as weapons; clumsy, prepubescent sandbox flirt ploys that had never worked on Rory before. Still, there was something about this one that gave her pause. When the noise from the gigs, the money wrangling, the sideline cretins poisoning their livers by downing shot after shot in the dwindling midnight audiences receded, she had time and space to pick apart the thought of him.

She considered how a pretty boy like that could be useful as an advance guard, a buffer, a penknife to whittle down the edges of Katy. How the ever-present indictment, the scorn in Katy's voice became perversely delicious to Rory. How it echoed with savage force every time she fucked Eamon and thought, with only a twinge of guilt, that she and Katy might be more evenly matched now that the threat of him loomed; he, the hick interloper who had designs on the pittance that would be left over when they put the flowers on her. If there was one thing Katy excelled at over all others it was penury, all the dough they made in the early days fastidiously counted and recounted, inhaled, initialed, then secreted away into the mini bunkers she dug in the backyard garden in Cotton Plant.

Katy, ever the rainy day woman, always looking out for her baby girl. Til death do them part.

"No one will ever love you more than I love you," Katy said after each gig, pecking Rory on her forehead as she sat in front of the dressing room mirror, her skin embroidered in Katy's purple lipstick. It was the shade she'd requested for burial so she could be presentable for Jesus, for the devil, or for the worms, kidding that any one of them was a strong possibility. She died the day before Rory's birthday, a final act of spite. Then, shortly after, the nightly visitations began. The purple smeared lips announcing themselves to Rory in the darkness, taunting, soothing, plying her with questions and commands.

"I may not outlive that shiny nigger," the purple lips whispered. "But he's gonna learn to watch his back."

But first.

In the early days of the marriage, Eamon watched their dance from the sidelines, evading the heat of Katy's contempt, her attention focused on fighting the tax bill she'd gotten for '47 to '49. They moved into a railroad apartment near Harlem, taking furtive turns bathing in the kitchen tub. Katy camped out in the front room with a toy piano and a yapping weasel dog she'd smuggled in for company. Between gigs she filled in as a substitute cafeteria worker at the corner elementary school. She was a machine at chopping orange slices, coaxing mounds of creamed string beans into tin platters under the line supervisor's pop-eyed scrutiny. The supervisor once caught Katy doing mock glissandos on the counter and docked her pay. You gonna boogaloo your country ass right out of here, she said, snickering under her hair net, the halls bursting with ravenous little United Nations kids sprung from their math drills.

Winters were the hardest, the tightest, the driest for bookings in New York. After work, she came home and tied up the hallway phone with calls to clubs and promoters, sharks who wanted to jam Rory into four-a-night, back-to-back sessions or a backing band with tin pot amateurs who'd get paid the same as she did.

"If you trying to make these deals you gotta get down off that highfalutin shit," Eamon said. "Ain't nobody care what she done did back in the '40s. Shit's gotta grab 'em now."

"Don't tell me how to work this," Katy bristled. "Your ass' been here for all of two damn minutes and now you the expert."

"Well I know one thing, my baby ain't gonna slop no toilets and look after no ashy brats the rest of her life if you can't bring nothin' in. Hard as she work and with her talent she should be on all of them major shows, Ed Sullivan, Perry Como, Dean Martin, all of 'em. Now, in order to do that you gotta know how to work them white boys. Otherwise, all they gonna throw you is crumbs."

The apartment overflowed with his wardrobe. A suit for every occasion and mood, piled haphazardly on a chair in their bedroom next to a milk crate full of his color-coded handkerchiefs, ties, scarves, socks. The collection spilling out onto the fire escape where Rory went to practice when the four walls started to close in on her, and she wished Eamon and her mother would both vaporize.

By the end of the fourth month, the married couple had settled semi-permanently into their opposite ends of the bed, ocean floor sediment undisturbed, Rory's hand only grabbing for his hip in the funk of a nightmare about a fumbled intro, a series of misplaced sharps, her clothes blown off, hanging in shreds as she stumbled on stage in front of the church kids she'd grown up with; pointing at her, dissolving into a froth of laughter.

"Aw girl, you done had the nekkid dream again?" Eamon teased, holding her until she'd settled down. "Everybody in the world has had that at least once."

"Yours was never playing in front of a hundred people."

"True, but try waking up refreshed after you've dreamt of being a grown ass buck naked man in front of your grandmama." They laughed. He got up and went into the kitchen and lit the stove, careful not to wake

Katy, who was snoring on the day bed in the front room, entangled in her dog. Harlem's monstrous cold bore down from every corner. He put on water for coffee, fixed Rory a brandy to get her back to sleep, savoring their softest ritual in the hours before the building jumped with people going to work. Seventh floor, a family of seamstresses; eighth floor, the boiler technicians and pipefitters; ninth floor, the window washers and nurse's aides and laundry attendants; and then him, looking down his nose at them. His only marketable skills were his smile, moxie, cunning, or so he believed, chewing through a cocoon of cocky self-doubt.

Late afternoon, when Rory and Katy were at work, he called up the labels where Katy had bombed. Rory was under new management, he said. Thought you'd like to know. Everything's negotiable. She's ready, just give her a chance. Why mess around with imitators when we got the original right here in New York fucking City.

"That nigger barely finished the first grade and he's trying to run you," Katy said when Eamon went out at night, making the rounds playing pool for bets. "He got no business representing nobody, least of all you."

"Least he's trying," Rory snapped.

Katy took a breath. Her tone measured, the quiet of Holy Tabernacle church pews, right after the Prophetess had banished another unwitting victim. "You suggesting I'm not? Ain't fair, baby girl. Who got you work in the early days? Put your, *our,* name on the map when you were still littler than that guitar? Those white boys on the labels would never give an inch to a Negro woman playing race music. And just 'cause that nigger's got a few peanuts between his legs they give him a smidgen more respect than they would give me."

"He ain't a nigger."

"What's he done to show otherwise?"

"Stop calling him that."

"Well, his Christian name's suspect. Ain't never heard of a colored man with that kind of name."

"He got me a spot in the Village for two weekends."

"Fancy that. Backing?"

"Lead."

"What's the pay?"

"Good enough."

"Don't get cute."

"I don't have specific numbers right now."

"The specific number for our rent, heat and water bill is fifty dollars. I haven't seen him give a thin dime to any of it since he's been here."

"He paid last month with his tips from the restaurant."

"You mean from gambling."

"What difference does it make, Mama?"

"Gambling is illegal, girl, don't act like a damn fool and don't play me for one. He got half a brain, two working legs and all his faculties, tell his ass to get a real job or get in the service—"

"He got a heart murmur. They discharged him. Besides, you say all the time yourself this ain't our war no way."

"I said that about those of us who've already sacrificed. What sacrifices has that Negro made, other than laying up getting frostbite in this rattle-trap and looking less pretty than he would in a place with decent heat?" She paused. The dog panted and fussed around her feet. She reached onto the counter and picked up a ball of yarn, throwing it into the next room, the dog skittering after it. "You settled, baby," she said in a low voice. "A lot do. Practically a disease women have. I thought you would've been stronger than that."

"What are you talking about?"

"Opening your legs for the first shiny nigger looks your way."

Rory took a step back. The dog rolled around the floor, ravaging the yarn. "He wasn't the first… and what if he was? That's my business."

"Wrong, baby, it's our business. Don't you understand, if the labels think you a tramp, if they think you a dyke, a junkie or whatever the hell else they got in their heads… it's our business, it affects whether there's food on the table, whether we get to stay in this rattle trap a few more months or get thrown out on the streets. You ain't Miss Ann, girl. Miss Ann gets all kind of second, third and fourth chances."

"I know that, Mama. You ain't telling me nothing new. But what do you think Eamon's trying to do? He's out there trying to get me signed somewhere. I can't do nothing if I don't have a fighting chance at a contract."

"Don't fool yourself that all the so-called hustlin' he's doing is for you, Miss Rory," she said, holding the nickname bitterly between her teeth.

"If he finds himself what he thinks is a better, prettier, faster piece of tail you'll look up one morning and all them shiny clothes and shoes of his will be gone. Lightning quick. Then you would be better off with one of them gals you been sniffin' around."

"I'm not sniffin' up around nobody."

"Hurts me when you lie, girl. I see what you do. God sees, He knows what's in your heart and He don't approve."

"What makes you think God approves of what you do?"

"We ain't talking about me."

"I get a man, you slam him. I pop a string or so much as breathe the wrong way—"

"You don't have to speechify with me. And don't get with a man just to lay up under him, lying through your teeth that you love him when he's screwing you. I'm just trying to protect you. You trust too much, you'll fall hard."

"That go for trusting you too?"

Katy lowered her voice. "You trusted me for one hot second and that was before you were born."

Keys rustled outside in the hallway. Eamon lurched through the door, blowing into his hands, tip of his nose tinged with red. He nodded curtly at Katy, slinging his arm around Rory's neck, ice stung lips puckering into her cheek. "Hey baby. Got some good news. Even the battle axe landlady out there on a warpath can't spoil it."

Katy hoisted the pot of water onto the stove. "Well, what is it?"

"Saw Northrup Stein in the pool hall today."

"That peckerwood still around?"

He released Rory and plopped down on the wooden stool by the stove, wrestling his boots off. "Alive, kickin' and lookin'. Wants to pep up his line-up."

"What kind of numbers is he talkin'?"

"Forty percent."

Katy banged her fist on the stove. "Fool."

"First single she cuts that goes platinum; he'll raise it fifteen percent."

Rory slumped against the door, listening to the landlady make her way down the hall for the rent. "He told you that with a straight face?"

"Peckerwood ain't changed since the government shut his penny ante label down because it was run by the mob. Now he's sniffing around for a new scam and new marks and hit pay dirt when he found you."

"Who's he signed?" Rory asked.

"A few Carolina gospel acts, scat trio from Baton Rouge and a little white girl, teenage Texas cracker trying to sound Negro."

Northrup Stein helmed "race music" at Artrola records. Artrola… named after the words "art" and "Victrola". A revelation he had, sitting in his office, circa 1945, the world swirling in postwar liberation as a corner busker looking for her big break screeched a few notes of Billie up at him from the street. We're going to give the average American the best, most primo listening experience ever. Like they can smell Lady Day's gardenias, catch a drop of Satchmo's sweat sitting right in the comfort of their living rooms. Get a fat juicy little piece of the Negro experience at the turn of a knob, all for a nominal price, a pittance, a steal.

A month after he ran into Stein, Eamon, Katy and Rory waited in Artrola's outer office for over an hour before the peppermint-slurping secretary ushered them into Northrup's inner sanctum with an imperial wave of the hand. He occupied little more than a walk-in closet, a dirge of an office festooned with plastic plants and diagrams of musical dynasties that stared dingily onto Thirty Fourth Street. He was a Country and Western encyclopedia, a student of Rory's collaboration with bluegrass harp player Spence Martin, priding himself on mastering all the muck and mire of the project's stillbirth, selling fewer than a hundred copies.

"Unfortunately, there's no money in Negroes collaborating with hillbillies," he said, flashing snaggle teeth. "Too bad too, 'cause I've always thought you and them had natural affinities. Two groups beaten down by rich landholders and all." He flashed a conspiratorial grin. "You know, they say an Alabama redneck is just a Negro with white skin, a double gauge shotgun and no home training. By the way, call me North."

Katy snorted, unimpressed. "I don't know who says mess like that. Rory wants the freedom to experiment or go traditional and not have to worry about ya'll breathing down her neck. That bluegrass pecker was stone crazy. If you people can hook her up with songwriters and producers that are worth a damn—"

"We've got some of the finest ones around. Question is, will Rory work with them?"

Rory swiveled in her seat. "What's that supposed to mean?"

Eamon bristled, puffing himself up. "Yeah, what the hell are you talking about, man?"

"There've been a few complaints."

"About what?"

"Reliability. Consistency."

"Who's saying Rory ain't reliable?"

"It would be... indelicate for me to reveal my sources."

"Bullshit!" Eamon snarled.

Katy held her hand up at him dismissively, as if ordering a dog to heel. "That's because they don't exist or they jealous. When we get booked, we there on time, no ifs and or buts. Most of the time she schooling the producer, teaching him on what he should be doing."

North trained his gaze on Rory. "I know you're a pro, Mrs. Tharpe."

"Then treat her like one," Eamon said.

"I heard you gave those high yellow caterwaulers from Sarasota, one's that don't even know how to play instruments, a pretty little advance. Rory's got more talent in her fingernail than all three of 'em put together," Katy said.

"You mean the Withers' sisters? They're top of the line."

"They're pieces of tail." Katy pointed at a poster of a musical revue on the wall. "You can line 'em up with that other gal right there."

North squinted to where she was pointing, a silhouette of a white woman at a mic, dark hair blasting out from her head. "Jude Justis' a Texas sensation," he said. "Used to sneak into Negro churches in West Texas and pass for colored. Stayed from sunup to sundown. Drank it all in."

"Pastors should start charging white folks an admission fee," Rory said.

Eamon picked up a strip club matchbook from North's desk. "Or make 'em slop toilets and serve chitlins in exchange for all the music they be stealing."

North smiled weakly. "She's part of a stable I'm putting together. Girls with big voices and an ear for a beat. Trainable, teachable. No comparison to your talent, Mrs. Tharpe. What you can do with a guitar...

man," he shook his head, pressing his gelatinous body into the desk as he offered Eamon a cigarette.

"I'll take one," Katy said, reaching past Eamon. "Now you say you putting together a 'stable'? You running a horse show, Mr. Northrup?"

"Just a figure of speech."

"It's a bad one."

"It's just words. You know the saying, 'sticks and stones' and all that. Rory, we'd like to offer you a three-year contract with flexibility to do session work for some of the girl groups…"

Rory didn't flinch. "Five years and freedom to hand pick my own band. Any session work I make double the rate."

North paused. "Provided you pick from the Artrola roster first."

They went home triumphant. Eamon buzzing, Katy grudgingly aglow, the El train hurtling them back uptown in a clean line of promise, the other passengers a Babel-esque soundtrack to their outsized meditations on what would be next; the heat bill that could finally be paid in full, new dress shoes for Katy, a long-delayed doctor's visit for the tremors in her hands, a bullet proof safe deposit box to keep her shit away from Eamon's prying fingers.

Katy flipped through the pages of her Bible, pretending to be absorbed, a defense against Eamon's chattering, his showy petting of Rory for the disinterested audience of the train car, an odorous group newly sprung from ten-hour shifts at the seaport, picking the mire of fish gills off their clothes. The train slammed to a stop. The Bible slid off her lap onto the floor. A burly white man with a crumpled grocery bag leaned down to pick it up.

"Here you go," he said, giving it back to Katy.

She nodded thanks. He looked over at Rory. "Your sanctified music's my favorite," he said. "Used to practice to it when I was learning electric bass." He extended his free hand to Katy. "Mick Kincade. You must be Mother Katy Duren."

"How you know about me?"

"Have some of your old Nickelback records."

"Crooks."

"Saw you coming out of Artrola."

Eamon sat up in his seat. "You stalking us?"

"You might say that. I mean no disrespect though."

"Look, man, my lady's tired, she ain't got time to—"

Rory interjected. "You any good on that bass?"

"I can run and walk with the best of 'em."

Katy let out a dry laugh. "Boy, you sure is clever, I'll give you that. But clever don't mean you good enough to back Rory Tharpe."

Eamon whipped out a business card. "I'm her husband and business manager. Any demos you got send 'em to that P.O. Box and we'll take your proposal under advisement."

The train stopped, disgorging the seaport workers, sucking in maids in wilted uniforms, servicemen slurping down egg creams, panhandlers rattling tin cups over the cries of babies being shushed by their mothers. Katy tightened her grip on the Bible and squinted mockingly at Eamon. "Take it under advisement. You talkin' proper ain't foolin' nobody. The word 'manage' shouldn't even be in your vocabulary." She turned to Mick. "If we interested in you, we'll call you, but don't hold your breath."

Butch looked at himself in the motel bathroom mirror and frowned. His head floated in the sickly light, smudged, misshapen, lifted from a passing ghoul's body and plopped down on his neck in ¾ time, the backward travel of the morphine zigzag he'd been riding since they left California.

Mick sprawled lumpily on one of the double beds in the other room in gym socks and sweatpants, flipping through one of Rory's *Jet* magazines.

"What time are we up?" Butch asked, straining to see the centerfold as he walked out of the bathroom.

"Leaving here at 9:30. Rory's getting grub from the ptomaine palace across the way."

"That'll ground her. Even if it's crap, at least she's got something in her stomach other than booze."

"She's dry, brother. Haven't seen her take anything but a recreational hit in over a month."

Butch raised his shirt up, rolling deodorant under his arms. "Stop coverin' for her."

"I'm not."

"Bullshit. Katy never coddled her."

"Katy's been dead for donkey's years. Practically beat Rory down when she was alive."

"Well, maybe she needs a little stick."

"What's that supposed to mean?"

"British term for getting things done."

"You saying she's not doing shit?"

"What's she written over the past year? We're doing the same old covers over and over."

"That's what people want. Or have you forgotten what happened when she did that country stuff?"

"It's treading water."

"You're eating aren't you? Got a roof over your head?"

"Stop covering for her."

Mick put down the magazine and turned on the TV, banging it to get rid of the fuzzy picture snow. Football players rolled on a field, fondling each other in a big flailing heap of spent flesh. He blinked at the scene then banged the TV some more.

"I know she was real disappointed about losing that gig to Jude's sidekick," Butch said.

Mick kept his eyes on the screen. "Uh huh… I used to want to do that."

"What?"

"Color commentary. Calling plays and shit."

Butch put his shirt on then rustled into the saggy black jeans he'd worn two days in a row. His weight had been dipping from crammed-in meals on the fly, pork rind dinners, creamed corn breakfasts, all you can eat onion rings from gamey truck stop buffets glopped with griddle grease.

"Yeah, another shit-fisted white man making millions on Black bucks. You would've been a real natural."

The phone rang. Mick put it up to his ear, then hung up.

"She's ready."

Butch tossed him the deodorant. "Here you go. Showtime. Weee."

Mick turned the TV off. He took the cap off the deodorant and sniffed it, holding it to his nose for a few seconds. "Keep that critique to yourself, hear?"

"About the writing?"

"About everything. She doesn't need it right now."

"Doesn't want it, you mean."

"Not the right time or place."

"You're not her fucking gatekeeper, Mick."

"If you don't have shit to offer by way of a solution then why raise it?"

Butch was silent. Someone was coming up the stairs in a series of wheezes and hacking coughs. A fist pounded on the door.

"Yo, let's go, mates!" It was Thurston's voice. He jiggled the locked doorknob then pounded again.

"We're coming, you maniac!" Butch yelled. "Don't make me have to drop kick your Okie ass."

"Ah, keep dreamin'!"

Butch rushed out onto the balcony. Thurston bounded down the stairs, swiveling around to give Butch the finger. The motel owner Cruz's sister leaned over the railing, pockmarked cheeks encrusted with dried mascara, a paper cup of piss colored lemonade dangling from her hand. "Okie, yeah, that's right. Cocksuckers all look alike."

Rory patted the loaded .45 in her bag, watching the empty stage, gleaming, immaculate. The stage was eat-off-the-floor spic and span, the cleanest she'd ever seen in a dive bar, save for when she played the fringe of the '68 Democratic Convention in Chicago. She'd opened for Mickey Mouse hometown advantage blues rock untouchables who'd just been kicked off their label after mooning the company's chief exec at a fundraiser they claimed was for Ethiopian refugees. Her performance had been in super slo-mo, Black kids dotting a sea of hopped up white ones from the North Side, cooling their heels and looking for shelter, cheap dope and conspiracy stories after the protests flamed through the city. She'd tried to quiet her insecurity, smooth the brain smudges of doubt that Katy had stitched into her about whitey on the hunt. She ripped into a private solo for the Black ones, picking them out when the light hit the crowd and giving them names, back stories, temperaments. These were the same faces she'd watched from the sidelines as she traveled the country, bedding down for a hot second hither and yon, fighting back the murmurs of Cotton Plant and the squirm of 6 a.m. Sundays when she and Katy were still in bed. When Katy held her close, nibbling, tickling at her ear to distract her from the tin soldier march of the simpleton who made the rounds collecting rent for the landlord, taking down names of those who couldn't pay in a ledger.

They called it the slave book, the rape book. Sunday nights after the first of the month were awash in the screams of the women the landlord came back to fuck, musk oil slathered over the fortress of his body, fresh from church and a home cooked meal, fresh with the sweet doting kisses of his baby daughters.

That was why Katy kept a loaded pistol by their bed. *Pistol-whipped cracker stew is always in season*, she said. Don't keep a home unless you're protected, don't leave home unless you're packing.

Rory found the gun among Katy's things when she died, realizing that she'd blocked out the sound, smell, taste of the scene one night when she'd fired it in self-defense at a Black man, not the cracker.

Joberg, the bar manager, led Rory and the rest of the band to a makeshift dressing room next to the boiler and shuffled off, biting his grimy nails between barks to the staff about doing a sound check, skin the color of smashed silverfish.

"Get them a round!" he yelled to the bartender, emptying blenders of Bloody Mary sludge down the sink. "Pronto, whatever they want."

"Water for me," Rory said. Thurston, Butch and Mick fanned out into the room with their equipment. Sid shadowed Rory cautiously, cupping her mouth to a comic book she'd found on the bus.

"Your manager Russ and I go back decades, poor bastard. Way back. Before he became a traitor to us little guys out in the sticks," he chuckled. "First time in Boise?"

"I went to a funeral here once," Butch cracked.

The manager went on, extending his hand to Sid. "Hello, young lady. You got to keep your head down, lest we get busted." He turned to Rory unfazed. "Make sure you keep an eye on this little lady. You're lucky this is assbackward Boise. Kiddies in clubs don't fly once you go past the state line over to Billings. Russ said you all were going overseas after this?"

"That's news to me," Rory said.

"He's got something up his sleeve. Read it in the trades. Big blues-gospel extravaganza revival thing. The limeys are still crazy about your shit. Punk and the disco ball haven't totally mowed them down yet. Way more money to be made over there than here."

Rory took her guitar out of the case, eyeing him strategically. "Read what in the trades?"

"That the limeys want you over there for a big shindig at one of those roundhouses."

"Nobody told me about it."

"Don't you read your own press?"

"When I can afford it."

"Go over to the limeys. Fatten your paycheck. They love retro across the pond."

The building shuddered with the roar of people coming in, stamping off the cold, shedding their fur-lined jackets. Their vision adjusted in the feral dark as they honed in on the bar, open seats, familiar faces, replays of President Carter's speech to the U.N. jumping frantically on the busted set mounted overhead. Practice time had been scant since the studio session. Rory felt Katy stirring, spoiling for a rematch. How can you stay in the game if you don't work these knuckleheads? Them bottom feeding thieves from the record companies gone lick you dry and pass you by so fast your head'll spin. You got to get rid of doll face, just like you ditched that shiny nigger. Distractions and side mess'll bring you straight down. Your boy Russ said there might be a record label scout out watching y'all tonight. Don't sleep on these hayseeds.

She punched her knuckles against the strings to get the voice out of her head.

Showtime.

She stood up and walked over to Butch, Thurston, and Mick. "Come the fuck on, it's time." The men gazed up at her, startled. "We got a scout in the audience and we're going to be a quartet tonight. Card's coming for the second set."

Thurston snorted, grabbing his drumsticks. "How charitable of him."

"Card and a scout? How come you didn't tell us?" Butch asked.

The bar manager went up on stage to introduce them. A waitress plopped a Stetson on his head, and he jiggled his ass in time to piped-in

Merle Haggard, sending her off with a silverfish leer, his squat junior G-man's body backlit by the disco ball hanging over the drum kit.

"Alright, ladies and gents, as you know we mostly dig and support local talent. We've been blessed with some of the best shredders in the business to come through these portals, straight from Boise, Pocatello, Billings, Bozeman, Helena and the list goes on. But tonight, we gots the good stuff. Straight pipin' hot from the Mississippi Delta."

Butch cut his eyes at Rory and Mick. "Mississippi Delta? Dumb shit's been shooting up."

"Naw, that's on purpose," Mick said.

"Mississippi's more Negro to him than New York," Rory said.

"Please put your hands together for the incomparable Rory Tharpe and her merry band of minions and misfits!"

Butch clenched his harmonica tighter, trailing Rory out onto the stage. "Dumb shit," he muttered.

The space was two-thirds full. Funhouse mirror shapes floated on the floor. Thurston drummed the first rolls of Trouble in Mind, their standard intro, waiting as Butch took his seat at the rickety piano and Mick settled into the background, checking the amps. Rory waved her hand at him to stop, twirling her guitar in the air.

"What?" he asked.

"Let's switch it up."

She trilled, launching into the first punchy bars of "Satisfaction". "Well, good evening, everyone. Some of you might be familiar with this ditty. Made its way from Otis Redding to England to this limp dick band called the Stones. I taught them everything they know."

Puzzlement swept over the room. Then a woman raised her beer bottle and let out a whoop in tribute, bobbing her head as she poured the bronze rotgut down her gullet. "That's right, let 'er rip!" she yelled.

"Tear the roof off this mother!" another voice howled.

The band started in, following Rory's lead. She ripped through two country songs, dead-ending with "You Can't Always Get What You Want", Thurston and Butch hustling to keep up with her. She took a sip of water from a cup Mick handed her, wiping the sweat off her forehead, trying to latch onto a face in the audience to give it a back story, some fire, purpose. But the only thing she could make out for certain was Katy watching from the back, strobe lights glinting off the crucifix swinging around her scraggly neck.

Usually she could tell the label types by the high rent booze they ordered and their appraising stares, the boredom seeping in their eyes if they couldn't get their rocks off in five minutes. She didn't know why she'd said a scout was definitely going to be there. Maybe if she willed it to come true, it would.

Her stomach churned with all the maybes piling up. Damn Katy, she thought, afraid to look back out into the audience.

She eased into the microphone. "So it ain't true that all you do 'round here is cook potatoes morning, noon, and night?"

Rotgut woman let out a screech, "Hell fucking naw!" The wall of bleary-eyed white men to her left jolted awake, rustling ominously against the stage, beer bottles clinking in time to the undertow of pressed together bodies as more people staggered in from the parking lot, laughing, panting, cussing about the high cover charge for that Negress bending them motherfucking strings like Clapton.

Rory gripped the mic. "Well, I don't know… Can this crowd take a joke?"

"Keep it movin'."

"This ain't no stand up hour!"

Butch pumped at the piano pedal, wondering what Rory was getting at, why she wanted to rile the horde this early in the game. Sid hovered at the back of the stage, a wraith in the guise of a flesh and blood girl, feeling like she was being ripped into a thousand particles by the noise. The front door opened again and Cruz came in with a pug-mugged man in a green parka. They settled down at the bar, swiveling around to face the stage.

Joberg paced in front of them, shaking his head at the bartender.

"This is fucking crazy."

"Lady's got some nerve."

"I took a risk booking her Black ass in the first place."

"The last time she had a hit record was when?"

"Hasn't been on a label in years. Bringing her here was a little charity thing, a favor I did for her manager. Get me a club soda, will you?"

The bartender took down a glass, filled it up and slid it over. Cruz intercepted it.

"Thanks, Joberg. You gonna pay a round for us?"

"Miss Delacruz, what brings you out in this freezing cold?"

Cruz nodded at Rory and the band. "Don't like seeing pearls cast before swine."

"Haven't lost that acid tongue I see."

"She's doin' you a favor playing this dump. Maybe even give you a little legitimacy for a while as you bribe your way into expanding the empire. I hear you've taken out a permit for that parcel north of my property."

"I don't know where you got that information."

"Don't shit me, Joe. The city council minutes are public record."

"Congratulations for reading the fine print."

"You try and get within striking distance of my property with that glorified whorehouse—"

"And what? You're going to sic the Injun mafia on me?" He chuckled, glancing at the stage as Rory launched into an electrified version of *Precious Lord Take My Hand.*

"Oh yeah… Good one," he said, turning back to Cruz. "You should listen carefully. You might learn something."

On stage, Mick hovered in the wings, monitoring the movements of the crowd. Rory had started doing electric versions of gospel staples years before on the revival circuit. When the shows raged late into the night, plugging into her amp was an easy device to keep the flock awake and alive, bleeding whatever pittance they could into Jesus' collection plate. Rory's wailing Gibson became the pastor's top earner, the secret sauce for submission to the wayward hard luck men who thought God's word wasn't worth shit.

There was a commotion at the back of the room as the crowd parted and Card Jefferson strode up to the stage with his bass guitar. His signature salt and pepper pompadour was slicked down tight on his skull, fingers aglow with a thousand rings, expression shut down and stoic against the seamy, gyrating whites.

Mick waved him up to the mic beside Rory. "'Bout fucking time."

"Amtrack broke down in Big Sky. Ten hours with no grub except for some beef jerky one of the good ol' boy ranch hands gave me. They got any food up in this joint?"

"Nothing but gourmet roadkill, man."

The band finished the song and Rory stepped into her mic. "It's not often these days that I have the pleasure of playing with an actual legend. There're so many fake ones running around. Some of you may've heard about a little record company called Motown. This man is the real power behind it. Please welcome, Card Jefferson!"

Thurston did a drum roll, segueing into the intro for *My Girl*. Card played a few bars in game response. Rory turned, signaling for him to stop.

"This is for the women in the room," she said. "It's called *Bury Him Head First*."

Someone lobbed a beer can onstage.

"Animals," Butch hissed.

Card kept playing. "That's some seriously cowardly shit."

Joberg's bouncers barreled into the crowd, looking for the perp. Rory kept strumming for a few bars then stopped, clenching the top of the mic. She bent down and picked up the beer can, holding it out in front of her. "Mr. Berg, can someone clean this up? Thank you. I guess home training is hard to come by in these parts."

"Dumb ass bad apples!"

"No matter, we getting paid regardless of whether you act a fool or keep civilized."

Card whispered into her ear. "Stop tryin' to humor their cracker asses."

"Look, we got a week left up in here and we need the money."

"At the expense of what? I didn't drag all the way clear across the country for some backwoods mess."

"Don't preach to me, I got a band and a bus to support and probably the IRS too."

"That's real heartbreaking, girl, but it don't justify bendin' over to them."

"That what you did when you played all them Jim Crow clubs back in the day."

Card scoffed, shaking his head. "Now who's in the pulpit? Shit, Jim Crow never died, just got a new name and took up residence in shit holes like this."

"Somebody's scouting me. Scouting us, tonight."

"Well, good for you. Where is he? Call him up here and give him a cookie." He made like he was going to grab the mic. "Will the big money label man come on up here so these desperate ass fuckers can jump your bones?"

They wound down the set with a few Motown tunes, segueing to the opening bars of *Happy Trails*, Rory's nod to her country and western dabbling. The dwindling crowd scurried over to the bar and bathrooms staking out a dingy knot of tables by the pool room. She searched for the scout among the idling locals, stir crazy on the musty little stage.

Card turned toward Thurston, egging him on to do a final clash on his hi hat cymbal. Rory took off her guitar and handed it to Mick, tapping Card on the shoulder.

"Let's talk."

He followed her back into the dressing room where Sid sat fiddling with Rory's tape recorder.

"Hey, little Miss? Who's she?"

"Sid, go wait in the bathroom."

"Ok."

"They're going to lose their liquor license with her around," Card said.

"Next time wait for my cue before you go in with my drummer, hear?"

"Whatever you say."

"Coming into the middle of the set like that was sloppy and you ain't gonna fuck with any chance we have to get signed."

"Get signed by who? This ain't exactly Madison Square Garden."

"I don't play CP time, Card."

He smirked. "I could've stayed back in Cleveland and gotten this kind of abuse."

"You that delicate, huh?"

"On an empty stomach and two hours of sleep, fuck yeah."

She took him in, pacing her reaction to the cheeky XY chromosome insecurity he was radiating, his gaunt body bending forward, snappable. She looked outside the door, searching the shadows again. No obvious candidates loitered around. She would try Russ after the show. Run his ass down for the umpteenth blood-from-a-stone time. She came back in, nodding in assurance at Sid sitting on top of the toilet, waiting, then turned back to Card. "What are your plans after all this?"

"Open-ended. Studio in Los Angeles canceled on me right before you called. If you want me, I'm here."

"Good to know. When's the last time you had a checkup?"

"So, you a nurse now too?"

"I just don't need anybody dropping dead on me again. We had a situation a few years ago with a guy who had heart problems, liver problems, every damn organ in his body was jammed up with something and he lasted three days into my tour."

"Bet he wasn't half as good as me no way. Haven't seen a doctor in years. Are you gonna foot the bill?"

Thurston and Butch dragged in. Thurston pawed at a bag of popcorn, licking salt off his fingertips. "Here," he said, tossing it to Card. "Delicacies from the bar."

Card caught it and sank into a folding chair, hoisting the bag up to his mouth. "You know shit is bad when a stale thing of popcorn tastes like prime rib." Thurston grinned, crow's feet crackling to his hairline, jagged from years of quickie blond dye jobs in gas station bathrooms.

Card fished a kernel out of his teeth, nodding to Thurston. "You were pretty good out there with your banging."

"Thanks."

"Where'd you do your time?"

"Say what?"

Butch rolled his eyes at Thurston, hating every dirty blond iota of him. "Training, fool," he said. "He means what's your training."

"Listening and just playing mostly, beating on pots, trashcan tops, whatever shit I could get ahold of. Wearing out Krupa, Max Roach, Ginger Baker on my little Woolworth record player up in Blaine, Washington."

"In other words, all the usual name-dropping clichés," Butch said.

"I'm self-taught and self-made. My mama and daddy couldn't afford to stick me in no fucking string quartet like yours did."

Card perked up. "You did classical, Butch?"

"From elementary to college, before I dropped out."

"Boy's got talent," Rory said. "Modest about it, but I like that." She looked pointedly at Card. "He backed church choirs, did session work with some of the race labels."

"Didn't know they had Orientals on those labels."

"I ain't no damn 'Oriental' and they snapped up anybody they could get for cheap who could throw down on an instrument."

"My mother Katy connected with Butch when we swung through Dallas."

Card scarfed down the rest of the popcorn. "The late great Katy Duren. May she rest in peace. I remember seeing ya'll play Faithful Temple Baptist Church. Some kind of TV special. Had the prettiest matching velvet blue suits. What you think she'd make of all this heathenism?"

"Heathens are paying the bills these days," Mick said.

"Don't believe I was addressing you, Sherlock."

"Well, I'm answering you."

Card crumpled the popcorn bag, turning to Rory. "Tell your boy to lighten up."

"I'm nobody's boy."

"Ya'll been trying to make us yours for three hundred years. Turnabout's fair play. Rory, where's the scout you was talking about?"

"I thought I saw somebody by the game room."

Card grinned. "A water mirage, I used to see them driving through the desert."

Rory held up her hand, defensive. "Look, we have twenty minutes until the next set. Tighten your asses up, I'll have Sid tape us. Maybe we can package it and sell it on the tour Russ is supposed to be scoping out. Mick, you tell Joberg I wanted to see him about the money?"

Mick shook his head. "I'm going, I'm going."

Rory stood up. The men flipped in front of her like dazed guppies on hot concrete, Thurston rubbing at his pocket, Butch chewing his lips raw, his usual game face appearance of being calm, cool, collected sucked into the vortex as the specter of her bank account draining to a negative balance jabbed a finger into her eye. The bus repairs, the three months back pay she owed the band, the medical bills from the hernia operation she'd finally gotten after Mick's badgering. Joberg's check would cover a fraction of it. Then it would be back to scrounging, scraping, wheedling session work in New York or busking in the infernal funk of the Times Square subway station for the grand rate of ten dollars an hour if she was lucky to ever make it back there and the competition was slim.

She looked at Card, shaking off chills. "Butch, Thurston, can you give us a minute?"

"You sure?" Butch asked.

"Yeah."

They shuffled out warily. Card rolled his eyes. "Your highness can't find no brothers good enough for a permanent slot in the court."

"That what this is about?"

"Right now, it's about eating and getting paid. Long term, it's about payback and redemption."

"And what exactly are you needing redemption for?"

Joberg poked his head in. "You people decent in here? You wanted to see me?"

"I need another advance."

"You're on in five minutes and that's what you wanted to talk about? I'm already doing you a favor letting you keep the kid back here."

"Why can't she talk about it? It's her money."

Joberg stuck out his hand to Card, nodding sourly in acknowledgment. "I don't believe we've had the pleasure of meeting yet."

"Cardinal Jefferson."

"Welcome to The Roost. Had many a wild night banging chicks in the back of my '57 Chevy with your shit as a backdrop."

"Well, maybe in addition to the cash for this gig I can get a retroactive commission for my 'shit' helping you score."

"That's funny… You know, I admire your work, I really do. But if you're going to continue with this gig you can't step up on my stage late."

"Yassuh, boss."

He looked Card up and down, digesting the reference, the acid in his voice. "Just opened up a new club on the strip in Vegas. One of these days I'd like to do a full-on Motown revue. Dancers, horns, strings, the whole nine. Smooth but with a cultural feel. Give these disco kids a taste of the history of real music. Think you could hook me up with the Motor City G-man?"

"That ain't my jurisdiction. You so much as breathe a note of his shit in public without meeting his price and he'll haul your ass into court."

"I heard you've had rough sledding with them. This revue might be an opportunity to make amends. Be one big happy family again." A timer went off on his watch. He raised his eyebrows. "Alright kids, everybody back in the pool."

Rory stopped him. "Hold up. What about the advance?"

"You finish the first week, then we'll talk."

"I got folk who are going to get evicted if they don't cut a rent check by tomorrow."

"That's unfortunate, but it's not my problem."

He pushed through the door, disappearing into the roar of the club. From the stage, she heard her name announced to the crowd, then the wayward drizzle of applause.

Filthy Lucre

THE GIRLS KNEELED in order. Oldest to youngest, gracefully descending like falling snow, Vaseline slathered elbows touching in weathervane formation.

"The Lord is my shepherd, I shall not want," said Adeline Moore, aged ten. Scruffy voice hitting the line in pitch perfect Standard English. The younger girls followed suit, lathered in envy, lapping up her pluck, itching to be just like her. Clementine, Harper, Rory, June, Divinity. Ducklings waddling behind Adeline, determined to get every word right before supper, to suck the poetry from the bone, to be the Black angel atop baby Jesus' Christmas tree. Their ashy knees dented from marathon kneeling on the clapboard floors Divinity's grandfather Daddy Simmons built.

Daddy Simmons was the first ex-slave to own land outright in Cotton Plant. When the other trifling denizens were drinking, whoring and sinning; he saved. When the night roared with wasps, stinging any exposed scintilla of human flesh; he saved. When the rat-faced piss-in-his-pants cracker bank manager tried to charge him seventy percent interest on a construction loan, he balked, spat in his face, and saved some more.

The motherfucker came after him with five friends and a pickaxe between them. Cut a dollar sign into his shoulder. Stepped back, wiped the blood off their hands, and admired their handiwork.

"That's the way they did us, back then," Pastor Divinity said into the phone, sitting in her church office, cream-colored high heel boots dangling over the edge of her imported cherry wood office desk. "But Daddy Simmons knew self-reliance. Even after they'd maimed him. The church was our shelter from the storm, bedrock in our fingers, sweet unity. When all the white folk were coming at us with their sin and madness that was all we had."

There was a pause on the other end of the line. She waited, picking a piece of lint off her blazer, irritated by the plague of indecisive Negroes. She'd been head pastor of Revivals for nearly three years, tossed about by the headwinds and backbiting; the Good Book wielded against her to check, qualify, rate her every move as an untested leader, a temptress who bled every month, a turncoat who'd betrayed the world with one slithery bite of an apple in the Garden of Eden.

"C'mon, Gerard. You either shit or get off the pot," she cackled into the receiver. "Corporate HQ is in for $50k and a matching donation from your people will put us on track to break ground for the sanctuary and youth center come March."

She waited, bracing for the hemming hawing excuses, the counteroffer or non-offer of in-kind crumbs. It was the fifth such call she'd placed that day, speed dialing through a Rolodex of sweet talkers to solicit funds for her new church cathedral complex and community center. The faith dome she was building was going to be a revelation smack dab in the middle of up and coming downtown Little Rock.

"Chocolate City Central in the Deep South," she said to the Black elites, the American Express gold cardholders, the bootstrap conservatives with a touch of Back to Africa Garveyite about them. She never hesitated to remind the bootstraps brigade that Arkansas had been the site of a full-blown repatriation movement. *Lord, to have had the courage, backbone and spirit of those Black pioneers*, she gushed. They all liked the idea of being secretly in on a tempest in a teapot, keeping up with the Joneses in donations, patronage and bump and grind Jerry Lewis slobbering telethon appeals.

Daddy Simmons would be right proud. The mama who'd run off shortly after she was born would be right proud. The kneeling girls would be jealous as ten green-eyed monsters.

A much more domesticated version of the bootstraps speech was pitched to the white gatekeepers, termed out politicians, and yacht slumming philanthropists aching to do tax deductible missionary time reading *Cat in the Hat* to kids in the ghetto one weekend of the year. They all wanted to keep the flashbulbs popping and the sob stories coming. It helped their wives reel in bigger fish for the society pages, one-upping each other on who could score more glossies handing out care packages and Easter Sunday hams against the backdrop of shotgun shacks. Divinity had already decided that there would be no photo ops for lowballers. Only those who pledged above a grand would be granted holy access.

Her secretary Miss Patton came in bearing a pastel fruit basket from a local florist and a planner embossed with Divinity's initials in gold. Divinity plucked an orange from the basket, dug her nail into it and put it in her mouth, sucking juice and pulp.

"Looks especially ripe today," she said.

"Should be, given all the business we send their way. Take a look at this shit." Patton slapped the front page of the local newspaper on her desk. "Cult murders of Black folk all the damn way out in the boonies. Running up after some white man, apparently."

"Would've been the same outcome with a Black man, except he would've had the brains to take the madness straight to the Motherland where nobody would've given a fuck what happened." She gestured for the planner. "Negro, white, Oriental or Spanish—with these off brand religions it's all the same difference."

"How's the fundraising?"

"Shitty—I mean, so so… My New Year's resolution is to clean up the potty mouth."

"Just don't let one of the deacons or any of the elders hear you."

"They can kiss my Black ass, cellulite and all. You see how they behaved at the board meeting the other day? Haven't raised a red cent and carrying on like heathens, acting like they still run the place."

Patton took a container of protein powder from a file cabinet. She shook it, then poured a few scoops into a blender behind Divinity's desk. "The usual?" she asked, grabbing fruit from the basket and stuffing it into the blender. "The natives is restless is all. They been in these hick Arkansas towns most of their lives and here you come—loud, female, moving too fast." She turned on the blender. The fruit churned, urine gold. She poured it into a glass and put it in Divinity's outstretched hand.

"Thanks, babe. Looks lovely. You see the blueprints?" She slurped at her glass, whipping out a poster from the top drawer of the desk. "Feast your eyes. State of the art gym. Library. Day care center. Kitchen, cafeteria, one-thousand-seat sanctuary. Meditation room. First Colored congregation in the whole entire Southeast to have that big of a facility."

"You sure that's enough?"

Divinity smiled, smacked to earth by Patton's usual edge, one of the many goads that had fueled her when she was an associate pastor slogging through decades of petty jealousies and skirmishes with the church board over money, direction, message. A cesspit under the watchful gaze of the crucifix-grasping moralists of the women's auxiliaries who churned around her in perpetual judgment.

The church pew girls collapsed into each other, knees raw. Blinking back at the older Divinity, brows stiffened with rage. *The Lord is our shepherd. We shall not want.*

Divinity swallowed, stuffing the church pew girls down onto the gleaming floorboards. Patton shut the protein powder, watching, waiting, to catch her if she fell.

"If it's good enough for the faith healers and the snake wrestlers it's good enough for our people," Divinity said. "They deserve this in spades, Pat—"

"*You* deserve it."

"For the groundbreaking, I want to bus in every storefront and penny ante church from Cotton Plant to Arkadelphia. Doesn't matter what their color or politics." She downed the drink, dabbing her lips with a cloth napkin. "Going to do a fund drive for battered women. In fact, the meditation room will be exclusively for them the first month we open. Anybody else so much as steps a toe in there they get fined."

Patton scribbled some notes in the planner. She stopped, waiting for Divinity to continue, following her gaze out of the window to the dusk light twinkle of downtown. Scaffolds for new construction grinned against the skyline that Divinity had coveted since childhood when she was ravenous as a bottomless pit beast clawing her way out from the church walls. She frowned, blinded by the smudged negative of her eight-year-old self, kneeling with the other girls in descending order as Daddy Simmons inhaled the Easter basket talcum powder, the Dixie Peach from their fried pigtails, the odor of bubble bath rising from their necks.

Take your pick, the deacon whispered to Daddy Simmons, as she smashed his eardrum, her hands growing into mallets.

"Our own oasis in downtown Little Rock. Ain't that a blip."

"God's house."

"The one and only."

Patton eyed her, taking her glass and pouring another round. "What about a benefit concert? A real, old time revival. We could bring in more money, get the local press off their butts to cover something positive for a change."

"Yeah, maybe… Why's it so goddamn hard to raise money for this? If it was a juke joint or a chicken shack all the white boys who like to jack off on sinning Negroes would be all over it."

Patton put her finger up to her mouth. "Divinity, hush."

Divinity took another swig from her glass and looked skyward. "I can't help it. I promise you; He understands. It's a test, just like raising $100k in three months on three hours of sleep at night is a test. As they say, whatever doesn't kill us—"

"We haven't done a gospel thing in a while. We could call some of the sanctified people on the circuit. Or what about Aretha or Mahalia? Don't you have some contacts with their record companies?"

"We ain't got Aretha or Mahalia money."

"What about that Tharpe woman, then? Speedy fingers, the guitar player. Weren't her mama and yours friends?"

Divinity perked up, crossing her legs. "A million years ago, then her mama up and died. We grew up together. She bounced back and forth between Cotton Plant and Little Rock. Practically owes all of Black Arkansas a favor."

"How so?"

"Whole town pitched in to get her new shoes, a fancy dress, and an amplifier to play what her mama lied and said was gonna be this big debut at Carnegie Hall."

"The mama lied?"

"Through her teeth."

"Well, I'm quite sure it wasn't Tharpe's fault. She was just a kid."

"She carried on and put on airs like she had a private audience with Jesus and none of us peons were good enough to so much as breathe on her shit… Knows her chops though. Can play the hell outta anything you put in front of her."

"What makes you so sure she would want to come back to this place then?"

Divinity paused, icy fingers needling her vertebrae, tracing a picture of Rory's chubby face, dark, immobile, taunting, sticks and fucking stones, tongue lolling out of her mouth Medusa-ish as the Deacons' hench women searched up her underpants to make sure she was still a virgin.

"I'm not sure. Bet she's curious though. Who wouldn't be? Who wouldn't want to see what the stranded townies are up to after all these years? To see what's up in the hole she busted out of. Especially now that homegirl's star has dimmed and the calls have stopped. Hell, maybe we can arrange to give her a key to the city."

"Feels good to be the big woman on campus."

"Big? Little 'ol me? They ain't selling me in overseas markets. At least not yet. And that's where all the serious missionary bank is… Naw… I'm a fan of Tharpe's stuff. To still be standing in that industry, even if it is peglegged, ain't nothing to sneeze at. She was the shit with a maraschino cherry on top. We were all so envious of her talents growing up."

"Her mama played organ a few nights at our church in Pittsburgh. My auntie got a copy of a 78 she'd just cut. She autographed it Mother Katy and the 'World Famous Rory'. Vain as sin that woman. Carried on like she was the Queen of Sheba reincarnate. Most un-Christian."

Divinity snorted. "Katy didn't give two shits about being un-Christian."

"Evidently."

"Shrewd in business. Ran Rory like a stopwatch. Would've swallowed all these snake-in-the-grass deacons and elders whole and still had room left for—"

Patton put her finger to her mouth. "The walls have ears."

And that they did. The flock's reigning preoccupation was with why Divinity remained unmarried after all these decades, swaddled so airtight in the arms of da Lawd no other man could fuck her, they snickered. The deacon board willed itself between her sheets, hanging from her bedroom ceiling like bats in a belfry, making it the most titillating place to be during her sermons when she lit into the Judases who wanted to see the church expansion fail. She ran her finger across the blueprints, shivering with pride. Outside, construction workers snaked down to the ground from their perches on top of the new cathedral, a sorcerer's clap of dust rising in the air. As a kid she'd been obsessed with telling the future, intoxicated by the pell-mell of "what if"; wrapping her head in a turban, reading palms for five cents. Didn't care that it was a sin in the eyes of God. A nod to false idols and hoodoo and uncivilized savages who didn't have the benefit of the good book.

That was long after the sessions in Daddy Simmons' office. The hench women had called them "cleansings". She wondered if they still stalked Rory, fanged chimeras massing in her dreams. She wondered if all Rory's traveling, ripping, and running were a balm for remembering what happened between all of them four decades ago. The coiled spring six-year-old inside pushing her aging self to the ends of the earth.

Patton nodded at the blueprints. "You could drop a hundred shotgun shacks right in here and still have room for a swimming pool and a golf course."

"That's a thought. We could dump all the deacons and elders in the deep end for a re-baptism."

"Don't forget their wives. But none of them folks know how to swim."

"Exactly. Easy fix to our problems then."

"You're wicked."

"That's why you love me, remember?"

"Selectively. Conditionally."

She clutched her chest. "I'm wounded... naw. Bringing Tharpe in is an interesting concept."

"She still have people in Cotton Plant?"

"Her mama was the last one. They were on the road playing clubs and church revivals practically every day she was in grade school."

"Who could blame her?"

"Now look who's saditty, Miz Pittsburgh, Pennsylvania."

"Ya'll would've killed to be in Pittsburgh in '33."

"Bullshit. They were raping and lynching in Pittsburgh too. Just knew how to clean up the blood better."

"Well, anyway, I think Tharpe will take a shine to what you're doing here, preaching the gospel and pumping jobs into the local economy. It'll make for good press. Two Nigra girls from the sticks done good, credit to their race and all."

Divinity chortled. "I like that. But don't hold your breath. She's no altruist. The only presidents she and mama Katy acknowledged were dead ones."

"As it should be. Last I heard, Rory was on the dark side of the moon somewhere playing for spare change."

"Shame. Track her down for me, would you?

The Loner

It took a while before she realized Katy was sprinkling water on her face, so nestled in nightmare was she, the Boise motel bed sodden with sweat. The wake-up ritual was a thing from their Paleolithic past. A wet shot to the eye, the cheek, the ear, a calling card laced with vinegar or sugar, depending on Katy's mood.

The parking lot rumbled with truck engines turning over, dying in midsentence against the snap of jumper cables and muttered motherfuckers drifting up through the air as the cleaning woman trundled door-to-door, knocking, calling, busting into the unholy stench of straggling 10 a.m. checkouts.

Rory forced herself up. Sid sprawled at the bottom of the bed, worn out from being at the club the night before, a spitty thumb dangling from her mouth. She'd recorded their second set, proudly showing it off, playing and replaying it on the ride back to the motel when everyone was blasted, bent out of shape about the lie Rory had told about the scout.

Russ blew off her calls, his secretary running interference. Every day she postponed what to do about Sid plunged her deeper into the muck of indecision. The aunt had been a fraud, a grifter from the cult, trying to collect insurance. When Rory called the police, they kept her on hold, promising a hand-off at another dingy gas station on the highway, then backing out at the last minute, passing the buck to the next jurisdiction, all to Katy's morbid delight.

"This shows why it was good you never had no kids. Our genes die with you," she said, hanging from the ceiling, agile as a bubonic bat. "Did the Jew bloodsucker give you the advance?"

"Yeah."

"Don't lie to me."

"I'm not, Mama."

"Might do you some good to have that Negro Cardinal with you next time as backup when you try and negotiate with these fools. He got clout."

Rory disentangled herself from the damp sheets and went to the bathroom, swigged a bottle of mouthwash and started the shower as she closed the door on Katy, still talking.

"Get your money straight and ditch that little girl," Katy said on the other side of the door. "Police'll track you down for kidnapping, and besides that, she'll start eating you out of house and home."

"You think any of them gives a damn about a Black girl, Mama?"

"You got a point there. Probably pay you to keep her then."

Rory put a scarf on her head and got in the shower, turning on the hot water full blast, feeling her skin melt as she sorted through the mess of the night before. With Card joining them, their playing had been ragged. They hadn't had a decent rehearsal in weeks. Butch and Thurston's sniping derailed them while Mick sulked in a cloud on the sidelines. All three stomped down on her, lodestones drilling her into the ground with the worms, her own loyal legion of undertakers waiting patiently for her since birth. She could see nothing beyond Boise, save for the distant promise of the beer commercial getting national airplay and a crack at maybe cutting a record with a z-list independent label in the San Fernando Valley in Los Angeles.

She turned off the water, steadying herself against the mildewed wall. Cruz had come upstairs to intervene in an argument between the cleaning woman and a disgruntled man, giving him shit about his loudness, the trail of dirty dishes, chili cans, and rubbers he'd left on the floor, all topped off by the declined credit card he'd given her that had been issued to his mother.

Rory peered out the window. Cruz pointed a gun at the man, a ferret with human features and a stump of a nose.

The man whined and retreated back inside at the barrel of Cruz's gun as she fussed at him to clean up his mess. Rory stepped out of her door wearing a bathrobe and slippers, a crinkly spiral of hair snaking out from under her damp bed scarf.

Card was slumped at the bottom of the railing smoking a cigarette. She took an envelope out of her robe pocket and handed him three twenty-dollar bills. "Here. Joberg gave me this after ya'll left."

"That's mighty white of him. This on top of our cut?"

"It's yours. He's buttering you up. Thinks he's going to convince you to do a cheap run at his dive. You know how white folks love them some Motown."

"It's the soundtrack to all their cheatin' and fuckin'." He stuffed the money in his pocket. "Boy's gonna have to do better than that."

"We need to rehearse. Sounded like shit last night."

Mick walked over to them, his face creased, marshmallow puffy from a hard sleep, waking up hung over and seeing elves dancing on the bathroom floor. "I was thinking about going to the diner to get something. You two want to come?"

Card sized him up. "You buyin', Mister Charley?"

Mick bristled at the slight, fire in his cobalt eyes. "Depends on whether you're a cheap date or not."

"Hell yeah, I saw him recycle his tea bag twice." Thurston slunk up to them with a paper cup of tea, pinky raised.

"Who said I drank tea, motherfucker?"

Thurston smiled.

"Can you call Joberg and see if we can get some rehearsal time at the bar?" Rory asked Mick. "If you're buying at the diner I'm in. Although I think Card should treat us, what with his newfound riches and all."

Card slapped his hand on the railing in mock disgust. "Moochers getting carried away with life. Little Miss want anything or did you eat her for breakfast?"

"Go on ahead," Rory said. "I'll meet you over there after I get dressed."

Mick frowned. "Pretty soon the police are going to come sniffing around again looking for that girl. If you get busted all our prospects go to shit."

"Stop whining. I'm two steps ahead of them and this ain't no gravy train."

"If you're two steps ahead of them, I wish you'd let me in on the plan."

"I *said*, stop whining." She tightened the belt of her robe across her stomach and went back to the room.

The men walked downstairs, ravenous, the sky a manic blue, clear as cut glass. Sid poked her head out the door and watched them leave. She'd never seen anything like that color sky, envying the kids who could have it year-round, feasting on stars, planets, unobstructed, while tucked in their warm beds, wooly covers up to their fat, secure chins.

Rory came in and put her clothes on. "We're going out for a little while," she said gruffly. The church girls rose from the floor, prim, judging, the spitting image of Sid. She clawed at the air, checking herself, stuffing her talons into her pocket.

"Stay in the room, I'll bring you back some food."

She thought she'd heard Rory talking to someone during the night. Muttering, debating, a singsong pitter-patter about dressing for church. Toe-pinching patent leather shoes, frilly dingy ankle socks, white skirt that she couldn't play stickball in. There was a half-asleep gentleness to her voice, as though she'd forgotten herself; hijacked someone else's molecules. Staggering deformed through the blackness of the room.

She'd forgotten where she was when she woke up. The digital display of the radio desk clock busted, stuck at 12 p.m., red demon teeth flashing on the walls. She'd awakened in fits and starts to her mother Genetic's scowling face, her ranting about the boogers in Sid's nose, how filthy she was relative to her adoptive siblings, butterscotch-dipped dream cherubs who gave her no trouble at all.

Sid was lighter than Rory, who was darker than Genetic, who was darker than the siblings who were lighter than the women who worked the compound, hacking wizened banana plants with machetes from sunup to noon. When she'd asked Genetic about the color differences she'd been smacked into silence, told we all bleed red, told the worm on a corpse'll suck you down to the same shade when you die, doesn't matter whether you're black, white or purple.

The Lord is our shepherd. We shall not want.

She sat up in the middle of the bed, playing tic tac toe on a gas receipt from the tour bus, floating on the mattress, an island tossed by the riptides of the outstretched hands of her sixth grade classmates, dead as doornails, begging her to pull them up out of the water.

"Fuck ya'll," she said to herself, then took it back, half-assed. In life, they'd tormented, pissed on her darkness, her turned up vowels, the frantic white boy rock music she listened to. No one would know, no one would judge her for condemning them if she didn't say it out loud. After she'd come back from the compound, she'd seen newspaper photos of the bodies rotting in the sun. Heard the titillated disgust of the grown-ups at the rest stops as she and her uncle drove to California. He smothered her with his promises that no one else would ever be able to take care of her except him, his princess, mature beyond her years.

The phone rang. She picked it up. Before she had a chance to speak, a white man's voice sounded on the other end.

"Rory! How you and the boys doin' up in that cold, babe? I know you're killin' it. Listen—"

"This isn't Rory."

The man paused, confused by the smallness of her voice. "Oh… who is this? Is she in?"

"No."

"Who are you?"

"Who are *you?*"

"This is Russ, Rory's manager." He paused again, waiting for a response. "You a relative of hers?"

"No."

"Look, sweetheart, can you take a message for Miss Tharpe? It's real important."

Sid scrounged around for a piece of paper, settling on a prescription that Rory left on the nightstand. "Ok," she said.

"Jude Justis wants to speak to her, wants her to go on tour. That's J-u-s-"

"I know how to spell it," Sid said impatiently, recalling her mother's secret fixation with Jude's music, the steamy, burnt bat out of hell mornings when she would commandeer the record player and bang through one warped record after another.

He chuckled, humming a snippet of a Jude song. "Right. Everybody in the world knows her. Tell Miss Tharpe to call me asap."

Sid hung up the phone. She looked at her neat cursive handwriting on the prescription, comparing it to the doctor's scrawl barreling off the end of the page. Vesperax by mouth at night for Rory Tharpe, not to exceed two tablets in twenty-four hours.

Sydney, Australia

The white girls at the snack bar took turns eating French fries, swirling them in the ketchup splatter on their paper plate of mini corn dogs... a ten-for-a-dollar delicacy in honor of the American holiday, the gala of fireworks and big flags when George Washington broke away from England and created America the Beautiful. They were waiting for the bathroom line to shrink. Watching the boys slouch by in mock indifference. Jaunty asses in shorts and dungarees, arms swinging with leonine purpose. Toned to flabby, sunburnt to translucent, lethal weapons unsheathed in the hurly burly of neck craning, reefer toking, corn dog scarfing white youth, pawing and snorting at each other as a clown did a dance routine and squirted water from the stage.

All afternoon they'd swum in sweaty suspense, counting down for a glimpse of the woman of the hour. A week of hopped up anticipation for the high priestess of blues. The lucky ones in their neighborhood to win tickets on the Full Tilt Boogie express midnight radio show, wearing their fingers down to the nub while speed dialing on grocery store payphones so their parents wouldn't know. They ratted their hair like hers; crossed their eyes, draped themselves in purple feather boas and went into conniptions in front of every mirror they passed. And now here they were, a few thousand bodies away from her, the ground rippling as the crowd stamped their feet, chanting *Jus-tis, Jus-tis, Jus-tis.*

A helicopter dipped down from the sky. It landed on the amphitheater helipad, cutting through an electric wave of gasps, squeals, paroxysms of excitement.

The white girls broke from the line, French fries flying as they barreled into the crowd, determined to get near the stage at all costs.

The helicopter door slid open and Jude Justis stepped out in a beam of empyreal light, her band positioned at their instruments, the shadows of the stage deepening.

"Evening, Sydney!"

"*Jus-tis, Jus-tis, Jus-tis!*"

She gestured to the chopper, rimmed by an iron knot of police, billy clubs at attention. "Courtesy of Australia's finest. Don't worry though, I ain't trying to go military on you. It's just that we were out partyin' last night, the band and I, doin' a little of that oh so fine Mexican reefer, and this fourteen hour time difference had us bent over gettin' reamed. So there was no way we could get a limo to get us here in one piece and God almighty, the traffic up in this joint is like fucking Times Square during rush hour!"

The crowd roared back its approval as the band struck up the melody of her signature song, *Down 'N' Dirty 'N' the Delta*, the white girls locking arms, swooning.

She sang a few wobbly bars, growling. "You float my boat, Sydney!"

"You're a beaut, Jude!"

"Ya'll know that Down Under accounts for twelve percent of my sales? The numbers man told me that right before we got on the plane. Scrunched up his numbers man face all screwy and said, 'Jude, you got to knock their socks off baby or all those cute aboriginal boys in the Outback will switch to Laura fucking Nyro,'" She covered the mic, wincing at the prospect, the stadium erupting with groans and boos.

"Alright, alright, ya'll… I'm not trying to throw anybody to the wolves up here. It's still all about peace and love… giving, and, *especially*, getting lovin' in a world that don't know the first thing about what that is… So, this one's for the gals who're tired of sacrificing for some no-good man!"

The band exploded into a driving whiplash beat as Jude kicked off her shoes and wriggled around the mic stand, sputtering baby talk, snaking her fingers in the air, throwing a beefy leg around the lead guitar player chomping on his fifth cigarette. The stadium burned with the frenzy of ten thousand damp, moldy, insomniac bodies burrowing into each other and bleating like tree frogs at the crack of dawn as the police hung back, a silent shroud exuding light menace, scanning the crowd with megawatt beams for dark-skinned belligerents.

At the end of the concert, fireworks cascaded through the sky. Stars and stripes forever rained down on the gamy throng glued together in gelatinous bliss. After the last encore, the crowd fanned out into the parking lot in the darkness, groping for their cars, some murmuring reverently about what they'd just seen, searching for quick communion on their hoods, hatching plans to steal to the US of A, launch Jude colonies and evangelize the dull, stupid, disco gorging, booty shaking Americans.

Vintage Jude took a bow, left the stage, and crashed into heroin-encrusted infinity.

It was the same lurid shimmy of give and take and posing and sussing out the cosmic slop vibe of the audience on a stopwatch. It was the same punch drunkenness of being blasted from a ten-cylinder jet engine into the ether, each city blurring into the next. She was so fucked up by time zones and mangled flights and freeze-dried food and handlers and minions slurping every inch of her down their gullets. But her hometown of Port Arthur was watching and eating their hearts out. Port Arthur would be licking her asshole squeaky clean by the time she got back there, triumphant, bigger than motherfucking dead Jesus, dead Elvis, and dead Marilyn combined in a Tootsie Roll.

The next morning, back at her hotel, white bodies flickered eel-like through the pool, water sloshing at the feet of the servers who ferried past with shiny Day-Glo drinks and deluxe beach towels. Jude trudged out of the private elevator for her suite and flopped on a patio chair, blinking in the sun, wrestling a piece of the room service eggs from the post-concert buffet and boozing bacchanal out of her teeth. A series of mammoth international conferences had converged on the hotel at once. The ground aflutter with building retrofitters, airfoil frame engineers, metal detector manufacturers all clogging the sleek twenty-dollar-a-head buffets fit for oily on the lam potentates. The bliss of fresh bacon grease lighting up their faces.

No one had noticed her yet. She reclined, enjoying the pocket of anonymous calm amid the bustle. She could sense eyes on her from the patio. A bus boy, awareness dawning on his weather-beaten face. A bellhop juggling a trio of tank Samsonites up to the penthouse suites. These were the awkward moments. The nails on a chalkboard countdown in her cranium for when some random rubbernecker who'd seen her a few times on late night variety shows would call her out and shatter the peace.

A boy with sun block gunk on his nose rose out of the pool and stuck his tongue out at her. "Dirty Yank! Dirty Yank!"

"Motherfuckers hate Americans, and who can blame them. Happy birthday, baby." She looked up, irritated. Russ stood over her wearing a party hat, a tiny American flag dangling from his fist. He plopped the hat on her head and slid into a chair, stretching his stork legs out. The boy in the pool frowned at him. Russ gave him the finger.

"Backwoods Aussie S.O.B. Mum should've aborted him. What is this world coming to when a boy from Scranton can't feel safe at the Hilton Grande?"

A waiter glided to his side and handed him a piña colada.

"Compliments of the house."

"Nice start, my man. Gonna need something stronger though. Double martini will do. And my little sister here will have—"

"Nothing for me, thanks."

"You were brilliant last night, Lone Star."

"Don't call me that."

"They were eating out of your hand."

"That's the problem."

"What?"

"The shit's getting stale, Russ."

"Oh, please. I'll tell you when it's getting stale."

"What the fuck do you know? You signed all those bubblegum shysters last year, that country and western album you begged me to do tanked and the drummer you stuck me with blows."

He nursed the drink, waiting for the storm to pass, feeling the sinister little swimmer boy's underwater eyes on them as he chomped down a box of cheese crisps on a kiddie tray at the edge of the pool.

"Deal I just struck with The House makes you the highest paid sideshow in the states. Want to bitch and moan about that?"

She watched the boy wriggle back into the water, wondering how his skin stayed so white, translucent in the boiling sun, bottom feeder gills exposed. He was one of the sleep biters, undigested orphans that bubbled up in the mish mash dreams she had on planes, buses, airport lounges, taking various guises, gnawing away with judgment and recrimination.

"Thank you, oh great and powerful Oz."

"Don't sound so aggrieved, Lone Star. You've singlehandedly revived a lost art form."

"Bollocks."

"Jude Justis, working class hero, fearless channeler of the souls of Black mammies."

"Eat me."

"That didn't work out so good, remember?"

"You're a miserable eunuch."

"I don't give head as dexterously as your no-talent girlfriend."

"Leave her out of it."

"You were the one who put her in it. Can't keep hiring your conquests and putting them in starring roles."

"Men do it all the time."

"You're not a man, Lone Star. Least not yet anyway."

"What's this deal you're talking about?"

"They want you to do five live albums back to back. There's a possibility that the whole division could be eaten up in the merger they're negotiating with Standard Oil. This time next year the company could be divvied up and farmed out to the Asians and the Brits. There won't be any kid glove treatment and indulgences like New York does. Once disco dives, the whole industry is going down. Albums, 45s are dying. Cassette tapes are going to be the next 'it' technology. Eight tracks, all that clunky low rider grandpa shit's going the way of the dodo. The world will be poised for a blues-rock revival with Jude Justis at the helm."

"How much upfront?"

"One million apiece. Back-to-back North American and European tours for the next five years."

"That's insane."

"It's all about mind over matter. Cut back on the booze 'n' blow, cut out the late nights, the sideshow fucking—"

"Who I fuck is none of your business."

"Wrong. It's all my business. Every fart, fuck, transaction, and conversation. If I find out that any of those charity leeches you got on the payroll are dealing smack to you, I'll have their work visas revoked. The last leg of this tour's got to be immaculate as a newborn's ass, Jude. You rest up, go to a sanitarium for a month, then we go back to the States and do battle."

"You done?"

"Just getting started, Lone Star."

"This is the end, Russ. No more touring, no more flying forever, dealing with these time zones. I'm losing half my goddamned hair and my equilibrium."

"Give it a few more years."

"I want to go back into the studio."

"You are going back to the studio."

"No, with my own shit."

Russ paused, kicking his head back, slurping down the remains of the drink. The boy had disappeared under the pool waves, diving lustily after a toy ring, the water closing over him in a grim blue sheet.

"I want to go in and do my own shit, dust off some standards, underground stuff the honkies haven't found yet."

"You mean *the other* honkies."

Jude yawned, reclining back in the chair. Russ was an unworthy sparring partner, his mind a little nematode encased in primordial blubber, a floating piece of zooplankton that only glowed to life with the promise of profit, sex, or some pale approximation of it. She handed him a tube of suntan oil.

"Left shoulder. Looks like you need some too."

Russ squirted the oil on. Conference goers swarmed around the pool, dissecting the fine points of airfoil design in a welter of Anglo accents. Every now and then someone zeroed in on Jude, scanning her up and down with a raised eyebrow, confounded by her tip of the tongue celebrity and the sour gnome kneading suntan oil on her liver spotted shoulders. It was surprising that no one had formally approached her. The record company usually posted its plants to strategic spots around the pool to spy on her, monitoring bad behavior for the risk management insurance company bean counters calculating the probability that she would still have a heartbeat a year later. Banking that she would be pert, ready and able to deliver them a meatier market share from sales to the throngs overseas.

Or not.

Baby, you'd be worth more dead, the voices had begun to whisper.

"Dirty Yank," she heard the boy chortle again as he edged toward the deep end, certain he was one of the naysaying chorus trying to strangle her in her sleep.

"Ah, there they are," Russ said, as though reading her mind. Two grinning white women approached from the shade of a fake palm tree by the bar. They sidled up to her, clinking and clanking in bangles, hood earrings and puka shell necklaces shellacked to a blinding sheen. The taller one tittered and stuck out a clammy hand to Jude.

"Your music. Your voice. Your presence on this earth." She clutched Jude's hand grandly then released it.

Russ snapped the cap on the suntan oil. "Can I help you with anything, ladies?"

The woman continued, ignoring Russ. "I'm Lavender Smurch."

"Ash Nicks," the other one said.

"We're from *Womyn's Roar*, the new American start-up mag from the Gavin Corp—"

"Yes, I've heard of you," Jude said. "You do the women's lib stuff, right?"

"You could say that. The concert last night was phenomenal."

"We've followed you all over the world. This is number ninety-six for me. Ash, what's yours?"

"Eighty-three. I'm a piker in comparison to Lav."

"We'd like to do a cover on you."

"A special issue devoted to the Equal Rights Amendment."

"We'd like you to become a national endorser."

Russ put up his hand. "Hold it, Jude doesn't endorse political campaigns or issues."

"This isn't an issue, it's a movement."

"Are you going to let her speak?"

Jude raised up her chair, taking a deep saffron whiff of the aboriginal wrap she'd gotten on a drive through tour of the Outback. "Naw, it's ok, man. Equal rights, I'm down with that. Where do you want me to sign?"

"Well, there's nothing to sign just yet. We'd like to set up an interview time."

Russ cleared his throat. "You can send a request through our London office."

Jude waved him off. "Bullshit, whatever we need to set up we can do now. Ya'll staying here?"

"Couldn't afford it."

Jude smiled and stretched luxuriously, giving the women a show of an emancipated nipple, the pale dimpled skin creeping up from below her browned solar plexus. She drew her wrap around her shoulders and burped into her fist. "I'm on the thirtieth floor," she said to the women. "Come up and see me sometime."

It was the humming of random passersby that got her. The spontaneous eruptions at the grocery store when Rory was in line with her lethal favorites, a bottle of Jack Beam and a can of creamed corn. The floating slips of atonality that dragged her by the ear at the gas station when she was putting another round of diesel in the bus with the last of Mick's state disability checks. The gurgling snatches from a cracked car window cruising by at the end of the day; the driver finally settling on a radio station that wasn't playing commercials.

The song you couldn't beat out of your head with a two-by-four. Her invisible nemesis. Her Waterloo. Bloody hot damn.

It was that miserable like a stuck pig summer when it seemed the whole globe was blasting Jude's new riff in unison. A twelve-bar Monstrosity that she claimed she'd dredged up from the bottom of the Delta, tobacco-stained fingernails dirty and squirming with the muck of the ancestors one generation removed from the Middle Passage, she drawled in exclusive interviews with the European trade mags.

As crotch-sticky and miserable as the tread of June to August was, there was no worse torture than the hijacking of the airwaves and every inch of the audible world by the Monstrosity. It burned up the U.S., British, and global charts, staying on top for five weeks, dethroned by an Oklahoma white girl group in matching blue gingham dresses twanging *Maybelline* to ukuleles, cowbells, and booming snare, proud one hit wonders on the variety show circuit.

To counter the noise, Rory swore off all media, then Jack Beam, creamed corn, Solitaire, any whiff of diversion or corruption that would take her away from practicing. She accomplished it by going up and down the fret board in her head, on the back of her seat in the bus; trying to tame the petty niggling argument between her mind, telling her she was a spent wreck, and her disobedient fingers.

Meanwhile, Jude had signed with the Proteus label, a subsidiary of 'The House', or TBS International records, film and TV, home of the gingham girls, pioneer in spreading artists across multiple platforms and bottling blackness to stuff down ofays' gullets. The deal was lauded in the industry for its fairness to "talent". All the A&R executives clucking in their echo chambers about the wide berth it would give Jude to control the production of her albums.

Rory's upcoming appearance on Jude's tour was barely a footnote in the trades. She was supposed to explode with gratefulness to Russ and the label for giving her a chance. Shit sunshine and rainbows even though her royalty checks had begun to dwindle each month and the accountant from her last label was perpetually out on medical leave.

"What about the scout you promised?" she asked Russ, tracking him down two days after Sid took his message. "Somebody was supposed to be checking us out at The Roost. We're busting our asses every night."

"Never promised that, babe. But I know there's interest from uh, San Fernando—"

"They do novelty records, Russ. Biggest hit was five years ago with the Chipmunks."

"Don't knock it, the Chipmunks are making them bank."

"What's happening with my publishing rights?"

"What's this I hear about you toting around a kid? Joberg said he was practically babysitting at the club."

"My publishing rights, Russ. For once in your life answer me straight."

"We're looking into it, babe. On it night and day. But, I gotta tell ya, with the peanuts you've been bringing in, I'm practically paying you. We can't afford to keep shelling out for an attorney with the chump change we're making on gigs," he paused, letting it sink in. "And, Rory, listen… whatever you got going on with this kid…"

"Nothing's going on."

"I'm not trying to get too deep into your personal shit, but you need to fix that entanglement before Nashville."

"Does the varmint even know how to write a song?" Card asked, carving up a plate of pigs in a blanket. Jude's record deal was plastered on the front page of the entertainment section in the *Boise Star*. The band had hunkered down for a late breakfast in the diner near Cruz's motel. Thurston sucked down a Bloody Mary, Butch poked at a cold clump of corned beef hash, Mick watched Card watch the human traffic shuffle in and out of the door.

"Starts to get a little hazy for her once you go past a-b-c and 1-2-3," Butch said, grinning. He had started to court Card to get at Thurston. Lapping up Card's dirty jokes, fawning over the tossed off flourishes he did to liven up simple songs during rehearsals as Thurston showboated drum licks he'd stolen from Stax Records.

"What difference does it make? She can afford to hire anyone she wants to cook up shit."

"Record company pays them fan clubs of hers to buy her singles as soon as they hit the streets."

"It's collusion on the deepest level," Thurston said.

"Guess what. She wants us to open for her in Nashville," Mick said.

Butch sat up in his chair. "For how much and what's the boss think?"

"Tight lipped. In fact, don't say anything about it to her until she brings it up." He looked at Card. "I get the sense that certain terms aren't solidified yet."

"Meaning she hasn't decided about hiring me on."

"Step up your game for the next week."

"Son, I don't need you to check me."

"Sounds like this is Russ' consolation prize for not getting us signed," Butch said.

Thurston drained his Bloody Mary. "Right now, who gives a fuck. It's a chance to get the hell out of here, get noticed, get laid and get paid."

"In that order," Card said. "Must be nice being taken care of like Aunt Jemima's cleaning up after you."

"Practically raised your rusty butt from the dead," Mick said.

Card leaned over Butch, jabbing his finger in Mick's face. "This rusty butt's gonna stay on yours, water boy. Nobody fucks with my pay." He took a drink from Mick's water glass, setting it back down with a slosh, wetting Mick's pants. "Dixie'll suit me fine just so long as the white girl is putting money on the table."

They'd been in Idaho a week, rattling around the motel like rotten teeth in a corpse's skull, gobbling down grease bombs that made their hearts race when they collapsed in their bed bug cots at night. Kept on a schedule of two meals a day to stretch the budget; after that it was Teflon slices of community pizza, a bucket of fried chicken or TV dinners fired up on the hot plate in Cruz's office. Card had ventured out to take in the lustrous sights of downtown Boise, the storefronts studded with bargain signs. He browsed in a few sparsely stocked gift shops, looking for cheap souvenirs for his kids, the skeet shooting eyes of the white women clerks following him from aisle to aisle in every store. He settled on two snow globes at a dusty flea market, one globe gleaming with the state capital, the other sparkling "Wish you were here" in a Winter Wonderland scene. The white lady at the counter wrapped them up, snapping her fingers to the Supremes.

"That's three for three dollars if you want another one," she said.

"I have two boys and a baby girl."

"Maybe they'd like to share an extra one, or you can give it to your girlfriend back home."

"Doubt that," he said, ignoring the suggestion. All the Black men who'd been ripped from limb to limb because of some white girl's lies rose up in his head. He barely had the $2.50 for the two globes, but he shrugged, ambled back to pick out a third one, not wanting the white girl to think he was either scared or just another dirt-poor nigger passing through. He would give the extra to Rory's stray, Sid.

He put the globe down on the counter and pulled out two quarters. "You know, that's me on the radio."

"Diana Ross?"

"Naw. Me, Card Jefferson, on bass."

She scrunched up her face, listening to the song more closely. "Gee. Well, good for you. What was it like to play with Diana? Missed her when she played up here. Hear she's a tough cookie."

"You could say that." He waited for his receipt. Other customers in the store milled about, the stench of eavesdropping in the air.

"Are you listed on that song?" she asked, a too casual, flirty lilt to her voice.

"Yeah, I'm listed. I built the backbone of that shit."

She raised her eyebrows, smirking. "Thinking about seeing the sights this evening?"

"Naw, I got a gig at a club over on Main Street."

She wrapped up the snow globes, stuffing a crumpled business card into the bag. "Beautiful country up here. But I wouldn't get caught out after sundown."

When Sid woke up Friday morning, Winter Wonderland was staring at her from the nightstand. A miniature sled, reindeer, pinpoint crystals of silent snow sparkled behind the glass. Things she'd never seen before, except on TV, longing for the vast, unsettled whiteness of sudden blizzards.

"Up and Adam," a faraway voice sang.

She ignored it, searching for Rory's form in the dark. The light of a siren lit up the wall, flashing back and forth over the bureau mirror.

"Up and Adam," the voice sang again, closer to her ear, doubling down. She rubbed her eyes and sat up. Winter Wonderland was gone. In the mirror, a woman stood next to her, holding the globe over her head, bringing it down with force.

Sid jerked away, falling onto the floor. The door opened. A Black policeman stuck his head in cautiously, squinting in the dark, scanning the room, empty, save for the girl.

"I'm not going to hurt you," he called out. "I'll give you a minute to get decent, then we're gonna get you back home."

"I don't have a home."

"Don't be silly, honey. Everybody has a home."

Cruz walked in, keys jangling on her belt. "What the fuck's going on here, Wayne?"

"We're taking this minor back to her family."

"Uh uh. I own this motel. This is my jurisdiction. Nobody told me nothing about this. She's been staying here with Rory Tharpe, the musician."

"Miss Tharpe called us."

Cruz folded her arms across her chest. "You're not taking this child nowhere until Tharpe gets back."

"I have a court order, ma'am."

"I don't care. Boise County's fucked up more Native kids taking them out of their homes last year than the feds. Lay a hand on that child and I'm suing the department."

The officer shook his head. "I'm only going to ask you once, Ms. Cruz."

Cruz picked up the phone, dialing the bar. Joberg answered, guitar feedback blasting through the receiver. "Joberg, this is Cruz, where's Tharpe?"

"Heading to your place."

She put the phone down. "She'll be back in ten minutes."

On the balcony, guests in robes and pajamas peeked out from the rooms next door. "Go back inside, dammit," she growled. "Absolutely nothing to see here."

Sid huddled down into the covers. The policeman was searching the room, poking at Rory's suitcase with a flashlight, peering under the bed, rooting through the bathroom. The snow globe had fallen to the floor. She glanced down at it, wondering how long it would take to grab it, to smash it into his head as the vanishing woman had tried to do with her. She picked it up. It was cold and smooth and hard in her small fingers, silently insistent. She walked to the bathroom. The policeman was snooping in Rory's pill bag, shoulders broad and unyielding in the uniform, body humming with a bog water blend of cologne and Dial soap. If he turned around, he would have her uncle's face, speak with his traitor lips, lie with his dewy brown eyes, caressing. She raised the snow globe.

"Sid!" Rory stood behind her. The policeman jerked around as she took the snow globe from Sid's hand, blinking in the hard light. Rory led Sid back to the bed, lurching. "Come on, come on, sit down."

"You're drunk," the policeman said. "And this little witch tried to kill me? I should bust all of you."

Cruz inserted herself between them. "They had a rough night."

"I'm going to need someone to come down to the police station with the girl and give a statement."

Cruz hesitated. Rory slumped down on the edge of the bed, nursing the snow globe to her chest.

"I can go," Cruz said. "Just need to lock up downstairs."

Rory slept off her hangover on the floor, waking up to the sound of Mick knocking on the door about rehearsing. Told herself in the blear of getting up, washing her face, scraping the vomit off her shoes, checking her teeth to see if they were all still there, that she wasn't going to think about the girl. Wasn't going to think about the girl 'cuz she was shit on a stick warmed over. Incapable of higher order functions. Done with charity. Done with being a sucker, mark, patsy going over the rainbow for strangers, strays, dead on arrival man-boys. Told herself, told herself, told herself. She yelled at Mick to fuck off and flopped back on the bed, nursing the snow globe.

She dreamt of being on stage in Nashville, playing to rows of empty seats. She couldn't see the end of the arena. It faded to blackness, white ocean waves lapping the cheap seats where Sid sat grinning out at her, whirlpool eyes glinting in the dark.

Sid had been reunited with a pair of relatives who'd come out of the woodwork from Arkansas. A fidgety elementary schoolteacher couple she'd never seen before on her mother's side who finished each other's sentences and huffed about a lawsuit against Rory, Cruz, and the whole state of Idaho. Cruz bit their heads off, labeled them ambulance chasers, said a prayer for Sid and went back to the motel, ending the night in front of the TV; the test pattern watching her baby three shot glasses of bourbon.

At Friday's end, the band piled into the diner on Rory's dime. It was the capper to a middling workweek of flat shows. The period to Sid's departure. Monday, the bar bathroom flooded. Tuesday, they were the midnight diversion for a bachelorette party. Wednesday, the backdrop to carousers smashed and reeking after a high school football game. Thursday, the soft landing for a bunch of Montana-bound pool hustlers who'd just missed their Greyhound bus to Pocatello.

Card had minded his ps and qs through the last two performances. Dutiful on each sound check. Dutiful to Rory's tempo change signals, adjusting his tone to complement the dip and keen of her voice on the slow numbers. Hoping she'd appreciate it, give him a smile, a sign. In truth, he had nothing to fall back on. The unemployment checks he'd gotten from a six month orderly job at a Detroit state hospital had run out. Back child support he owed had shot his credit to hell. In quiet moments he melted down to the little boy he'd been on a Charleston train platform soft shoeing for nickels. Begging with Papa at 9 years old, the white passengers chucking quarters at them for the extra thrill of a crocodile grin and a buck dance. He was certain Rory could see it, smell it, taste what he'd been through; that sinister stretch of real estate where he'd despised his grandfather's obsequious blackness, wanted, for a few seconds, to put a rope around his neck himself.

Two white truckers came in smoking and talking loud as they plunked down in the booth across from the band, eyeing a woman sopping up toast and butter at the counter. Card watched them settle in, tracking the clumsy balletic oblivion of their entrance, the way the waitress moved instantly to give them space; handing them menus, chirping about coffee and how many sugars, reciting the day's specials in succulent prose as she emptied full ashtrays.

Envy. He was on elevators all over the globe, motherfuckers. One sixteenth of his piss, blood and pus had made it into the Muzak of every office building, grocery store produce section, waiting room, bill collector telephone hold. Motherfuckers like these bopped to the latest travesty covers of his shit as they had cavities filled and bought T-bones.

"Oh hey, look, it's them," one of the truckers said, pointing at Card, Butch, and Thurston. "I'll be damned. You boys tore the roof off that joint last night with that Tharpe lady."

"You know I got a vintage record of hers, a 78, 1949, mint condition, probably worth something."

"You all are geniuses… don't make 'em like they used to what with all that faggy crapola on the radio."

Butch put a sugar cube in his mouth and chomped hard. "I happen to like that kind of 'crapola'. What you think your daddy used to call rock 'n' roll?"

"Nothing. Daddy was a dimwit. He knew Roy Rogers and Patsy Cline, with the car radio dial stuck on the same one-horse town station and that was it."

"You folks were a damn sight better than the usual half-assed honky tonk boys that come through. We're out here every month from Bozeman and it's the same script—a little music at the club, a little hash browns at Hattie's and a little pussy in the parking lot."

Rory opened the door and walked in. It was a test to stay upright, stay collected. Even after the hot shower she took, the soiled clothes she dumped, the slapdash purge she made of all traces of Sid.

Mick patted for her to sit down next to him.

"Good work tonight, boys, but we have to tighten it up," Rory said. "Russ called about touring with Jude Justis. First show is in Nashville next week."

"Praise be," Thurston snorted sarcastically. "Are we driving or flying?"

Rory cracked open the menu, still unsettled by the dream of the arena and Sid watching her in the dark. "Driving, but management's paying for gas. There's a possibility of a global run."

"What's she paying us?"

"We're still in negotiations on the contract."

"Better get that shit notarized by God and signed in blood."

Rory studied the menu for a beat, then rested her gaze on Card. Their eyes met, a shy quicksilver smile playing on his lips then vanishing. "Are you interested if the numbers are right?"

"Numbers'll never be right enough to back that no talent—"

"We'd be opening for her, not backing. I'd like you to come if you're interested."

He hesitated, calculatingly, square jaw hardening into a scowl again. "Yeah. Yeah, I'm down. The sooner we're up outta the boonies the better. I want to speak to Miss Lady directly though."

"No, I don't think so. She doesn't even know you're part of the equation yet."

The flow of bloated tick customers and semi drivers washed past Rory. They patted their paunches and stroked their gizzards, breath mints crammed between chipmunk cheeks as they contemplated jumping back into the white noise of the highway and putting in eight, twelve, sixteen more hours behind the wheel before they dumped their cargo. Lumber, cars, steel, tubing. Reports of semis smuggling Vietnamese refugees stacked in the musty maw of their cabs had cropped up on the local news. Highway patrol cars camped out on the shoulder at each exit, descending on Native families going to work, returning to the Duck Valley reservation in the south. The cops rousted them for being so-called drunk and disorderly, jamming their flashlights into the eyes of kids blinking away sleep in the back seat.

"The tour will get us back out there," Rory said, wanting the comfort of a unified front for the first time, the knife of the town at her throat. Mick hadn't said a word about the deal. She could feel his disdain flowering into anger, as he slouched down in the booth, erecting an invisible wall between himself and the others. Suddenly, she was afraid he would bail on her.

"What's your issue, Mick?"

"You know I wanted us to go out on our own. Not ride trailer trash's coattails."

"Huh? We *are* out on our own. We're out in the fucking middle of nowhere being scenery to twenty jerkoffs a night and I'm sick of it. I can't play hard to get with Jude or Russ while I'm lying down at the bottom of a ditch with the four of you and no lifeline."

Card laughed. "That's right then, just let Jude polish up her white-girl-does-darkie credentials and sell another million dollars' worth of crap."

"So, what's the alternative?" Thurston asked. "Ride the coattails of a rich as fuck fraud and get a little exposure or stay broke and obscure?"

"Speak for yourself," Butch said in defense. "Rory's hardly obscure."

"Obscure meaning that we sit back and rot in shitholes like this." Thurston looked at Card. "We ain't got royalty checks coming in from Motown every month."

"Who told you I got it that way, son?"

"Just assumed."

"Assuming will get your ass in trouble." He stretched his legs out into the aisle, casting a gaze at the waitresses.

"Motherfuckers are paying me fifty percent less than what they're paying you, i.e., negative zero to the nth power. They'd bury me deeper than hell if they could. Me and every other Black man who played on their records and kept them in gold pots to piss in."

"They would've been watered down schmaltz without you and the rest of the Funk Brothers backing them up," Thurston said.

"Tell us something we don't already know," Butch retorted.

A new waitress took their plates, balancing glasses, silverware, and dirty napkins in her arms as Card slowly retracted his legs. It was the woman from the flea market pretending not to notice him. "This job number two or three?" he asked.

"Two."

"I did a little sightseeing last night, like you recommended. Still alive and kicking."

"Good for you. And it's two and a half jobs."

"I've got two and a half jobs too. That nuke-happy bastard Reagan gets elected I'll need another two and a half. In a few weeks I'll be touring the country with these good people."

Rory shifted. Card cleared his throat. "Excuse me, touring with Miss Rory, ace guitarist, and her band. Our shows were as good as greased lightning, girl."

"That good, huh."

"I can get you backstage at Madison Square Garden if you behave."

"Oh, is that right? That's always been one of my ambitions. How you propose to get me there?"

"Fly you on his back," Thurston said.

She grabbed their empty saltshaker. "When hell freezes over."

The white men at the other table had begun to perk up, getting riled by the second by Card's easy banter with the white waitress, her reciprocation, her leg bumping dangerously up against his.

"Say, partner, you extending that invite to everyone up in here?"

"What? To fly you on his back?" Thurston howled.

"Boy, shut the fuck up," Rory said to him. "You trying to jump-start the Confederacy again?" She drummed her fingers on the edge of Thurston's empty plate as she leaned across the table and addressed Card. "Don't use my shit as a ticket to getting laid, hear? I told you the contract's still being negotiated and adding you is going to cut into our take."

"I ain't no charity case."

"Stop acting like one then."

"Me on the bill will mean more profit. All the gold records I played on with no credit could fill Fort Knox. And look at them punk ass bastards Jude has on her tours—Axelrod, Heaton, Wysocki—they get paid to mail it in and here I am rattling a tin cup."

A salesman hustled through the aisle, hawking handmade belt buckles at five dollars a pop. The truckers looked on admiringly, their attention diverted from Card. "We'll take the check," Rory said to the waitress, nauseous suddenly from the claustrophobia of them all jammed into the booth together. She could feel Katy's claws tightening on her shoulder in rebuke. *One misstep and God has a spot for you down there with Satan, no trumpets, no angels, no pearly gates. Gabriel would only shake his head at how pitiful you is.*

When they lived in New York, Katy would plop down in the tub and take a long bath, submerging her entire body in the water. The tip of her nose skimmed the surface like a telescope, her press and curl going gloriously back to nappy while she communicated, she said, with the dead slaves that waited at the bottom of the river with blackjacks and pitchforks in Cotton Point. What the fuck did they do to keep from going stir crazy, forced to suck Massa's dick every night, she slurred, a fifth of Scotch gurgling inside her, soapy water pooling over her eyelids, and always the dare that she would go under and never come back up again. Rory would listen from the kitchen, half-scared, half-hopeful. Tuning out the run of the toilet, the neighbors clanking skillets in prep for Friday fish, the A train conductor's groggy call from the 190th street station stop. *Stand clear the closing doors. Thank your lucky stars you was born when you was*, Katy said. Her grand finale, when she climbed out, dripping, body speckled from years of skin rejuvenation quackery; miracle rubs and salves and tone improvers that she slathered in every crevice to ward off the darkness.

Card took out some crumpled bills and put them on the table for the check. "My contribution," he said quietly. "Look... I need the money for this gig, whatever it's gonna be. My bills got bills. However much more you can wring out of those tightwads—"

"They'll do right by us, believe me. Otherwise, we can get some of your Detroit boys to kneecap 'em."

Ashes to Ashes

THE ORGAN BLASTED Pastor Divinity's ear, sending pieces of pus and skin dribbling down the front of her satin pastor's robe. After three hours of pacing and jumping and shouting before a wilting congregation zapped by that morning's news of the continuing investigation into a fratricide in East Little Rock, she stopped, took a swig of buzz worthy communion grape juice and looked out into the crowd, trying to curb her disgust. A yapping weasel peered out of her throat, googly-eyed at the double-decker hats, powder white gloves, freshly patted wigs and pastel polyester suits floating in the putrid tide of the over-perfumed sanctuary.

Attendance was down for the second week in a row after she'd dismissed the gossipy deacons scheming to stage a coup over the alleged excesses of the church's expansion. If the expansion had been their brainchild it would've been golden, hailed as genius, an inspired nod to community building and the future of Negro uplift.

Now the audience was divided into factions. The sea anemones and informants who pined to see her crash and burn. The furrowed brow fence sitters. The dewy-eyed loyalists parched and desperate, lapping up her every word like it was milk about to go sour. The loyalists cycling through office hours, volunteering time, money, food, consolation, quivering for answers and a Grade A taste of God. She lay awake at night feeling irritated, thinking about what she could not give them, masturbating in despondent, sludgy bursts between vampire films and the dawn parade of newscast horrors. The East Little Rock murderer was a Vietnam vet who'd cracked after his lights were cut off because of an overdue electric bill. Buckets of blood all through the living room and out into the driveway. Kewpie dolls and teddy bears in his crosshairs as he picked off his daddy and mama for bringing him into this world. Mowed down his wife and baby girl just for breathing. When the police pulled up, he was lodged in a tree, monitoring enemy lines through the scope of his rifle.

Pastor Divinity had received the call to lead prayers at the scene. To lay the carnage at the Lord's feet for him to deal with. They'd rung her up only after it was determined that all the county's big preacher men had decamped to Little Rock for a faith jubilee and they needed a surrogate quick fast and in a hurry.

Fuck 'em. Fuck 'em all, she thought, after making an imaginary paper airplane of the fourth draft of her sermon and launching it down to Hades. If it had been up to her that night, they would all stay unsaved and simpering. Besides, the collection plate was barely paying utilities. Nobody owed them nothing. Not a tinker's damn. She swam in her bed, backstroking, a sixth of an insomniac. Sleep loomed, delicious, playing hide and seek with her body. She lined No Doz pills on the shelf, sucking them down with coke every time her head banged forward. All she could smell was the baby oil and isopropyl hospital stench of the shut-ins she visited three days a week; a goulash of a stench knocking her awake to watch the clock again, cursing the savage rush of the minute hand on its mission to lay waste to her.

She could pluck their faces from the throng like hard candy, stale on her tongue. Her secretary Patton being the brightest, the most brittle stalwart. The venal voice of reason in her head. The one she vacillated about wanting to bend over and do, to slather with Vaseline as they marveled at the girders and cranes for the new development shuddering in the dark.

"Yea though I walk through the valley of the shadow of Death, I will fear no evil, for thou art with me." They bowed their heads, repeating after her, lambs to the slaughter. She met the fluttering bashful gaze of a skittish maroon swaddled woman in the third row and winked, amused by her peeking.

"So, the Lord is my shepherd ain't powerful enough for some of ya'll?" she boomed. "Or is it because pastor has a vagina, X and Y chromosomes? Yes, I said it. The Lord has blessed us with these bodies. Short, fat, tall, thin, male, female, what have you. There's no shame in the flesh we're in, no shame like you've been brainwashed into believing. God don't make mistakes."

"No, he don't, but who's doing the brainwashing, Pastor? Scripture is clear about the shame."

Divinity stared her down, rearing forward in the pulpit. "No shame in the bodies we're born in, sister Styles. Just the earthly filth, the treason some commit, betraying God's plan for these temples."

"What kind of sabotage was that?" Patton asked her later in her office. A pitcher of iced tea sat between them on Divinity's desk.

"Hate. Envy. Two of the Seven Deadly Sins. Girl was on biddie patrol."

"I'd like to wring her country neck."

"Now, Patton."

"Or see you lay hands on her."

"Need some disinfectant for that."

"She's running for school board, you know. Maroon hat and all."

"That's a logical next step. That kind lives to fuck up the heads of impressionable chilluns."

"And you?"

"I like victims to be legal. As you know."

"Well, in addition to harboring political ambitions, Maroon is a prolific writer... check writer, that is. Husband sits on the water board, the sanitation board, the police commission."

"Fuck her."

"Few weeks ago, I approached her women's group about providing an advance for Rory Tharpe."

"Motherfucker."

"They were amenable before that tirade of yours."

"Wasn't a tirade, it was a schooling."

"I recommend you bring her in and apologize. Have her to high tea. Hats and gloves and all that."

"They ain't buyin' it. Besides, remember, I don't have a husband to cover for me."

"Make some of them English white lady fluffy things, the teacake imposters."

"Scones? Aw hell..."

"Think of it as an easy atonement. Unfortunately, Rory's people have another offer on the table."

"From who?"

"Jude Justis."

"The bullfrog?"

"Does that rip off number with the stuttering and carrying on."

"Big Mama's song."

"Ran it into the ground and making ducats hand over fist. Gossip sheets say she got a little 'nose' problem."

"Snorting?"

"Yeah. Shooting up too."

"A woman after my own heart."

"Maybe we can get her to stump for our new rehab program. Could start a sub unit exclusively devoted to the traumas of white lady lushes and smack shooters."

"I like the sound of that. Ministry moves on that we could make a killing with a few high-profile clients. Only problem is the Negro quotient."

"Right."

"I bet ol' Jude is the good Godfearing type, would love to help some poor Deep South Negroes of the cloth like ourselves."

"She was over in Australia talking sovereignty to the Aborigines. Dedicated the proceeds of her last concert to—"

"Fuck 'em, she's got a bigger debt to pay to the natives here."

"Right."

"Her earnings off of Black folks could make the GDP of a small African nation. And now Rory's gonna be her undercard. There truly is no God."

Patton shook her head. "Divinity... girl. Cut that shit out."

Divinity smiled. She liked needling Patton, undoing her thin straight laces one by one and watching her flail in curdled righteousness. Patton, the efficiency maven turned high finance minister to her empire, soon to rival the Lone Star televangelists. Rory could put them over with the old guard who adored her before she went secular. Could reel in the bushy tailed whites who cannibalized anything black, raw, and breathing. Divinity stretched, impatient with the slow pace of the planning. She would need a bravura act before the cathedral groundbreaking to raise her profile and make a splash in the press well beyond Little Rock.

"Ok, I'll tone it down. Put a little more money on the table for Rory's people from our rainy day fund. Maybe then they'll bite. I'll squeeze out a little bit more from the developers. Long as I have some white folks bleeding their hearts into their beer paying reparations we got it made in the shade."

Patton shook her head, arranging phone bills from the call center into neat piles. Voices rumbled below them as groups from the domestic violence shelter flowed into the meeting hall for the first spring community dinner, raffle, and bazaar.

"Show time again," she said. "Get the white woman. The Little Rock uppercrust loves her dirty drawers."

The nasally nicotine-starved voice on the other end of the phone line told Rory that her bank account was overdrawn by two hundred dollars and she would be swiftly dispatched to the nether region of debtors pestered at all hours by robot monster collection calls. Living at the motel for nearly two weeks had temporarily relieved her of the honor of their constant chatter. Someone had given up her location in the grapevine of has-beens on perpetual tour. Sid grinned from the back of the arena, top row of her teeth vanishing.

After the meeting in the diner, she went back to her room and waited for Cruz to finish her poker game with the VFW men, vets from Vietnam and Korea who funneled the occasional relative or conventioneer to her motel. The smell of fried baloney and weed wafted up from the cracked door of Cruz's office. Rory tried not to listen to the flow of the game, the arcane rhythm of table slaps, guffaws, card shuffling then silence, as they sunk into deep strategy deliberation. When the last man left grumbling and defeated, Cruz came upstairs with a bag of baloney sandwiches and potato chips, a cat that ate the canary grin plastered on her lean face. She brushed past Rory and laid the food out on the bed.

"Homemade delicacies."

"I ate earlier."

"I cleaned them out. You play?"

"No, never had the time to learn."

"I can teach you if you want."

"Never been too high on the list."

"What is then?"

"Guess."

Cruz nodded, rooting around in the bag. She pulled out a sandwich and put a few potato chips between the bread. "The girl was bust up about leaving."

"Don't want to talk about it."

"Got it."

"Thanks for what you did."

Cruz shrugged. "Only decent thing to do. Given your situation and hers. Between bailing folks out and trying to keep the chief honest, I've been to that station a million times. They jam Shoshone kids anytime they get a thought… Maybe you're wondering if I've ever thought of leaving… I've been outside of state lines for a 'leisure trip' maybe once, twice in fifteen years. This place, all the taxes, insurance, maintenance, payroll, has sucked up everything in sight." She took a bite and sank down on the bed, tilting her face up to Rory, lingering barefoot and droopy in the middle of the floor.

Rory felt off kilter for a moment. Aware of the thin walls, the pulsing of the washing machine and dryer downstairs as guests' kids played tag in the parking lot around a Ford on concrete blocks. She wondered where Sid was for a moment, then put it out of her head.

"Damn, it's past those little critters' bedtime," Cruz said. "Car is a safety hazard."

"Why don't you get it towed?"

"Lazy. That and it's an heirloom of sorts. Mother's. She never went any fucking where either."

"Mine couldn't sit still."

Cruz nodded, kneading bread crust between her fingers. "She sung real good. The stuff I heard of hers. You take after her."

"Not really."

"Not looks-wise, I meant temperament."

"Naw."

Cruz leaned back on the bed, propping herself up with her elbows, her shirt sleeves damp with mustard, rolled up from her toil at the game, an ant trail of sweat on her lip. Her key ring jangled on her belt loop, one for every keyhole in the building. She gestured to Rory. "Sit down, stay awhile."

"I gotta schedule a rehearsal."

116

"What are you doing with all those cocksuckers? All those men backing you, stirring shit up?"

"It's business, we've been together for years."

"Turn you on?"

"What kinda question is that?"

"Do they know how to obey, not muck it up trying to get personal or trying to run shit?"

"You sound like Katy."

"She kept your shit running right all those years, I heard. Shrewd, take no prisoners, hellion with the record companies."

"You know an awful lot."

She wiped her mouth with her hand. "My business to know. I got files on most of the people passing through here. Insurance, in case anybody gets ideas."

The kids howled downstairs. A car door slammed, followed by the snare drum rattle of little feet stamping on a hood. "Critters are playing in that wreck again… this land is worth a pile to the government. Speculators are forever trying to get me to sell."

"How much?"

"Millions."

"Why don't you then?"

"Why don't you put on some tight, half naked shit and do disco? Or better yet just outright hook."

"Alright, I get you."

"I don't think you do. That was a light analogy. How about when they ripped ya'll out of Africa and made you try and talk like Massa? This place has been in the family for forty years."

"Good for ya'll. Negroes couldn't stay in places like this, Indian blood or no."

"What do you mean, girl, we had Negroes in the tribe."

"Heard a bunch of 'em were expelled for being too Black."

Cruz took an open bottle of beer from the bag and sipped it. She stood up, offering the bottle to Rory. "Now where did you hear some bullshit like that?"

Rory shook her head at the bottle. "You know you want some," Cruz said.

The kids stomped fiercer, the shadows from outside deepening, carving monster heads into the dingy walls, pressed together in dull communion around the glopped on picture of a sailboat, Katy's fingers playing at the mast.

"You making me look bad," Cruz whispered, putting the bottle to Rory's lips, tilting her head back. Rory gave in a hair, just a whisker, the tang of the beer punching at the hidden nooks in her throat, making them cry uncle. She hesitated, then guzzled at it greedily, conceding to the taste, bittersweet, long denied, turning to face Cruz, avoiding her gunmetal eyes, tuning out the crack of her knuckles, the fighter's swing of her hips like she was readying for a boxing match in quicksand.

"I got a reputation to uphold," Cruz said, taking the bottle from Rory's mouth. She put it on the table and took off her jacket.

"What's that?"

"Can I tell you in the morning?"

"You really think I'll be around."

"Wanna bet?"

"You're cocky as fuck."

Cruz put her arm around Rory, drawing her down to the bed under the pixilated squeals of the stomping kids, ignoring the limp command of a drowsy adult voice to come inside for fried chicken. Cruz cursed at them and kicked her shoes off, sliding on top of Rory, pushing her to the headboard, rickety and hanging on by a rusted hinge, bracing for the jackrabbit creak and tumble of their bodies, smudged up against Cruz's mother's hand-me-down comforter.

"I used to have nightmares sleeping in this thing," she muttered, kissing Rory's eyelids. "Forgot I put it in this room. Bloody hell and it smells just like her still, what the fuck is washing with Tide good for?"

Rory undid Cruz's belt, the motel keys clattering to the floor as she put her hand down Cruz's pants, rubbing her clit. She settled back as Cruz moaned, drifting, opening her legs wider. "Get her out of your head."

"Aye, aye, captain," Cruz said, staring at the ceiling, at the cobwebs the cleaning women hadn't hit, a lightning buzz ratcheting up her toes to her temples, Rory's lickable majestic hair forming a nest in her hands as she came too quick, wailing in defeat.

Rory flopped down next to her. She stroked Cruz's cheek, kissing it shyly. "Be gentle with me, ok?"

"That's my middle name."

"You're funny."

"Barrel of laughs is my second middle name."

"I'll take a little more of that beer. Funny, that was our last big payday. A backup jingle for a fucking beer commercial."

"Maybe you should pace yourself, babe, especially after last night."

"Not your babe."

Cruz smiled and handed her the beer. "Not yet," she said. She lifted Rory's shirt, sucking, teasing her nipples, tonguing her navel where she'd once been joined to Katy, licking her to a deep, slow thundering climax that had the beer rumbling back up in revolt.

The phone rang. Cruz put her finger to Rory's mouth and snatched it up. "Rory Tharpe?" The twangy voice on the other end said.

She handed the phone to Rory. "Sounds like some white woman."

Rory took it and sat up, arranging her clothes around her. "Hello?"

"I can't believe I'm finally talking to you."

"Who's this?"

"Jude. Jude Justis. Russ done told you about everything right?"

"Yes."

"Well, I'm right excited about us gigging together Ms. Tharpe. *Rory*. Can I call you that? I just thought we could sorta huddle on the phone a little before the tour begins. Honored to have you aboard."

"Your album is doing well, I see. Hear it practically everywhere."

"Yes, it was just a modest little offering to keep the record company off my back. Finished my old contract and on to the new one. TBS International. But they're all leeches. Fuckers got me by the balls."

Rory rolled her eyes. "Pity."

"Don't get me wrong, the company did right by us in the beginning. I just ain't gonna compromise on my sound."

Rory was silent, plucking F sharps out of the air. Katy was playing the piano, her back to Rory.

Rory recalled a Thursday when she'd been kept home from school again, because the mumps was going around. Seventh anniversary of the murders in the town of Elaine. Seventh year Katy vowed to keep her mouth shut in commemoration of the more than one hundred Negroes killed. Seventh time she'd sat down at the piano in silence, not a word, a mumble, a peep the entire day, doing chromatics, wearing the keyboard down to a nub, Rory's head throbbing from the repetition, the scraps of field holler songs she tried to interject, her brain moving faster than her fingers. The playing was supposed to be fair warning about the A&R men who came through with tape recorders, scouring the sharecroppers' bar, skulking around the churches after Sunday afternoon service, lapping up every drop of what they thought was the grittiest and dirtiest of the Negro id. *These Negroes will hand their lives to them on a silver platter,* she said. *I tole them to keep their shit under wraps. They gave it up without a fight, easy like the dumb backwoods coons the ofays saw them as anyways. You make it your business to get up on out of here for good the first minute you get a chance,* she told Rory. *Ofays would suck up your earwax with a straw, bottle it and call it champagne if it was gonna make them money.*

Jude rambled on about the album, "They tried to prettify it with Spector strings and overdubbed horns."

"Must've cost a mint."

"Oh, it didn't come anywhere near what those limeys spend on their production costs, what with their smack and whores."

"I want Card Jefferson to come on the tour. He's been backing me on our tour for nearly a month."

"He clean?"

"Yeah, far as I can tell."

"He's a genius and all, but I need him to be clean."

"He will be."

"Russ, the insurers, and the label are just waiting to jump down my throat on any kind of using."

"What about you?"

"I ain't doing junk anymore. Just a drink once in a while to stay limber. You can't begrudge a girl that. What's your poison of choice, Ms. Rory? I'll make sure you're well-stocked when y'all hit Nashville."

"Clear liquids," Rory lied.

Cruz got up and put on her jacket. She swept up the paper bag, stuffing her feet into her shoes. "Got bills to pay and work to do," she said curtly.

"I'm sorry, you have somebody there with you? Didn't mean to interrupt," Jude said.

"Tell her I'm one of her biggest fans, proprietor of the North End motel in East bum fuck Idaho," Cruz said.

Jude paused, then cackled, her voice rising through the receiver. "Hell, that's the funniest line I've heard all day. I ought to hire your old lady to do security for us."

Cruz took the phone from Rory. "I'm not for hire, sweetie. Not unless you plan to pay the mortgage on my property for another three years."

"Mortgages are for the man. Banks'll suck you up to the point of no return. Parents have one and—"

"Any idea who owned the land mommy and daddy are squatting on a thousand years ago?"

"Squatting?"

"Inhabiting illegally, yes."

"Ah shit, that's deep. Squatting, right on."

Rory took the phone from Cruz. "Is Card in or out?"

"Yeah, yeah. Bring him along, and that firecracker you put on the line."

Cruz put her hand down Rory's shirt and gave her breast a parting tweak.

She squirmed and pushed her hand away, gripping her by the wrist for a second, not wanting her to go. "The advance is forthcoming?" she asked Jude, strained, suddenly paranoid that the white woman could see her and Cruz half-dressed.

"Yeah."

"Need it before we head out."

"I'm gon' get on Russ about it. You'll have a check beginning of next week."

Rory hung up the phone. Cruz shook her head. "I wouldn't trust her as far as I could throw her."

"She pays her people alright."

"Sure she does. When will I see you again?"

"The tour lasts until the end of the year."

"Well, if you ever need help whipping those shits in line..."

"You're on call?"

"I'd need to find someone competent enough to run this place. The second I'm gone developers would be crawling around scheming on how to turn my property into a glorified whorehouse." She paused, rocking back and forth on her heels, antsy. "I hadn't fucked anyone in a year until this."

"That what we did, fucked?"

"I just wanted to go on record."

"For?"

She hesitated, skimming the right side of Rory's face, controlling her eyes. "It was nice. You were nice."

Rory nodded. She wanted to tell her that it had been a long time for her too, a long, hungry wretched Kalahari dry spell, but she didn't, homesick suddenly for Marie the night they killed King; the taste of her roaring up in her mouth.

"Look. I know you said you didn't want to talk about it, the girl wanted me to give this to you," she took a crumpled fan out of her pocket. "Kept it from her church." Rory took it. Doodles in the awkward hand of a child scrawled across the back, punctuated by a radio station's call letters and lyrics to one of her songs.

The desk bell rang out from the lobby downstairs. Cruz cocked her head. "Frozen food salesmen, made reservations this morning. Visiting for a week to stake out Northwest Territory. Gotta go."

"C'mon, wait." Rory took her in her arms. Nose to nose they were the same height, their breath matching each other's in slow, trying to play it cool and calm bursts. Rory kissed her swan's neck, swimming in the scent of bleach, cigarettes, sandalwood soap.

"You smell like a drainpipe."

"One of my many life aspirations."

"Maybe I'll take you up on your offer."

"Hot piece of ass like me? You'd be a fool not to." Cruz pecked her on the cheek, avoiding her eyes. She motioned to the fan as she walked out of the door. "Now, go read your fan mail," she laughed.

Rory picked it up and turned it over. The words *Revivals, Inc.* were stamped across the bottom in black type. She threw the fan on the nightstand, watching Cruz dash down the stairs without a backward look.

The House that Black Built

THE BUILDING GLOWERED down on the Lilliputians. Fifty floors vaulting up to the empyrean in an express elevator eye blink, casting bat wing shadows on the jammed summer street of midtown Manhattan.

When it opened in '65 it was a tongue-wagging marvel. The golden child, industry mecca jammed with five hundred employees in domestic and international sales, marketing and promotion of tailored sound for a ravenous middle America drugged up on cheeseburgers, Pepsi, Monday night football, the black on black on black of Sonny Liston, Muhammed Ali, Floyd Patterson boxing match bone crunches washed down with Ben Gay and police chases looped on prime time after the kiddies were tucked in and whining about missing out on the stage-managed murder and mayhem.

When the House's records were pressed, they rolled out to a national list of anointed dee jays for rotation. The white ones in Top 40 pumped new titles non-stop for seventy-two hours to make them stick, to get the melodies seeping like greased lightning into every waking moment of anyone in earshot. They hoped to make the listening stiffs part with a few cents in the record stores, department stores, the five and dimes, to get their tongues wagging and pressure rising orgasmic; have them massaging the steering wheel, pounding the dash, making love to the windshield in an eight-tentacle running-the-red-light frenzy. Even though Jude's new groove wasn't strictly pop, it fired up the white girls in the deepest pit of Akron, Ohio. Got them twisting and spitting in the shower so when their mamas and daddies saw her album cover in the store they sighed, thinking, 'at least this caterwauling gal ain't a genuine darkie', and shelled out two bucks; one for Jude Justis' *Back to the Roots* jam, and one for Perry Como's Christmas double album extravaganza. On weekends, the white girls prowled around the radio, waiting for the dee jay anointed to give the tenth caller, at the beginning of every hour, a 45 or LP and a shot at concert tickets when her highness came to town.

The top floor of the House was where Jude held court with a phalanx of accountants, managers, promoters, and A&R moles jamming up her ear. Marty, Moe, and Jack, a trio of scene chewers dribbling over her chart numbers, grinding each unit of revenue into sub-atomic dust in strategic planning. How many tickets sold in the Midwest versus the South Atlantic. How many in Bismarck, North Dakota versus Bridgeport, Connecticut. How many giveaways at the big urban stations and the ones out in the sticks with the traffic signals that flat-lined out in the cornfields, the path to deliverance for little outcast girls listening late under the covers in the dark like you once did, they said.

Jude perched on the edge of the desk, nursing a beer bottle in one hand and a cigarette in the other. "Don't steal my shit," she blurted.

"What?"

"My memories, my experiences. Ya'll don't know what I went through back there."

"Nobody knows the trouble I've seen—" Marty crooned.

"Cut it out, Marty. How much are we netting from the free stuff?"

"With word of mouth and buzz? Who knows? Can't put a price tag on it."

"Long as your name is out there on everybody's lips."

"Lennon said the Beatles were bigger than Jesus, well, we're going to Golgotha, Mt Sinai and… what was the other one he did?"

"Jesus didn't do Golgotha, Golgotha did him, idiot," Moe snapped.

Jude pointed the bottle at them, drawing a shaky bead on their limp bodies. A secretary shuttled in with a tray of club sandwiches and seltzer water. "I ain't trying to stir up none of that Jesus crap going through the Bible Belt. I got two concerts in Memphis and—"

"Nashville and Little Rock. They'd sop you up with melted butter and put you on a biscuit down there. Love you something fierce. We could make two hundred grand just from you reciting the yellow pages on the commode," Jack said, his pool cue limbs weighted down with spreadsheets.

Jude took a long swig. "Dirty motherfucker."

"She's gotta watch her chart position. Those fruits are edging up with their ass-wagging and synthesizers."

"And they got commercials too. You see that peanut butter ad they did in the club with the Muppets on roller skates? Chunky, not creamy, too."

"Must've cost a mint."

"The next single is gonna be field hollers. Chants they used to do during slavery days to subvert the uh, 'Massa'. I'm thinking maybe Jude can team up with Rory Tharpe on a live cover of it—"

"How's that gonna go over with Jude Core? They don't give a fuck about her bringing Rory and her hand-me-downs on the tour."

"Throw the Jude Core fascists some cookies and they'll keep quiet. A few in store promos with the dee jays and a prefab holiday greeting from Jude."

"They'd scarf down her smelliest dump if they could."

"The cover will give them a blast of back in the day—"

"History don't move records."

"Get her back on the variety shows. Flash some tits 'n' ass, tried and true formula—"

"We're working on that, but she pissed off the networks last time."

Jude took another swig and belched. "Don't talk like I'm not here in the room, dirty motherfuckers."

"You can't do reefer and scotch on air, Judie."

"Who says? Most of them Gulf and Western execs leave work smashed blotto at the end of their five-hour days."

"They control over half of the known universe. Sure, we generate good profit, but with all the oil and gas pipelines and developments they've got going in the Middle East you're just one more bitch they want to keep on script."

"Oh, so you a poet now."

"My life's ambition. Nowhere as grand as Judie here."

"Pretty soon the disco Muppets are gonna be nipping at her heels."

"Trick is, how to stay ten steps ahead. The Tharpe chick could be value-added."

"Value, what?"

"Drive through the ghettoes and what do you hear? Jive practically pouring out of the windows of every car, tenement, and corner store."

"Still say Tharpe's a throwback, though. Twenty years from now most music will be automated. You enter a formula into a machine, it churns up Beethoven's Ninth into some unlistenable 6/8 time goulash. You can customize till the cows come home."

Moe waved away the seltzer the secretary offered him and took a jar from underneath his trench coat. "Check this shit out. Adam Clayton Powell and 125th Street, Sunday night, 6:05 p.m. The last church services are getting out, the subway is emptying, and you got a bunch of knuckle-heads throwing sneakers up on the phone wires, a lady scolding some yapping mutt, snippets of Merengue in the park, ketchup being glopped on a half-burnt hot dog." He put his ear to the jar. "Who wouldn't want to buy that sound for fifty cents?"

Jude snatched the jar from him. "Let me see that." She put her ear to it. "This ain't no seashell, Moe. Stop running games."

"Precisely. That's why you hired us. To run games. Listening to an empty jar and marking it up a million times is no less authentic and no more a game than what you do with Negro music."

"I was born and raised in the Deep South."

"Port Arthur isn't that deep. But, dream on, and get back in the saddle. Let's do a Justis in Jivetown revue in the flyover states—"

Jack blanched, stroking his goatee. "We can come up with something more politic than that."

"Sho nuff."

126

Pissing Gold

THE SOUR BEGINNINGS of Nashville peeked out from between Rory's seat back and Mick's jughead. It had always been a whimper of a drive-thru city for her, concocted in regretful spit out bars by Katy who claimed to have ditched two white boy suitors 'cause they wanted to auction me off to Atlantic Records, she sad.

Hadn't practiced in days and the first rehearsal was that afternoon, with Jude's menagerie of reeking third stringers who thought they were heaven sent, gold-plated neophytes with fancy Euro axes bonded to their bony swivel hips. Mick and Thurston took bets on how quick they'd fall in line, how free flowing the white boy slobber would be when they roasted them and put an apple in their mouths like pigs.

"She's ready for you now," one of the reeking ones said as he led Rory into Jude's sanctum sanctorum.

Jude faced the window, oily hair snarling around her shoulders. She held a baton between stumpy, nail-bitten fingers festooned with turquoise rings.

"Always wanted to do a symphony. Just pluck out a cello or a flute, bend 'em anyway I wanted. Never saw any chicks conducting though. Want a drink?" She swiveled around to face Rory, cracking a snaggle-toothed grin. "We finally meet in person and I'm like hog's maw sweaty. Damn this heat in October! It's ungodly."

"Nice switch from Idaho. We've been on the road for three days."

"So I heard. Well, Russ has upgraded you from the fleabag you were in back there. Better grade of hitchhiker, hangers on, and room service."

Rory sat down on a folding chair. Sludgy food cartons, music scores and costumes were scattered all over the room in dejected heaps, making an ant trail path to a sunken bathtub and kitchenette.

Jude gestured to a bubbling pot on the kitchenette stove. "If you're not gonna have a drink, try some root tea. Got seven different herb plants. Latin shit I can't even pronounce. Totally organic. Works like a reverse aphrodisiac. Keeps me woke, alert, and on my feet for hours. Stable as a model fucking citizen."

"I'm good."

"Are your boys settled?"

"Getting there."

"We're gonna work them tomorrow."

"We always take a half day to rehearse."

"Nashville accounts for one quarter of my sales. Motherfuckers know every line, every solo—"

"Those 'motherfuckers' have been mighty good to you, like loyal little lambs—"

"To the slaughter?"

"Your words."

Jude waved her hand. "They're fickle. Just waiting for me to die. The House's stock will go up and all the girlies with mint condition records in Dixie will have collector's items to hawk."

"You're breaking them violin strings hard milking the sympathy. You know where Arthur Crudup is now? Sweeping up bathroom floors at the Mobile, Alabama bus station."

"Shit, I didn't know that."

"How 'bout creating a fund?" A voice said. A white woman in a terry cloth bathrobe flounced through the double doors from the bedroom, squinting dazedly at Rory. She fiddled with a clipboard tucked under her arm, pulling her robe up to her neck. "Morning, er, I mean afternoon. I'd shake your hand but I haven't properly washed," she said shyly.

"Lavender is working on a deadline."

"I'm from *Womyn's Roar*, the magazine. Maybe you've heard of us. We're super huge admirers of yours. My mom… mama, had all your records."

"Their motto is a few good pussies against the Establishment with a capital e," Jude said.

Lavender blushed. "Not quite… but I overheard you talking about um, unsung blues artists. What about a fund to benefit folks like Big

Mama Thornton? We could blow it up and get some traction on it in *Womyn's Roar*. We've got a readership of 10,000 and counting including Guam and the Virgin Islands."

Jude pointed the baton at Lavender. "Your street clothes are hanging up in the bathroom." She made a slashing motion. "Now get."

"Jude—"

"Did I stutter?"

Lavender backed out of the room, hanging onto the clipboard for dear life.

"A fund. The indignity of it. These girl reporters have been flitting around here all week like white gnats."

Rory picked a piece of lint off her shoe. "She's not on your payroll?"

"Hell no."

"The House probably owes Big Mama half of its domestic sales. No whiny little white girl fund is going to make up for that debt. Should've been her living large at Graceland."

Rory stared at her hard. The TV went on in the next room. Gas fiends had siphoned gas from cars in ten suburban Nashville blocks, slurping it up like ice-cold fruit punch.

"Damn that squawk box. I got an appearance on one of the variety shows next week. Look… about her."

"None of my business."

"They follow me, it's like getting rid of the clap."

"You love every stinking minute of it."

"Must be something… having them pop up from every toilet and flowerpot drooling your name."

"They don't know me. They see all this shit and it's, it's like a five-course fucking meal spiked with arsenic. They won't want to get down with me when I'm old as dirt with a catheter on my clit."

"You got some years before that yet."

"Not the way I feel now."

"Well, have her lick your wounds."

"That your m.o.?"

"On the contract it says we're guaranteed at least an hour of rehearsal with your crew."

"You dodging my question?"

"I don't have an m.o. where that's concerned."

"Girl ain't my type and they want me to fly the flag at some ERA march or something—"

"*Caucus*," Lavender said from the back room. "It's a caucus to blow the lid off corruption in five industries, and the corporate scum in music and entertainment are right in our bullseye."

"Caucus, march, same animal—"

Lavender reappeared from the bedroom. "Practically every women's lib group in San Francisco is down with us now that you committed."

"Who said I committed?"

"What's your name again, Purple?" Rory asked.

"Lavender."

"You think her services are for free, Lavender?"

"What do you mean?"

Rory turned to Jude. "I need a record deal. What can you do to make that happen?"

Lavender rapped her fist on the clipboard. "Everyone, every woman in the industry is getting fucked on their contract terms at the House. Black, white, pink, purple, whatever. We surveyed a thousand sisters from the mail room to the executive suites and it was the same chicken-shit litany—"

"But I'm not talking about everyone," Rory said. "I ain't pink or purple and I certainly ain't white. Whatever your 'thousand sister' survey told you, it wasn't relevant to me and my situation."

Jude raised her glass, nodding in agreement. "Apple juice. It'll loosen your bowels and make your mind tight as a steel trap."

"For example, your idol, girlfriend here just inked an historic, three-album deal with the House."

"Heard about it, and she's not my idol or my girlfriend."

Jude took a swig. "That hurts."

"So, not everyone is getting fucked by the man. The House didn't sign any solo women's acts last year or the year before so she's the lone Great White hope."

"Maybe none was good enough," Jude croaked sarcastically. "According to the dicks cutting the checks. Like I said, them fuckers think I'm just a few years away from wearing a catheter." She sipped her drink, slow, self-conscious. "Look, one of the reasons I wanted… one of the reasons why I asked for you to come on this tour was I wanted to work in the same space with you after all these years."

"You've worked in the same space with me; I just didn't get paid for it. I'm still trying to get all my publishing rights back through Russ and his braindead legal minds."

"Yeah, that's fucked up. Sometimes the attorneys working for you are just as corrupt as the ones on the other side. That's why I got smart chicks like Lavender to expose the dirt the labels do talking good vibrations while they're stabbing us in the back. Hate those Beach Boys surfing candy asses by the way. Did more to fuck up the West Coast with their wet dreams than Ronald Reagan."

"Only a white boy would get called a genius because he stuck some glockenspiels and train whistles on an album."

Jude drained her glass. "Candy asses are pissing gold. Their people run rings around Russ with licensing and distribution deals. They got dolls made after them, wind up toys, ugly as sin, speaking in Japanese, Swedish, Russian. They got coasters, pool cues, beach blankets, panties, laundry soap."

"Mobster money," Lavender joked.

"Mobster money is small fry. They practically got their mugs on Kotex," Rory said.

"That might not be a bad thing, depending on the woman wearing it," Jude snickered.

A knock sounded on the door, followed by the plaintive bleat of 'room service'. Jude opened it. A skinny bellhop wheeled in a cart jammed with silver platters and a metronome plopped in the middle.

"Caesar salad, medium rare steak, potatoes au gratin, lemon cream puffs—"

"Who ordered this shit?"

The boy shrugged, startled.

"My so-called management team?"

He handed her a note card. "Eat drink and be merry?" She scrunched up her face at the fine print. "Another feast courtesy of the boys in the House." She threw the card down and picked over the food. "Salad's packed with pesticides." She stabbed at the steak with a fork, shoveling a bloody morsel into her mouth, offering a piece to Rory, then to Lavender, who took it, swallowing defiantly as though in a dare. Jude's porcine eyes roamed up and the down the bellhop's body, resting on the prize of the cream puffs.

"Should've had a food taster," she said.

"What's the metronome for?" Rory asked.

"I like to have a beat when I eat."

"She can't sit still," Lavender said.

Jude unbuttoned her jeans, jutting her stomach out as she lay waste to the steak. "Sitting still equals death. I didn't fucking get here by sitting still and neither did she." She paused, munching, looking moistly at Rory. "I can hook you up with some better legal eagles but they don't do pro bono."

"I'm not looking for a handout or a pity party."

"I know, I know, not suggesting that you are—"

"The only reason why I'm here besides the money is to raise the profile on my situation and give my boys exposure."

Jude nodded weakly, zeroing in on the bellboy, shifting from leg to leg as he awaited further instructions. "Aye, aye. They just want to make all of us cogs in the capitalist machine. The parent company of the House owns this hotel, so this tender young lad's services and those of thirty other lapdog concierges come with the bill. Most of these places got disease-free dial-a-fuck for the dudes."

"And rich white ladies too. White boys ain't got no monopoly on fuckery." Rory held out a dollar to the bellboy. "For keeping the animals fed."

Jude put down her fork and pulled out a fifty-dollar bill. "Go buy yourself some chewing gum, boy. You can be my eyes and ears if any funny stuff jumps off. And remember who this lady here is. This lady here blows Page, Clapton, Beck and all those other pretenders from across the pond away with a twelve gauge. This lady here is Hendrix incandescent, though she was tearing the roof off the mother when he was in diapers."

"I'm hoping maybe I can get an exclusive with you, Ms. Tharpe, about your amazing career," Lavender murmured.

"You said you have global distribution? It needs to be the cover and I have to see what you type before it runs."

"Umm, ok, ordinarily I don't—"

"Is it your magazine or corporate's?"

"Mine, mostly, I mean an editorial collective of grassroots womyn with a 'Y' decides the final cut and we would be so honored—."

"It's hers 'mostly', after they take a few dimes from the House just to keep the lights on. The women with a Y ain't never had no Black woman on the cover."

"And they buy records by the boatloads. No cover, no interview, and I want it in writing."

"I don't know if I can do that."

"Fuck that shit. You'd draft Gidget to do it with my voice coming out of her mouth if you could."

"That's not true, I mean, you're correct, there's never been one on the cover, but I meant I can't give up editorial control—"

"Righteous," Jude blurted out, the tendrils of her hair overtaking her face in a greasy hive. "You know, the last city we were in, they put glass in my food."

Rory shook her head. "Who's 'they' and why would *they* want to do that?"

"Record company. I'm worth more dead than alive."

"What kind of sense does that make? They playing you on every radio station in the country."

"The House's got beef with Grammophone, which is owned by Dutch Shell. They're losing market share to them. Sharks just signed a bunch of new Top 40 and high grossing touring acts, lured 'em away from the House, plus Shell's prospecting for rare petroleum reserves near Little Rock. Ain't you from there?"

"Just east of there. Town where the Union stomped the Confederate Army into the ground."

"Uh huh, well, look what happened with Elvis. If I buy the farm early, my back catalog goes through the roof. Simple math's in the House's favor."

"Least you got a back catalogue. Fighting for mine. I need to make sure I got a career five, ten years from now when you're kicked back in the South of France making millions off of royalties."

"I hate snails in butter sauce, and we *both* worth more dead than alive."

Rory walked over to the cart and picked up a cream puff. "Ain't no we," she said between bites. "But I'll take the number of your attorney. And, Lavender, if you got the dough to pay me for the magazine interview get ready to fire up your camera for some onstage shots tomorrow night. Let's get the womyn with a Y shitting bricks."

The Playlist

5 A.M. IN THE BUTT CRACK of a gloomy Tuesday, plowed roads slick with salt. When Mooch Morrison, one-quarter lace-curtain Irish, three-quarters skeet shooting Pequot nation-stealing WASP, spun it, crooned it, yodeled it, squealed it on the radio in the morning at the beginning of his shift, it was golden. He played it ten times at rush hour, ten times during lunch, booming over the loudspeakers at the corner juke joint drive-thrus overflowing with chili-breathed secretarial pools kite-high on Crisco grilled onions and patty melt cheese scraped black and bubbly onto fat mattresses of rye bread. Mooch told them in his high-pitched, scrotum squeezed auctioneer's voice that it was the best dollar investment when they got their paychecks on the fifteenth and all their household expenses had been accounted for. After they'd paid for formula for the baby, carfare for the bus, Junior's football cleats, the ceiling leak, the busted kitchen faucet, the last installment on the Robin's egg blue Easter layaway dress at Penney's. After all of the household essentials had been attended to it was on and cracking. In the bottom of the mason jar, a little leftover for their own two-and-a-half-minute piece of vinyl paradise plunked down on the doddering Panasonic turntable after the house had been cleared of grasping hands and begging mouths. Only then, could they summon the swamp goddess and let 'er rip.

"Goddamn, how does she get that sound, Ladies and Gents?" Mooch sputtered to the four corners of the Earth. He had the biggest signal in the U.S., the largest number of extraterrestrial syndicates, a reach so gargantuan and intergalactic that nobody could exactly pinpoint where he was broadcasting from at any given moment, guiding deejay caravans across the South and Midwest, a comely distraction to the clouds of nuclear war. If the Russkies are gonna bomb us, we may as well end it all with a fine little number from our blazing lady talent from Port Arthur, Texas.

Mooch liked to claim in publicity interviews that he'd hatched up the idea of Jude long before her parents ever fucked or laid eyes on each other. She was just a vessel for a bigger concept of commerce. If he'd copyrighted her, he'd be a more gonzo multi-millionaire than he was already, going down in history second only to Sam Phillips building Elvis with spit shine Negro-fication from the ground up in the most lucrative social experiment in the music biz.

The execs at the House tracked him down in Memphis and said: "How can we bottle that magic that you're makin', get the keys to the collective brain of the mass audience you built over a decade, the formula to what makes 'em tick, cream, squeal out in the pitch black of REM sleep?" Mooch would be their platinum ambassador, delivering stratospheric market share and brand loyalty with his drive-time bonanzas, steamrolling the asleep-at-the-switch program directors and their turntable toadies, a bloodless coup won by the soothing thrum of his Pied Piper of Hamlin voice.

The House beat out Capitol, Atlantic, RCA, Columbia, and Asylum to cut an exclusive five-year deal with Mooch… renewable if he kept their tunes on the lips of every hinterland hick and high society barnacle in the fifty states. No market or station too small to conquer. No time zone too obscure to spin a salutary medley or do a plug. No regional sales office too piddling to have his minions spread Jude's clarion tunes in a margarine slick melt behind their news, gossip, and weather patter.

There was Mooch in a bear hug with the House's CEO on the front page of Billboard magazine. There was Mooch at a ribbon cutting for a children's cancer ward, donating ten percent of every House LP sale to oncology research. There was Mooch at the biggest record convention in the Southwest, chewing the fat with hardcore, deep-sea-diving collectors in Corpus Christi, Texas on the lost art of pops, hisses, and jumps on 78 rpm Blues vinyl. There was Mooch hawking an all-expense paid trip to Jude's "Southern (dis)Comfort" tour, front row center, backstage pass, photo-ops chased down with a hot toddy of Jude's choice.

There was Mooch touching down in his turbo prop plane on the steaming tarmac at Nashville International, a clutch of reporters storming him, screaming for Top Ten Grammy predictions. There was Mooch mugging for the cameras, playing the thumb on the scale soothsayer.

Lavender got a spot in the concert's press corps, fresh from the wee hours spooning and slurping with Jude. Her hopes for slow burn intrigue and petting dashed when Jude glued her nose to her bong, practicing her Big Mama Thornton intro for the next day's show, fending off stage fright, nausea, dry mouth, the ringing in her ears that she got in phantom anticipation of the concert din. Still, Lavender had come thunderously, twice, going soft as a baby's bald head in Jude's limp arms, unsure of how she'd wound up snoring in the bathtub, fully clothed, lukewarm water ankle deep around her while Jude's bodyguard stood outside the door smacking his fish lips in glee at a Frazier-Ali fight on the living room TV.

She was one of only two white women reporters in the windswept gaggle that huddled on the tarmac, smoking and shooting the shit, waiting for Mooch to touch down. He galloped off the plane, flinging copies of the Yee Haw compilation he'd rushed out to market with the House's blessing to capitalize on Jude's tour.

"Smokin' hot covers and a few originals!" he bleated to the gaggle. "Number one seller in all the Soviet bloc countries. Gal is going to clean house behind that Iron Curtain. Keep us out of World War III. Stuff's better than washed up Washington diplomacy if we got the Commies dreaming of Jude when they fall asleep at night."

"What's your cut, Mooch?" Lavender shouted from within the thicket of alpha males. The others stared at her quizzically from behind their fat aviator shades, all primed to plant their thin leathery lips on Mooch's ass to land an exclusive with Jude.

"You're impeding progress, wankers," he said, cutting through the gaggle with a knobby middle finger. "I mean, ladies and gents. I'm spinning at Nashville Hitz from 3 to 7, then it's Jude on a stick—"

"And Rory Tharpe," Lavender interjected.

"Correct. A long, storied career, that one."

"She can't get a record deal."

"Well, this foray into redneckery will help her. 'Sides, they love her to pieces in Wales, Belgium, and lower Iceland. This thing goes down well, we're looking at a global rollout. Merch, TV, film, the works. Then the old girl will really be cooking with gas."

He wriggled past, striding to the open door of a black Lincoln Town Car, patting the receding sprigs of his Teddy Boy comb-over. Lavender bolted in front of him and slid into the Lincoln.

"What the fuck!"

"Did you get a hair transplant or is that a straight up rug?"

He groped at the sprouts. "Who the fuck are you?"

"Tell that goon to close the door."

"Shut it, Amos. What rag do you write for?"

"*Womyn's Roar*. We've gotten 'Excellence in Journalism' awards from New Zealand two years in a row."

"That so? What do you want with a countrified plebe like me, young lady?"

Lavender curled her lip and pressed on. "What can you do to move a deal for Rory Tharpe?"

"Who do you think I am? I can't do shit."

"C'mon, you personally account for millions of record sales a year."

"I don't do charity unless it's bald orphans. Terminal, bald kids with lymphoma. The neediest of the needy."

"And good photo ops."

"That helps, yeah. The world needs to know that kind of painful shit exists and, yes, my conscience will be clear on Judgment Day."

They pulled away from the curb, reporters bumping across the tarmac like pinballs. Rainclouds glowered overhead. The car phone rang. Mooch waited for three rings then picked it up imperially.

"Nobody gets a quote except for this enterprising little chick I got here sitting next to me," he wheezed into the receiver, tapping Lavender on the knee. Raindrops splattered on the tinted windows. "Anybody wants an exclusive gots to pay for it, either in ducats or albums." He tapped her knee again, fingers lingering. The outline of the concert stadium rose up in front of them. Jude's name was wedged between the Day-Glo words "Sold Out" and the logo of the tour's beer company sponsor.

"Yeah, we're passing by it now," he said. "Looks beautiful, lit up like Christmas. This shit's gonna smash everything else on the books. Bud Beer says it's gonna open up a plant here. Concert will be the launching pad. Three thousand manufacturing jobs in the works and Jude gets at least five years' worth of sponsorship."

"Union jobs?" Lavender asked.

"Yeah, Teamsters or something." He put his hand on her pants leg, probing the fabric as he talked and barked out directions to the driver at the same time. "Take me back to the Seville." He leaned into Lavender. "I got a suite there, whirlpool tub with those fancy jets. Good therapy for the dregs of childhood scoliosis and any other ailment you got."

Lavender moved away from him. "I have a deadline to finish this story by tomorrow."

"That could be arranged. Why not tonight? Need a ghost writer?"

"Stop the car."

"You're giving women's libbers a bad name. I consider myself one, by the way. Strong women make the world go round."

"Let me the fuck out."

Mooch flipped through a tattered appointment book, slipping a pair of reading glasses onto his nose. "Relax. You really think I'd risk getting VD screwing around with sloppy seconds like you? Plenty more where you came from. Amos, drop this individual off at the curb."

"Sloppy seconds my ass, you dirty, dried up motherfucker." Lavender snatched the book, grabbed him by the collar, and pushed him down onto the seat.

Helter Skelter

ON THE TOILET, Rory could make out the sounds of tentative gasps and grunts, demon beating, pint-sized exorcisms rising symphonic in the next stall. Tan white girl, backup singer, drum majorette boots pointing sideways accusatorily. Katy would wait like clockwork for Rory with a bottle of Milk of Magnesia thirty minutes before big performances when her stomach was in an all-out palace revolt. *If your belly's not on fire, then the stage won't be lit either*, she'd proclaimed, shoving the bottle in Rory's face for her to drink down in one gulp.

"You got anything, baby doll?" the girl shrieked from next door.

Rory rustled up half a Milk of Magnesia tablet from her pocket and passed it under the stall.

"Pardon me, baby. Pardon me," the girl said, letting loose a fantabulous fart. "This gonna be where we can hide out when the Russian warheads get launched," she cackled. "Whole state of Tennessee will be safe as a steel trap bunker in here."

Rory flushed the toilet and left the stall, washed her hands, dabbed water on her makeshift spit curls.

In the mirror, Katy frowned at her disdainfully from behind, appraising the white girl's doughy thinness in the silver sheath halter dress Jude's designer had slapped together for the backup singers stitched in the dead of night as they brooded over late tax returns, bounced checks, clingy mates, ditched file clerk jobs, and children left haplessly behind for their shot at the road and their deep dark heart's desire.

Jude had assembled a crackpot sisterhood of Fleetwood Mac refugees around her. An iron wall of bottom feeders who warbled, scratched, and punched through Jude's bootleg blues repertoire. Rory kept a careful eye on the drama of fourth string white women backup singers. Watched their unspoken assumption of being catered to. Noted the cunning, solicitous once-overs they got from the crew. All the breaks and excuses that rained down on them like candy when a harmony or a dance move went sour. The white women, in turn, were always watching her for a misstep, a slight, a trespass in the wee wrung out hours after they'd dragged off-stage, talking shop over a joint and Jack Daniels, waiting for dawn in a flea-bitten trailer before they got up and did the same sub-Vegas shtick all over again, prancing around, oozing omnipotent control down to their pink fingertips in the presence of Black men musicians.

"Don't think we've met," Rory said to the white girl.

"Mooch brought me on. Dirty goat, promised me at least two month's worth of work."

"If you fucked him?"

"Something like that. More diplomatic about it. Perv's got a foot fetish so just wants me to stomp on him a little bit, like they do the grapes in Greece, 'er, I mean Italy."

Rory grunted goodbye and walked out to the arena. A man pushed an industrial-size vacuum cleaner across the stage as a crew of attendants in gray uniforms and rubber gloves did a final sweep of the seats for trash.

"Afternoon, ma'am," the vacuum cleaner shouted over the din, face alive with a hundred creases. "Finally made it back."

"Pardon?"

"I caught you and your mama at the Imperial back in '55."

"Yeah?"

"Coming down in buckets and mama did a solid five nighter, kicking around on a cane but still a sparkplug."

"Recovering from a hernia."

"Nothing could stop that woman."

Rory nodded, looking around. "How long you been working here?"

"Since they started hiring Colored. Put me in charge of maintenance ten years ago when the white boy they had doing the job rolled in drunk too many mornings."

"Figures."

"I tell these pups to take pride, 'cause every square inch of this joint's got our mark on it, whether the bosses acknowledge it or not. Gonna be nice to see you up there."

"What's the hourly, if you don't mind my asking?"

"Just under two bucks."

"Hard to take pride in scraps."

"It's either that or starve."

"From what I've seen around here, looks like some of us is pretty close to it."

"That's long behind you, sister Tharpe. It'll be a blessing to see you play."

Rory took out her purse, fishing a twenty from her wallet. She held it out to the man. "Take it, please. Car fare, bills, something nice for your lady if you have one."

"Good of you, but I can't. Bosses' eyes and ears are wired into the stage. Besides, might want to save it for rainy days in the next city."

He turned the vacuum cleaner back on and started working the wings, hoisting the cord against his sagging hip, the stage gleaming back at them.

She felt a hand on her shoulder and turned to see Mick.

"Thurston and Butch are going at it again. You got to stop this."

"At it over what?"

"Just dicking around. Miscellaneous shit. Card's stirring the pot. Gets off on it."

"They like performing for him."

"I can't have it."

"What do you want me to do, lock them down? We're on in three hours."

"Can Butch."

"Butch? You mean Thurston."

"He's a three a.m. junkie drunk and a thief. Lifts small shit from stores, lifts food, any little crumb that ain't nailed down."

"I never seen that."

"A lot you don't see, baby."

She paused.

"Butch's playing—"

"Is going soft. You can't see it and you can't hear it. Motherfucker's coasting."

"*You're* soft on Thurston."

"Please."

"Always have been. Birds of a feather."

"You know that's crap. Butch can't do the distance and now we got corporate watching. Think about what's best for you, for the band, for making a half decent living for the first time in ten fucking years."

"You blaming me for that?"

"Course not."

"You want a break to ditch it all, cool your heels, just say so. Don't make Butch the excuse."

"He's a liability. Card too."

"I'm smelling something else, Mick. Jealousy. Stinks to high heaven."

"I'm not jealous of him."

"It's about the bass, isn't it? Him showing you up? Shit, we got Jude's people and her white trash audience set to eat us alive in a slow munch if I ain't at the top of my game. Folks from the House are going to be watching hard. Not the time or place to start nitpicking Butch."

"We're bleeding and he's stumbling over every other note, disappearing after hours to god knows the fuck where."

"Why don't you put a tail on him since you're itching to know?"

"What sense does it make to keep on deadweight with all the bills we have and the debts you're under?" He was in her face now, wincing from back pain, a phantom of all the years he'd tried to play bass, his rock god daydreams galloping over what little grit and discipline he had. Years ago, at thirty-three, he'd surrendered to the drumbeat of doubt about his abilities, rescued from the walking dead by Rory's job offer to road manage the band.

They did their angry twostep, eyed from the wings by the vacuum cleaner. He monitored the white man's tone and body language for signs of transgression while he watched the staff double check the aisles for trash. He wanted everything to be correct. Polished down to the studs, maneuvered by Black hands fading into invisibility for the chanting, overspending, stoned out of their skull whites out for a few hours of packaged abandon. It would be the smoothest ride for her until the deep bend of the Delta, where there had been rumblings of a possible service workers' strike at the big arenas.

"You know this isn't just about me," Mick said. His voice went hoarse under the roar of drilling in the bathroom. "Not trying to jam you up at the last minute and suck you into some mess. It's just that you've turned your back on this for too long."

"And brought Card in, right? That's what this is really about."

"Horseshit."

"Go on, lie to yourself."

He looked at her hard. "You ready to go back into the studio?"

"Unless the House or some other wizard pays for it, we ain't going nowhere."

"After all this, they'll give you some time, maybe even a better than decent deal. But that wasn't what I asked you."

"Nobody's *giving* me anything."

"You ready?"

"When have I had any goddamn time to write or think or pee straight, holding together the gigs, the bills, paying for the roach motels we stay in."

"The last one didn't seem so bad. At least you got a little leg for your troubles."

"Don't know what you're talking about."

"It's ok to have liked someone, to have fucked someone other than Marie. Cut yourself some slack."

"Back off."

"You've got to be shitting me. It's been years since you and she were together. Move the fuck on. For all intents and purposes the lady's dead." He paused, waiting for a glimmer of recognition. "You hear anything about that Sid girl? Anything about how she's doing?"

"No."

"Case closed on that too, huh? I know it's still eating at you. That night you were too sick to go down to the police station."

"I was drunk. Flat out drunk. Don't sugarcoat it. Or are you fucking with me? You know, you're a bad psychologist."

"I'll stop psychologizing then. Just thought you might want to talk about it. You keep this crap bottled up—"

"You're doing it again, Mick. I fucked up. I'm living with it. If I could snap my fingers and make it right I would, hear?"

"Alright, I'm done. Just stop acting like a damn martyr."

"Deal." She hesitated, looking past him to the backline crew fumbling with a toolbox onstage. "Listen, can you find out what the numbers are for the crowd tonight?"

"I told you, 20,000 or so… How's your stomach been, you been taking those pills?"

A figure advanced quickly toward them in silvery Beatle boots. "Rory, Ms. Tharpe! Can I talk to you for a minute?" Lavender strode up with a commanding flourish, mustering a dry smile for Mick as she edged towards Rory. She crumpled a package of Saltines between her fingers, cracker bits spraying from her agitated lips. "Mooch Morrison, know who he is?"

"Vaguely."

Mick drew himself up, irritated by the intrusion. "Obnoxious radio guy out of Ohio."

"He wants to interview you before the show, one on one, live, in studio, broadcasts to mega millions, syndicated across the entire country."

"I'm Mick, her road manager."

Lavender looked Mick up and down. "Mick, the trusty dusty vicarious thrillster. Yes, I'm familiar with you. The not quite so big man on campus in Vegas and Atlantic City."

"What?"

"I guess craps is better than shoving shit up your nose. Are you down for the interview, Ms. Tharpe?"

Mick pointed a finger in her face, "All queries need to go through me."

"They just did. Ms. Tharpe?"

"When and how long? We got a sound check two hours before."

"He can do it asap, just need to get you to the studio and mic-ed up." She stepped closer to Rory, eyeing Mick contemptuously. "And keep your damn hands to yourself."

The plane bumped up and over the bloated cotton candy clouds, then down again, giving Divinity's stomach a little beating, a tweaking reminder of the capriciousness of God, his knuckles balled inches from her body in a fat fist full of wriggling creditors. All the money she owed. All the checks in the ledger. All the phone calls Patton was making back in Little Rock as she slept. All, all, all, drizzling out to her in dream sludge, sweaty on the cramped coach aisle seat.

She'd been awakened to an elbow in her side, the undisciplined mollusk in the center seat sputtering about stock dividends from a bullish market that was finally going his way. She waved off his investing tips and downed the last bit of club soda in her cup. Nashville, a balmy sixty, touching down in twenty minutes, seats back, tray tables up, soundtrack to the white kewpies humping in the bathroom under the averted gaze of the flight attendant. The dishwater white woman attendant roamed the aisles, double checking, her tone predictably sharp when she got to Divinity, who took her time complying. When they found out she was a pastor, a lady reverend, a menopausal wild card interloper in the Negro pulpit, the public's tone always shifted to quizzical, halting regard.

"Down for business or pleasure?" the mollusk asked after the attendant swept away.

"The former," Divinity said, clutching the gold cross she'd received from an annual 'Walk with God' apostles' retreat, hoping it would ward off probing creatures.

"Good time for it, oil crisis is over and the OPEC boys have settled down for now. Quite sure you don't follow all that madness."

"To the contrary."

"What line of work you in?"

"I run several ministries, charitable initiatives, flying in today to negotiate a radio program."

"TV's the future but radio's gold. Wake up to it, go to bed to it, wall of noise, chatter and happy talk but you can't get away from it. The wife orders these health vitamins from this WLAC show on natural life rejuvenation and still got the televangelists out of Texas jabbering on at the same time. Double teamed on the quackery if you ask me," he paused, eyeing the gleaming cross in her hand. "No offense meant."

"None taken."

At the airport she was met by a car provided by Bethel Faithful, a favor she'd called in for making a donation to the ministry's roofing fund. Most of the time she preferred to drive on her own, but today she wanted to see the city unimpeded by the micro calculations of turns and stops and figuring out street signs. The driver put her suitcase in the trunk and left her to her thoughts.

As they drove, she rode the train tracks in her head, track ties slick from a humid glancing rain that poured down, then evaporated in an eye blink. She'd memorized the pant of the low-slung houses, men hanging on the porch smoking, feet up, playing the dozens, kids walking from the bus stop after school in anxious threes and fours, jubilant over having lived to see another Friday.

At her grandparents' church, hugging the tracks in Germantown, she'd learned to play a middling piano concerto, swimming in resentment after all the painstaking instruction and wishful laments of the breath mint gnashing white teacher. Fridays, she was his charity case number seventeen. Bleeding heart was galvanized, levitating in rage about the Negroes having been unjustly denied access to the musical canon he'd cherished since he was knee high to the belly of a grasshopper. Inwardly, she'd bitten his smooth, patient white hand, its sandalwood putrescence stroking her knee as she carved a bow and arrow from his right vertebrae.

More and more she found herself jolting from memories. Fully awake, sitting, working, agonizing over what came next, they'd descend, nibbling at her eyelids, gleefully blinding her until Patton came to the rescue with claptrap from the deacon's board, a laundry list of parishioner complaints, bank statements that didn't square. Concentration, focus, she thought, commanding the dirty urchins to line up in drill sergeant rows.

She checked into her hotel room, took a bath, made a few calls, watched the sky darken. Someone had left a handbill advertising Jude Justis's week-long arena concert on the front desk, Rory's name silk-screened at the bottom.

"Two birds with one stone," she said to herself, turning on the night-stand radio to WLAC's spiritual renaissance hour, brought to you by hemorrhoid ointment and denture glue, fade cream for those stubborn liver spots.

"Life everlasting," a voice bleated.

"Get me some fucking chicken. What's the point of being down here in this swamp if I can't get any goddamn fried chicken?" Mooch got up from the couch, snatching Rory's last record album out of its jacket.

Sound engineers swept through the studio around him, readying the console and the microphone. Rory was escorted in by an assistant wearing a headset. Mooch walked toward her, extending his hand briskly.

"Welcome, Miss Tharpe. Anything we can get you before we start? Water, soda, gin?" he snapped his fingers at the assistant. "Get Miss Tharpe something to drink then get on that chicken." The man sauntered off. Mooch shook his head. "Straight out of Tennessee State and dumber than a doornail in a donkey's ass." He handed her some headphones. "Here you go."

"You're on in five," one of the sound engineers said.

"We'll begin at the beginning. Early life in the backwoods, flight from Arkansas, ditching gospel and shacking up, figuratively that is, with J. J. for a late career revival."

"I'm not from the backwoods."

"Well, I stand corrected."

"And this ain't a late career revival."

"Let's save the semantics for the interview."

The sound engineer beckoned Mooch into the booth. "You're on in two."

His theme music rolled and Rory plunked down in the seat beside him, trying not to massage her churning stomach, the antacids Mick had given her torturously out of reach.

"Hello and good afternoon, evening, twilight and all points in between, ladies and gents out there in the musical universe, get your ears in gear for the Mooch, bringing you vinyl inspiration and aspiration from across this great big beautiful US of A. Today I'm fortunate to have in the flesh in studio and totally all the way live, gospel singer, axe wielder and fret blaster par excellence, Sister Rory Tharpe! How ya doing, Sister?"

"Call me Rory, no one's called me sister in a million years."

"Rory, we're excited to have you down here in good ol' Nashville for a stupendous concert tour with the one and only Jude Justis."

"Yes, I'm... looking forward to playing tonight."

"You have a long, fabled career coming out of the down and dirty blues tradition of Broonzy, Son House, Robert Johnson, Charley Patton and the list goes on. You were playing guitar in church practically before you could walk and talk and your mama was a gospel star in her own right."

148

"Right."

"Maestro Katy, may she rest in peace. I'm not too proud or vain to say that I grew up listening to you and your mama's records back in Columbus where we were the only white family on the block."

"Must've been trying for you."

"Well now I wouldn't say that, but talk to us about how you got started. You got a unique picking style, cross between slide and electric guitar, makes the axe sound like blue steel and greased lightning."

"Bending strings and making them bleed with my left and working a strong pick with my right."

"Sounds gory."

"Playing is gory and you couldn't be no slouch backing the gospel choirs when I was coming up. Folks think it was all just shouting, passing out, Bible thumping and carrying on but the playing was serious."

"Yes, but you left gospel for the godforsaken sinful world of blues rock with a good little lineup behind you. Drafting Card Jefferson, the Motown bassist, for a few runs was a nice touch."

"There's plenty of sin in gospel, that's what keeps it interesting."

Mooch cackled. "Your mother would turn over in her grave if she heard that."

"Maybe."

"So, are we gonna see a collaboration between Rory and Jude come out of this?"

"Don't know if Jude would be able to hang."

"Ouch, you got a real sense of humor on you."

"I'm not currently under contract. Haven't been in over a decade."

"Darn shame. Hopefully, Nashville will rectify that," he whipped out a 45 record. "Here's one of your down home favorites, we'll spin this in a sec."

Rory took the record. "I don't get a thin dime from you playing this."

"Well, I'll be a monkey's uncle. That hardly seems fair. Ladies and gents, sad to say that Miss Tharpe has been engaged in a battle royale with some of the publishing companies over copyright."

"Story of our lives in the industry. Ain't a single Black artist living or dead who hasn't been burned on the plantation chasing after royalties they're owed—"

"Plantation? Wow, that's a pretty strong metaphor there—"

"Anyone wanting to support my legal challenge can sign up for the Rory fan club out of Glasgow for a small fee."

"Glasgow, Kentucky?"

"Glasgow, Scotland."

Mooch slapped the table. "She's an international impresario, ladies and gents."

"I'll be playing all of my staples tonight and a few new songs. Bootleggers who try and record us will be cut off at the balls. My latest is called 'Swallow You Whole'. Ode to the ocean bottom feeders in A&R."

Mooch raised his eyebrows. "Well, sometimes you can find buried treasure on the bottom of the ocean. Titanic's still down there, far as I know. Anywho, I know you and Jude are gonna burn up the stage tonight. Folks, if you're within a one-hundred-mile radius of the Arena this week, run don't walk, and con a teenybopper for tickets to see two of the most electrifying lady musicians in the country run rings around disco and tear up some blues and rock 'n' roll. We'll be back with more in a sec." He ripped off his headphones. "You're quite the spitfire. Sparks make for good radio, but I wouldn't hold my breath waiting on the House to sign you. Shareholders won't bite. For them you either gotta be jailbait if you're a broad or a psycho junkie out of rehab if you're a dude. Payday is smaller, but you'd be better off at an indie where you wouldn't get lost in the shuffle."

Mooch's assistant popped back in, vibrating with importance. "Boss, you got a visitor."

Jude bustled in, sidestepping the assistant. "Moochie, baby doll, it's been a minute!" A feather boa dangled from her neck. She swigged from a half full wine cooler, Lavender hovering behind her, clicking her heels like Dorothy in Oz, face creased with sleep.

"Caught a little of the interview on the drive in. Can you give me and Rory a spin together after the commercial? Another promo for the road?"

Mooch cocked his head, avoiding Lavender's steely glare, the jingle for a new cereal commercial chirping from the speaker. "Yep. We got four minutes."

He led Jude into the studio. Rory spun around, surprised, as Jude clapped her hands with glee. "Guess what, mama? Show's sold out, wall to wall!"

The cereal jingle ended and Mooch tossed Jude some headphones. "Ok, all you ladies in radio land, when you're going down the grocery aisle, desperate for something for the kiddies, remember Angel Flakes melt in your mouth cereal, packed with all the vitamins and minerals your angels need to do the Indy 500 in their tricycles. But, in all seriousness, very pleased to have another special and unexpected guest to close out the hour, you know her as the voice that ate Texas and everything below the Mason Dixon, the take no prisoners hellraising mistress songbird bard of the blues, Miz Jude Justis, esquire! How's tonight shapin' up, Jude?"

"Mighty fine, Mooch."

"I see you got on that lucky boa that all your fans go crazy for. Tell me, in your own words, how did this meeting of the minds between you and the one-and-only Rory Tharpe come together?"

"Pure admiration. And, we happen to have the same manager. Cut my teeth on Sister's records. Without her and her god-sent music I wouldn't be here."

"Sho nuff. A lot of us feel the same way," Mooch gushed. "You got five sold out nights here in Nashville and the rest of the country to conquer—"

"I ain't hip to that kind of violent, militaristic language."

Mooch chuckled, motioning for his tech to cue up another 45. "Ok then, along the trail of lilacs and roses that you ladies are spreading across the nation, what are gonna be some high points? The Sister is the first woman you've ever had in your band."

"That's just happenstance. Growing up, life wasn't relevant for me until I found Jesus in the blues. Twelve years old, getting the stuffing kicked out of me riding the school bus and it was love at first listen. Mama and daddy didn't know what to do with my big mouth anyway. Would've wound up disowned and face down in the gutter if it weren't for getting royally saved by a few bars of Howlin' Wolf I heard a bricklayer playing in our neighborhood one day. All the church kids used to tease me 'bout how Wolf was the devil incarnate. Racist mother—"

"Suckers," Mooch interjected. "Have to watch your language, sugar plum, you know this is a family station."

"You're saying Wolf's responsible for getting you in this business? Well, he ain't here to defend himself," Rory said. "But seriously, I'm glad for the opportunity to return to Nashville after ten years of being on the road, getting acquainted with practically every motor inn and travel lodge in the country."

"Planning on going back home over the border to Arkansas after this?"

"Planning on going to California, or overseas. Hook up with some producers that want to cut a new album with me. Wider audience."

"Like a rolling stone. The Brits and the Krauts are in a full-on blues revival, I hear. Well, no man could ever keep up with you two liberated gals of the South."

"Half the proceeds from the tour's going to a charity for battered and neglected children," Jude interjected.

"You hear that folks? Not only do you have the opportunity to see these living legends in a musical match made in heaven, but it's going to a good cause."

"After Uncle Sam and the House carve it up."

Mooch coughed, leaning into the mic as he signaled for the engineer to wrap up. "Again, folks, run, don't walk to the Arena or to your local record store to get a smokin' hot copy of Jude's latest LP. Until we meet again tomorrow, the Mooch is officially out of session." He put his hand over the mic, glasses askew, the staff bracing for a volcanic tirade as he snatched a mug of coffee out of his second assistant's hand.

"What in hell was that all about?" he growled, lurching toward Lavender. "You put her up to that, talking that insurrectionist crap of yours. Thought we had an agreement to keep it nice and light."

"What agreement is he talking about, babe?" Jude asked.

"The one where I keep quiet about finger fucking him with lab gloves in the hotel elevator. Sorry for the detail. It's this thing he has. Quite sure any woman working for him knows the score."

"Aw get the fuck outta my face. Your career puts the 'w' in whoredom and that shit mountain newsletter of yours—"

Lavender jabbed her pen in the air. "The House gets an international rep as a savior of orphaned urchins when all it's doing is funneling money back into executive salaries and big oil—"

Mooch groaned. The phones had started ringing off the hook. The switchboard operator fielded calls like an octopus on speed, nodding, grunting, scribbling messages. "The ladies are going ape shit over Ms. Tharpe," she said, reading the first few messages. "They wanna know when the new single she was talking about is coming out… Wanna know whether Jude is going to cover her old songs… Wanna know whether she uses a pressing comb on her hair and if she has any kids or a husband."

"Earth shattering questions. If you've got legs in Hicksville you've got a career. The housewives are the soul power behind the industry. Case in point, take Judie here. Her side piece wants to bite the hand that feeds her but I notice she's not volunteering to return all the dirty bonuses she got for performing at corporate junkets. The House and my production company put together all the promos for her latest, might I add, middling effort. If it wasn't for the sweat equity I put behind it the shit would've landed in the remainders bin next to Disco Duck and Muzak's greatest hits."

"You got your pound of flesh just like everybody else. You didn't have nothing to do with my record sales."

Mooch chortled. "I made you. Every time they fire you up on the jukebox in some toe crud grease trap it's because of me, *baby girl*. I guess the women's libber here has got your memory prematurely fuzzy."

The switchboard operator plopped a handful of messages in front of Rory. "Here," she said, "You got some housewives, a few heavy breathers and a little girl who called in, didn't leave a message."

Rory tensed up, the white people's squabbling fading into background noise. She stared down at the pieces of paper, willing Sid's name onto them, warring with her tiny nub of a self, cowering in anger, relief, fear. She regretted having given the backup singer the antacid tablet. Regretted her terminally weak stomach, the remoteness of indoor plumbing, the lie she told Mooch about going overseas; steeling herself for Mick's hissy fit about it.

"I need some air," she said to the white people.

Katy guided her out of the room, hands cold as a patch of black ice on the highway. "You was always itching to be grown. Well, now you grown," she whispered. "You crack up they'll be all over you like flies on shit. You got to keep that girl away. Stop fixing on her." The hallway stretched in front of them, vibrating with the snickers of the girls in her Sunday school choir. They were pop-eyed in frilly dresses, jeering because Rory'd gotten her period, a smear of blood lighting up her hem like a comet's tail.

Katy pushed her into the elevator. Downstairs, the doors opened onto a crowd of white teenagers. Jude Core hardliners flopped around in boas and bell-bottoms, yellow-tinted attitude glasses slipping down their noses. A security guard shooed them back, frothing at the mouth, tight uniform splitting open over his bulbousness. They pushed past him, surging in a pimply tantrum toward Rory.

"Look, there's Aretha!"

"Naw, dumb shit, that's Rory Tharpe, she's backing Jude, can play the crap out of some guitar."

They gawked with vague interest, a chant for Jude rising up from the bowels of the crowd as it barreled into the hallway. Some ripped the station's promo posters off the wall for souvenirs, others high-fived in glee at penetrating the inner sanctum of the ground floor, casting sidelong glances at the defeated security guard panting into his radio for backup.

"Jude! Jude! Jude! Jude!" They bellowed, advancing to the elevator, wielding albums, coke cans and autograph books in a tight shield in front of them, fingers jabbing at the elevator buttons, the smaller ones jockeying for position and better sightlines, a scraggly Big Bird clone beating on a bongo drum, keeping time to the ruckus in staccato bursts, angling his elastic body past Rory.

"My daddy's the fire captain," he shrieked, "Ain't nobody gonna tell us that we're in violation at this joint so let's get on up there and see the queen!"

The swarm roared in approval as Rory ploughed through them. Somebody snipped a piece of her hair with scissors and laughed, jubilant about the big game souvenir they'd snagged, a hank of Negro hair for long life, good luck. The elevator lit up suddenly in slow descent as the swarm surged against it, listened, waited, awash in jittery speculation about Jude's appearance.

The door to the building opened and Divinity entered. She squinted at the swarm, then rummaged through her purse, pulling out a cherry leather-bound Bible. She had on a new two-piece suit. Beige, her favorite power shade. The high yellows on the deacon board couldn't wear it and look half as fine as she did. Double-pressed and pleated for the occasion. Test drive for her keynote speech at the Black Baptists' convention. *If any of these varmints so much as blink in my direction*, she thought, picking lint off her shoulder as she strode through them, Bible to her breast, first page of Ephesians as her talisman.

Castles Burning

THE RED BIBLE soared over the swarm, a sail of doom splitting Jude Core. Rory watched it as Divinity's face came into view; a disembodied head on a TV screen doing a weather report, her cheeks powdered and rouged, exuding a newscaster's impenetrable time sensitive cool. The crooked mouth and left of center features of the girl who'd stared back at her from the front pew of church had deepened with age, challenge, seeking. The gut level cunning was still there, lurking behind the quiver of her top lip, stiff now as she continued walking, Jude Core parting like bowling pins.

Rory had been dimly aware of Divinity's career in the ministry. Katy had followed it, clucking disapproval at mentions in the local Negro paper that her sister sent from Cotton Plant. The Arkansas stations ran commercials for her dial-a-prayer service in the wee hours.

Makes sense that the brightest one from that heathen family followed in Daddy Simmons' footsteps, Katy said. Pretending like she was sticking close to God. A good actor, just like her grandpa. Them buzzards would never let a dark gal like that have her own church. Them buzzards would pick the meat right off her bones even though she was kinfolk. Shit. Them buzzards tried to deny I gave them money to help start up the church. Daddy Simmons couldn't make the down payment for the land or the building. And them buzzards came crying to me at the eleventh hour, Shucking, jiving, panting after the money I made from Vee Jay records.

Them buzzards were all of the naysayers, doubting Thomases, and backroom skeptics flapping their gums across Cotton Plant. They'd barely let Rory play electric guitar. It could knock a womb out of balance, they said. Make her barren. Just like getting her rocks off would make her go blind, crippled, crazy, like Onan. Then what man would want her. To have and to hold. Honor and obey.

*Them buzzards wanted to put their hands on you, but I wouldn't let 'em.
Would soon as have God turn me into a pillar of salt.*

Little Divinity had started preaching soon as she learned how to speak
with that stereophonic voice of hers. Testifying to the rafters like she was
her own sanctified brass band marching down the church aisle. Holy
visions of apocalypse and plague. Hexes on the rival crosstown church
headed by the bishop with advanced degrees in fuck missions with a new
woman in every port. Little Divinity couldn't compete with that. God
knew it and cursed her to bleed every month.

Jude Core raged at the elevator doors. Someone smashed the fire alarm,
the sound bleating through the air. Divinity had never seen so many
unwashed, underage white people jammed in one small space. Claustrophobia kicked in, her head exploding with another migraine. She caught
Rory's eye in the crowd, pushing the tangled bodies away, the Bible locked
firmly in front of her.

"You ok?" she yelled to Rory.

"Fuckers cut a piece of my hair. Other than that, yeah. What're you
doing here?"

"Had an appointment with Mooch Morrison about some advertising on his show," she lied. "But given all this madness it'll have to wait.
C'mon, let's get the hell out of here." She hoisted the Bible above her
head. "Move back, blasphemers! Move back! Jesus don't sleep on sinners
bowing down at the altar of sonic iniquity."

Divinity led the way out of the building. Rory followed her, dazed
and sluggish, into the steamy Nashville sun.

"What time you go on stage?"

"Two hours."

A black rental car rolled up and blew its horn. Mick leaned out of the
window, squinting at Divinity and the magic Bible, her megawatt gold
earrings stabbing him between the eyes.

"Looks like your people are here to get you," she said.

Rory stepped to the car and opened the door. Mick frowned, checked
his watch, the radio squawking on about new nuclear power plants and
days-long gas lines crisscrossing the Midwest and the South.

Divinity put a hand on Rory's shoulder. "I'll be there tonight. Be praying for you. Break a leg."

Sound check. Dendrite-frying feedback. Tuning till doomsday, then more tuning. Roadies flopping and panting across the stage, lion taming cables, speakers, amps.

C to E minor was home for her. Shudder, slide, shudder. Then thump the strings with the right hand, pop 'em upside the head like a sobering smack for a falling down drunk sprung from a dive. They were the first chords she got down cold. Ear candy that gave her a tingle lasting for hours until Katy intruded with demands to do laundry, wash dishes or practice hymnals until her throat rang raw.

She should have told Divinity to save the fucking prayers. Save that dizzy shit for a more willing dupe. A captive audience. A roach spinning on its back.

Nothing ever happened from above. No heavenly lightning strike, no incinerating rebuke. Something about Divinity's posture, her big show with the Bible in the studio, gave Rory an inkling that she knew the jig was up too. Grasped a bit of it at least; her preacher thing now running on fumes and terror, the prized Negro gift of oratory honed in debate contests, bathroom mirrors, pews damp with waiting and comingled body fluids. She'd always been blessed with speech, magnificent cut-glass diction, the molasses voice that men who wormed their way into the ministry would die for. Divinity never had to really work for the killer close, the hushed hook, line, and sinker. Came into a room and owned it with the alchemical curl of her lip. Spread her arms and poof. The women gave her grudging respect because of it; the men dissected, debated, and waited for a misstep. When she applied for Revival Church's first building loan none of the banks would gamble on a single Black woman. A white land speculator named Sprat ponied up for a lease on a storefront nobody wanted. *It was the stomping grounds of them godforsaken End Time loonies that had gone out and been swallowed up in the West Texas desert, the leasing agent said. Some buildings have too much damn unfinished business. Remnants lingering, ornery spirits.* Before she moved in, Divinity did a purifying ceremony to drive out the interlopers. To put them in their place, before they put her in hers.

"Get in your fucking places, blokes!" A roadie yelled at the arena attendants picking up junk in the aisles. "Shit, we don't need to eat off the floors. Fuckers will probably trash the place anyway after Jude leaves. Miss Tharpe, we're ready for you and your boys."

Card, Thurston, and Butch filed onto the stage silently, corralled by Mick hours before, their backbiting put on hold for the moment. Rory plugged in her guitar. The air rippled with bustling attendants, some stopping to watch as she cued up a fast arpeggio churning blues number. The three men plodded through their parts. Thurston cued up too fast on the downbeat, Butch let loose a scattered bridge. Card whacked at his bass with his open hand.

"Get it together," Rory growled, as they shambled to a close, the clock ticking down to Jude's entrance. It had been years since she'd been in an arena that big, cavernous, bumptious, baby goblins of stage fright coming at her. Suddenly she was antsy about Divinity being in the audience sitting in judgment with her cartoon Bible; tossed among the record company execs, assassins with submachine guns lurking in the exits. The band would throw in an original that Rory squeaked out after months of stewing inactivity, procrastination, doubt. She'd tried to write at the end of meals, hiding in the toilet, collapsing on the edge of her motel bed with the guitar, mixing up chords at every angle, the C to E minor old faithfuls failing her in the face of figuring out installments on four months of unpaid doctor's bills for her stomach pain and gallstones.

These were all alien matters to Divinity, she was sure. Judging from her painstakingly color-coordinated suits, she was shielded from calamity by her god force field, her sharp nose for profit and hoarding and saving every penny she got. In the news clips her aunt sent from back home, Rory had heard something about the cathedral and community center Divinity was trying to build with the aid of white donors, rumors that she'd fucked one or several of them spread by her nemeses on the Baptist convention boards. A secret part of Rory relished the smear, the whiff of freshly ground dirt spread over the old neighborhood's prudish high regard for the budding junior prophetess of 1930.

They finished the rehearsal and went backstage to their dressing rooms. Card and Thurston haggled over a joint. Butch did his ritual finger dunk in warm water and Epsom salts to keep limber, bracing for a long night at the keyboard. Mick lingered in the corridor, going over the set list, busying himself with the smallest logistics. He broke out his inhaler for strategic hits when no one was looking, avoiding Rory's orbit, swallowed up in the turbine of Jude's handlers and sycophants.

"Fifty minutes to show time, fuckers," a voice screeched over the loudspeaker.

"Let's blast these Dixiecrats back to the swamps," a tech chortled from behind the towering Marshall stacks anchored in an iron wall around the stage.

Rory walked back onstage for one last look. The attendants stood poised in place at the arena exits, seat rows bathed in the dank glow of the footlights. Katy sat in the back, nodding, a blue put-on-airs Monday night revival meeting hat perched on her head.

Precious Lord. Take my hand.

Cotton Plant, Arkansas, 1930

Route 9 quivered with the distant menace of sputtering engines. Congregants walking, driving, getting the hang of the rattletraps handed down to them with a wink and a prayer for at least another hundred more miles before sudden death on a two-lane blacktop. The backbone of Calvary Church headed to an after Sunday service fish fry for the Browns, Clemons, Langhornes… off to Cleveland in the morning for railway jobs, weekend shifts in sanitation, road maintenance. A damp evening showcasing child prodigies on piano, guitar, drums with the most suspense and anticipation over the first pulpit appearance of little Divinity Mason Mulvaney offering blessings for new beginnings.

Divinity had practiced her delivery again and again in the mirror. When everyone had gone to bed she was still practicing, drawing out words, pausing for emphasis, making musical notes of end phrases like she'd heard bishop do, his kindly russet brown face pushing her to new heights of mastery.

Again and again, in front of him, with Sunday school finally over and a barrage of lessons baring down on her, she wended through the scripture lines she'd chosen all by herself. Romans, Jeremiah, First Corinthians. Full to bursting with pride at her powers of recall. How clever, what a big smart girl, what a credit to her family name. The others so plain, less blessed. A few paces farther away from God.

It was the russet stench of the bishop's shaving cream that woke her up, trickling sweat, tingling with exhaustion in her empty hotel bed. She always asked for at least a queen-sized bed, to contain her thrashing, blunt the endless chain of night visitors.

Ten years and three months. That was how old her fingers had been. Just long enough to fit over the head of his cock. To give her the strength to suffer God's silence. To give her the strength to devise the countdowns. Count for the missing tiles on the ceiling. Count for how many floor tiles she could jump on before hitting a crack. Count for the number of pinstripes on his suit pants. Count the creases in the long black preacher's robe draping like a sickle over the swivel chair in his office. Count for the time it would take between the end of her practice sermon and the footsteps approaching in the hallway to reach them. For the doorknob to turn, for the crescent of Rory's face rising in front of them as Bishop repositioned her cursed with age fingers to his shoulder.

She got up from bed and took an aspirin. The room shifted into soft focus around her. Warm rain pissed in fits and starts on the roof. It was only the third integrated hotel she'd ever stayed in in the South. She could feel the tremor of the white bodies who'd slept there before, shrouded in comfort and dream, furtive fucks, sour business dealings over a smoke and *Kojak* reruns. She fished out her concert ticket. A good night for a first salvo, to root for our electric girl, for Cotton Plant's long heralded resurrection. She laughed to herself, went to the closet, picked out a new outfit, new armor, not too pastorly, straight, or prim for the gutter heathens who'd paid top dollar to see their clay footed goddess Jude.

She settled on pinstripes. Showered off the night visitors, dressed, and went downstairs.

Thousands of Jude Core raised their lighters toward the damp Nashville sky, flames flickering like flairs from a ghost ship. Decades ago, in London, they'd fawned over the legendary Negress on guitar, come out in droves in a blast of nostalgia, followed her around the shops, whispering and gawking in awe as she bought toothpaste, burbling about how she'd set them free with her bog water music birthed from centuries of torment and woe.

The crowd rippled and pulled back as Rory wound through her set, keeping her focus on the outer limits of the cheap seats, away from thoughts of Sid and Katy. There was comfort in the anonymity of the cheap seats. Refuge from the three straight nights of having her hotel phone ring with no one on the other end of the line when she picked up. Maybe it was the white women from the radio station crank calling. Or the labels keeping tabs on her. Or Sid getting the last laugh. If she fucked up and fell off the wagon again, she'd be less bankable pushing sixty, staring into the deaths-head's dreamy eyes. If the House shat on her she'd go to California, take up the indie on its offer. Drown her boys in the Pacific Ocean like a litter of mewling kittens and never look back.

Attendants scooped up a man howling about his beard, singed to a dirty blond crisp by a woman's lighter. The sound of the place was off. Every note she played bounced back in triplet, soaring for a second, then crashing to the ground in distorted murk. The band missed its cue for the second song and limped through the rest of them, discombobulated. Thurston and Butch stared woodenly out into the darkness, Card plodded through his licks, the whole lot of them marooned in separate galaxies. Standing in the wings, Mick watched for patrolling record execs, any rotund well-fed faces he'd seen in the glossy company informationals or Billboard magazine mugshots. He saw one white man who looked familiar tug at his fly and head off toward the bathroom. If their third song tanked, the set would be beyond redemption. He'd be indirectly blamed for starting shit with the others, resented by Rory in another silent wave of fresh high dudgeon on the ride back to the hotel.

Chants had already begun for Jude to come onstage. Jungle bellows rumbling from the back and reverberating to the front. A mezzanine brigade of white girls warbling the signature song Jude had stolen from

Big Mama. Masses of them staggered off to the bathrooms before inter-mission, fanning out from the concession lines, stuffing candy corn into their mouths, trading roach clips in front of the arena staff with a fuck you flourish.

Divinity sipped a Diet Coke in the third center row, itching to make her own particle accelerator and smash the heads of the two mangy recalcitrants sitting next to her wearing Flying V guitar t-shirts. The recalcitrant to her right banged his fist on the seatback in front of him, yelling over the muddy opening chords of Rory's third song. "Ain't you the preacher lady we saw at the radio station? If you got a private line to Jesus tell him to move this shit along."

"Yeah, we got a zillion people sitting hot as fuck in the fucking humidity who paid good money to hear Jude Justis," his comrade snarled.

Divinity downed her drink, crumpling the paper cup in her hand as she turned toward them, their blunt features twisted with the special misshapen rabidity of bored, anxious, on the brink white teenhood shooting fish in the barrel with bb guns. *I know you better get out of my face*, she thought, then corrected herself, sniffing out an opportunity. "Y'all believe in Jesus?"

"No. Sometimes."

"Yeah."

"I'm going to let you in on a secret."

"What?"

"Your girl Jude asked me to pray over her because she had a premonition, a vision that she might not make it to the next city."

"Fuck that."

"Threats have been coming in."

"From who?"

"Good ol' boys who don't like the integration stuff she's doing, putting Blacks on the bill, traveling around with them. Y'all know how dangerous that is for a white woman."

They stared at her, hollow-eyed, turning their attention back to the stage where Card had stepped out front, playing a duet with Rory on the song *Shotgun*, her guitar scissoring out big and full as she took on the saxophone part. A few waifs crept from their seats, gyrating fitfully in the aisles. Divinity pulled out her business card and gave it to the recalcitrants.

"Line to my radio ministry. A new service every Sunday night. Prayer reps standing by twenty-four hours a day. The meek and the brave get saved right on air, no distinctions made."

She got up and moved into the aisle, the waifs parting like a red sea as she walked toward the snack bar, backlit with a blinking Slurpee logo. *No god on heaven, hell, earth or in the squirming imagination of woman could save these doomed fuckers from themselves*, she thought.

Forty minutes before last call, and the band and Mick sat at the hotel bar, slumped over withered bowls of popcorn and peanuts. The aftermath of a presidential candidate's debate flickered on the black and white tube mounted on the wall.

"Ain't voting for neither of 'em," the bartender yelped, jamming the buttons of a ramshackle remote.

"I second that," Thurston said.

Mick brushed peanut dust off his lips. "When have you ever voted or given a shit anyway?"

"I vote every election, junior."

"You stay in one place long enough?" the bartender croaked.

"When nobody wants me."

"Quite sure all that moving around breaks you down after a while. But least you don't have to stay put for any bullshit, the nagging and tugging at you when you're settled into the ball and chain. Jesus. Drives me crazier than Manson. Not that I would go the fuck off like that dickwad. Can y'all spot me some comps to the concert?"

Card laughed. "You ain't making enough here? Big tips from high rollers, the record people, politicos?"

"Naw. This place is small fry. Try and stay in one of them luxury chains next city you roll through and the liquor will be better."

Butch lit his fifth cigarette, scanning the room. Dim figures sank down in hushed duos and trios in the stiff, burgundy vinyl booths rounding out the empty dance floor. After the set, he'd resolved to keep safe mental distance from the vampiric suck of Card and the rest. The rut they'd fallen into made him homesick for Seattle's droning gloom, the slant of the frame houses perched in cold judgment above the I5 freeway, the chop of whale watching boats groaning with bored white-bread tourists on Puget Sound.

"Rory coming down?" he asked, hoping she would stay away, calculating whether chewing on the anticlimax of the fucked up set or weathering the indifference of the hotel dregs would be worse for her, in recovery from watching Jude prance, caterwaul, and shake her ass into a drenched frenzy all night. They were due for a rehearsal early in the morning. His fingers dangled from the joints in a cramped mess from trying to match Thurston's bashing.

"Mind if I sit here?" a sandpaper and salt voice said in his ear.

Lavender slid into the seat next to him, gnawing on a corncob from the mystery meat buffet in the lobby. He'd seen her lurking around Jude's crew before the show, scribbling showily into a notebook, another cog in the hype machine.

"Good job out there tonight," she said. "You soldiered on well despite your mate here trying to raise the dead and the living in three continents. Can I buy you a drink or do you run dry between gigs?"

Butch shrugged, trying to place the sandpaper voice in a specific region, the white woman's insistence a buzz fly distraction on his shoulder.

"Sure, whiskey and soda."

She waved the bartender over with an assured flick of the wrist. He glided dutifully to her side, a simpering smile on his face as she gave him the order and turned her jaunty attentions back to Butch.

"I'm doing a story on this tour, why it's historic, who the players are. Wondered if you'd be willing to give me a little of your time."

"I ain't a 'player' and why is this historic in your mind?"

"You're critical to the band's sound. And it's historic because two women blues rock performers are touring together, interracially, kicking off in the Deep South, where they just love that kind of shit, right? Peel back some of the paint on these train and bus station doors and the For Colored signs are still there. Most of these inbred crackers would rather have their cousins lynched than see that shit taken down."

"I got news for you, Nashville ain't the Deep South. But I digress. Your name is?"

"Lavender."

"The women's libber."

"You heard of me?"

"Heard you were stalking Jude."

"Stalking? Hardly. I don't want anything from Jude, or Rory for that matter, other than their truths. I'm trying to do a magazine cover on Rory too."

"What do you think nosing around me will get you?"

"You've been in the band for a while now and you're well respected in the field."

"Idle flattery."

"I bought you the best whiskey and soda in the house. That should count for something, right? Why do you think Rory decided to do this gig after all these years? She doesn't exactly have the highest opinion of Jude."

"Why do you think? Money."

"That it?"

"It ain't a genius conclusion, lady." Butch took another swig. He was reminded of all the solicitous white girls who clustered around him in elementary school when he won the Spelling Bee, their funhouse faces perking up in hot suspense on the scent of something new, scary fun, and repellent, like licking the congealed oil at the bottom of a sardine can on a dare.

"Don't you have better things to do than dig up mess?"

"I don't write 'mess'. Quite sure if had a dick between my legs you'd be more enthusiastic."

"To be on the record in your little rag?"

"Ever had a desire to go solo?"

"Naw."

"Would be nice to get away from that no talent white boy on drums."

Butch stared at her and kept drinking.

"Why's she keeping him around?"

"Ask her."

"Comes off as amateur hour. Now, Card Jefferson on the other hand."

"What about him?"

"Motown wizard, super nova talent, big step up, but a bit undisciplined, yes?"

Butch glanced over at Card across the room, talking bitterly back to the TV screen. He was ignoring the bartender's mounting scorn, stoked by the aroused gazes of the dwindling moths-to-a-flame white women conspiring over neon-colored drinks in pairs at the lounge tables. Lavender was dangling the bait hard, spindly fingers wrapped around the sickle of her pen, poised, like he was going to spill that easily, part of him amused, flattered by her bushy tailed desperation. All the years being at Rory's side and no one had ever buttonholed him for anything or paid him any mind in the piecemeal press that trickled her way.

"Card does his own thing," he said.

"And well, too. Even though his former bosses treated him like shit, didn't credit him for his own work, I hear."

Butch shrugged. "They're crooks. All of 'em. Meanwhile, back at the fucking ranch."

Lavender smiled, crocodile big, fingers tapping out a melody on the rim of the newly drained shot glass. "I used to play drums. Snare in marching band, snare at keg parties, then a little group I pulled together in high school. It was always, look at their asses, look at the cock teases trying to hook dudes. Look, look, look."

"Try being Chinese in a snow blizzard town with two stoplights, lady."

"That's why this is so important, the two of them getting together on stage, showing the world."

"Rory wouldn't use what's-her-names sheet lyrics as toilet paper."

"Ok. That's strong. What about the road manager, the one who's been around forever? White man who's got all the answers. Wouldn't talk to a peon like me except to grunt."

"Mick? Ask him."

"Ask me about what?" Mick stepped up beside them, tugging at his pants, riding his beer bulging middle into the curdled sunset.

"This here's Purple."

"*Lavender*. We met already. Butch was speaking highly of you."

"I'll bet."

"Says you're not as hard-assed as you act."

"Like hell I did," Butch said.

"Says you would actually stoop to talk to me."

"She's poking around with her stick."

"I prefer shit stirrer."

"Semantics."

"You an educated hombre."

"You a dumb, white motherfucker." Butch watched Card, at the other side of the bar, pound his glass and throw his head back, laughing in the wooly ear of the swaying paisley-bedecked Caucasoid who'd been trying to grab his attention for the past hour. He didn't know how Card did it, veering between courting and contemptuous, ten steps ahead of the Ofay's eternally munching jaws. Lavender smirked at Butch's insult, the tip of her boot brushing up against his shin as she tracked Rory coming in the room. Rory walked past Mick and straight to Lavender, narrowing her gaze.

"Still hanging around?" she asked.

"Slow night in Nashville."

Rory nodded at Butch. "This one don't need any more distractions."

"I was just picking his oh so quick brain. I'm sure he can speak for himself."

"Yep, and my response is the same. Dumb. White. Motherfucker."

"I see y'all have gotten close," Rory said.

"Butch was showing me the error of my white ways."

"Yeah? You learning anything?"

"Think I need a little more time be schooled."

Mick summoned the bartender for a drink and walked over to Card. Butch rolled his eyes. He could see Rory was borderline lit, voice cracking like it did when she was wrung out on stage, her focus darting from them to the swirling backdrop of stooges and drunkards. He got butterflies in his stomach all of a sudden, tired of playing the head game of measuring where he stood with Rory in the pecking order of the others. He slurped the last drop in his glass. How nice it would be to have an android fuck, automatic pilot, pure matter over mind. He glanced at Lavender, then decided against it. A roll with her would needlessly complicate shit. "Keep dreamin', lady," he said. "I'm turning in."

Butch walked away.

Lavender shrugged, turning to Rory. "Sweet guy. Low on the totem pole."

"What's it to you?" Rory asked.

"I watch and I write. I know how big a heart you have. How much you care for your boys. Coddle 'em. Bailed the chip on his shoulder piano guy out from a druggie who wanted to beat the crap out of him. Rescued that other one from certain cirrhosis of the liver and the flophouse. Brought the flailing dingbat with the gold drumsticks up from diapers to now. Can't exactly call that a man, more like a teenage chimp who needs his zoo cage cleaned. Then there's my man Mick. Always a shiny, bright ray of sunshine when you need him. Dependable port in a storm."

Rory drew up a barstool in front of Lavender. The TV screen jumped behind her in a psychedelic splash. "Stop rubbing up against my boys, hear?"

"What are you talking about?"

"You ain't slick. I saw what you were doing."

"Look, I don't want anything from them other than their views on your creative process."

"Butch is too smart to fuck and tell. You'd have better luck with Thurston. How's my cover coming? I need to see any pictures you took of us tonight."

"S-sure. I got plenty. Remember, I said I could do a story."

"Did you hear how many people were calling in for me during that show?"

Lavender paused. "Mooch has half of those people on his payroll in some capacity."

"Well, the half that he ain't paying want to hear more of me. They're sick of Jude's canned shit. When I was over in Europe—"

"Yes, Europe, but Black people over here aren't buying your records. I kinda want to explore that in the piece too."

Lavender's voice seemed to come from the TV, pulsing, disembodied. The newscasters roared about the election and bombs, the prospect of a nuclear disaster under the megalomaniac Republican Reagan, the earth burnt down to a charcoal brick.

"And wouldn't that just be what God ordered to punish the world for its sinful ways?" a voice said from the door.

"Well, if it isn't the good pastor," Rory said.

"Depends on your idea of good."

"Thanks for getting me out of there the other day."

Lavender stuck her hand out as Divinity walked up to them. "Lavender, a journalist for—"

Divinity bypassed Lavender's ingratiating grin, touching Rory's elbow. "Can we talk privately?"

She followed Divinity to an empty booth by a broken pinball machine. Divinity slid in, adjusting the thin gold watch on her wrist, her navy-blue pinstripe suit standing in cool rebuke to the slouchy dishevelment of the boozers hanging around the bar, the white ones quietly aflutter at the sight of yet another Negress.

"Want anything? Coffee, tea, wine?"

"No thanks."

Divinity picked up a menu from the holder at the side of the table. "Heard they got a good prime rib. Sure you don't want to share?"

"Just ate."

"Seem to recall you didn't eat much red meat back in the day."

"You got that elephant's memory. How's your church?"

"Booming and growing. We're developing a new complex. Have a few investors' meetings here in town," she paused, thumbing through the menu, gold watch glinting. "We've been trying to get in touch with you."

"About what?"

"Coming back to Little Rock to do some benefit concerts for the church."

"If you're doing so well why do you need me?"

"We don't need you. I mean we, the board, want to give back to the city. A slice of our heritage. You'd get paid, of course."

"When are you looking to do this?"

"After your tour. We'd do some marketing, play it up. Stage a gospel revival like the old days."

"I'm off gospel."

"Yes, I noticed from your set last night. Don't let those white boys sway you away from your roots. There's plenty of folk back home who'd like to see you reclaim your spot at the top, doing the Lord's music like it should be done."

"Oh, I doubt that."

"Why?"

Rory watched Divinity's face a second, looking for a twitch, a poker game tell, a ripple going backward to the clatter, still, clatter of the church basement as the moaners, wheezers, and coughers from the ten a.m. service stomped around upstairs in climax. At the end of it they adjourned to punch and cake and rushed fellowship in the pale June sunshine because it was so pretty outside and it was a sin to waste the honey of late morning on being cooped up indoors wilting from fresh paint fumes.

Why would anyone want to miss the joy of the littler ones playing Mother May I in the courtyard? Miss the joy of watching them go to war, snipping and braying at each other on the sidelines when Mother called them out of the game. Rory was always one of the first to be taken out. She hadn't mastered any of the sidewinder twists, the cunning, the foresight, the up-the-sleeve tricks Divinity and the Sunday school girls used to stay alive in their to-the-bone sandbox smack downs. Divinity had delighted in them, reveling, lording over the others, rooster feathers aflame. Watching her now, Rory felt something else tingle, a sudden urge to capture her larynx, keep it as a pet, walk it, stroke it, listen to it purr in the privacy of her room. That would be half a punishment, a cure for all the times she pretended to ignore her.

"I'm assuming this concert tour is a good chunk of change."

"But the benefit in Little Rock could be even more lucrative... that is, in terms of your spiritual balance."

"Not interested."

Divinity picked up the plastic centerpiece of yellow daisies from the middle of the table, fondling it for a second. "Not interested in what? In the money or the spiritual balance? Mama Katy is spinning in her grave."

"She was cremated."

"Rustling in her urn, then." Divinity paused, smiling, bemused suddenly by the sidebars and random flutterings in the room. "She had a good sense of humor. Thought you walked on water. Rest her soul. Well, I know one thing, she wouldn't have let you be stuck in these misbegotten hick dumps playing second fiddle to Miss Ann eating this indecent crap."

"These are the biggest arenas we've played in years."

"It's not the size, it's the symbolism," she put down the centerpiece. "Playing big arenas ain't no substitute for spiritual balance. Even if you claim not to subscribe to it now," she looked around, snapping her fingers at no one in particular. "What I wouldn't give for a good prime rib. Might have to go out and slay one on our own. Oh, come on, don't look panicked. It would be nice to get some fresh air anyway. What do you say?"

"It's late, I haven't seen you in god knows how many years, and you're lecturing me about spiritual balance?"

"That's what I'm called to do. Cotton Plant, and some of these other little towns in the state, are dying on the vine due to the recession. Most of the ladies that work in my call center are either moonlighting at the poultry plant or the strip club. I don't need to tell you which pays more."

"You pay them benefits?"

"Medical and dental if they're working at least thirty-five hours. But, again, I'm struggling."

"Struggling, how? Thought y'all got a free ride on taxes."

"We got some out of town unions sniffing around. And I still have to bust my ass raising money for our charitable programs. They don't get funded by themselves and the preacher men gobble up every last philanthropist crumb and panty that gets thrown in the collection plate."

Rory laughed, her wet puppy dog childhood crush on Divinity rearing up again in slivers of dread longing. Would she find herself still there if she went back to the house she and Katy had lived in; the Rory that she woke up to every morning, the grizzled imposter who stared back at her in the mirror, shriveling to dust.

"Nice to hear you laugh," Divinity said. She raised her water glass to her lips, sipping slowly. "You know what it's like to be out on a limb every damn second, fighting, rolling the same damn rock up a hill. I do. My ladies do. Every Colored woman with 2.5 jobs, common sense, and a baby, a man or both to take care of does too."

"Does your offer include my entire band?"

"If that would tip the scale, yes, for the first few performances at least."

"Including Card?"

"Mr. Motor City? The peacock? I hear he's a handful trying to stay off blow."

"Reefer's his Achilles. But that would be right up your alley. I know y'all get your jollies off of collecting sinners and deviants."

"Collecting. Interesting word. Always the contrarian. I like that," she chuckled drily, stabbing her finger in the air. "Notice we haven't been served by these fuckers. Surprise, surprise. Waiter, waitress! Garcon!"

Rory shifted in her seat. Divinity's performance was a throwback to her top dog jockeying. Always hungry, always roving, greedy for a forum wherever there were other bodies to bear witness and be awed by her studied daring. Suddenly, she felt sorry for the gnomish white waitress who'd been trying to ignore them. Her beat down blue eyes darted back and forth as she slouched toward them, arms full of spaghetti and meatball splattered plates and glasses dribbling coke. A set of false teeth that someone had left behind sat anchored in goo on a chipped saucer atop her pile of dishes.

"Be right with y'all in a sec," she wheezed limply, two booths away and making it seem like a mile.

"Your ass better," Divinity said. "Shit, I make more in a year than her mama probably did in a lifetime. Make more in two months than she does in a year, and still these peckerwood girls act like they're to-the-manor born… Look at your gal over there, the journalist, blabbering till doomsday. What's her game? She just another predator or is she going to help you?"

"She's attached herself to Jude. Started doing a piece on me."

"The press, the traditional ones, are worthless. You'd get more play doing slots on our radio and TV network. All ages, races, backgrounds, listen, watch, and walk with God. Whole subset of rich white Sun Belt retirees with pensions put their money where their mouths are."

"I'm not selling anything like that."

"The hell you are. You just said it yourself. Redemption, hoisting your asses back in the saddle is three quarters of what getting press is about. The pensioners don't want no Pollyanna Karo syrup shit."

"If the white girl puts me on her cover and it blows up, some of the other trade mags might take a chance on me and the House might—"

"You holding out for the Big House?"

"Don't put it that way. I'm not holding out for nobody… I can't afford to, at least not where my band is concerned."

The waitress bustled up with her pad. "Sorry for the delay, ladies. Lou, our usual cook, is out sick."

Divinity picked at the centerpiece. "What looks good, sweetie?"

"Honestly, at this time of night, split pea soup is safe," she raised her eyebrows, turning to Rory. "You played with Jude in her band?"

"Opened for her with my own group."

"Her voice is everything. What she sings about, how she bends the words. I had to drop out of high school too to go to work, went back and got my GED after I had my second baby girl."

"Well, congratulations. That must've been hard on you," Divinity said. "How'd you manage to get through it?"

"Late nights and a whole lot of prayer."

Divinity cracked a beauty pageant smile. "The good Lord always finds a way."

"That he does."

Divinity took out her business card. "If you're ever in Little Rock and want a church home, or an infusion, look us up. Or better yet, dial up the hotline. God don't work shifts so his servants should be on call twenty-four seven. I'll take a cheeseburger, medium rare, a double vodka, and a cup of that delightful split pea soup."

The woman looked doubtfully at the card. "A hotline like Reverend Jim Bakker and the PTL club?"

"Yep, but bigger. International. A whole UN of god servants at your fingertips."

"Hmm, ok. Your food should be up soon." She walked off, stuffing the card into her uniform pocket.

Divinity flicked Rory a card across the table. She examined it, frowning. "Counseling 'At your fingertips'? What's the catch?"

"No catch. I have trained personnel at my call center just outside downtown Little Rock. Ladies can work from home if they got babies and other obligations, want to pick up hours on the weekends. We cater our prayer messages to anyone with ears and a phone. Worldview don't matter. Most of my girls are quick studies. With a little bit of vocal training, timing, rhythm, tips on how to go in for the soft kill, they can sell ice to Eskimos."

"They sign up sinners by commission or are they making an hourly wage?"

"Hourly and performance bonuses. Helps keep turnover down."

"And you're running the show on your own, or you have overseers?"

"Ouch, that's harsh." She wound up her watch, taking a folder out of her bag. The glossy imprint of the church's insignia blinked out at Rory. She whipped out a sheet from the folder, running her finger over a sprawl of figures and pie charts. "The Vision Complex. This is a blueprint of the facility I'm building, courtesy of the funds we're taking in from the call centers and a dash of Ofay philanthropy. The smart white boys know it's better to keep us off the streets, pony up and invest in programs. They can talk that Reagan up-by-the-bootstraps bullshit all day long, but do they really want to see black folks in their neighborhoods trying to boost car stereos when folks don't have enough to eat."

"That how you sell them on this thing?"

"By any means necessary."

Rory looked at the folder. Divinity's snake oil saleswoman-on-speed pitch was daring for its nakedness. She'd heard it a thousand times and ways from the white pimp missionaries hawking blackest Africa porn and magic carpet rides to India at six a.m. on the local stations. Coming from Divinity's mouth it was tragicomic, a sour flashback to all the times she'd harassed the lower grade girls, then courted them with candy, cookies, flattery about how pretty and smart they were over all the others living dirty. Jesus is shining his little light on you, she told them. He sees everything you do, every move you make, every crap you take, every lie and half step. It was the same thing Katy told her to keep her in line, scrunched up in the palm of her fist.

Rory got up to leave. "I have an early morning."

"Pity. The night is young, and I haven't even gotten my food. Y'all, *you*, were magnificent last night, by the way."

"No, we stunk, but thanks for not kicking a woman when she's down."

Divinity held out her hand to shake Rory's. "Consider my offer. Break a leg tomorrow."

Sunup on Nashville, a bitter tease of it coming in unbidden through the drawn shade. Rays dappled on Katy's legs, stretched imperially on the hotel bed, her feet in the pink puffball slippers that had been her one high-end indulgence before she croaked.

"I say take the money," she drawled. "Take it and run. Negotiate a little something for your boys. The white one and Butch, provided they behave, stay in line. Ditch the prima donna Negro. Reminds me too much of your handkerchief head ex-husband. Who needs all that cutting up and carrying on from a man you ain't even married to?"

"Take it, and then what?" Rory asked, wet sheets up around her neck. An alarm clock went off somewhere in the room.

"Keep moving. Sharks ain't sleeping on the bottom of the ocean waiting for blood. They owe you."

"That all you have to say?"

The phone rang. Rory contemplated it, then lay back down, flush with the urge to masturbate. That and the speed tablet dancing in the drawer were the only things that would divert her from drinking. She'd been too worn out lately to even get off. Divinity's overture rattled through her head. She picked up the phone, waiting for the familiar click.

"Don't fuck with me," she said, in Katy's bullwhip smacking voice. "I know where you live." She opened the drawer and crammed the tablet in her mouth.

That night, all she could see was blackness from the stage. The audience scrunched down in dollhouse miniature, mutant angels dancing on the head of a pin. The callers were out there, plotting their next move. The band pushed sloppily through the set. Thurston, Butch, Card barely looking at each other, roaring to wake the dead. She cued up "Swallow You Whole" and watched the black mass part into a row of empty streets, the first gilded glimmer of Cotton Plant teasing from the highway as the boys meandered around, improvising rhythm parts for the unrehearsed song.

"The fuck's the matter with her?" Butch muttered, riled by the herky jerk change and Thurston's ear shattering hoofbeats, Card's tempo lurches. Rory threw down her guitar and walked offstage. They wound down and slunk after her. Jude staggered on, spit out by their headwinds, raising a Jack Daniels' bottle in the air as she let out a clubbed seal wail and jumped on an amp, a helicopter buzzing overhead.

Butch ran after Rory, grabbing her arm as she went into her dressing room. "Hey, what's going on, what's the matter with you?"

She pointed up to the ceiling. "Eye in the fucking sky helicopter. Every fucking where we go, the House is siccing that shit on us."

"Yeah, Jude practically has her own military detail," Butch agreed. "But you can't leave us hanging like that."

"That's corporate's helicopter!" Thurston screeched. "Record execs use it to monitor their intellectual property. They own every ass shake Jude does and they want to practice that voodoo shit on us!"

"Man, shut up! She doesn't need any conspiracy shit now!" He turned back to Rory. "Babe, what's going on, when did you sleep last? C'mon, somebody get her some coffee," he squinted into her face. "Are you using?"

"No."

"Don't lie to me."

"Not lying."

He sat her down in the chair, peering into her eyes. "You're lying. Who gave it to you? Jude? Lavender? That preacher lady?"

"Nobody gave me anything… I just need them to stop calling me all the time."

"Who's them?"

"People."

"What people?"

"Nashville parasites calling in at the studio. Don't act like you don't know. Whose side are you on?"

"Yours. Always."

"Act like it."

"C'mon, take a sip of this. Stop talking crazy."

She drank the coffee and spit it out. "That's fucking dirt!"

"Keep it down."

"I don't want shit from Jude's people."

"It's from the machine down the hall."

She put her head on the makeup table. "Fuck me."

"Drink up."

"Don't leave."

"I'm right here."

"I mean, don't cut out on me."

"When have I ever cut out on you?"

Mick poked his head through the door. "What the hell was that exit all about?"

"Give her some space, Mick."

"Russ is on the line."

"He can wait."

Rory sat up. "Naw, that's ok, I'll talk to him."

She waited for them to put the call through. Next they would be in Memphis, then Alabama, then Georgia, dipping down into Florida swampland, back up to South Carolina, wrapping with a deflated whimper in Newport News, Virginia. She drifted back to the dingy basement office where she'd met with Russ, the tour managers, and record company handlers a week before, hammering out the language of a potential contract. Russ never raised his voice. He slapped a calming paw on her shoulder, his beard slicked down with the gas tank aftershave he rubbed on when he was in doubt and wanting to smell respectable.

You need something solid to pay your bills, to keep you on your feet, get you back in the game, even if it's a temporary compromise. Ain't nobody getting any younger, ain't no crystal stair as your folks say, right? And who the fuck knows who'll be nipping at your heels next in the new decade. The eighties is gonna be where anything goes. Space colonies. Robot symphonies. Can't go back home again to the golden age of Black guitar, can't go back to the little church socials and the speakeasys where they wanted to get drunk on a tub of your bathwater. Bloom is off being fawned over, besides who knows how long we have to live on this rotten beat down motherfucker and they're for certain gonna elect that nuke happy cowboy Reagan.

It was Russ and Katy double-teaming in her ear that made her consider signing the contract. Both of them standing behind her pushing as she stared over the ledge. She was tired. Scared. Shitting bricks. The ulcer she'd been nursing for five years divebombing up through her throat. Getting her hopped up over where the money for the stomach specialists was going to come from, where she would get the two grand to keep the band together until the end of the year. How she'd keep the overhead down on maintenance for the bus, the instruments, the Marshall stacks they rented. Every nanosecond, the loan company was baring down on her with piranha jaws and compound interest.

The contract they dangled would grant her one studio album, a dry run before she became lead guitar for Jude's backup band. All the years she'd tried to keep the boys together as their own independent band blasted in a pen stroke.

You in this sorry place cuz you ain't right with God and you ain't right with your past, Katy said, slipping a pair of rhinestone pumps on her feet. The kind she'd taken off to stab the gold-toothed rapist who'd tried to fuck, then rob, her outside the Cotton Club. *You get right with those two; God, and the past, and all this confusion in your head will resolve itself.*

Drove Rory crazy when she wore those pumps. Katy knew it. Didn't care. Didn't give any quarter to anyone else's recollection. I don't have to get right with nobody but me, Rory would tell her, if she ever worked up the nerve. Disbelieving in God and the past equally. Both would kill you, leave you for dead.

"Well, well," Russ boomed through the receiver. Jude's first encore raged in the background. "Never a dull moment in the Southland. We going to have to call out the cavalry?"

"For what?"

"We didn't come this far for you to have tantrums trying to show Jude up."

"What the fuck are you, the CIA?"

"You on the sauce?"

"No."

"If I hear you're using, *and* on the sauce—"

"I have a new song. We've been fighting to get rehearsal time—"

"'Swallow You Whole'? Sounds like a whorehouse anthem or a Saturday night porno. Next time you want to get political tell me beforehand so I can massage it."

"I don't need your 'massages'."

"All I'm saying is don't blow up your trial balloon while you're flying in it."

"Whitey loved it. They flooded the radio station with calls after my interview with Mooch Morrison. What's the House saying?"

"About you? The House is quiet. They're still waiting, babe. Curveballs only work if you're Elvis, and look where his ass is now. Remember what we talked about before you signed onto the tour. I like my ladies, all my clients, to be independent, but I need fair warning before you do it."

"Jude's got another copyright attorney for me."

"Good for her. If it's Bludorn he's the best in the business, but expensive."

"And I have an offer for another gig."

He coughed. "I'm all ears."

"A revival concert in Little Rock."

"Revival?? So now you're going full on kamikaze. Help me understand how that's going to get you from point a to point b?"

"I've got an audience there. People who actually listen to my records."

"Babe, I don't know if I can be any clearer. Back to the roots ain't gonna cut it at your age. You got one shot at this."

Jude wound down the encore with "Hound Dog". A jillion foot stomps wrenched the arena off its foundation. *You ain't never caught a rabbit and you ain't no friend of mine.*

"Just watch me, Russ. Just watch me."

You know, Pastor loved the smell of us under his fingernails, she would tell Katy if she could. Mustering up the courage, the gumption long denied. Star-angel, Candace, Etta Mae, Divinity, me. Pastor was pig smitten with the odor. The inner dare of how long he could keep it on without washing it off, before he set himself on fire with cologne, breath mints and barbecue sauce to keep his wife, First Lady Almight-y, off the scent.

First Lady was the one with the inheritance, the one who ran the church empire from the wings. She wrote all the checks, drafted the reams of official correspondence to the county building inspectors, cleaned up the debt Pastor racked up trying to create an international institute in Cambodia, a scheme to import refugees so the church could qualify for more dough and a plum, annual humanitarian award the Pentecostal councils pulled out of their asses. Divinity apprenticed with her from afar, sopped up her tactical genius, sharpening the organizational template in her head for decades until she took the reins of Elysian church in a fluke vote that cancelled two rival male pastors.

They had less of a public shine to them than the molester, Daddy Simmons.

The women in the congregation howled the longest and hardest about her victory, secretly feeling upstaged. They questioned her allegiances, her ability to right a ship riddled with bullet holes, staying up late at night, panting after every sweet misstep she made. Rory would tell Katy about all of this, standing in front of her in the mirror. The two of them, who'd once looked nothing alike, identical now from top to bottom. Age twinning them, mocking their old antagonisms, giving them a scythe to cut through the weeds of bile. The same countdown to death ticking inside their heads, faster every hour.

Starless 'n' Bible Black

THE PHONES AT THE Vision Complex screamed in unison, pinging off the walls of the conference room, a vortex of metal tables, bent heads, gum smacking, chit chatting, nail biting, Fanta slurping. The worker bees of Revivals, Inc. studied the pitch script, cleared their throats, took one last belch and dialed, tiny plastic crosses flapping from their tablets for inspiration.

Patton walked up and down the aisles, listening in on the conversations.

"Never too late, brother, never too late to lay it down for the Lord Jesus."

"A man just out of jail and looking for a job is a perfect candidate for redemption."

"Don't cost a lot, just a few pennies a month."

She warned the callers about countrified talk. Get familiar but not too familiar. Be the sympathetic ear, the down to earth buddy, the gentle light at the end of the tunnel. If they need a shoulder to cry on, bump them up to our regional trainer for massaging, management, trouble shooting. Most of 'em just want air time with a live body but they ain't paying the bills.

Patton felt she was an able taskmaster. Doing Divinity proud when she was away on one of her many business-prospecting trips. She met with the contractors who were prowling around with change orders. She handled the city permits, tangled with the accreditation paperwork for the daycare center located on the first floor of the complex. Women could drop their babies off and keep going. Roll into work on time and wrack up bonuses if they signed ten new clients in five hours. Small donors would be named to "The Disciples Corner", medium donors to "Angels'

Flight", big kahunas to the vaunted "Jesus Circle". Six-figure high flyers to the "Holy Ghost Empyrean". Categories beyond that were top secret confidential. But Divinity made it known that every little donation, every cent and pledge, were welcomed, cherished, valued just the same as the big yields.

They had a core of women associates groomed to do the advance scouting. Intergenerational troops riding the city bus in from the projects at 7:30, then leaving promptly at 4 to go to night school or other jobs, cleaning toilets, changing diapers, working the Jack 'n' the Box fryers for the carousing white kids jamming the drive-thrus after their lawless blowouts at the high school football games. Stripping at the club. The next shift began a half hour later. That one was staffed with associates who had received deluxe training. Older, more seasoned reinforcements were marshalled to handle doubters, fence sitters, the misinformed who gushed about Revelations, prophecies of Armageddon, a ripe season for doomsday sonnets and Reagan prognostication.

"We just circling the drain of the bathtub," one screeched. "Dirty Americans circling the drain, staring down into the pit of deliverance. Me, I can't wait to see the Glory. Gonna be a beautiful thing after living in this shithole."

Patton imagined the man on the other end of the receiver sitting on the toilet half-naked in holey gym socks, sniffing at the classifieds as he talked back to the TV soaps in the middle of a work day. Multiply him by a few thousand and he was half the white male population in the pinprick towns outside of Little Rock. Ramshackle ghosts laid off in that summer's round of fryer plant closures or filing for disability from the trucking companies, chewed up and spit out after twenty-five years. The associates half-listened to them, twiddling their thumbs, daydreaming about quitting time and the math exams they had to take to pass accounting class to get in line for a real job with a future, the growl of rotgut drenched white men waking them up in the middle of the night.

In the training sessions for callers, Patton counseled the associates to handle the men with care. Learn their psychology. "Even if they dirt poor they got a little more than we got. They all got wives, girlfriends, mamas. The women is the ones to get. The wives, girlfriends and mamas will always be willing to pony up for God when the men turn tail and run."

She patrolled both shifts, beat down and breath stinking, running on diet drinks at the butt end of night, proud of the pristine order of the conference room and the steady hum of phones. Proud of the mood setting happy talk that loped back to the script she'd written about the beauty of Jesus' word. High off the contact sheets flush with names and addresses from across the nation. Had her hawk eyes and ears on who could best deliver the message, who had the gift, the supernatural knack, the mad mojo, Olympian skills to turn her words into solid gold.

On her watch, Revivals, Inc. had signed fifty dependable subscribers who were kept waiting, anticipating new limited-time-only goodies every month. Silver cufflinks, silver engraved Bibles, prayer shawls, blessed beach blankets big enough to wrap the whole family in divine prophylaxis. Praise be to Him in the darkest hour, in the bowels of need, in the deepest infernal pit of depravity we got the tools to help you step out of the void and come out shiny, saved, and victorious at the end.

Shit yeah, she believed the hype deep in the marrow of her bones, in every fiber of her gecko skin, in every depraved second lost to the world in damp perimenopausal sleep.

When Divinity was traveling, Patton wondered about the line of succession, sketchily outlining the tragic story of her boss in a rush hour crash. How it would begin with something teeny tiny, less than a hairsbreadth. A split second when she looked down at a mustard stain on her suit lapel as some off-brand motherfucker on the highway to Tallahassee or Chicago or Binghamton, New York came out of nowhere, flipping the radio channels, distracted by homegirl Jude's new song. Swerve, impact, fireball, pandemonium, lane closures, snarls, then tag on the toe in the county morgue.

Every disaster had a mathematical sequence. Could be immortalized in an equation. A string of hidden code set to spring at the right moment. Calculus had been one of her favorite subjects in high school. Deemed an afterthought for the Negroes, a sacred treasure for genius white boys. She kept her head down, doing her work with the other Black girl in class, becoming each other's hope to die for, even though she hated her prissy, double-talking guts, the two of them unseen and underestimated until she took first runner up in the countywide computing championship.

Wasn't as though she was wishing for a calamity. God would back her up on that. There'd be cosmic reckoning for anybody wishing fucked up shit on Divinity. For wanting to see her squeal, atone. Wasn't like that though, Patton told herself when the associates had made their quotas and dragged home. All she could hear was the gurgle of the busted coffee-maker and the security guard making his rounds, mumbling to himself in the parking lot, counting down to payday, watching out for her like Fido, eyes turning milky when she finally shut down for the day and staggered to her car.

"Need anything, Miss Patton?" he always asked, studied, drippingly solicitous, angling for a perk, a way to make the skeleton march of the night more bearable at the beginning of his shift. He flashed his rent-a-cop credentials at the scavenger rats that stormed the dumpster behind the church, commanding authority, order, obedience from all four-legged malcontents. During the entire time she'd been working there, they'd only had one disruption. A member mixing his blood pressure meds with booze on a micro suicide rampage, telling the office receptionist he'd chisel his carotid artery out with a screwdriver if he didn't get to see the file the church kept on his family.

Rumor among the ex-members was that Patton and Divinity documented every move folks made and kept the files in a basement vault. Them gossipy women couldn't help themselves. God had cursed them to talk perpetual trash like in Genesis. Having security around made Divinity look like a player, a mogul on the verge, another steel gloved fuck you to the scheming brother man preachers who licked their chops over the prospect of hijacking the televangelist business she was building from a handful of mostly anonymous investors. If Patton had given a shit about courting men, she might've sat rent-a-cop down and told him some bed-time stories about what happened to boys who got too curious. Every time she saw him sniveling in her corner, she hoped Divinity would fire his ass, secretly wondering if he was a snitch for one of the companies she'd hooked up with to fund the complex.

He kept a transistor radio at his post, a void filler spewing sports, weather, a steady stream of breathless traffic reports, interplanetary music shards, and wall-to-wall Jude on the rock stations, making him forget he didn't have a gun to pose with. Rent-a-cop curled his lip.

"This one just wrapped up a tour with that old blues and gospel singer from around here," he said. "Tharpe's her name, right? White gal ain't exactly no nightingale. Now, my niece, sings at Tabernacle, got some Mahalia pipes on her—"

"Delightful."

"Heard from the boss that you're bringing her here for some kind of benefit concert."

"It's in the works."

"That'll be a breath of fresh air. Hope y'all are offering discount tickets to the folks up in here, otherwise nobody's gonna be able to afford it, what with gas and food going through the roof."

"We'll make sure our people are taken care of."

He looked at her too long, the bones in his face cutting through the ragged skin.

"Take care of us. Right. Praise Jesus."

The Sell-Out

Gas lines began jumping at 6:45 a.m. A ping-pong snap of pumps being slammed into gas tanks, topped off, then disengaged. The national soundtrack for the month. By noon, premium spots in line were going for five bucks, then ten, twenty. Station managers flush and smug, turning a tidy under the table profit. Cashiers rolled down the aisles selling gum, road maps, cigarettes, laxatives. Six o'clock p.m. and it was Carter flailing around the evening news, bloviating promises about fuel conservation and standing up to the Iranians.

At the end of the tour in Memphis, Palladium strikers from the service workers union came out, cornering the bus, daring Rory and the boys to cross picket lines.

"We sympathetic to what y'all doing, but we gotta eat too," Card said, standing up in his seat, curling his lip as he watched the strikers' signs and banners stream by. "When we needed a union in Detroit to deal with the record company's bloodsucking motherfuckers their asses was nowhere to be found."

Thurston reared up from the backseat. "Union dues go straight to the union bosses' whores, cars and houses. Same as pastors."

"If we had one maybe we wouldn't be in the shit we're in," Butch said.

"Doubtful," Mick added. He maneuvered around the strikers, going to the back of the building into an empty space next to Jude's hulking fleet of custom designed buses.

He eyed the gas gauge then switched off the engine. "We're going to need another forty bucks to fill up."

"You know what to do. Jude's road manager will give it to us from our allowance."

"An allowance, like we're fucking ten years old. I don't want to have to go through him again."

"Not my problem."

"What is your problem is telling us what comes next after the tour ends."

"We've already talked about it, what else do you want?"

"Decided to join preacher lady's traveling circus?"

"It's work, Mick."

"You don't even believe that spiritual crap anymore."

"Don't have to believe."

"You left there to get away from all that."

"It's either that or fall in line with Jude."

"You're going to piss on the contract, then?"

"Haven't made up my mind yet."

"They're not gonna wait for you forever. Think maybe you need to fill me, fill us, in on what you're gonna do before you do it?"

"Don't push me, Mick."

Card, Thurston, and Butch shuffled off the bus, unpacking equipment, gathering for a final smoke. Mick shifted his bulk, one foot off the stairwell, the other on the ground, bitter voice raw with strain. "Been letting all these leeches play you."

"Focused right now on finishing up the rest of the tour."

"You can't treat me like an errand boy."

"That line's getting old."

"I need an answer from you."

"Just let me get through the next two nights."

"Why were you using the other night."

"I wasn't. Butch came crying to you about it?"

"I have eyes. Everyone could see you were off. Butch is the last person who'd come crying to me about anything and if his junkie stash ever accidentally on purpose winds up with you I'll personally fuck him up."

"I was tired the other night. I keep getting these calls. Butch was the only one who came in to check on me—"

"He can't even tie his shoes straight. He was in your dressing room doing what? Stroking your ego or feeding you more junk?"

Rory watched the men skitter around the strikers as they trudged into the stadium, amps and instrument cases shielding their bodies from the chants, cussing; an undulating wall of janitors, ticket takers, cooks, servers and cashiers, black, brown, and white, faces wrung out in the hellfire heat after days of failed negotiations.

"Look, I—I've been trying to give you breathing space," Mick continued. Sweat trickled down his temples. He'd skipped his high blood pressure meds for the past two weeks and started chugging any liquid he could get his hands on. "But I need an answer."

"You want a how-to manual, not an answer."

"You owe me more than this, Rory. You can pull rank on Butch, Card, and all the rest of them, but you can't hoodwink me with this falling apart act."

"I said wait for two more days. Then I'll have a decision all wrapped up in a bow for you. They're not coming after you, you can't hear what they're saying—"

"Who? What are you talking about?"

"The callers at night."

He closed his eyes. "Quit with that shit. Please. The last twenty years of my life have been put on hold for you, tearing around the country making jack. I got no savings, no place to live, don't know when the fuck I'm gonna be able to retire—"

"Put on hold for what? So you could drink yourself into the ground and get fired from minimum wage jobs you had to work morning noon and night? And retiring is some fantasy land white shit." She pushed past him, wobbling, falling onto the pavement, pain knifing her back. A warm trickle of pee spread through her semi-new slacks, the sour taunt of age. She sat there, bolted to the ground on her ass for a second as red ants marched cockily up her boot heel. The holy rollers sent them, sent everything. Every smidgeon of bad luck that was happening to her.

A man charged forward, extending his hand. "You ok, Sister?"

She grasped it and got up. "Thanks. Appreciate it."

The man glared at Mick, resting his sign between his spindly legs. "Anytime, sister. Been following your music since you was rockin' them choirs down in the boondocks. Hope you understand why some of us won't be up in that stadium tonight, but we'll be cheering you on from out here. Your record company the House tried to cut us off at the knees bringing scabs in from all over the state just to work this tour."

"The House ain't my company."

"Well, then maybe you can make a statement in solidarity from the stage—"

"Ask her why she crossing the picket line in the first place!" someone yelled.

"Ain't no better'n a scab."

"She act big and bad in that radio station in Nashville then come here with her tail between her legs."

"It ain't my tour," she muttered, brushing past them.

"Your name's up there on the marquee. Getting beaucoup dollars to step on our necks."

"It's the city you got a beef with, not us," Mick said. They moved ahead. Lavender floated in front of them, balancing her notebook and a canvas knapsack big enough to stuff a body in.

"Ms. Tharpe, do you have a comment on the strike and why this tour's siding with the pigs in corporate?"

Jude Core chants bulleted down on them as the band took the stage. Card thumped out the opening hook of "Swallow You Whole". Butch and Thurston followed with the melody, loping in and out of a twelve-bar blues refrain. They played for two minutes. The crowd fixated on the empty mic stand center stage. Jude's handlers paced in the wings, insectoid in black headsets.

"Where's your boss lady?" they hissed at Mick.

Rory sat at the mirror in her dressing room, looking at her lopsided false eyelashes. She could hear the band stumbling through the intro of the song it had taken a grizzly year for her to write; could feel the buzzards massing outside her door with Satan-sharpened beaks, her stomach lurching with indecision.

Mick bust in, crushing a Coke can in his fist. "Bloody hell, they're going fucking crazy out there, what're you doing?"

The buzzards were over her head now. She grabbed at them, crushing them to pieces so they could never mate, multiply again.

"Pull the plug," she said. "Tell the boys I'm not coming out."

He knelt down weakly in front of her, offering her a sip of the Coke. "Don't do this. This ain't your fight."

She took a sip, stroking his cheek. "Pull the plug."

"Dammit, Rory! What have these people ever done for you? Most of 'em wouldn't piss on you or your music if it were on fire."

"Your name's not on the bill, mine is—"

"I know, and I'm trying to make sure it stays on there—"

"Just do it."

"I'm not looking like a damn idiot in front of twenty thousand people, promoters and the label just so you can keep playing the martyr."

She gave him back the soda can and got up. "You're right. Guard this with your life then."

The stage was lit up like a lake of fire when she went out and told them they weren't playing the set. Jude shrugged off her departure and launched into more purloined shit, mugging for the photographers in the front row, inviting Jude Core up to dance with her, sopping up every drop of adulation with a warm biscuit.

In the white newspapers the next day, Rory's walk out was spun as a cat fight. A tabloid fit of pique over pecking order and dressing room size. A footnote to the revelation of Jude owning the stage in the wake of adversity, riding a bridge that her band had picked from the corpses of Stax B-sides and the Grand Old Opry. The House would squeeze the next big thing out of Jude if they had to blow up the Federal Reserve. Marty, Moe, and Jack had bet Rory would be it. Would be the jackpot formula to get the white girls hopped up again, living at the record stores, bombing all the postage stamp radio stations along Route 66 with requests for that hummable, infectious new song.

"After that stunt, your bankability's in the toilet," Russ told her the next morning on the phone. She was soaking her feet in Epsom salts. Mick poured hot water into the tub and eavesdropped. He'd come back to check on her after the blow-up, pride swallowed, hungover. The service workers' union had run a press release in the local Black paper praising her action, vowing to shut down arenas in Mississippi, Georgia, Alabama.

"Babe, I know you want to be sympathetic, but that working class hero thing doesn't cut it when you got no leverage," Russ said. "I mean, what in God's name were you thinking? After all the work I've done, all the time and energy I put into getting the labels to look at you—"

"You're still getting your cut and you don't run me, hear? You and the House just want to beef up Jude's three ring circus. Nobody's going to program me, Russ."

"Either you want a manager who lives in the real world, or you want to be spoon fed by a lapdog who lives in a fantasy world."

"I'm going to Little Rock, then I'm going to California."

"You do that, and I'm walking."

"I have offers on the table to headline, maybe finally go into the studio and cut an album."

"Little Rock? That's fucking DOA. Can't have you going off the fucking reservation every time you get an itch. Get straight, finish the tour. I'll see if I can put Humpty Dumpty together again—"

She slammed down the phone. Mick sprawled on the floor, rubbing his temples. "Give him a little room to blow off steam, then kiss and make up," he said.

She shook her head.

"You fly solo then what?"

"Freedom. I don't know… Fuck him, I need room to think."

He sat up and crawled over to her, taking her right foot from the tub, massaging it, hot water trickling down his fingers.

"You've gotten rusty," she said, grimacing, shifting closer to him.

"Naw, never. Never with you."

The P.O. Box registered to Rory Eudalia Tharpe in the shipping and office supply services complex on 1405 Springer Lane in Baltimore was about to be shut down for non-payment of rent when the fat check arrived. The mailman slapped it on the counter along with a wizened letter from a Dutch musicology society seeking a quote on the Big Bill Broonzy song Rory Tharpe played at Tabernacle Holiness Church on the evening of June 19, 1945. Yeah, that June 19th. The Juneteenth when her mother had some kind of virus that sent her several times to the toilet, then out to the healer in Cotton Plant with ten dollars she'd borrowed on the sly from the deacon's middle daughter.

Katy had told Rory she was going to get rid of it. The virus. The space alien wrapping around her intestines, babbling in interplanetary code. The only reason she knew Katy was sick was because Katy had taken to falling asleep early. Wasn't like her to waste any juice from the day. *Don't never ever let it happen to you*, she said to Rory. Avoiding calling it a baby. Driving like a Tasmanian devil out to the healer's in the bald-tired Buick they took to revivals. If you keep a bastard, God will mark you. Fuck up your fingers. Then where would we be, moneywise. Fucked and fucked again.

All day, Rory had been waiting for a call about the fat check. Veering back and forth in her head about Katy's slapdash abortion and the walkout in Memphis. The fat check was supposed to be the insurance policy and passport to a bright, sparkling future. When it finally came, hundreds short due to the walkout, she quietly took it on the jaw and paid the band their full share. Card used his cut to send money to his kids. Butch paid off his weed debt. Thurston put a down payment on an Italian motorcycle he'd been lusting after, watching American bikes burn past him from the filmy midnight windows of the bus.

Mick sulked about the fizzled out tour, socked his money away, contemplated paying his maxed out credit cards. He'd go home to Jersey City and look for an apartment, insinuate himself back into the good graces of a gullible squeeze, a claims adjuster who'd dumped him when she found out he'd fucked a few men. Maybe they'd hole up for a spell and think about what to do next. Maybe the novelty and wham bam of reunion would carry them until they ripped each other from limb to limb. Again. The specter of rootedness bit at his balls, vampire teeth rousting him from sleep, sending him pacing in his motel room while the usual mob of hangers on drunks grasped onto the waning hours of the tour downstairs at the bar, trying to wheedle past last call. Who would really want him? Ravaged, skidding past middle age. Who would look away from, forgive the frittered years since he'd picked up a bass, been disciplined, been a ghost of a model citizen, paid bills on time, paid rent, a car note, anything you could sink an anchor in; increase your market value to get a heat seeking human to simply stick around.

Mick was paranoid about Rory reading his mind, sussing out the chinks, the dependency. He'd watched the slither of foreign journalists around her and Jude during the tour. Toadies from Canada, England, South America jamming the pay phones, lobbying their editors for deadline extensions. He watched, drank, spent, and drank some more. Pale envy throttling him when he least expected it.

Four days after Rory cashed it, most of the money from the fat check was gone. Once she'd doled it out to the boys, she paid off back taxes to the feds, then settled the past due note on the bus; the hunk of junk barely escaping repossession. A company affiliated with Russ had bought the bus and leased it to her for twenty percent interest.

"Limp dick bastard has more money than God, Satan, and the Holy Ghost combined and he's still fucking you with that interest rate," Card snarled, plopping down next to her on the bus as they drove to the final stop of the tour in Mobile, Alabama. Jude's management had diverted the tour to Mobile to avoid strikers in Birmingham. The Alabama gulf coast glittered out at them, backing darkened clusters of storefront churches and frame houses, watchful as cats on a fence, still festooned with banners from Mardi Gras.

Card gnawed at an apple, eating them several times a day to keep himself "regular". After Nashville and Memphis, they'd danced around each other, making an unspoken truce in the margins of the tour. "Don't know why you let that white man continue managing you no way," he said.

"A Black one managed you and where'd that get you?" she said.

"Motherfucker came from the United Nations of thievery but he ain't representative of the race."

"Didn't say he was, just that you're one to talk. You buy those kids of yours five years' worth of Christmas presents to make up for the ones you missed?"

Card paused. "Naw. And we don't celebrate that commercial shit."

"How old are they?"

"Old enough to be twenty-four-seven ornery. Large and in charge in their own heads. You never had none?"

"Didn't want any."

"Every woman does."

"Glad you feel qualified to speak for every woman."

Card speared an apple peel, popping it into his mouth. "'Scuse me. Sacrilege for me to lump you in with all them. The common folk who get knocked up, that is. All the one's still stuck back home that your mama warned you about ending up like. Damn shame," he chomped on the peel, rubbing the knife clean on his pants. The blade glinted back at Rory, jack o' lantern style. "Yeah, they got buried out there while you here shucking and jiving with the rednecks."

"Right. Shucking and jiving and signing your checks."

"Check came from the record company."

"It wasn't the record company who gave you a second chance, brought your ass back from the dead."

"What kind of sound would y'all have had without me, baby? Working half-cocked with the three stooges here whining like little girls—"

"Like boys. Girls don't whine like that, and somehow we managed to get along for over ten years without you."

"That ain't nothing to brag about. Time's passed you by and you still acting like hot shit from back when Ike was president… Fuck, we could go into the studio, get a real rhythm section and cut a record that'd sell, be bigger than that drowning cat sounding motherfucker Jude."

"It ain't a competition with her."

"Damn straight. You're on Jupiter and she's six feet under."

"Sounds about right."

"What's that preacher lady dangling in front of you?"

"My own gig, a chance to stay in one place for a bit. Play for our people."

He chortled, watching the houses roll by. "Our people. Didn't our so-called people bail on you when you stopped doing gospel?"

"I'll take it over having to show my ass groveling for the House."

Mick looked at her in the rear mirror from the driver's seat. Thurston and Butch stirred in their sleep, buried in a mess of flannel coats.

"That was gutsy what you did in Memphis, sticking your neck out."

"Yeah, but we can't eat on it."

"Not doing anything for our people we can't. White boys show some conviction and they wanna give 'em a Nobel prize and milk and cookies for life. What are you going to do about the contract?"

"Try and renegotiate. I don't want to be up under Jude, collecting Social Security."

"Now that would be a crime against humanity." He smiled, lowering his voice. "Ever thought about cutting them loose for good, hooking up with some new blood?"

"Like a purge."

"Yeah, a purge. Shake the cobwebs off. Cut a demo, funk it up. Put some horns in there, electric keyboard. Worrell, Bootsy, and that whole p-funk shit is outta sight. That's where it's at right now. You, me, and a few low overhead p-funk brothers, we could be a force."

"Naw, I'm too old for all that."

"Girl, you ain't never too old to squeeze into no space suit. You seen how they do 'em in the Mothership performances?"

"Nope." She paused. "Funny, that little girl Sid asked me about them though. Wondered how come I don't get played on the radio like them."

"I'm played on the radio all the time. Fat lot of good that does me." He looked at Mick, still eyeing them in the rear mirror. Card raised the apple to him in a mock toast and finished it off. "So, what do you say?" he asked her.

"I'm not interested in a duo."

"You mean you're not interested in one with me, a Black man. You all set to rip and run for that preacher even though they treated you like a stepchild out there—"

"It's steady pay for at least a month."

Mick slammed on the brakes, sending them lurching forward. "Which means she's not gonna carry you, man!"

Card jumped up. "You fucking trying to kill us??"

Thurston poked his head out from a coat. "What's going on?"

"Mr. Cardinal's plotting insurrection," Mick snapped.

Card moved into the aisle. "Handle your business and butt out of mine."

"Thinks he's god's gift to every woman living and breathing, got a medal on his dick to prove it."

"You better bow down then, you spineless honky tonk motherfucker or you're gonna be picking up your dentures from the freeway. This lady can't get a contract because of y'all."

There was a knock on the door. A white woman started pounding on the glass.

"Did you see what you did?" she yelled as Mick opened the door. "That car there practically tore up my porch swerving to avoid hitting y'all."

"Aww shit, forgive me, ma'am. I was having a seizure," Mick lied.

The woman screwed up her face, then her nose, peering inside the bus. A metal bat glinted in her hand. "Seizure my ass. Reeks to high heaven of booze in this thing. Where are y'all off to anyway at this time of night?"

"We're playing at the arena."

"Oh yeah? With that, uh, Judy gal? One that gets buck wild with the Nigra stuff? Ain't my cup of tea personally, but my kids love her." She considered them for a moment, her gaze deepening. "Well, kiddo, this is your lucky night," she nodded at the wrecked car. "We happen to know that gal in there. Seems to be basically ok, but you never know what aches and pains could develop over the course of twenty-four hours." She tapped the bat. "Instead of calling the police or doing a citizen's arrest, my alternative proposal is you pay me eight hundred dollars for the damage and we call it a night."

Rory walked to the door, elbowing Card aside. "We don't have that kind of money."

"And who are you?"

"This is my bus and my tour."

The white woman took a step back. "Well, sweetie, if this is your rig, I guess you better get to finding the money somewhere."

"What do you think you're going to do with that bat, *sweetie?*"

The white woman balanced it on the railing, turning as the car door opened and a white girl with a baby on her hip teetered out. "A gal's best friends are a gun, a knife or a bat, in that order. Lucky for you, I just happened to grab what was closest when I heard the car coming up on my property... I can take cash or a money order." She patted the bat. "Or, if that don't suit you, I'll have some of my boys from the highway patrol come collect it before the show. Maybe you can score them some free tickets. Where y'all staying again?"

Rory kept her eyes on her sallow, dancing-eyed face. A semi-truck trundled past, blowing its horn. The white woman waved at it. Card and Mick looked at the bat then at Rory. The white girl and the baby approached, fussing, wailing.

Rory walked to the bathroom at the back of the bus where she kept her safe. She entered the combination, emptying the dregs of the fat check onto the floor, the white baby's wails clawing wolfishly at the night.

Part Two

BLACK WINGS

Ransack, Butterfly

WHEN SHE WAS SIX, Sid cut open a radio to see if there were people in it. Disappointed by the sprawl of colored wires and electronic gunk she saw inside. The explanation of voices traveling through the air on waves was less magical than the prospect of little friends she could keep in her pocket forever. To have and to hold. 'Til death do us part.

She'd been flipping the dial on the car radio, waiting in the Kmart parking lot for her auntie Zinnia, when Rory burst through the static. It was what they called a syndicated show with white people playing white music; all folk guitar and country twang, all riding off into the sunset harmonies hawking manufactured heartbreak, murder, and mayhem. Some of it she liked deep down on the sly, not wanting to fuck around with white boy shit and get teased by the blacker than thou sentinels who ruled elementary school.

Listening to Rory's interview with the deejay on the radio took her back there. To that dumb little six-year-old. To the ass whipping she got for the dismembered radio. Each station a gateway to tiny worlds; new pop hits she memorized in one sitting, forbidden sugar rush candy commercial jingles, weather reports screeching at her to rise and shine and brace herself for another eye-gouging West Texas morning scrubbing toilets at the church.

The night the police took her from the Boise motel she turned into a poisonous butterfly, freeing it from the gut cage she'd built after the massacre when she was on the road with her uncle, and he promised her the moon with his hand between her legs. Promised her the moon when he let her take the wheel sometimes in the deepest deadest dead zones of the highway.

The butterfly would repel the demons, fuck them up, keep them in check. She willed it to be true, flying through the night above all the stable homes with stable children asleep in stable beds.

Before they sent her to foster care, the motel Indian lady came and sat with her. Held her hand, cracked silly jokes, gave her an envelope full of money, rustled up a used book of Mad Libs someone had left behind. Drilling her for verbs. Ransack. Pillage. Destroy.

Sid, you got such a big vocabulary for a young 'un. Use them words, they'll serve you well.

She listened to Rory's singing coming staccato through the speakers and felt her stomach drop leagues. Telling herself that she wasn't mad at her for giving her up to the police. Nobody in the world owed her jack and she didn't owe nobody. All she wanted was to play like her, surf the bloodstreams of millions to big shit immortality.

A week after she'd been picked up by her shifty relatives, she ran away, hitching rides with any Black or Brown woman who would stop. Sometimes she hoodwinked them into thinking she was a boy right on the innocent cusp before his voice cracked, plummeted. A cast off in sagging jeans and baseball cap, pen knife warm in her pocket for the predators who wanted her to suck them off in exchange for a few miles. Adults, the demons, saw what they wanted to see. At the Wyoming border, a nun going to Pine Bluff helped her buy a bus ticket to Little Rock, pity shining in her hard eyes. On the bus, Sid took a window seat in the middle, sleeping with the knife blade between her fingers.

Then the butterfly went back into its cage, and waited.

The person had called five or six times and always hung up before saying something. The seventh time was when they heard her breathing hard, coaxing a fussing baby to silence, soaps blasting in the background.

"Another head case?" Patton asked Divinity. Divinity had just come back from a pastor's lobbying trip at the capitol. She waddled into the office with her stockings rolled down to her ankles, skin riddled with mosquito bites, advance guard of a plague she was certain was intended for her. God was testing, making his might and displeasure known. *Fuck him/it/they*, she thought, noting the disheveled slant of Patton's suit coat. It was unlike her to have even a thread out of place.

"Maybe she's a head case. Or maybe a sinner looking for succor. Same fucking difference. You get some new clothes?"

"Yes, from the consignment store."

"Ever the frugal one."

"Better a tight belt than a loose one."

"That's why I 'preciate you, captain. Can't have expenses ballooning out of control, not when we're trying to launch phase two. I have a few more funding prospects I think I can reel in."

"Keeping that information classified?"

"What can I keep classified from you?"

"The building commission isn't going to approve a twenty-foot extension for a handicapped ramp to be put in the front. That's going to add another $10k we don't have. In other news, we got five callers out sick, the boiler needs servicing, and your girl is coming in this afternoon with her entourage."

"Entourage? What do you mean? I ain't paying for those white boys."

"You tell her that?"

"In so many words. She knows we have our own people."

"Strikes me as hardheaded."

"Wouldn't be the best around if she wasn't."

"Well, that may be in dispute these days. Reviews on her last fling with Jude were lackluster."

"Depends on who you were reading."

"Watching local TV news."

"What do they know?"

"You sure this is going to be a good investment? Word from Memphis was she walked off stage in some kind of half-assed, fist in the air protest over the service workers' strike they were having out there."

"Well, good for her. Girl's got a spine at least. Long as she don't pull nothing like that here we're A-ok. I don't make risky bets."

"How long are you going to keep her on?"

"Month or so."

"We can't afford much longer than that. Can barely afford this round."

"Which is why folks calling in sick on the regular will kill us. I'm sympathetic to emergencies that come up, but I ain't running a charity."

"We're in agreement there. Just keep it in mind when Miz Rory comes through."

"Don't second guess me on her."

"You hired me to keep finances in line. She and her people smell like a big damn money pit."

"Depending on you to make sure they're clean as a whistle."

"Right, you do your part then. Otherwise, we're gonna have the IRS swooping down."

Divinity looked at her. Patton had always shot straight, drawing a bead with careful measured aim, calm as still water in moonlight.

"The IRS is for private industry to worry about," Divinity said. "Long as we keep working for God—"

"That only goes for white folks and the minstrel Negroes slick enough to slide through the loopholes."

Someone knocked on the door. Divinity yelled at them to come in and Mick walked through. The women tightened their lips into flat lines of sour solidarity.

"Afternoon, Ms. Mason and—"

"It's *Pastor* Mason and this is Ms. Patton, director of operations."

Mick shook Patton's hand, appraising the well-appointed office. Plaques and pictures of Divinity grinning with politicians and church dignitaries stared down on him.

"I trust y'all had a good drive out here."

"Yep. This command central? Impressive. What kind of product do you sell?"

"We don't sell products. We promote spiritual wellbeing by establishing personal connections with seekers through phone and direct mail."

"Oh, like a telephone ministry, like those televangelists on, uh, what's that station called?"

"Televangelist is a crude term for it," Patton said dully.

"We prefer the term life coaching for mental and spiritual fitness."

"What's the difference?"

"You ever tried it? Ever tried to get control of your life through—"

"A direct line to God. That what you all are dangling?"

"We don't dangle. We got real needs in the community we serve—"

Divinity waved her hand at Patton. "Don't waste time explaining." She picked up a brochure from her desk and thrust it at him. "Here. Read up, get educated. Your boss still holed up in her motel room?"

Mick took the brochure. A picture of Divinity with her arms folded took up the entire front cover. The façade of the Revivals, Inc. building, loomed up, weather beaten against a downy blue sky. Scripture verses cascaded across the back of the brochure, punctuated by eight hundred numbers and a P.O. Box address.

"She's resting up," he said. He put the brochure back on the desk. "Business booming? I always wondered what the inside of one of these 'boiler rooms for Jesus' was like. Maybe if I got a sneak peek I'd be inclined to make a donation."

Divinity snatched up the brochure. "Like you give a fuck. Excuse my French. You wanna mock us, take your ass out to the parking lot."

"I wasn't trying to mock you. Just making an observation."

"How about we take a cut from your paycheck to advance the cause then?"

They watched him flinch, the hallways pinging with the racket of the callers going on a 20-minute lunch break, timed for the lull right before the 3:00 newscasts kicked in. A roar taking over the afternoon air.

Divinity liked to walk through the call center every now and then, giving pep talks about rising to the challenge of God. Strove to be the shining light of holy inspiration next to Patton's taskmaster. One eye on boosting the women's egos, the other on getting them to join the congregation. Relished the thrill of molding reluctant soldiers. Took pride in her sister-to-sister pitch. Some of them brightened up when they saw her coming, pretending to be transfixed by a Black woman running shit... or at least seeming to run it. They listened, nodded, murmured along as she held forth, brooding about their paychecks, the rumors of a hidden hand behind Revivals, Inc. Their suspicions dominating the small talk on the evening bus ride home.

"Go on," Divinity said to Mick, savoring every cereal crumb of his doubt. "You need translation?"

"That's not fucking funny," he said, edging out of the door and into the flow of women bunched in twos and threes at the vending machines, plugging them with coins for beer nuts, Doritos, beef jerky. They stared dully through Mick, a non-entity interloper. A line snaked from the payphone to the bathroom, toilets flushing and churning from the strain.

"Motherfucker's gonna be afraid of his own shadow now," Divinity said, rising from behind the desk after Mick left.

"He's a liability. You can tell from his red cheeks he's a stone drunk. Not sure why she didn't ditch him long ago."

"Insurance. Having a white boy along for the ride makes her look legitimate. Maybe they had something going between the sheets back in the day—"

"Now, now."

"I was thinking of having Rory and them play at Pilgrimage Methodist for two weekends as a warmup. We have a few donors that would be happier than pigs in shit to see her in a down home Negro church."

"Get out the habit of saying that. We ain't Negroes anymore. Sounds handkerchief headed."

"It's just between you and me. They love them some civil rights prayer breakfasts with us on the menu. Speaking of which, how many girls can work overtime tonight?"

"For?"

"Follow-ups on hard cases. Folks that need a little more massaging and TLC in the I.V. drip hours after they've finished dinner. Special friends with good ears and empathic skills. Not like those corporate Baptist convention jackals who'll skin 'em with a Kool-Aid grin and leave 'em for dead."

"We can barely afford to pay them their straight salaries, Divinity. And now that you got Rory and all her rejects on the payroll—"

"Gotta spend money to make money."

"We have to *have money* in the first place."

"That's why I got you. Train 'em up, smooth out the rough edges, make 'em talk like you talk. You know how much buying power Black folks have? We can fund, power several nations with what we spend on hair, movies, records, booze. That Back to Africa, Back to Liberia movement stuff launched right here in Arkansas."

"My grandmother was part of all that. Used to sit at the kitchen table writing letters to the feds. Her whole church went on caravans to the state capitol just after the stock market crashed in the thirties."

"Yeah?"

"None of her people wants to set up nothing there now. Least not the ones that are still alive. Congregation spun all sorts of fantasies about being real liberated Africans. Deacons and their wives went over there for a month, got their bubbles burst and came back broke and homesick."

"Big dreams to remember, as Otis once said. Get some of them girls in here now."

Patton hesitated, listening to the receding bustle of the women in the hallway. Most of them had stepped outside for smoke breaks or a snatch of sun. They huddled around their cars, flopping down on the crusty strip of lawn in front of the office for quick sidebars about money orders, talking about who and what would need to be paid with Friday's check, slapping ghoul-fanged June bugs off their legs as they calculated and recalculated, down to the last penny, how to make it stretch for another two weeks.

Patton walked up to them, a clipboard pressed in a tight shield against her chest. "Reverend Divinity wants five of you, five volunteers for a special project," she announced. "Possibility of overtime pay,"

"I'll do it," a woman shuffling baseball cards said. "Needed the money yesterday. How late and how long?"

"Just a few hours after your regular shift ends."

"What you want us to do exactly?" another one said, stepping forward, giving Patton the side eye. She popped the key chain to her two-door GTO stick shift across her palm, proud that she had wheels that weren't in the shop every week.

"Reverend Divinity's identified some folks that we need to reach out to in a more methodical way."

"What that mean in plain English?"

"Means we gotta close the deal," baseball card tittered.

Patton gestured for them to come back into the office. "Those who're interested follow me."

White Light, White Heat

AFTER SHE'D SHELLED OUT all the money she had to the white woman in Mobile, they'd finished the tour with a sorry whimper; bickering, festering in their separate sections of the bus, watching Jude take a victory lap in the press before going to New York to record her next album. Rory ignored Russ' calls for a week. Checking her Social Security statement, calculating what the payment would be if she decided to take it early. A taste creeping up on her. A monkey on her back squeezing her neck. Marooned at the bottom of the ocean she tried to shake it off, fix her mind on Little Rock.

She knew Butch knew how to get junk out in the middle of nowhere. He could conjure up some enterprising motherfucker and have him serve it up on demand at any random highway gas pump. Trick was how to make sure it was clean shit, safe shit; the kind that would send her to the clouds for a blissful little while then hang glide her safely back down in one piece.

She'd first seen her mother shoot up on the toilet in the spring of '46. End of the war, skinny sloth toes splayed on the cracked seat sagging from the strain of a thousand phantom asses. Reverend Ike on the radio, congregation aflame. *You didn't see nothing*, she said to Rory the first time. *It's new medicine from the doctor to reduce my flow, knock out the kinks in my back.* She was talking to Rory like she was toddling around in diapers, thumb up her butt. She rode the heroin high like a stallion, ecstatic and gushing love one moment, paranoid and raging the next. Soon she was living for Sunday afternoons in the bathroom, set to the Rev's dulcet voice. Living for the crash bang. Afterwards, pacing around the communal phone in the hall, waiting for the club bookers to call. Throw them a bone. Enough for half the rent, a week's worth of stew meat, carfare and a tin of the new lightening cream all the Negro magazines were hyping.

Wartime had been a blur of scrubbing white ladies' homes clean enough for them to eat off the floor with a vanilla wafer. Waiting for them to fall into a valium-induced stupor so she could steal a few coins from their kid's piggy banks. Her lazy white lady stash had funded a raincoat and a capo for Rory's guitar. Had kept her from floating away on the hope that war's end would mean more money in folks' pockets to spend on a stolen night to booze it up, drown, and escape through music.

Every time she closed her eyes, daydreaming, worrying, on the drive to Little Rock, blame curdled in her mouth. How she didn't stop Katy's using. How she watched, fascinated; her mother's eyes dimming, burning down to the wick, rolling back into her head, face hijacked by that sloppy harlequin grin she got when she was high. Part of her wanting Katy to go to sleep and never wake up. Part of her thinking that that wasn't punishment enough.

They pulled into town from highway 630 at dawn. Flopped at the motel Divinity had booked for them. Rented a car on Thurston's credit the next day. Abandoned houses and apartments rolled by, dark and gap-toothed in the sunset. The brick high school she'd dropped out of shuttered, beaten down to a tornado pulp. The liquor barn she remembered moons away from its groundbreaking when protesters snaked through the streets, railing about how it was going to make the neighborhood a drunkard, junkie, pusher cesspit. A fortuneteller house with a glittery neon palm-washed past, abutted by a fried chicken chain drive-thru choked with idling cars. Press and curl special beauty shops, vacant lots shifting to tall buildings, leonine sleek in the dusk.

"Hungry as fuck," she muttered, looking at the quarter full gas gauge, doing the numbers on how much more they'd need for the week. "We should've stopped at that drive-thru."

"You don't need that shit," Mick said.

"Don't tell me what I need."

"You're right," he said. "How many grease traps have you eaten at this year? I met with Divinity and her sidekick while you were resting up yesterday. They got a boiler room situation with all these women on the payroll doing dial-a-dollar for Jesus. Probably a fire hazard. Didn't say nothing about gigs or expectations as I predicted, then had the nerve to hit me up for a donation."

"She took you for a gullible white boy."

"Mistook. That Patton woman sticks close up under her. Where do they get the money?"

"Hell if I know. Baptist convention? Divinity always was good at the business end. Skilled at sweet talking white folks, trotting out their afflictions."

He paused, gauging her mood. "Look, about Mobile… I'll pay you back for all of it."

"That's why this gig's pro bono for you."

"Son of a bitch."

"The 'bitch' ain't got nothing to do with this. You just keep working that white boy charm of yours as my advance guard with the House. Time I got some profit out of you. Help me get my foot in the door some fucking where… C'mon, pick up the pace on this rattletrap, I need to eat."

"Nervous?"

"About what?"

"You only get hungry when you're nervous… planning on spending serious time here after the dog and pony show?"

"'Course not. What gave you that idea?"

"Just a feeling. Preacher lady's got a grand vision and you're the cherry on top. Gonna legitimize her with the sinners."

"She don't need legitimizing with them. Divinity probably snuck and did her share of smack back in the day, pretending to be prim, proper, and shiny."

"Called at a young age."

"Her and millions of others. Throw a rock around here and you hit a preacher, wannabe preacher or ex-preacher. Was the only job besides a janitor a Black man was guaranteed, and then they turned around and made damn sure to dog any woman who tried to be one."

Mick kept his eyes on the road, riled by the lunar crawl of the cars ahead of them. A man darted out from the bus stop, waving packs of incense, fluorescent necklaces, Timex watches for sale. He tripped onto the median strip just before a delivery truck barreled through, the passenger cackling, "Fuck you Father Time," out of the window.

"Sooner we get out of this place, the better," he muttered. They approached another liquor store, lit up with two-for-one special signs, dust-caked ads with half-naked women popping out of liquor bottles, squatting under black silkscreened beer logos while a procession of evening shoppers waited in line at the cash register.

"Stop here," she said. She jumped out and went in, walking past a group of men congregating outside on milk crates, smoking, playing cards, watching traffic, nodding at her glassy-eyed, disinterested. The once-overs they usually gave were reserved for disposable women on the cusp of aging out of the men's big game hunting rituals. She headed straight for the beverage freezer, rocketed to the moon for a split second, titillated by all the bottles, the choices, the smooching cold of dry ice against her ear. *How did you manage to live this long?* she heard Katy whisper. *How did you dodge God's bullet with all the mess that you did to yourself, frittering away your destiny like a damn fool?*

The shop owner craned his neck to monitor her. Kids swished through the aisles comparing candy bars and jawbreakers in rainbow relief. The shop owner scrunched up his nose to the odor of the outsiders, the Black woman stepping through aisles like she owned them while the white man trailed behind her croaking like a frog footman.

Mick ambled around the foot tappers in line and caught up with Rory. "What are you doing?" he said. "Trying to get high sniffing dry ice? We got an appointment with the preacher at 7:00, a demo to rehearse for early in the morning, and the motel wants a deposit for our rooms before 9 or we'll be sleeping on the bus again."

She ignored him, coasting on the ice and cold, the winter wonderland of booze it would take a day of nirvana to drink by herself on an exoplanet she'd invent.

"Rory. Rory?" Mick called out. "C'mon now, you ok?"

A woman brushed around him, opening the case next to them to scoop up a six-pack. She looked at him twice, suspicious, a glint of recognition in her eyes. "You that man that was at the church call center this morning."

He hesitated. "Yeah, why?"

"Looking for a job?"

"Naw."

"Miss Divinity never hired no white boys to make calls, wonder why."

Mick ignored her, coaxing Rory. "Rory. You ready?"

"It's either 'cause you ain't as competent as we is or 'cause you cost more."

"Maybe it's both," Rory said, pulling her head out of the freezer, a can of screwdriver mix in her hand.

"You with him?" the woman asked, looking at the two of them with piqued interest.

"He's with me."

The woman leaned into Rory, rubbing the six-pack against her cheek. "Well I heard that. But if y'all shacking up you better watch it. Even if you just passing through. Use common sense and the eyes in the back of your head."

Rory laughed. The woman came up to her nose, dyed black hair snarling in a halo around her hot poker eyes, a familiarity to the cocksure inflection, the way she bobbed back and forth, like a body popping up from the sea then sinking. Shouts rose up from the line as someone who'd tried to cut got sent to the back to a hail of snickers. "I'm just about the oldest one she got on the phones, baby. Rest is so wet behind the ears they drowning. I pulled in the top numbers for the month. Fifteen regular subscribers, paid in full right up front, no installments. Got a brand new color TV from Ms. Divinity. TV does everything but fry flapjacks and make coffee. Now everybody on the block's my new best friend when the fights is on."

"What are they subscribing to?"

"Ms. Divinity's sermons, daily dose of wisdom, special bonus gifts, extras for—"

"How much are they?"

"Depends on the package. VIP, Deluxe, platinum, silver—"

"Tin?" Mick retorted.

The woman sucked her teeth, taking out her wallet from her purse. "What you smokin'? Disrespecting Ms. Divinity. We ain't no fly by night operation like those motherfuckers running churches out of storefronts."

"Well, you sure are doing good PR for her. Hope you're making more than minimum wage."

"It's none of your business what I'm making. You ain't signing my checks so go on ahead then."

A man in the next aisle, studying ten varieties of potato chips, clapped his hands together, squealing. "Better watch it girl, he could be the police."

"Doubt it. Piglet wouldn't be seen in public with her if he was."

The three of them got in line. All eyes drifted to Rory, appraising, spinning tales with lip smacking curiosity about her and the white boy who'd come out of nowhere.

"They together," the woman announced to the line. "He her body-guard or something."

"You got I.D. for that?" the checker asked, pointing at the woman's six-pack.

"Naw, how many damn times am I in here a week buying groceries, keeping y'all in business. My grown Black ass is my I.D."

"Can't sell that to you unless you got I.D."

Mick stepped up. "I'll buy it." He gestured to his silver ponytail, pulling out his driver's license. "Good enough for you?"

The checker rang the six-pack up and moved them along. Mick gave her the beer. She trailed them outside.

"Can y'all give me a ride to the church?" the woman asked.

"This to help Divinity get through the night?" Mick asked.

"Naw, it's my dinner."

"She not paying you enough for you to buy real food?" Rory asked.

"Can y'all take me or not? You all about the twenty questions like you the County or something."

"Sure, c'mon." Rory said.

The woman slid into the back seat. She stretched out her legs and plopped the six-pack on the floor, then pulled out a container of Vaseline and slathered a fingerful on her lips.

"Must be nice to have a white chauffeur. Give you a little bit of protection. Slow 'em down when they're coming after you. That is, if they still do."

"What're you talking about?"

"Don't recognize me, do you?"

"No."

The woman laughed, lips shimmering in the dusk. "Just can't place me, right, superstar? Come across so many folks in your walk of life, I bet. Hard to keep 'em all straight. All the little people out in the audience. Back in the day, you used to wear custom made wigs. One for every performance. Sorta like Dinah Washington almost, but not as stylish as her. She could do them wigs real slick, just over the eye, cut down dumb motherfuckers with one look."

They stopped at a light by the railroad tracks, the semaphore waving faintly in the wind. At the crossing, cars were always getting caught by the gate coming down. A Dodge packed with five kids was sliced in half in '54. Car innards, school books, piles of a white lady's clean laundry mangled in the hot rail ties as the whole lot of them fled; bodies weirdly intact, split second before the train hurled past, the taste of near death salting their days from then on. Sometimes, she dreamt that she was in the car, savoring the aftermath, the rush of attention that came with survival. Sometimes she dreamt up new roles for herself; how she'd saved them, how she'd gone back and plucked them from their seats, how the arm of the gate had almost sliced off her head and had her jerking around like Ichabod Crane.

"I hate trains," the woman said.

"Some kids nearly got killed right here, years ago. Car stalled."

"Yeah."

"You familiar with it?"

"I wish they'd all died, nasty asses, teased me for being fat."

Rory paused, swiveling her head to look at the woman, moist caterpillar brows crawling off her face.

"Damn, a death wish, just for that?"

"Why not? This world's got too many people in it. We could stand to toss some of 'em off the ship. Sure you'd agree, ripping and running all around the country the way you do."

"Ripping and running—"

"My name's Zinnia, like the flower. Hated it when I was growing up but now it's golden. Sets me apart from all the other chicks trying to score on the phone. They ain't got half the skills I do... We all looked up to you, superstar, how you could play. Blindfolded, one hand tied behind your back. I always wanted to play the piano or something. Wasn't nobody musical in the family, though... Can your boy here drive faster? We got an exorcism to do." She laughed, moving up in her seat until she was talking into the back of Mick's head. "Kidding. Don't have that kind of training, not yet."

The car got quiet as they pulled away from the tracks, past the park where Rory had gone to play on the swings years after Negroes were officially allowed to. Past the grassy knoll darkened by the shadows of all the dead children who'd never had a chance to feel the cool of the sandbox between their toes, build castles up to the sky, have raging turf fights with fairies and gremlins.

Zinnia had worn a white sweater encrusted with plastic beads every Sunday to church. These are diamonds, she'd lied to the younger girls, stoking their tender envy. When it was her turn for a private confessional with Daddy Simmons, she offered them a diamond apiece to take her place. One could buy you a new car. Two a new house. Three a new head of hair. Long and soft and shiny, the to die for prize. The tiniest girl had fallen for it. Holding the diamond up to the light in the basement bathroom, delirious, expecting a horse mane to sprout down her back at any moment. *Save it*, she'd said. *It'll only work if you swallow it before bedtime and not tell no one.*

Divinity's church rose up in the distance, a trio of low-slung buildings anchored by new construction. All the courting, wheedling, and scrounging Divinity did for donations rippled through every modest beam of the church. The lot had once been home to a succession of bootleg businesses. A fish place, a temp agency, a smoke shop, a massage parlor, all trying to make a go of it with shitty credit and high interest loans amidst the stew of bad traffic, break-ins, unpaid back taxes. The lot had crumbled into an unholy eyesore until it was rehabbed by Methodists who built a church in the late sixties during the race riots, then lost it to the Baptists, who lost it to Divinity after the Baptists went down for embezzlement and the bank foreclosed on the building.

A woman came out of the main building with a record album under her arm. She watched them pull into the parking lot, eyes fortified behind thin black glasses. The moon spread in slivers over the two church vans stationed by the entrance. The slogan "God's love in the mood for miracles" was emblazoned in ornate cursive on the side doors.

"That's Deaconess Patton," Zinnia said. "Or, General, if you know your history."

Mick shut off the engine. "Met her earlier today and became good friends."

Zinnia motioned to the six-pack. "Mind if I keep this in the car? I don't want to hear her mouth about it. Woman is all about no shame no gain."

Patton walked over to them, locking her gaze onto Rory as she shook her hand firmly then took out the album. "Yvette Patton. We've been speaking on the phone all these months. Enjoy your music. *Sanctified Kingdom*, straight to number one on the gospel charts in 1955. Sold out at all the Negro dime stores. Whole family wore out the grooves on this one back home. You played and sang like an angel. Every time we put it on it was like a cyclone hit us, like Clara Ward and Mahalia combined. Listened for many years. Good you could join us for the revivals."

"Where's back home?" Rory asked.

"Pittsburgh, but grew up here mostly. Your mama played at our church once."

She tapped the liner notes of the album. "This was your best year, in my humble opinion. Both barrels blazing."

"Now that's a strong image," Mick said acidly.

Patton turned to Zinnia. "Where is it?"

"Where's what?"

"The booze. You hide it in their car?"

"Ain't none."

"Don't lie to me."

"Ain't lyin'."

"You're bad at it. You should be one of them Southern Baptist convention preachers. Bad liars, amateurs. Rather lie than pee when they get up in the morning."

"I said I ain't lyin'."

"Ok, baby girl, have it your way. Just trying to keep you clean and honest." She turned back to Rory, tucking the album under her arm. "Pastor Divinity's been waiting for you. Maybe I can get you to autograph this later."

'Mosquito shampoo' were the last words Jude heard out of Lavender's mouth before they fell asleep in a snoring heap on the king size bed in her hotel room. At 7 a.m., she staggered up, a riff pestering her, dragline chords in the key of F, or something. She'd started learning how to read music on piano in her teens, then gave up, reasoning that the best, the masters, the fingers to the bone picking Black men writing the book on slide guitar never needed to; you either had a golden ear or you didn't. Either had monster timing or didn't. If God hadn't blessed you, then fighting to overcome the handicap was the journey that stiffened the spine.

She drank in the quiet of the street down below. The hotel was in New York's Chelsea district, a half mile from where she'd played to an invitation-only crowd oohing and aahing and right proud of their philanthropy as they did the hustle to benefit gunshot wound victims in Harlem. *How the fuck could they do that disco dance shit to my music?* she'd complained to Lavender afterwards, entranced by the fresh grove of sweaty curls that had formed at her neck in the theater's steam bath heat. They'd gone back to Jude's room, nibbling each other in the Lincoln town car; Lavender a quarter stoned, Jude jittery about the doctor's prognosis on her shifty bladder revolting at the end of every show.

Lavender was an easy low-calorie distraction. A desert island, a beachhead away from her cascade of traitorous body problems, or so Jude fantasized. They stayed up until 3 a.m. watching a z-budget gumshoe series, then a rebroadcast of the presidential debates. Reagan shucking and lying fast and loose against the backdrop of a Tums crunching Caucasoid Minnesota audience waving toy flags to punctuate every sentence. Reagan sucking off true believers eighteen to eighty, decked out in electric stars and stripes. Reagan stale as a rubber chicken on a banquet dinner plate, the wet dream of coked up day traders.

Lavender raged back at him in paragraphs, while Jude secretly rooted for his anti-tax shtick. Her capital gains taxes had been through the roof since 1966 when her first album went platinum and her accountants prophesied doom unless she socked every last penny away in a Cayman Islands tax shelter. Back in Texas, her parents had said Reagan was the last great white hope to smack down the Russkies. The last righteous gunslinger to expose all the stateside Dem turncoats reveling in their godlessness and the devil of high taxes.

This was one of the umpteen reasons she avoided that corner of Earth when they toured the Lone Star state. Her parents and the whole lot of sidewinder relatives scraping by in the same dinky houses they'd owned since the forties, when prospectors found oil a half mile away and rooked them out of the profits.

Lavender kinda favored her mother around the nose. She hadn't realized it until they were eye to eye, tumbling off a cliff together in slobbery by-the-numbers kisses. She could tell Lavender was a reefer virgin. She'd take a puff, a hit, then, blam. Spilling over the sides about her deadlines, her phobias, her life's dream to be a women's lib revolutionary. All this and too fucked up incoherent to go down on Jude properly.

The phone rang. Jude struggled to pick it up, the room blurry, swimming in front of her, before a certain time she was useless without her eye drops. "Get your cracker ass out of bed," the voice on the other line said.

"Who is this?"

"The Candyman, who else? It's your friendly neighborhood publicist. Still shacking up with that writer bitch?"

"Told you not to call here before ten, Bill."

"Morning to you too, baby. You gonna be able to be functional in thirty minutes or do we need to call a bouncer?"

"Thirty minutes for what?"

"Photo shoot with *Omega Man* magazine, rehearsal with the boys, new contracts the label's sending over. Got to head out for Jersey City at five, before the traffic goes to shit."

"*Omega Man*? All they want is T&A on a stick."

"You agreed to it two months ago."

"Agreed to an interview, no pictures."

"Look, how can I say this… you're getting up there. *Omega*'s got nearly a million subscribers. *Paid* subscribers, no padding, no fluff. You need to run with this. Gloria Steinem doing pillow talk, whispering in your ear about scruples or morals or whatever the fuck she's on is gonna hurt your market share."

"Last time I checked, Bill, I was paying you."

"Correction, the label is paying me, or I guess you didn't notice. My last check direct from your production company was rubbery as a bathtub duck."

She stood up, cradling the phone against her shoulder, smell checking the blouse and pants she wore yesterday for freshness. She rustled a vial of perfume from her purse and smeared it on the clothes. "How much for the photo shoot?"

"A few grand. Main thing is it drops just before you go underground to record the blues album with Tharpe. It'll be a valentine for folks to remember you by, distract them from freaking the fuck out over Reagan and the election."

"Got it."

"And one more thing… What's Gloria bringing to the party? Where does she live when she's not freeloading off of you? That fuck-up paper she's writing for has all of four, maybe six eyeballs on it. Hers, the editor's, and the publisher's."

"She's doing a profile on me."

"She's running a scam." He paused, lowering his voice. "I know I can ride you hard sometimes, but it's only because you're too trusting. Can't let yourself be a mark for flattery. At the end of the day you got no one, no heirs, no ties. Sometimes that can be beautiful, the best. Not being beholden to anyone. But if you croak tomorrow who's going to pick up the baton?"

"I dunno, maybe I could will it all to those kids in Harlem… you see the way they live?"

"That's real noble. If I believed in heaven, I'd say that might guarantee you a slot."

"That ain't my intent."

"Come now, it can't ever hurt to be strategic, especially when every Tom, Dick, and Harry in Texas is gonna come out of the woodwork and claim you when you die. How're you gonna decide who to bless, who to pluck out of obscurity? Eany meany miney mo?"

Lavender let out a foghorn blast, nestling into the pillow, her wallet turned upside down on the desk, change spilling out amidst a withered press pass, two-for-one coupons, a Polaroid picture of a shirtless man with tattoos branded on his liver-spotted trunk.

"Haven't figured it out yet. And it ain't about blessing nobody neither."

"Oh, really now? Like I said, that might ease open the pearly gates for you, offset the sinning and debauching, in addition, I might add, to boosting your image right here on planet Earth. Again, market share and eternity, not a bad combination."

"Right. Appreciate your looking out for my welfare. I'll be down in a sec." She hung up the phone. Lavender stirred, jolting up, fumbling for her glasses.

"Head feels like somebody stepped on it."

"I have to go do an interview."

"For those chauvinist pigs at *Omega*? All they want is your legs open and your mouth shut. The interview is just a formality."

"I'm doing it on my own terms."

"Please. You're not controlling the image or the copyright. They pay you once then they can do whatever the fuck they want with it forever. That's why we need our own newspapers, magazines, and publishing companies."

"Yeah, yeah."

"And you got all your millions."

"So crucify me. You see the IRS' cut? The label's? The insurance company's from all the meds and doctor visits my crew needs every year? One of my men goes belly up and his whole family is on the line. His kids' school, his wife's car, the rent, mortgage or whatever, most of these millions I only see on paper when it's time for my accountant to itemize in April."

"My condolences. What's Tharpe's cut and all the other Blacks you lifted from?"

Jude started pulling her clothes on. She picked up the picture of the man from Lavender's wallet. "Nice of you to ask. Don't worry, they'll get theirs with interest." She walked over to Lavender, rubbing her bare foot against her leg. The word "housekeeping" echoed through the hallways as the maids called out at each door, trundling down the corridors, tapping, pausing, listening for movement on the other side, in advance of the whir of vacuum cleaners, the smack of mops and dirty towels and toilet paper being put on dispensers.

Jude leaned over, dangling the picture in Lavender's face. "Who's this? Hubby, boss or pops?"

"Nobody. What do you care?"

"Somebody you're fucking? Would've thought that you had higher standards. Or are you married and undercover. Always so pumped up about this women's libber bull crap, always riding everybody else about

218

what they need to do, seems strange that you'd be toting this little keep-sake around."

"Go on to your photo shoot."

"Tell me who he is."

The phone rang again. Someone pounded on the door. "Hold up, motherfuckers!" she shouted. "Tell me or get the fuck out of my room."

"What do you have to be jealous about?"

"You haven't written or run a word about me in that so-called paper of yours."

"Your mug is all over that paper in the entertainment section, Jude. Last week, front page, the road map to your blues revival, the studio musicians you're gonna use, your favorite fucking ice cream flavor, that bouffant drill team girl from your high school who dogged you and has a shrine to you in her house now. We got major hits from the big presses, even *Rolling Stone* and *Creem* were citing the last piece, tried to steal from it. You too drunk or stoned to remember that?"

Jude grinned. "Naw, just under your spell, darlin'." She reached down and massaged Lavender's leg, rubbing the calf, snatching away the covers. Lavender backed away from her, lumpy body pressed up against the headboard. The pounding on the door resumed, one of the roadies called out about the time, scolding Jude about the waiting crew and money going down the drain.

Jude ignored him, drawing closer to Lavender, the white calf under her thumb. "Never told you how much you favored my mother around the nose. Wonder if you look like her in other places."

"Jude... what the fuck."

"Give me a name, bitch."

"Kilroy."

Jude shook her head, squeezing the calf to a ripe pink. Lavender flinched. Jude squeezed again, putting her face up to Lavender's. "Cute. You know, not a single man on this tour wanted to fuck you. Means your asshole repellent mojo is working. That's a marketable talent. You should bottle that shit. Rest of the female world would pay for it. When they finally fire your ass you can live off the profits."

"Jude! Open this goddamn door!"

"Tell me that fucker's name or else you'll be out sleeping in the lobby tonight."

"That where you exile all your rejects?" Lavender yanked her leg away, jumping out of the bed. "I'll take my chances with them then."

Jude lunged for her. "C'mon, c'mon, c'mon now... wait. Thought you was tough as nails."

"Get off me," she snapped.

Jude encircled her with her arm, stroking her hair. "Don't be that way, ain't nice."

"Jude! You got five fucking minutes before they cancel, then the bill's on you! Photographer, designer, reporter, the label's docking you every cent."

Jude tickled Lavender's ear. "I need you to go with me to this thing."

"No."

"I don't feel safe."

"Not my problem."

"The way they look at me."

She released Lavender, raked her fingers through the mess of tumbleweed tangles in her hair, smeared Chapstick on her lips and pulled an orange smock over her head, sniffing under her arms for a presentability check. The pounding stopped. The roadie's retreating footsteps boomed down the hall on a trail of Welsh curses.

Jude looked at herself in the mirror, grabbing the whisky bottle on the dresser. She shoved it up to Lavender's mouth.

"How 'bout a little hit, huh? This'll brighten your day. Get you out of that bitchy mood."

Lavender slapped the bottle away. "It's ten o'clock in the fucking morning."

"C'mon, just a little itsy bitsy one. A little taste to bring you down to earth with the rest of us. Itsy bitsy spider. Remember that off key garbage your mama used to sing to you at bedtime?"

She pushed the bottle back to Lavender's lips, the liquid spilled down the front of her shirt, dribbling to the floor just as the housecleaner pushed the door open, the roadie behind her, flushed and rumpled.

"Ma'am, I—I'm sorry," she said. "He—he told me you were sick—"

"It's ok, sweetie, you can leave, ain't shit wrong with me." She took twenty dollars out of her pocket and gave it to the woman, gesturing to the roadie. "Told you to get the fuck out of here. Two more seconds and I'm going to have you arrested for trespassing." She grabbed a mop out of the woman's cart, shoving it at the man. "Not unless you want to get down on your hands and knees and clean this motherfucker up spic and span, get a taste of what she does to earn a living every day."

He knocked the mop away. "Right, I'll let Bill know you're pissing around, playing games and you got your checkbook ready." He turned, directing the housecleaner and her cart out of the door.

Lavender rustled up her purse, struggled into her pants, rubbing at the darkening stain on her press shirt, wishing she'd worn an underwire bra for the perp walk down the hall in front of the housecleaners from Jude's three-hundred dollar a night suite. She glanced furtively at the cleaning women, tiptoeing in her stocking feet. They went about their business, making a show of not seeing the dumb ass gringa with a middling job. She slunk past the ice machine, getting nauseous, thinking about how she was a pig's whisker away from the unemployment line and no better than a common star fucker.

The women turned up their music, moving in and out of the rooms unfazed as Jude opened the door and screamed, "Like I said, it all goes to the Black kids, every motherfucking penny! None of them Port Arthur termites'll be able to touch it!"

Divinity's morning began with the return of the nimbus cloud that had been following her, promising retribution. It watched her pick out her lucky teal suit and a pair of matching hose. Swooned over the open toe Empire State building pumps she wore to tower over minions and crunch church board functionaries. It hovered as she scanned the chalkboard in the front office with all the names of new subscribers, the women Patton had triumphantly crowed about. The coup of getting each of them to tithe twenty-five bucks a month in exchange for a discount on personalized prayer pillows and a promise to snap up more converts from their rarefied corner of the world on Nutmeg Lane in Arkadelphia. What a blessing to have found these sisters in arms. A revelation for Nutmeg's champion bid whist team who'd heard about the sharp as a tack woman

221

preacher from Miz Bradford, dazzled by the swift returns Father God had given her. She'd petitioned Him for a burgundy Oldsmobile, then inherited one from a dead uncle ten days later, just as her prayer pillow had foretold.

In her daydreams, Divinity reached up and grabbed the nimbus, pounding it to the ground until it split into toy soldiers, wooden arms swinging to "His Eye is on the Sparrow", Pastor's preferred grooming song. It was the first one she'd heard Rory play, flawless on the church dais, looking older and more righteous than everybody combined, wearing a handmade crepe dress with frilly sleeves, the junior usher girls riveted by how fast she moved up and down the fretboard.

Divinity paced behind her desk, sifting through newspaper clippings about the expansion of the complex and all the kids with leukemia the ministry had spiritually adopted. Local coverage, fourth page, buried at the bottom, riddled with typos. White lady condescension over the various and sundry doings down in Negro-dom, a career of sniffing out titillating charity opps. Patton led Rory into the room, then went to prep the call center workers for that evening's pitch.

The two women faced each other. Silent for a beat, taking a match to the girls they'd been, warming up next to the bonfire.

"Sit down, sit down," Divinity said. "Made it without a hitch?"

"Let's just say we made it."

"Y'all doing ok in the motel?"

"We have a nice view of the dumpster and the ravine."

"We'll work on it. We got five churches lined up the next two weeks so all you'll be doing is resting your head in that joint. Highflyer like you is used to that."

"Don't flatter me to get me to settle."

"Wouldn't dream of it."

"What kind of rehearsal space can we get between now and then?"

"We'll set you up in the sanctuary at our church downtown. Best acoustics in the city. Your boy Card make it yet?"

"Yeah, he checked in last night with us."

"Folks still have some allegiance to his Motown work. He'll bring out a nice crowd if he can stay upright and focused."

"He will. You seem real preoccupied with him."

"Was one of my idols back in the day when I dabbled in a little singing. Good-looking man. Thought I was gonna have a private audition with him and Gordy, maybe replace that skinny gal what's her name in the Supremes. Delusional."

Rory took in the pictures, the trophies, the certificates of honor and distinction choking the walls. "Looks like you rebounded just fine from that."

"Dashed dreams can be a good thing. Otherwise, I would've been just one more mediocre Black girl with a bad voice pining for fame and fortune in that den of sin Detroit."

"Now you're in this den of sin, barely moved an inch."

Divinity stopped and leaned back on the desk, twisting up her mouth. She picked up a White Pages directory and thumbed through it, the teal suit coat bunching up around her waist. "Tarnation. Still got a way with words I see."

"How do you know what I still got? You never knew me."

"That's true, I'd never make that claim. Who'd pretend to know the maestro who got the fuck out of here when the getting was good?"

Rory flinched.

"Oh please, don't act so virginal."

"Thought you was a good woman of God."

"I am. Or at least I aspire to be. The language goes with the aspiration. The men who claim to be called are all about hypocrisy, show, double standards when eyes are on them. Me, I try not to let too much daylight pass between what I say and what I do. God forgives fucks up. We're imperfect humans. Primates. Say a few prayers, all is forgiven." She gestured to the sky.

Rory smirked. "I'm no monkey."

A sliver of skin appeared at the edge of the teal. Divinity shifted slightly to adjust her coat before Rory caught it, too late, the watchful disdain on her face hardening.

"What do you have those women in there doing?" Rory asked.

Divinity skimmed through the White pages. "Going through a modified version of this. Dialing every working number in the directory with a female name."

"For?"

"Outreach. Connection to the ministry. We had two companies close and lay off nearly three hundred workers, and guess who got the brunt of it. Last hired first fired as usual," she closed the book and put it in a drawer. "Heard you shut things down in Memphis not crossing picket lines."

"Yep. Probably cost me a contract with the House."

"True, but as Jesus said, 'It's more blessed to give than to receive.' You took a stand, sacrificed, our people know how much these big arenas shit on Negroes and don't nobody want to see a show fronted by a scab for mega millionaires."

Rory stared out of the window, into the darkness behind Divinity, to the lip of a ravine flowing silent and sure, water closing tight over junked auto parts, sunken balls, frisbees, slingshots, bones shifting in puzzle pieces, settling into the rich silt. Rumors of babies dumped, enough to fill a nursery, drowned after the only abortion clinic for fifty miles was bombed.

Divinity swiveled around, following her gaze to the ravine. "Clean as a pig sty. We're working on fixing it, though. Developing it, so kids can have somewhere to go play… Is this place, the city, like you pictured it?"

"Dunno. Ask me in a week after it's sunk in. I didn't have no picture really, just want to be back on stage doing new material—"

"For Black ears."

"Yeah."

"That's a beautiful thing. Folks' is hungry for it, gonna be the shot in the arm they need. So, here's how I see the concerts." She took out a diagram of a stage. "For the first set—"

Rory held up her hand. "I don't do diagrams. We like to keep it loose."

"And we like order and structure. Ensures the set's tight, on time and we can get the audience in and out for the second one. That one tends to go longer with all the testifyin' and fallin' out. Besides, we have three sponsors lined up."

"What kind of stuff they selling?"

"They manufacture our spiritual collection. All the goodies callers get for being faithful. Gotta cross-pollinate, cross-promote, or we'll be a few thou in the hole. Your buddies in arena rock have got that down to a science. By the way, does Card sing? Put him up front. Good looking Negro like that needs to be up front, especially if he can sing."

"My piano player, Butch, sings backup. Card plays bass, he's already up front and I prefer him keeping his mouth shut… Did he put you up to that question?"

"I've never spoken directly to the man."

"Him stirring up mess with my road manager cost me eight hundred bucks and grief with some white bitches in Mobile."

"That so. I don't want to get all up into your personal business, but don't you think it's time for some new blood? You got all these white boys riding the gravy train and what are they doing for you? Where's the quid pro quo? Now, Card might be a hard ass, but he's got genuine God-given talent and he's easy on the eyes. Easy on the eyes and Motown will help us sell more tickets. Besides, these kids in the new generation don't know your music, or you, from Beethoven or Mozart. It's Greek to them. Truth be told, some of our people have tunnel vision, limited mindsets, can't see past what they've been spoon-fed by these grinning gold-teeth deejays giving away Cadillacs and cruises to the first caller. Hell, you know how much those shiteaters make in Top 40 radio? The big ones in the syndicated markets?"

"Mooch Morrison's raking in six figures basically being a front for the record companies. He can make or break a record with the flick of his wrist. Won't push my singles because the House and all the majors have him in their hip pockets."

"And Justis is the dime store jewel in the crown. I'd rather eat glass than listen to the crap he's peddling. Got no message of any relevance to our people. Highlights again why we gotta do for self, start our own. Like I said, what have these punk managers done for you lately to earn their keep while you're working to the bone, fighting for your publishing rights?" She picked up a plaque from the Budding Black Entrepreneurs' Society on the desk, scowled at it and put it down. "Punk managers and punk men. Being on the road with all those men in your band. Don't know how you do it. Must be tempting sometimes to wring their no account necks."

Rory looked at her hard, wanting to agree, but wary. There was always an angle with Divinity, a slow burn cat and mouse game that got her eyes in the back of her head flashing. Ringing phones and the quick and dirty cadence of scripts being read and improvised bounced off the walls in the building. "Men are fucked up, but women ain't no picnic neither," she said.

"You got me there, but we ain't out lootin' and raping. Who stole your publishing rights out from under your nose?"

"And who was sitting up depositing the checks in the big house when we was being looted and raped?"

Divinity clapped her hands. "I'll give you that one… Now, about those women in the next room. Some of them got laid off from the plant and they're working overtime here, and Jesus knows what other jobs in addition to this one. But my goal is to fix it so they won't have to be on their backs or get on their hands and knees and suck dick to make a living and feed their babies. Better thank Jesus that you got the talent you do. If you didn't have the touch with your music who knows what you might've had to stoop to."

"Never that."

"How do you know? Mary Magdalen got redeemed, so nobody is out of Jesus' reach. You of all people should know, given your predilections."

"What are you talking about?"

"I forgive all my ladies their lowest sin so they can get on with their lives."

"*You* forgive them? Quite sure that helps keep them motivated to work long hours in that boiler room of yours. You shit out of the same hole everybody else does. What gives you the right to sit in judgment—"

"My motto is live and let live. See, unlike the labels you're groveling to get signed by I'd never piss on you for being queer. Hell, any woman with some sense who ain't hanging up under some man gets called that. Far as my ladies are concerned, I pay more than minimum wage. They get bus passes. We do carpools, and they got daycare for their babies if they need it."

"And how do you manage that supreme generosity?"

Divinity got up, perching on the edge of the desk again. "A coven, some white women, and a few black ones, with open checkbooks and closed mouths."

Rory sneered. "So, all this is white women's doing? You rely on them you might as well be on your back selling yourself."

"This ain't all white women's doing. They pony up and keep it moving. This church's forged in our sweat. They don't have any say in how we run it. When Black folks started the Back to Liberia movement here in the twenties white folks ponied up for that too."

"Ain't surprising, they shipped us over here, then when niggers got disposable they wanted to ship us back. You're fucking naïve. Show me a white woman who don't want nothing from a black one and I'll show you a faithful Judas. They're natural born thieves."

"What? Like your very own Miss Jude?"

"I ain't at her mercy."

"To hear her tell it at the Nashville concert, she brought you back from the dead."

"According to you I'm still dead."

Divinity smiled, listening. A whir of slamming car doors and goodnights sounded outside. "You know, I rather enjoyed that trip. Interesting seeing you in your element." She reached over and took Rory's hand, probing her wrist. "There's a pulse there, or at least the beginning of one."

Snatches of R&B music fizzed up over starting engines. Roberta Flack and Donnie Hathaway tangoed through the air, crooning "Where Is the Love". Rory stiffened in Divinity's grip. She was always listening for herself in the hum drum noise of the everyday; half vain, half scared.

"Relax," Divinity said. "The rat race ain't going nowhere."

Patton bustled in with her clipboard, stopping short at the sight of Divinity holding Rory's wrist. "Telling fortunes again, Pastor?"

"Thought I asked you to knock when I'm in a business meeting."

Patton dropped the clipboard down on the desk. "I will, when you're in one."

Rory withdrew her hand. Rain rivulets shimmered on the window.

"You'll have to excuse Ms. Patton," Divinity said sharply. "She gets antsy when she's kept out of the loop too long. Right, baby? We've had a lot of vultures descend and start pecking around for leftovers. Present company excluded, of course. Patton, Rory and her boys need to use the sanctuary to rehearse. Can you set up a time for them? We're bussing in two congregations for the opening performance."

Ghost Notes

CARD WATCHED THE Little Rock lightning crack through the sky and took another bite of his orange. Rind, sticky pulp, seeds, and all. He'd read somewhere that rind was medicinal. Would keep the doctor and the quacks away, would heal his small intestine, make it museum ready, something modern science could slap in a jar, keep him buzzing through the night on the bass guitar when everybody else was six feet under and punked out by God.

Heaven's a piss pipe dream mothafuckas.

He didn't know what he was doing now, other than hanging on by a thread. Following the others. Treading water. Drowning in a sanctified vat of wishful thinking. Matching Mick's desperation pound for pound with something mangier. Rory was still mad at him for the Mobile shit. If she docked him it would take months to dig out of it. He looked down at his hands, blistered, beat up, wanting to call the hooker service, tap the business card he'd found stuck on the gas station bathroom door when he was buying beer and Cheetos. He went back and forth on whether or not to do it. Telling himself not this time, Cardinal Jefferson the III. Not this time, son, be upright, be moral, be a secret knight in shining armor for the sake of your baby girl, nestled in her bed next to her mama wearing big fat foam curlers, snoring one fish two fish red fish blue fish.

He hadn't meant to stay gone from them for so long. Hadn't meant to become one in a long line of men who didn't stick around, who fumbled promises, became a shadow choking out the sun in their lives. As the years rolled by, the gigs dwindled and he drank more, it got easier to blow off picking up the phone. The next wasted day turning into the next and then the next. He told himself that he didn't deserve them, that they were better off without the rotting carcass of his body. The fungal regret seeping into every memory, every blown opportunity, every judgment, every millisecond he'd been smashed under a factory manager or producer's bootheel for being an untamable nigger.

The way he just looked at you with his eyes. Daring you to say his timing was off.

The band was promised a big crowd for opening night at the tabernacle. Top billing before the organ grinders, jugglers, and flamethrowers. Part of him looked forward to dazzling the holy rollers. They all loved them some Motown. Fucked to it, daydreamed to it, crapped to it, procrastinated to it, blew a month's paycheck to it, rode elevators to it up and down in an endless death spiral of work and snatched leisure time. Yes siree, Bob, the whole world loved it some Motown.

He unzipped his pants. He couldn't get hard if all of the Confederacy was forcing him to at gunpoint. The room was cold, his mind going in circles, fixing on the last conversation he had with the Motown accountant. It was the day he'd been purged out of the system. His old employee number reassigned to a desk clerk. For five years, he'd had his very own employee number. Seven golden digits. It was a passport to prove he wasn't just a temp, a shrug of the shoulder paid under the table with a few sticky mob boss Benjamins. For a while, he'd acted like he was the big shit. Proud of the normalcy of having a place to be in the morning, a clock to punch, a biweekly check he could use to build up his credit. Cocky proud. Treating aunts, uncles, even second and third cousins to Sunday catfish dinners, bowling parties, shopping sprees at the first boutiques that allowed Negroes to try on clothes. At the time, he thought it was all gonna lead to something better, deeper, permanent. His name in Klieg light white on his own record album. A roomful of studio musicians at his beck and call. A producer who'd snap, crackle, and pop to his commands. A pad that he could put first and last on, decorate a little, ride into the new decade. His baby girl and boys properly situated with their own separate rooms, weekends at the park, the roller rink, wherever, whenever.

Rain punched down through the roof. A biblical bullfrog-hopping flood.

Card ran outside with his shirt open, savoring the rain on his skin.

❖

The spit curl ushers took tickets at the church entrance, dancing a little to keep warm in the chill when no one was looking. Headmistress Divinity, as they called her behind her back, would've frowned at any deviance, wanting them to come correct, be upright, ladylike, inscrutable at all times lest the outside world gain the upper hand. Black queens can't be no slouches, she scolded. The queens she crowned feared and loved her, talking out of both sides of their mouths. Some were on loan from the call centers. Some were regular parishioners of Faith Reigns Supreme Tabernacle, hot for a quick lick of fame, a gilded night out, a diversion from the workaday dreary. *'Member when we'd close the joint dancing cheek to cheek to Motown and baby boy with the mole on his lip lost his virginity,* they whispered to each other, snapping up tickets with airy Kool-Aid grins. Later, they'd be raffling off an eight-track player, blue velvet slippers, a toaster oven, a collection of Divinity's limited edition inspiration tapes; words of wisdom interspersed with her trilling hymns like an opera singer. No downtrodden Negro spirituals for her. The church had been scrubbed to a zenith gleam by the new janitor, recently recruited to do a Saturday morning shift in the call center for extra cash.

The buzz in the church would be about what Divinity was wearing, who she'd have in her entourage, the subject of her sermon, then, the new band—in that order. Stragglers squeezed into the balcony pews, slipping their platinum Divinity fans into their purses. The thermostat had been edged down to teeth-chattering discomfort to keep folks from dozing off or, worse, sweating out their press and curls in the slithery grip of the Holy Ghost.

Mick dropped Rory off in front of the church, driving around back to park so the band could unload equipment. The lot was bumper to bumper with American beaters, Datsuns, Caddies, and the odd Mercedes. An attendant waved Mick to a spot by the alley, turning his flashlight on him warily as he, Butch, and Thurston staggered out of the car.

"Y'all comin' for the show?"

"Yep, we are the show," Thurston said.

The man looked them up and down, snarling. "Rory Tharpe's the show. Y'all backing her? Stage entrance is right there."

Inside, the curtain was down. The choir bustled back and forth in chiffon robes, swigging down honey and lemon tonics for their throats as the choir director herded them into formation. Patton appeared from the hallway, tapping at her clipboard like a metronome.

"I trust you're settled?" she asked Mick.

"Just got here. We need the drumkit and Rory's setup in front like we arranged it last night."

"Pastor Divinity wants a different configuration."

"What?"

"The choir needs to be centered. The band's going to be stage left. Miss Tharpe will play by the pulpit. The Pastor wants to be able to call audience members up to the stage, give 'em wide berth to move around, feel the spirit, can't have folks tripping on wires and cables while they're—"

"Getting happy?" Card walked up with his bass slung over his shoulder, face puffy, sleepless, worn slacks and miss-matched shirt, pleather maroon jacket and tube gym socks rustled up from the bottom of his duffel bag after he couldn't procrastinate anymore about coming. He hated churches. Hated the sight, smell, and taste of them. Their overbearing vampiric presence, gobbling every Negro street corner in sluttish command. Hated the way the howling bawling reverends, elders, and prophets made him feel tiny, a fetid pervert troll. He'd trashed their authority a thousand times in his teenage head when his grandmother emptied her rainy day coffers to bankroll yet another building emergency that God couldn't pay for.

"We don't get 'happy' here," Patton said.

"Oh, that's far too uncouth and niggerish, right?"

Patton took a step back, tightening the clipboard to her chest. "There aren't any niggers here, Mr. Jefferson, so that terminology doesn't apply, unless, of course, you consider yourself one."

"I ain't too proud to consider myself one. Those considered to be 'niggers' were the field hands. And, I got news for you, all that strutting and preening you're doing with Pastor Divinity... the second you leave all them philanthropists and big donors you're cozying up to, they got nicknames for you—Nigger one and Nigger two."

The choir director ambled over to them. He clutched two music stands, broadcasting his comments to the swirling crowd of chorus members, techs and musicians. "A few of our homegrown prodigies will be performing this evening. "His Eye is on the Sparrow", duet on flute and

French horn. Baby geniuses straight from the projects. Pastor Divinity paid to send 'em to a conservatory school in Sweden. We're blessed to have that kind of talent right here in the community."

"Ainsley, this is Cardinal Jefferson," Patton said.

"Card Jefferson, the ace bassist? We're all fans of your great work."

Patton cut him off. "Right. Ainsley, can you make sure all our people are in place, please? Not trying to have a CP time situation for the first concert of the tour."

"Of course not, Miss Patton."

"Appreciate you, brother. Always. God is good."

"Yes," he hesitated, then clapped his hands. "Places, ladies and gentleman, places, p-r-o-n-t-o, get your behinds in gear, curtain's up in ten minutes, sopranos, altos, front, row and center!"

Card smirked, propping his bass against an empty chair. "Trained seals and monkeys. God is so good."

Rory watched them from the wings. Mick dragged their amps in, directing one of the techs in curt bellows as Patton looked on disapprovingly. The choir massed in a semi-circle for a quick prayer then fell into position, robes aflutter, pomade christening the air. They turned in unison to see Divinity's entrance, like Venus docking at a stormy port on a shell.

Divinity gripped the pulpit, patted her forehead with a silk handkerchief and stepped off the stage into the audience.

"That David and Goliath story was going through my mind all night while writing this sermon. See, I had something a lot more sophisticated to speak on, y'all. I was going to dazzle you with Greek philosophy and an analysis of the upcoming election. Was going to let loose with some flowery words about who's trying to steal the White House this time. Y'all know our people, enslaved Black folks, Atlantic Creoles, Maroons, beautiful blue blacks descended from Goree Island? Y'all know they laid every rusty brick of that place, right? Built it from the ground up. David and Goliath. Little hombre had his slingshot hidden behind his back, ripe and ready for that behemoth. That's where we are now, sisters and brothers. Banks refused our first four loan applications. The first building over on Cimarron got flooded. The first floor plans for the new center got stolen. And y'all know the rest. Moral? Beware of things that come early and easy. Riches without struggle, without sacrifice, is the devil's secret calling card. Somebody want to hand you something you haven't worked, haven't sweated and bled for, better slap that hand and keep on moving."

She paused and looked around, acknowledging the seismic nods and murmurs. She clenched her fist to her mouth in a bittersweet smile.

"So, the boys told me when I was little that there were certain games I couldn't play. Certain lines I couldn't cross. I was quarantined because I had a... certain mix of chromosomes. Quarantined and dirty 'cause I was born wrong, born in sin. Sound familiar, sisters? We start out paces behind the men because of Eve's ruckus, spend our whole lives playing catch up. Again, David and Goliath. Hook up that slingshot. That's why my calling has been providing opportunities for women and their babies. When I go to meet Him at the end of walking my mile through the Valley of Death, the question will be, how did I serve them? Our telephone ministry just signed up its one thousandth member in Hot Springs. Subscribers who want an open pipeline to the good news. Straight, no chaser, no filter. Now we're expanding to the Midwest." She thumped the mic twice, squared her shoulders, waiting for the applause, gesturing grandly toward Rory.

"And this genius woman here is going to help us get to where we need to be. Grew up right here out east in Cotton Plant. Cut her teeth playing and singing in all our churches from sunup to sundown when she was knee high to the belly of a grasshopper. Us old-timers were raised on her music, easy as Sunday grits and biscuits. Brothers and sisters, please welcome Miss Rory Tharpe and her band to our humble service!"

Rory stumbled into the light, strumming her electric guitar in warm-up to a volley of polite handclaps, whirring fans with Divinity's mug on them, youngsters' bubble gum gnashing boredom.

At the back of the church, Katy marveled at the rainbow-hued glut of tired, over-rouged faces bristling with judgment; the daughters, granddaughters, nieces of all the women who had pissed on her behind her back generations ago when no organist east of the Mississippi could touch her. She heard two men whispering to each other about Divinity's intro. A thin one with slicked back turpentine hair and a rosewood cane, a plump one busting out of his custom-made suspenders. They were rival pastors from across town, guarding their attendance numbers like stock tips, hustlers who'd bootstrapped up from tinpot storefronts to five thousand square feet apiece.

"Strutting 'cause she just got that loan," the thin one said.

"Didn't get it yet. Still in the hunt as far as I know."

"Well, unless she's screwing one of them white boys at the Chamber of Commerce it might be a snowball's chance in hell, now. Pun fully intended."

"How you figure?"

"Look who she dragged onto the stage to so-called boost her profile. Ragtag and homo as they come. All of 'em. Every last one. Bulldagger turned her back on sanctified music 'cause it wasn't making her enough loot to keep her girls in diamonds and furs. Damn disgrace."

Katy jammed her foot into the plump one's gabardine bound thigh, testing it to see if he could feel any of it, a thrill and a letdown knowing he couldn't. She sliced the pulpy flesh into bacon strips sizzling on the floor. The two of them kept whispering, unmoved, ignoring the stares of the women next to them, as Rory ripped into the Charley Patton song, "Prayer of Death". The band struggled to keep up with her on the bridge:

If I never, never see you anymore. I'll meet you on that other shore.

Baby girl's fucking with me again, Katy thought, digging her heel into the thin one's ass and giving it a twist. A twist to send him into the night, in the path of a speeding car, a stray bullet, a samurai's knife. If she were dead, she could at least have that power. Otherwise, what was the mofo point?

All evening, Divinity had been watching Card and licking her lips. He moved like the daddy she'd only seen in old pictures her mother kept at the bottom of her nightstand drawer. A particular one from right before the time when he took off for Chicago to take a job at a big car battery manufacturer, or so her grandmother said. A failed preacher from a barnstorming line of failed preachers in the Father Divine vein. Thus, her name. A redbone, freckly, snaggle tooth pontificating-from-sunup-to-sundown dreamer who thought light bright skin and smooth talk would get him over. Divinity was her daddy through and through. Minus the skin and the mad love for car battery guts. They moved like two people separated at birth and it was this that had her licking her lips over Card. Mildly, just mildly distracted from her sermon and taking the pulse of the sanctuary to see what was landing and what was bombing with the audience.

She'd seen the pastors from Ezekiel and the Holy Ten churches hovering in the balcony doing intel. It meant she was getting closer. They wouldn't have come if they hadn't felt threatened by the chance that her development loan would go through. They were all grins and shucking in the church council meetings. All good, down home Christian solidarity when they were sitting up in her face. She'd gone to school with them, after all. Led prayers for the brothers they'd lost stationed in Hamburg during World War II. Voted "most eloquent" in the yearbook, spreading Jesus' word in the midst of grand tragedy with Negro families half wiped out and still fighting the government decades later over death benefits.

Her home church had taken up the crusade, every last parishioner chipping in for the political delegations to go lobby at the Capitol building. Junior pastors, ushers, Sunday school teacher aides, and apprentices stayed up late making banners and petitions for the cause, nodding off over glue and poster board, snoring into lukewarm plates of franks and beans. Whoever stayed vertical until the crack of dawn was deemed the most ride or die dedicated to Christ and the race. Whoever was committed to weathering the murderous dawn when the wandering hands of the junior pastors took on lives of their own, probing, swearing her to silence. That girl would be sanctified in the eyes of God.

Ezekiel and Holy Ten didn't even have the gumption to greet her before the concert. They slithered out with the oldest, most venerable, most tithing-besotted women they could find; hellhound ears pealed for stray gossip about Divinity's progress, the haul from that month's services, and who she was screwing this time. Ezekial and Holy Ten had built up a whole industry fantasizing a white cigar-chomping mogul with a pimply ass, fat checkbook and bottomless libido coasting on jungle fever.

Rory took the stage for an acoustic solo, head down, doing slide guitar like there weren't four-hundred eyeballs on her and she was playing deep in a crater on Neptune. Her breath slowed. The audience's faces shrank to starlit dots on a busted canvas as she reworked "Sparrow" into the rolling jaunt of "Swallow You Whole".

I'm alive! she screamed in her head, certain that they could hear her, certain that Russ and all the instigators from the House were closing in, certain that the choir director, bowing and scraping, would rise at Divinity's command and yank her off the stage with a noose.

"This one's for the industry jerk offs," she croaked, barely audible, into the mic. A gasp came from the front seats, the choir director quickly signaling the singers to start up again, trilling to the rafters in the Key of C.

"Good job, tonight," Divinity proclaimed after the flurry of the last encore. "Done us proud as usual. Trixie, Evelyn, y'all had Jesus spinning in bliss with those trills. Demetrius, you knocked the whole back row on their butts on that encore." She stopped, watching Patton huddle with Ainsley in the wings. The choir members braced themselves, flicking off the praise. They could set their stopwatches for the moment when the sourness crept in, the nitpicking over a missed cue or phrase, a blemish on her otherwise perfect soldiers.

It had gone off without a hitch, except for Rory's transgression.

"All y'all acquitted yourselves well, especially backing the new band." Divinity continued. "When we go to the next church home in Arkadelphia, we gotta move as one big united front." She spread her arms wide with an added flourish, scanning all the choir members for eye contact. A few parishioners lingered at the foot of the stage to get their programs signed. "Ms. Tharpe's been on the road most of her life and we're blessed to have her. Specially blessed to have the talent she brought straight from the Motor City. Now, y'all can say you heard two legends play up close and personal in your lifetime."

"Format gonna be the same for the next go around?" one of the choir members asked.

"We're still calibrating that," Divinity coughed. "We'll be doing tents in the more rural parts of the state. Taking it right to the people."

"Thought these were the people," Rory said.

Divinity took the parishioners' programs and signed them, handing them to Rory to sign. "They are, but we got the home team advantage here. We're a known quantity. Out hither and yon it's a different story. More competition, more doubts, more second-guessing," she leaned into Rory. "And folks ain't going to let the profane mess y'all pull in the so-called 'industry' slide."

"That means you better watch yourself then," Rory said.

"Ouch," Card said. "Well, with a busted steeple on every corner and no jobs in sight it's not surprising that y'all are in hand-to-hand combat for converts."

"Busted steeples? Where you been hanging out, Mr. Jefferson? Maybe that's the way they do it in Detroit—"

"I ain't from there, not originally that is."

Rory signed the programs and handed them back. "Nobody was. Y'all fled out there looking for jobs and a better way and found out it was just as fucked up as—'scuse me, Rev, ladies—as this place. But, remember, that's why we're here, Cardinal. To redeem the good old Southern Baptist tradition of uplifting the Negro race."

The choir held its breath as Mick chuckled from the back, hoisting Thurston's drum kit on his stomach while Butch steadied it.

"Get yourselves some food downstairs and we'll see everyone in the morning," Patton announced, sending the choir to the exits in a murmuring mass of disdain.

"We gonna get the travel allowance Pastor promised?" a voice sputtered.

"It'll all be taken care of," Patton said breezily. "When have we not stepped up for y'all and kept our word?"

The call center women and ushers had laid out a lukewarm feast in the assembly room. Divinity watched Card trip past the procession at the buffet line, plate piled high with mashed potatoes and pot roast gravy, desiccated pieces of icebox lemon cake leftover from a bake sale. Everything was to be recycled for economy. Lean, mean, no waste. Even when the bootleg rivals at Ezekiel and Holy Ten were spending hundreds they didn't have on benefit dinners and charity confabs Divinity was counting every toilet paper roll and light switch flip.

"Enjoying yourself?" she asked Card.

"Growing boy needs good grub." He took a bite of pot roast, licking his fingers. "Shit's top notch. Girls here can burn. No surprise, I guess. What else they got to do in this place but cook, clean, work, fuck, repeat it all over again and go out of their minds planning to escape."

Divinity accepted a piece of cake from one of the congregants, stabbing the dry lump with her plastic fork. "You got some kind of mouth on you, Mr. Cardinal. Yeah, we put our heads down and work. Stayed here, toughed it out while y'all fled up North. So, did your mama or your daddy give you that uppity name? Sounds like a redneck's version of a fancy name."

"Neither. Both of 'em died in an explosion at the pajama factory they was working at in '34. Some local cracker blew it up for the insurance. Sweethearts holding hands until the bitter end. Or at least that's my dream. Grandpa gave me the 'redneck fancy' name."

"Sorry to hear that."

"Bethel New Canaan Church would always give my grandparents a bucket of hand-me-downs, powdered milk, and soup crackers during Christmas. We were right grateful. Mind if I take some of the pot roast back to the motel for later?"

"Take as much as you need. Maybe that'll make up for the powdered milk."

Card grinned. It was the first time she'd seen his teeth. White, straight, electrifying. She waited for him to smile again, to eat with abandon. Thrilling to it. Catching herself.

"Scarred for life, Rev," he said, laughing. "Once you get that taste in your mouth…"

Divinity walked behind the buffet table and started helping the women serve. "Agreed. Those Bethel-ites should be ashamed. So many of 'em traffick in that kind of tokenism. Can't give folks three square meals with some real protein then they should hang it up."

"Amen," the woman next to her said, ladling green beans onto the plate of a beaming white man. The man quivered with glee at the big portions, the hot meat, the sauces glistening in steamy puddles.

"Want to commend you on your performance," he said to Card. "I'm Josiah Sprat from the Chamber of Commerce. The pastor really did a number pulling this together."

Card eyed the door, looking around for Rory. "Oh yeah, she did."

Sprat snapped his fingers to a tune in his head. "Always loved me some Motown growing up. Born and bred on it. Soundtrack of my life. 'My Girl' was the theme song at my wedding. Protested to 'Ball of Confusion' at a Greenpeace rally with my oldest kid. Salad days, back when we were big liberals. Leaning towards Reagan now, though. Carter's wrecked this country. Run it into the ground with the tax and spend. Can't go wrong with new blood every four years if you're in a fiscal hole, right?"

"Depends on what method works best to plug the hole and how big it is," Divinity retorted. "Fortunately, we're bipartisan when it comes to the future of Revivals," she said, as she turned her attention back to Card. "Josiah is on our development team."

"Right-o." Sprat put the plate up to his nose and took a luxurious sniff. "Mr. Jefferson, it was a pleasure. And I hope, maybe, we can do business in the very near future. There are a lot of possibilities for cross-promotion through some of our companies here. We're always looking for innovative ways to boost the city and the region. We need musicians for commercials, corporate functions, press junkets, you name it. I know I don't have to tell you that music is the universal language. Don't matter whether you speak Oriental or English. Why, just look at how that disco thingamajig is practically taking over the world."

He wiggled his oily finger in a mock dance move and shuffled off.

Divinity put down her serving spoon. "Boy gets real excited when there's food around."

Card dug his fork into the mashed potatoes. "Like I said, this is some good shit."

"Cardinal. Watch your mouth in God's house... Sprat took a shine to you. Might be something we could parlay into a longer term gig."

"Longer term's gotta have at least six figures attached to it, and how does 'we' factor into it?"

"Come to my office tomorrow and we can discuss it."

Rory walked into the room, a cap smashed on her head over the pageboy wig she'd taken to wearing in public. She noted Card and Divinity huddling, the crafty glitter of their eyes as they chattered, sized each other up. She joined the buffet line, hot, queasy, oblivious to the well wishers murmuring about her performance. The ranks had begun to thin, as folks gave their regards to Divinity, plunked down a few more last minute donation envelopes, and headed to their cars with to-go plates.

"Rory knows the address," Divinity said. "Both of y'all should come along." She nodded towards Mick, hunkered down, sipping fruit punch on the other side of the room. "Leave the white lawn jockey home."

Big Shit Immortality

WHEN THE BUS HIT the I-40, and the highway sign said Little Rock in six miles, Sid's stomach knotted up at the cannon blast of being back home. Torpedoed by the first sludgy creep of menstrual cramps and anticipation, her seatmate's rag tag Beach Boys' marathon bleeding from his headphones into her ear. All the people that she knew who liked that stuff were dead. End Times white people smeared like margarine in the Texas desert. Fraudulent motherfuckers who called her parents 'brother' and 'sister' then took the lightest work details at the church.

The knife kept watch on the seatmate and the buses' murky reptile universe. She'd pulled it on an old man who'd tried to follow her in Boise, fondling it as she got off the bus, her aunt Zinnia rolling up in a borrowed Buick, pissed, chain smoking, late for work. She'd placed a collect call in Oklahoma begging her aunt to come get her. Zinnia, the oldest of her mother's sisters, the musical one who didn't want shit to do with churches or getting religion. The penny pinching, twenty questions one who scoffed at the End Times revival when Sid's mother joined, talking big talk instead about buying a record store, chain.

"Girl, you need you a bath, pronto, and look at that nappy hair," she said under ten pounds of blue eyeliner, gathering Sid up by the collar of her t-shirt in a stiff embrace. "You eat anything?"

Sid showed her a crumpled Snickers candy bar.

"You got to eat something more than that." She pulled out of the lot, kids' toys rolling across the backseat. "I got work now so I'll have to take you with me."

"What do you do?"

"Sell crap to people on the phone." She frowned, the radio squawking news about a Watergate crook who was just let out of prison. She turned the dial, shaking her head to the strains of "Where Is the Love".

"Heard this mush five times already today. Shame, though. Singer killed himself jumping out a building a few weeks ago. Thought white people had hooked a wire up to his brain trying to steal his stuff."

Patton decreed that phones shouldn't be allowed to ring more than twice. Folks had emergencies, overdrawn bank accounts, evictions, terminal illnesses, busted water heaters, flooded bathrooms, stove fires, or more simple calamities like ant infestations that needed troubleshooting. Any second wasted was a second the big white boy televangelists could jump on and ride into the sunset with folks' hard-earned ducats.

Besides, phones that rang more than twice made Divinity's skin crawl.

Rory and Card drove up. Divinity listened to their footfalls as they made their way to the locked security door, then buzzed them in.

"Nice digs," Card said, plopping into one of the high-backed vinyl chairs in Divinity's conference room. "How you manage this?"

"The pastor's an entrepreneur. Or didn't you know?" Rory said.

"That don't tell me nothing."

Divinity smiled expansively at the two of them. "Skeptical's a good fit on you. Means you're hungry."

Card widened his legs and leaned back in the chair. "Funny."

"I like that in a man... or a business partner."

"What you got in mind? Spit it out."

"Rory says you're not under contract."

"Been gigging with her for practically a year freelance."

"And before that?"

"Session work. Clubs, odds, and ends."

"Ever held down a regular day job?"

"This an interview?"

"What other marketable skills do you have?"

"Lady, I can play ghost notes with my teeth, behind my back and with one hand tied."

Rory watched a pack of squirrels dart through the garbage-studded trees in the ravine outside the window. "What are you getting at, Divinity?"

Divinity paused. She picked up a letter opener and polished it with the lace handkerchief in her breast pocket. "You're out in the streets for how many days a year? One-hundred? Two hundred? Out there making jack or less than jack. Aren't y'all tired of it? I would be. This is the era of enterprise. Tycoon motherfuckers and the peckerwoods who're scared of us and want to be like the tycoon motherfuckers are gonna elect Reagan. I can smell it. They're primed. And if we don't have our own industries in place we're going to be shark bait even more than we are now."

"Hollywood cowboy's got an itchy trigger finger and an end of the world complex," Rory said. "Whites like his anti-communist big dick of the Western world thing."

Divinity let out a controlled chuckle. "And all the little brown countries he wants to crush in the process. I like it when you get political. Card's the cynic and you're the pundit. Well, you both got more play out of last night than in two months being trained seals in Jude Justis' shadow. They loved you. Loved y'all, and ticket sales were up twenty percent from our last revival concert."

"We ain't no trained seals," Card fumed.

Rory reached for the pitcher of water in the center of the table, pouring herself and Card a glass. "So, you made more bank off us. Good for you. Did you ask us here to give us a raise?"

A phone buzzed in the room next door. Divinity twitched. "Y'all hear that? Callers. Even at this time of evening. Televangelism is a growth industry and virtually no Negroes in it."

"Blacks," Rory interjected.

"I prefer Negroes among family."

"We ain't family."

"Not yet, no." She strained, listening. The sound of a recorded voice echoed through the walls. "Hear that? That's an answering machine. Just got it installed. Top of the line. Tracks calls round the clock. Never miss an important one."

"Can't ever keep da Lawd on hold or in waiting," Card quipped.

Rory drummed her fingers on the table. "What about the raise?"

"What about that offer?" Card asked, voice rising over the muffled cadence of the answering machine.

"I'm set to close on this new vision complex center in a few months. I can guarantee you both employment for at least a year... in security and leading my backing band."

"Backing who? Your choir?" Rory asked.

"Them and me."

"What about the rest of my band?"

"My offer's only for you two, the real talent. Can't afford the others, and frankly I ain't interested. Throw 'em back in the pond, see if they can swim on their own for a change."

Card grinned, lapping up Divinity's bluntness. Rory watched him get comfortable, laying out strategy in his head, figuring out the best way to stroke the Pastor and not get burned. He loosened his collar, chest hairs curling a resolute gray at the neck. He had on the same world-weary Oxford shirt he wore for special gigs; pressed and starched just for this occasion. "You ain't telling her nothing new," he said bitterly. "But Rory's too much of a bleeding heart for all that. Lets soul brother Mick cart her around like a lovesick puppy."

"You piss-ants almost got us killed in Mobile."

"He did, your boy did, I wasn't at the wheel! The Rev here is just telling you the gospel fucking truth, which is why your ass is out here in the sticks instead of cutting an album—"

"I can't just turn Butch and Thurston loose out here with no back up," Rory said to Divinity. "Can you float me two hundred bucks until the end of the week so I can do right by them?"

"They under contract?"

"No."

Divinity rolled her eyes. "Then what you need to do right by them for? They grown ass men… Look, I'll have Patton get you a few bills, if it'll ease your conscience. Consider it an advance on your first month's pay."

The answering machine message clicked off. A woman's voice rasped, "Don't have money for my rent or my car note."

Divinity tapped the letter opener on the back of Card's chair, impatient. "We get maybe ten, fifteen of these a day. Sob stories wanting Jesus, Antie Pookie and Uncle Junebug to snap their fingers and save them with not a smidgen of effort on their part. Mama always taught me to do for self, help those that can't, teach a man to fish, shit like that."

Card swiveled around to face her, scooting his chair back for effect. "You know, you the foulest-mouthed woman of the cloth I've ever heard, but I like that. If them jacklegs back home had talked real talk like that

I might still be in the church. Scratch that, none of them looked half as good as you do—"

"So, when you get through teaching them how to fish and they still drowning in debt, then what?" Rory asked.

"Put 'em to work, offer them a job here if they're really hungry and want to make something of themselves. Plenty of horizons for folks who don't think they going to start at the top in management. That's how I groomed Patton. She was stocking soda pop machines in Arkadelphia, going to adult school, and practically raising three babies at night with one hand. Now look at her."

"And how much are your 'memberships'?"

"Sliding scale. Pay what you can, whether it's a few pennies or twenty-five bucks a month."

"That's a light bill or a gas bill," Rory said. "Month's worth of smokes, school clothes."

"We ain't saying starve or go broke. At some point though, folks got to prioritize Jesus to get ahead."

The caller hung up after a long, garbled rant. Divinity motioned for them to follow her. "Come on, let me show y'all the rest of the place."

Pictures jammed every inch of the hallway walls. Stoic families, victorious groundbreakings, men toting shovels and hardhats, women lifting babies and baked goods up to the sky sacrificially, a baptism on a moonlit lake.

Rory stopped at the baptism scene. A girl's face flashed out, eyes ambivalent, hair dripping with lake water against the haunted black and white print. "Recognize that one?" Divinity asked. "It's a little blurry, but I think that's your mama on the shore with her organ on the right side there."

"Maybe."

"Pastor loved her voice. Her rendition of 'What a Friend We Have in Jesus' was especially to his liking."

"She hated that song. Cloying piece of shit with a weak bridge."

"It's a standard, how can you not love it? I challenge you to do a better arrangement when we tour. Both of y'all are such hard cases. Resistance is good though. Toughens the hide."

Divinity continued down the hall. They went into a room filled with children's toys and games. A model city sat on a table in the middle, decked out with Styrofoam buildings, rolling plastic green lawns, miniature cars parked in a shiny black lot. A coliseum-style crystal cathedral gleamed in the center. A figurine dressed in white held forth from a tiny pulpit in the center, stick arms raised to the skies in exultation.

Divinity picked it up and thumped it. "Don't look nothing like me. Girl's a little too orange. White folks can never get our color right."

"So, this is your grand vision?" Rory asked.

Divinity gazed longingly at the spread, then snapped to attention. "Willing it into existence, Sister Tharpe. You know all about that, fighting for your music." She spread her arms theatrically swooping up the figurine in a tight grip, tracing its frozen features with a lacquered nail. "In the beginning there was darkness… You know, Pastor had a competitive thing with your mama."

Rory stopped short. Card slipped over to the other side of the room, suddenly absorbed by an Etch A Sketch pad.

"Why are you telling me this now?" she asked.

"She fought him tooth and nail over the way he was running the church into the ground with his… habits. Ball of rage all his life because he was just a common preacher instead of a business head, running his own company. White boys wouldn't let him be nothing else but."

"White boys didn't have nothing to do with that. They all run and hide in the ministry when they can't cut it anywhere else," Rory snarled. "And by habits, do you mean finger fucking little girls?"

Divinity put the figurine down. "That's a damn lie. He was a thief and a fornicator for sure, but not that."

"And she who casts the first stone," Card interjected. "For-ni-ca-tor, I love the way you talk."

"Stay out of this," Rory said. "It's not a lie, Divinity. You were there. Right along with me and the other girls. Harper, the others, can't remember their names… but there were—"

"No, you're mistaken."

"Don't give me that shit!"

"As God is my witness, you're mistaken," Divinity said quietly.

"You're protecting him, protecting all that sick shit, even though those men tried to take you down too, you're still protecting them."

Divinity walked over to Rory, putting her hand on her shoulder. "C'mon, calm down. I know it's painful… Let's pray."

"Take your fucking hands off me. You don't even believe in that shit."

"I believe in you, though."

Card dropped the game and approached them. "She said for you to back off."

"Why do you cover up for them?"

Divinity stared at them, rearranging a train set that fallen onto the floor. "Jesus loves you, no matter what you say or do."

"That and prayer didn't mean shit when we was getting fucked to death."

"Your mama made the down payment for the church after she turned a profit from the 45 record she cut on the Vee-Jay label run by Black folks," Divinity said, plumping up a doll with red yarn hair. "The ones who did the Beatles' first single over here. 'With love from me to you' or something. Never could see what the fuss was about them, white girls screamin', pissing their pants and carrying on. Anyway, them Negroes could've made a killing had they played their cards right in my opinion, but what do I know. Technically, your mama's one of the founders of Revivals. Pastor never acknowledged it. Quite sure, it drove her crazy to see him running all those women like an Arabian harem while he kept his light bright First Lady up in the big house popping out babies. Wanted to be so much like Massa he could taste it.

"Turns out the church was built on a sinkhole," Divinity continued. "He knew about it, but sold it to another Negro preacher for twice what the collective paid. Y'all were out on the road by then. Not looking back. Never got a return on her investment." She swept her hand over the model of the complex. "So, you could say that this is a tiny part of your inheritance."

Rory sat down, blood rushing to her head. "Then you owe me part of this new thing on top of whatever he made on the original sale."

"Don't get too excited. Granny said your mama kicked in a few pennies from her washing money. I owe you a few bricks," Divinity said. "What about my proposal to the both of you?"

"To be a rent-a-cop for you?" Card sneered. "Below my pay grade. Besides, who's coming for you? You certainly ain't got no bounty on your head, unless that Sprat motherfucker is trying to get his seed money back."

"You're smarter than you look."

"You saying he's after you?" Card asked.

"You really think they want an independent Black church in the heart of downtown Little Rock doing what I'm doing."

"Ofay was panting all over y'all and feeding his face last night, fat and happy with his fried chicken. What exactly are you doing that's so taboo?"

"How much did Katy pay?" Rory cut in. "Where are the records?"

Divinity turned to Card. "This is a tax write-off for Sprat, just like any other deal. Ain't doing it out of benevolence, godliness or uplifting the race. Same as when white folks was investing in our colleges. If we fail, it's on to the next boondoggle for these boys. You should know all about that, given your experience with the record companies. I want to give y'all a chance for a second act. You come on board with me and the sky's the limit—"

"I never had any direct experience with white boys at Motown, it was strictly Negroes fucking Negroes," Card said.

Rory cleared her throat. "I asked you where the records are."

"Haven't been able to find any trace in all the church documents."

"I don't believe that for one minute. When it came to money, that generation accounted for every thin dime even if they didn't know how to read and write."

"True. Pastor could've destroyed them. The agreement could've been strictly verbal at first. Can't account for what went down lifetimes ago. We can only deal with the here and now."

"I'll take you to court."

"That's your prerogative. We'll be ready... By the way, what's happening with your publishing rights? Made any headway nabbing the white folks who're stealing you blind?"

Divinity tucked a stray lock of hair behind her ear, penciled-in eyebrows settling in a flat, resolute line. She picked up the doll again, stroking the red yarn on its head. "I'm trying to do right by y'all by bringing you here," she said.

Card looked at Rory. "'Course you are."

"The bigger picture is how these white motherfuckers are scheming for land and Black pocketbooks, Black information. Mostly they want access to our membership base. That's the real goldmine for them. See, once I'm deposed and out of the way they'll still have Black folks from here to Kansas City in the hopper. Personal records, data, numbers, habits, profiles. Vital stats all at their fingertips."

The phone rang again in the other room. Divinity ignored it.

"I'm willing to play along for a little while, get a foot in the door, then shove it up their asses." She put the doll in the toy chest. "Y'all must be starving, follow me."

Piece 'O' My Heart

USUALLY, THERE WERE throngs. Sloppy strategic, pell-mell, willy-nilly. Hunters on the hunt for a teeny piece of her, settling instead for jellybeans and slurping crème sodas as they waited. Gobs of sullen Long Island expressway lizard girls, flicking their pin straight bobs, playing hooky from White Castle summer jobs and boiler room gigs. Wasn't entirely her imagination, but maybe they'd thinned a tad, scared off by the Midtown Manhattan sludge of late August. Recycled air from rush hour human cargo welled up from the Number 3 train subway vents, fierce, brackish.

Jude had been trying to get the buried alive tone of "Motherless Child" down. Sitting in the backseat of the stretch limo, the city skyline clear as a farted mushroom cloud, she'd asked the label gophers to have chicken fried steak, cranberry sauce, and a Tabasco spiked ginger ale with heavy ice waiting for her at the studio. Everybody knew that was the trick that kept her going more than booze, blow, weed, fawning, cunnilingus. The sugar/salt/carbonation cholesterol bomb, secret formula for steamrolling into the night, doing take after take after take with her producer Marv, coked at the board.

She'd ditched her road manager and the entourage for the day so it would just be her and Marv doing vocals before the session players lumbered in later that night. The gimmick for the "Motherless Child" cover was a jazz scat, not blues; a sidewinding road dipping down into country with a banjo and a washboard, ending with a disco spasmed horn lick channeling Sly and the Family Stone. Riffs they can shake their asses to, Marv said, pawing the fifteen-carat chain he wore for luck, relic of his dashed career as a star high school basketball forward who'd rolled into the recording industry by default after blowing out his knee in the thirties.

"We gotta get the college kids again," he boomed from the control booth, shadow dribbling with his right hand. "American fucking Bandstand, *Tiger Beat* mag, guest spot on the Brady Bunch. Gotta diversify, get ahead of the tsunami that's coming down. Slumming in the backwoods like you do? Getting old. Low tech? Getting old. Tsunami's coming, doll. Mark my words, it's gonna knock you flat on your ass. What goes up must come down."

"Ain't doing no Brady Bunch," Jude said.

"You'll do whatever and go wherever the label tells you to. After that crap you pulled in Nashville? If the label wants you to dry hump a tuba with a jock strap at midnight in Times Square you best be ready to snap to it."

"Fuck that."

Marv took off his headphones, training his Wolfman Jack growl into the intercom. "I'm serious, Jude. All I need from you right now is to just sing. Concentrate on your voice. It's the jewel in the crown that they're paying you shitloads for. Giving me lip ain't helping your cause. Let me plug in some coordinates and just maybe we can crack the Top 40 with this thing."

"I've been writing. All through the trip up here, ten new songs—"

"Best be better'n heartbreak and woe is me, doll. Otherwise, I ain't got time for it. Label's got Amelie on deck for me after I'm done with you. Forty-eight hours to knock a hit out. Flash in the pan talent compared to you, but shit... she's got some legs and some lungs."

"Bottle blond fucker's from Iowa. Got dust between her ears. Couldn't compose her way out of a paper bag."

"Iowa's where they start the presidential stumping, so must be something to it. And who are you to be prejudiced against the chick 'cause of where she's from, given that glorified hay bale your mother and daddy live in."

"Don't piss on my record, Marv."

"You sit out arranging this time, hear? The label's not gonna pay for another week for you to cogitate about how long you can hold an F sharp with your thumb up your ass, especially given diminishing returns and the buyout that's coming down."

"What buyout?"

"*The* buyout. Don't your people tell you anything? Big Japanese conglomerate. Been in negotiations with the label for months. Friendly takeover of the company and all its little boutique genre subsidiaries that aren't making jack. Like I said, if you don't adapt, they're putting you and all of us in amber, doll. You know the motto of stocks and bonds—past performance doesn't guarantee future results. Should've had that credo taped to your forehead the minute you signed that five-album contract."

She glared at him across the ganglia of wires, music stands, and chairs, spearing a piece of chicken fried steak and funneling it into her mouth. "Get Russ on the phone for me."

"Russ can't save you, doll. He's clueless. He can't snap his crusty fingers and make you bankable with one of his cockeyed deals. This session is about making Jude Justis relevant again musically. Period. Like I said, you reevaluate, adjust, and buck up."

A studio technician wearing a green beanie poked his head into her booth. "More ginger ale? Sound levels good? Is JJ signing autographs for the unwashed today? You got some eager beavers panting at the door. Want me to eject them?"

"Leave 'em alone, man. Next time make yourself useful and be my food tester, huh?" She waved him off, stomach starting to burble with cholesterol bomb regrets as he scooted out the door, humming an Amelie song in perfect pitch.

All the world was mocking her and she hadn't been able to see it until then. As if a flying saucer had crash-landed on her head, diesel fuel leaking down her temples making a spectacle. She croaked into the mic, belching the first words of the song, disoriented by not having the backing instruments.

"Pump it up now, you ain't Bessie Smith," Marv said.

She snatched off her headphones in a rage. "Let them groupie girls in then, maybe they can fucking do this shit better than me!"

"You going to give them some of the royalties on this song and the next five tracks we have to lay down? What about benefits, insurance, overtime? Or are you gonna let them improvise like the other peons on your payroll?"

"Nobody who works for me 'improvises.'"

"Know how Bessie died?"

"Matter of fact, yeah, and I don't need a history lesson on the label's dime."

"Bleeding and tore up after a car crash on the side of a road in Mississippi. Heard that none of the cracker hospitals would let her in. Now, what do you in your miserable little junked up life with all these sycophants fawning over you got on that?"

"Paid for her headstone, motherfucker."

"That's right saintly. Not enough to get you into heaven though."

"That supposed to scare me?"

"I know you don't scare easy, doll."

The technician came in again. "There's a woman out here named Lavender who says she has permission to interview you about the new album."

Marv looked at the clock. "These dimwits must got a homing device on you."

"Let her in," Jude said.

"I'm warning you, if we go over time, it's coming out of your pocket."

Lavender rolled in, beaming, waving copies of her latest freelance article on the front page of the *Seattle Intelligencer*. All traces of their Nashville spat were gone, plastic grin smeared from ear to ear.

"Big protest this weekend over the nuclear waste facility they're planning for upstate New York. Be good if you could lend a hand and speak out against it while you're here."

"Yeah, man, sure, but I try not to do causes while I'm recording."

"Will you go on record opposing it?"

Jude started singing. "Maybe. What are you gonna give me in return, homegirl?"

"Undying devotion," Marv cracked. "Once Reagan gets in office you can forget about all that no nukes stuff. Dumb megalomaniac shit thinks nukes can cure cancer. Miss, whatever-your-name-is, I'm going to need you to zip it for one hour, otherwise your squeeze will be out a thousand dollars."

"She's not my squeeze."

They blazed through five takes of "Motherless Child". Jude avoiding the murk of Lavender's eyes, her brow sour with judgment, hangover phlegm on her pancake thin lips.

Lavender scowled, pretending to write, jerking in time to Jude's manufactured yelps and moans leftover from the repertoire of fuck me sounds Lavender thought that only she, a beacon among all the other conquests, had been able to wring out of her.

"Sing this shit like your life depends on it, because it does," Marv said. He stood up, pointing to Lavender, shirt flapping open, a colostomy bag peeking out from his hip. "Whatever you write about her you've got to make it stick, you hear? Pitch something for the smut mags. Short of bestiality, and maybe that wouldn't be such a bad idea, you gotta give the world some new tangy angle on her."

"I don't write 'angles', I do long form pieces—"

Jude cracked her knuckles, cutting her off. "How's this for an angle? I'm leaving all my worldly possessions to Revivals. Get them to find some needy Black baby, a baby girl—."

"Huh?"

"Revivals congregation in Little Rock. Church of the pastor lady Rory's on tour with."

Marv sat down, fiddling with the knobs on the board. "Your people know about this scheme?"

"It's none of management's business. I got an attorney working on it and it ain't a scheme."

"No, I mean do your kin know."

"They never did nothing but come around looking for a handout. As God is my witness, this child's going to carry on me and Bessie's legacy."

Marv rolled his eyes, digging out the last Marlboro in his cigarette pack. "Now, Jude—"

Lavender frowned. "You think by throwing money at this child—"

"Give me more credit than that, soul poet. I got a clause in my will about blood transfusions. Having a certain percentage of my O universal shot up into hers. Small price to pay for longevity."

Marv gripped the microphone, chewing on his patience, an unholy bleating whizzing up through the colostomy bag. "Just don't let the Negro protest groups, NAACP, Rainbow Push and what not, get wind of it. Gonna think you some kind of Dr. Frankenstein. C'mon, baby love. Let's get this mofo moving again."

The Black music stations had been playing her shit on the radio in an endless cum-inducing loop. Mom and pop stations. Conglomerate-owned stations. Morning, noon, night, sea to shining sea. Eating through walls and eardrums, sound pillows Rory could rest her head on, caves she could live in, every flaw and tiny triumph of recorded music she'd ever made served up to the light on a gilded pitchfork, wriggling, Easter dinner pig glistening. Critics gnashing, gnawing, Hoovering up her seasoned entrails with salt and pepper and a backslap belch.

The sound of it gave her chills. And nah, she hadn't told anyone about the recurring nightmare. Not Mick, and certainly not Card, wrapping his spider legs around Divinity and her bootleg promises, holding on for dear life. Even wide awake she couldn't be sure that the noise she heard just a few decibels above a refrigerator's hum wasn't the stations playing her shit twenty-four seven with no commercials, no PSAs, no DJ happy talk, no random tests of the Emergency Broadcasting System, no earthly interruption, no toothless covers by vanilla twits.

Everybody in the city was listening, goose-stepping after her, on the prowl for messed up notes. Taking her to the winter of ten years old, when Katy had clipped clotheslines on her arms in rebuke of the travesty of wrong notes she was playing. The meal ticket wasn't allowed no fuck-ups. The meal ticket couldn't talk back. The meal ticket had to stay on schedule, keep eviction at bay.

The grayness of the day stretched ahead of Rory in steel fingers, ticking off the list of things she had to do. She'd spent the morning and early afternoon in bed, chewing on Divinity's lies, ignoring the bleats of the phone, the icicles on her feet from the cold motel room. She let herself go numb and went hunting. Back to Cotton Plant, to the moment when she'd allowed herself to be lost, sucked into Divinity's turbulent brown eyes. She'd gut the both of them, the trembling little deer in the headlights girl that she'd been, and Divinity.

Russ had left several messages at the front desk about the delayed air date of the beer commercial. He was working on bookings at a barbecue sauce convention in Toledo, a designer tracksuit launch in Boston, an oldies bar in Orlando. When they finally spoke at the end of the week, he scolded her through nicotine hacking coughs.

"The House is dead for now," he said.

"They're playing my music on the radio here."

"We can try again after you get back on solid ground in civilian life. It's all about moving chess pieces around the board, having a resuscitation strategy."

"Playing me back-to-back, Russ… why is it dead?"

"You know why. How many times do we have to go over it? They claim they lost a hundred grand from a sponsor 'cause of Memphis. Luckily I got a second cousin in legal to hold them off suing us for breach of contract—"

"I need an advance."

"Holy Mother of god, for what?"

"Property issue."

"Property? I thought you sold all your Baltimore shit after Marie flew the coop?"

"Need an attorney to get back some land I'm owed. Jude's so-called pro bono guy hasn't panned out."

"Can't do it."

"Don't give me that, Russ."

"What is it about the term negative balance that you don't understand? The rainy day fund and that shoestring you thought you had? Gone, done, over, ripped to shreds."

"What about the gigs you mentioned?"

"Ancient history."

"You just left a message about them yesterday."

"It was Monday, and they booked the Staples Singers. You snooze you lose."

Outside, in the motel parking lot, Butch and Thurston struggled through a tune up on the bus, poring over the tattered old manual, their grievances against each other calmed in the tedium of changing spark plugs.

She put on her clothes, swigged a little mouthwash, and went downstairs. Thurston stood over Butch, cradling a pop can, hair smashed down over his forehead, etched into barbed wire lines with worry, the death sentence of heredity come to roost. In every band he'd been in, he'd fancied himself the youngest and hungriest, the most sure and insecure all rolled up into one. Now, the tables had turned and he was staring down the barrel of forty, mind squirming out of his skull over where the time had gone.

"It's early to be drinking soda," Rory said.

Thurston patted his gut. "Never too early. Besides, the sugar makes me feel full, powers me through the day. Looks like it's going to be a long one trying to get this beast up and running."

Butch steadied the hood, eyes rimmed with motor oil. "Thing needs more work than we can give it. Maybe it's good for another one thousand miles."

"It's like a World War II bomber," Thurston giggled. "It might live to fly another mission. Maybe we can get your pastor to pray over it. May Jesus have mercy on its soul."

Rory paused. "She asked Card and me to stay on here, to lead her band."

Butch squinted, trying to find the dipstick. "I hope you let her down easy."

"A whole year stuck out here? That'd be hell," Thurston said.

"I accepted."

They fell silent. Butch wiped a clump of rust off the ignition coil, his face hardening. "What about Mick?"

"He has family in Oklahoma. I know he's always wanted to go there."

"She putting you guys up in an apartment?"

"We haven't worked that out yet."

"Probably be bedding down in her call center. Whole thing is shady."

Butch kept wiping, biting back his anger. "Card always manages to land on his feet."

"Always manages to land on somebody," Thurston said. "How many kids does he have now? A daddy for all seasons in all fifty states."

"Shut the fuck up," Butch said. He turned to Rory, steadying his voice. "We were fixing this thing to try and have it on the road by the end of summer. Wanted to save you from blowing money on a mechanic."

"I appreciate it."

"So, this is it for us?"

"What do you think? She cut a shitty deal and we're expendable."

"It's not a deal. You never wanted to stay out here to begin with."

"I never wanted to be broke and homeless either."

"Whose fault is that, Thurston?"

"I had other offers, all these years wasted with you I could've been working the studios or playing regular gigs—"

"Instead of riding Rory, waiting for her to break big again, right?" Butch said. "Stop blaming her for your fuck-ups."

"And what about you?"

A family checking out of the motel wheeled its battered suitcases to a station wagon. The children watched the two men go at it in cage match slow motion beside the dilapidated bus, tools scattered on the ground like costume jewelry pieces. The smallest one banged on a pilfered ice bucket, keeping time with their bickering, royally entertained, until his mother snatched him up and stuffed him in the backseat.

"Face it, nobody else wanted you, it's like sleeping with sloppy seconds," Butch accused, inches from Thurston's face. "She just needed two white boys to scare off the predators."

"Then what were you, her manservant? Better climb off the high horse, boy. You were no better than me or Mick, you never had a career to piss away in the first place."

"I had a career, a fiancée, a pad, my own wheels. More than you could say. She rescued your ass, scraped you off the bottom of Modesto's shoe."

"I came from Stockton."

"Same difference."

"Born and raised. Not shipped in trying to play catch up."

Butch grabbed a wrench from the ground and waved it at Thurston. The air around them went dead, rising up, a body floating in a rigor mortis sail on black water.

"Chinaman is gonna whip that white boy good!" the child shouted out of the window.

Butch looked at Rory. She met his gaze for a second, then looked away.

Selling me out, he thought. *Selling me out.*

Butch lunged forward, jamming the wrench under Thurston's chin. Thurston staggered backward, gurgling, turning twenty different shades of Aryan pink.

"Go, Chinaman!" the child trilled, banging the ice bucket on the door. He was hanging out of the window now, a moppet in conspiracy with Rory, Thurston, the overnighters, long termers, room cleaners, maintenance crew, desk clerks, prostitutes, johns; the whole world assembled, popping out from the motel rooms, the hallways, the front office, pointing, having a rollicking high old time at a Sunday afternoon double feature.

The body began to sink. The ass, the feet, then the hands, grasping chunks of wet sky in rigor mortis memory. Butch ran, knocking Thurston into the hood of the bus. He went over to the jeering child, snatched the ice bucket from his tiny brown hand, and swung it, hitting the back of the station wagon, the fender, the Louisiana license plate, bashing at the tailpipe. From behind the window, the children screamed for their mother.

"Going to kill you, motherfucker!" the father hissed. He dove at Mick to get to Butch again, spectacles falling down his nose. The cock of a gun gauge made everyone turn around.

The motel manager stood at the entrance of the office in a floral print nightgown, pointing a shotgun in the air.

"If y'all don't stop cutting up on my property you're going to jail," she said calmly. "Police come up in here they'll arrest all of y'all, no questions asked."

"Understood," Rory said.

Butch heaved, hacking a spiral of nervous spit into the ground as Mick put his body between him and the father. Mick held out his hands, contrite. "Please, lady, can you just put the gun down? Give us a second here."

The woman stood, unmoved, a mountainous force in pink flip-flops, hybrid races embedded into her switchblade cheekbones. "I want y'all off my property now."

The office phone rang. She wagged her finger at Mick. "If I lose one booking or get cited over this mess y'all paying every penny in damages."

"We've been playing for Pastor Divinity. She's doing revival meetings all up and down the state. That's why we're staying here until we find a permanent situation."

The woman sucked her teeth, unimpressed with Rory's defense. "Now there's one who knows what side her bread is buttered on. Her and her developer friends got an ordinance rammed through to put in a whole new set of stoplights for that complex she's trying to build. Going to mess up traffic big time, then probably jack up our taxes."

"I don't know anything about that."

"Of course, you don't. Y'all drag in from out of town and don't know nothing about this place. Those so-called revivals she's running are just a show to rake in more money for her boondoggle. What the Lord need with shiny buildings and crap? She's giving my maids a rags-to-riches line about joining a God club for five bucks a month while she's on the take with them developers hustling folks out of they apartments."

"What?"

"Recommend you do some research on who you work with next time. And on who you hire too. Oriental's got a screw loose."

Rory eyed the wig, itching to snatch it off. "His name's Butch. Not Chinaman, not Oriental. We'll be out of here in another hour tops."

Butch rummaged through his bag for the junk. He plunked down in the bathtub, wrestling a rubber band around his arm, making a neat tie, his veins screaming. He slid the needle in and sunk back against the wall. To his right side, piano keys rippled in the air, playing Little Richard's "Lucille", the first song he'd mastered without mistakes, attracting a goo-gly-eyed audience in the elementary school cafeteria, the exotic space of polyurethane chili and creamed corn and white boy gym sock smells and pledging allegiance to a counterfeit flag and being asked *why you wanna mess with that 'nigger music', as upright and brainiac as you all are.* It was the first time, gliding over the heads of mere mortals, that he decided that this, banging ivories, making people swoon, go bat shit crazy, was what he wanted to do with the rest of his natural life.

Please don't leave me alone.

Somewhere, water was running. It swept him up and under as he drifted to sleep, suspended in the corner of the cafeteria, signing autographs in the white devils' grammar books. How sweet it'd been, for a split second, until they pounced on him in the boys' bathroom for the curve of his wrists on the keyboard. Punk, queer, sissy.

There was a distant pounding. It was one of the white devils spearing him with a fishing hook, his fingers sprouting into castles, the sound of meteor showers that no one else could hear.

"Butch!" The pounding stopped. "Butch!"

Hands yanked at his arms, shaking him awake.

"Make it fucking stop," he muttered, as Rory snatched him up by the rubber band, splashing cold water on his face, banging his head against the porcelain. She slapped his cheeks raw, shoving the needle under his nose, enraged.

"Butch… Goddammit. Look at this! Wake the fuck up!"

"You look at it, I wanna go to sleep. Wanna go with me?" He reached out his hand and stroked her face. She pressed it into her temple, kissing each knuckle.

Lobotomy Wings

THERE WERE THINGS you could do with dead bodies that were most exhilarating. Things Katy had only dreamt of as a girl, lusting after the medical instruments the white boys tinkered with at the clinicians' school. She'd been a janitor there long before Rory's birth. Had secretly wanted to study the fledgling path of disease in the spotless white boy laboratories; how it blossomed, zig zagged, sank its teeth in, nestled, plotting for decades until climax, gloating, victorious.

She'd watched her two brothers waste away and die from tuberculosis, and been curious. Their once robust, always moving at warp speed bodies turning to dust right in front of her. Bodies that loved stick ball and sunset lake swims and melted cheese dripping from County fair hot dogs in greasy gobs. Bodies that sucked out the lynching stares of the white people, spat them back in bullets.

She'd been curious, then mold green with envy, finally, 'cause they gobbled up all the family's attention, commanded a circus of bawling adults, a war council of aunts in the kitchen conjuring spells to blast them off proper to the other side. We're gathered here, Dearly Beloved, to grieve sweet innocence. Their eleven and twelve-year-old splendor. Their dashed manhood. What was the taste, the sound, the musical key of the dearly beloveds' premature death? Did the memory of how they molested her in the outhouse go to corn meal mush, leaking into the ground, seeds planted for the next generation of boy wonders?

She'd heard the shrinks used to drill tiny holes into the skulls of the deranged to let the demons flitter flutter out into the world. Releasing satanic pollution into the air, the drinking water. Sub-atomic particles that fucked up crops and livestock, feasting on easy prey. She'd spent half her life obsessed with the invisible, and now she had become them.

Gratefully dead, ashes to ashes, an eighth of an eighth of an eighth of a dandelion sprig bumping around in the atmosphere.

The undertaker had cremated her in stages, as per the request she'd typed out on Rory's manager's Remington. A dank August Monday after her fifty-fifth birthday, 1965 in full bloody bloom, and she finalized the papers in the office of the pretty, city mouse lawyer who'd sleazed up to them with his card during a Memphis revival concert. In one part of her mind, she fucked him good on a brand new waterbed with goldfish backstroking inside. In another, she watched him fuck Rory then pistol-whipped him with Bugs Bunny sputtering on the TV in the background.

There were two sides of the brain, and she took turns hiding from herself in one or the other. A right and a left hemisphere that kept secrets from each other, she told Rory, whenever she tried to dig herself out from a gun barrel-to-the-temple night with ten audience members. Three in the toilet, two on the payphones, two at the jukebox, three doing shots in a half-listening, half-sloshing defensive crouch at the bar. Best keep them two sides separate, she told her, or you won't have nowhere to go.

She'd been suspicious of Divinity from the beginning. Had only a dim recollection of the girl from their time in Cotton Plant. Only a taste of her pining after Rory's talent like they all had; goddamn bitches in heat, she muttered to herself, biting down bitter on the memory, as she waited for Rory to wake up.

Divinity had worked her developer connections to get the band better motel rooms. The men were scattered throughout the building, grateful for the hot water, the working toilets, the springy bug-free mattresses that didn't cave mid-nightmare, the new hotplates for soup and stovetop coffee to steel their stomachs waiting for call time.

When sleeping beauty awakened, Katy was perched on the end of the bed with a brush and comb. She steered Rory to the mirror and attacked her hair, pulling off the pageboy wig she'd fallen asleep in.

"Don't sign ten months of your life away to being on preacher girl's shoestring express," she said.

"What else can I do, Mama? Ain't like I got people banging down my door with offers."

"What about that white girl Jude? She got money. Ride her for a little while until something better comes along."

"No."

"How're you going to make money? What are you going to do to support yourself and these sad sacks clinging to your tit? The preacher's desperate trying to make a name for herself and con you paying crumbs in the process."

"Now that's funny because that's exactly what you said about Jude."

"Least Jude's the devil you know. Preacher girl makes like she's a bigshot in Arkansas. What the hell is that worth, but some bullshit with some flies in it. Jude's got a label, white men eating out of the palm of her hand. All you got to do is ride it for a little while, turn it to your advantage, the world is waiting for you to climb back up—"

"The world ain't waiting for me to do nothing, Katy."

"Make yourself believe that it is, baby girl. That's your problem now. Keep your damn head up. Make that wish into fact."

"Have you looked at me, Mama?"

"Every day since you were born. And?"

"No amount of wishing, praying, hoping or busting my ass is gonna make me younger and white."

"Who's talking about that? I'm saying use Miss Ann's fear of spooks to your advantage. She claims she want to be us, then hold her to it. Don't mess with no third and fourth rate cut and run revivals with preacher girl. That's going backwards in time and twisting up God's word just to cheat women out of their pocket change."

"You didn't seem to have a problem with them niggers twisting up God's word in Cotton Plant."

"Don't call them niggers."

"Oh, that's right, I forgot, nigger is too good for them."

Rory looked in the mirror. Katy put her hands on her shoulders, massaging out the kinks she'd gotten from hours of playing bent over the neck of her guitar. The familiar reconciliation pattern they lapsed into after shows after they'd been at each other's throats over the arrangements, the tempo, the tone, the order of songs or a stray look that burned too long. Don't fuck with the audience loving you, even if it's just a lightning flash, Katy'd said. It was the first time she'd heard her mother cuss, a Sunday morning shit storm in a teapot when the show booker shorted them twenty bucks the day before their back rent went was due.

"Have you looked at me, Mama?" Rory asked again, avoiding her mother's grinning skull eyes while Katy kept massaging to take the pain away. The melt of her fingers like the boring of lobotomy holes into the scalp. The flutter of demon wings letting the plague out loose into the world. Rory took Katy's hand, guiding it to her breast, her thigh, sliding the skeleton knuckles between her legs, letting them come to rest where the good men of God did their communion.

Katy stood, unflinching, listening to the wings flap, the quiet rasp of her child breathing. She was older now in her late fifties than Katy had been in life. Older now. This peeping, half-blind sea creature that she'd spit out of her own womb decades ago, blast now to smithereens, to the four corners of Mars, barely recognizable in the cold light of day.

How had that happened? Could it be undone?

"Did preacher girl watch?" she asked.

"Yeah," Rory said. "Lied to my face about it."

Katy kept her hand between Rory's legs. Feeling her pulse, the damp crease of her lips. Their blood running in a river of alien women snaking through Cotton Plant to Africa, ending with Rory, leaving nothing.

"Someone has to pay for what she did," Katy said.

Zinnia parked the Buick in front of the triplex on Meridian Lane and waited for Divinity's righteous women. The righteous women got under the table commissions for making house calls to the wavering and the afflicted. With a new mouth to feed, Zinnia needed the extra money bad.

She looked in the rear mirror and sighed. Sid picked at a hamburger in the backseat, digging ketchup-encrusted onions from the stale bun, silent, a galaxy away. She had refused to stay in Zinnia's apartment alone while she made arrangements to enroll her in junior high; nightmares rustling from the floorboards, the ceilings, the monstrous steam heaters crouched like gargoyles against the walls.

The righteous women drove up, launched out of the car armed with purses and pamphlets, then rang Sis Hepburn's doorbell.

"Stay here," Zinnia said to Sid. "I'll be right back."

Sid watched her go inside, then took out a tape recorder from her bag and pressed play. The batteries were wearing down. The sound of the Boise club clanged out tinnily from the cassette she'd made. Butch's piano did curlicues in the air under Rory's voice croaking desolation. The audience wolf baying as they trickled to the exits.

The righteous women were an elite corps trained to handle the more difficult cases of conversion. Commandoes who kept meticulous intel on the neighborhood, job, family size, and horoscope of each woman who dialed into the Revivals' call center.

Eviction notices had been issued for Sis Hepburn's apartment building. Three months to pack up and make way for a strip mall or a Fortune 500 office complex that would put Blacks to work as janitors herding cubicle trashcans.

"Morning, Sister," the righteous women chirped in near unison as Hepburn opened the door. "We're God's secret army."

"Says who?" Hepburn snorted, peeking behind a chain lock. Suspicion crackled across her face as she struggled to keep two little children behind her legs. "If you with them lawyers trying to kick us outta here you can go to hell."

"Naw, we ain't. You called us, remember? Last week, Pastor Divinity gave a pocket sermon tailored just for you." The first one handed her a marketing pamphlet through the chain opening.

Hepburn examined it, frowning. "Yes, that's right, I guess I did. Place is a wreck, can y'all come back later?"

"No problem. Ain't nobody sitting in judgment on you, sis. We'll only take a minute of your time. Beautiful grandbabies you got there."

"I look that old?" Hepburn smiled weakly and hoisted the little boy up onto her hip. She glanced over at the Buick, squinting at the sight of Sid bobbing her head in the backseat. "That your baby in the car out there?" she asked Zinnia.

"Yeah."

"I suppose y'all can come in for a sec. Bring that girl in too, ain't safe for her to be sitting out there by herself long." She took off the chain. Zinnia got Sid and came back. The women fanned out through the cramped front room, rolling up their sleeves as they scooped up clothes from the floor. They straightened stacks of bills, snagged dirty dishes, scanned for trash to take out, shelves to dust, sinks to scrub, laundry to wash, plumbing to troubleshoot, appliances to revive, the heat in the apartment nearly knocking them over.

Hepburn stood back in a daze. "What are y'all doing?"

"We told you, we're God's secret army. Here to protect and serve. Prophetess Divinity believes you should get some rest. The Lord says you deserve it."

"Well, that's reassuring. She a prophetess now, huh? Got promoted? She come off real nice on the radio." Hepburn put the little boy down, sniffing his butt, refastening the safety pin on his diaper. "So y'all get paid by Pastor Divinity to go door-to-door to talk up her church? Good to see a colored woman heading up a big congregation, even though I know she gets mess behind it."

Sid watched the little boy toddle around, fascinated, his oblivion delicious as a sucker punch. He danced in the middle of the floor, making confetti out of a newspaper's headlines, pictures about stalled nuclear talks between the U.S. and USSR. He tossed the severed head of the Soviet premier gleefully in the air, gurgling at the women, trying to get their attention. A deejay's voice came from the radio in the kitchen, then a woman trilled about God sending a raven south.

Sid stood stock still. It was one of the songs Rory had done in Boise.

"That's a Rory Tharpe song," Hepburn said. "Always did like that one. Sound like a white girl butchering it though, like they always do."

"Sister Tharpe's featured at our revival concerts," One of the women said. "Next week she'll be at Holy Mount church in Arkadelphia with Divinity."

"Good for her," Hepburn said. She turned to Sid. "Baby, you ok? Can I get you some fruit punch?"

"She fine," Zinnia said quickly.

"Cat got her tongue? Where she come from, dressed up like a boy like that?"

"What do you mean where she come from? She's from here."

"Cross country," Sid blurted out.

"Excuse me?"

Sid pointed to the radio. "Came from cross country, with her."

"Who's her? What're you talking about?"

Sid was silent. Zinnia took her hand. The other women looked on, smelling something off. "Don't cut up in front of these ladies, here?" Zinnia said between clenched teeth as she nodded at them in apology. "She's my sister's girl. Almost never talks…"

"Sounds like she been on some journeys."

Zinnia paused, glancing at Sid. Sid stared straight ahead, eyes settling darkly on the little boy, drinking in how lucky he was not to have seen the world. She'd left her knife in her bag. She felt naked without it in the midst of these aliens chattering nonsense.

"Yeah, you could say that," Zinnia said. "She was in that End Times madness."

"Lord have mercy," Hepburn said.

"Her mama and daddy passed away."

"Sin and a shame."

One of the righteous women folded a quilt under her chin, clucking dolefully. "Pastor used to donate food to them End Times people. That was some nasty business what happened out there with that apocalypse cult stuff. So many beautiful lives lost. Poor child's lucky she got you," she said to Zinnia, handing the quilt to Hepburn in a neat square. "This place is going to be neat as a pin when we're through."

Hepburn clutched the quilt to her chest. "Neat enough for the buzzards circling around trying to kick us out."

"That's why I say it's best to go out on your own than to have them take you out feet first."

"That's why I ain't budging."

"We hear you, Sis." Zinnia said. "Trust and believe, God don't give you more than you can handle."

"Divinity would like you to come to the Arkadelphia revival," the first woman stressed again. "She got a situation for you… Why should you be on lock down, working 'round the clock, minding everyone else's lives? How many years you lived in this dump? Fifteen, twenty? What that rent add up to, thousands? A small fortune? Now they want to evict you and none of y'all up in here own a damn thing."

"Divinity has a situation, an ownership plan. A real future for your babies. All you gotta do is let God's army take some of the load," Zinnia volunteered robustly, thinking of the commission doled out in cash money at the end of their rounds.

Hepburn scanned the pamphlet, mindful of the hovering women, voices just below fever pitch. The End Times girl was staring at her, a telephoto lens going back and forth from her to the little boy.

"Can I have some of the fruit punch?" Sid asked.

"Why, certainly, baby. Follow me." Hepburn led her into the tiny, cramped kitchen. The song on the radio went off as the deejay sputtered, "For all of you that like that old time religion and gospel, Ms. Rory Tharpe's going to be in Arkadelphia this week."

Hepburn poured the fruit punch in a paper cup and handed it to Sid. "Funny, just like y'all said." She watched Sid gulp down the drink. "Jeez, baby, slow down, take your time, savor it."

"Why they want to kick you out of here?"

"Short answer is 'cause we're poor and Black."

"Seems like that's the long and short answer."

"You're a real smart one."

"So smart she ain't said more than two words to me the whole time she been here," Zinnia chimed in from the living room.

"After what she been through, she traumatized."

The righteous women cleared their throats, seeking to get back on track. "Pastor Divinity can take you out of any kind of trauma you feeling."

Sid put the drink on the counter and went over to the kitchen window. She could see the car with the bag in the backseat, the point of a church steeple rising above the apartment buildings, the rosebushes on the side lawn down below rustling in the breeze. A splash of color danced over the flowers, lighting on a pale pink bud. Friend and protector.

Hepburn walked up behind her. "What you looking at, girl?"

Sid shut down the symphony in her head and turned. "A butterfly."

The campaign signs had appeared overnight. A conspiracy of leprechauns and gravediggers organizing the lawns into a solid row of shit eating Vote Reagan-Bush 1980 grins stretching to the horizon. Gift bows on every shotgun shack, starter mansion, and old plantation house in the white neighborhoods. Divinity had put a sign in the driveway of the call center. She liked when the Negro preachers, functionaries, and sycophants drove past and ogled it. Most of them were too cautious to let their secret preference for the new regime be known. They blustered about traitors and sellouts in the pulpit, jerking off over their kickbacks from the city council when the lights went down.

One week she'd display the GOP shit eaters. The next week it'd be the peanut farmer from Georgia. Just to tease them. Keep 'em guessing, treading in a blue funk puddle over motives and strategy, the zero sum game. Variety was the spice of life, she told the call center workers. You want to get anywhere you gotta learn how to play both sides. Faith leaders can't appear to be beholden to any one until the results are in. When they bag the White House the sky'll be the limit.

After the fight at the motel, the band hunkered down on the bus. Butch raged through the aftermath of his high, puking in the busted bathroom in the back. Rory dragged back to the call center, spent from scrambling to get his ass out of the motel before the owner found out he'd nearly OD'd. The call center building stood spare and quiet, emptied of the day shift workers, shadows cutting like a scythe across the ravine behind it.

"Y'all managed to get yourselves kicked out of the Skyway Inn?" Divinity said, incredulous behind her big desk. "Imagine that. After I hooked up a special rate for you with that skinflint Zelda."

"She wasn't a fan of yours. Talked about you like you had two heads and a forked tail," Rory said.

"Cheapskate's jealous. She inherited a crappy motel and hasn't been able to turn a profit on it in the whole decade after it got dumped on her. Dumb bunny tried to get it declared a historical landmark 'cause Elvis supposedly fucked somebody there."

"What is she?" Rory asked.

"A mutt."

"Said she was going to go after us—"

"Bays at the moon. That's the most dangerous she's gonna get. Long as you're working for me she won't lift a finger against you."

Rory thought about Cruz and her motel in Idaho, how she was barely making it in a rattlesnake swamp. Always fighting, cleaning up after the rack and ruin of customers who just breezed through, replaced by a worm's regiment of new ones the next day, week, month. She did not want to admit to herself that she missed the woman. That the right side of her brain was dominated by flashbacks of their restless sex. That falling asleep alone she lived in the part of Cruz's hair, the tense of their bodies as they'd listened to footfalls on the balcony. It was the fear of being interrupted, found out, mowed over by Katy's stalking voice, the gnawing judgment that zapped her down to a pinprick.

I always suspected it, Katy said. *Even when you was little, you couldn't hide being off like that from me. You be that way just to spite me. If it wasn't messing with them nasty girls it'd be something else. You beyond God's or anybody else's help.*

Rory turned, taking a match to Katy's rant as she faced Divinity. "I can't stand another motel stay. Almost rather live on my bus."

"We can fix you up with a temporary apartment. I have a few units that are gonna be vacant soon. It'll be a little more deducted out of your check but probably worth the comfort and not having to deal with a cast of thousands coming in and out."

"How much more?"

"Fifty bucks a month."

"You know I can't afford that."

"Now that you're sending those boys home you should be able to."

"Still paying off the bus, loans, the advance from the record company."

"How long ago did you wrack up all that debt? Get rid of it and them, quick."

"Not up to me. They're grown men," she paused, looking down at her hands. "Butch is sick. Mick's broke… all these years, they've sorta been like family."

Divinity stretched out her legs, plucking at her stockings, the set list and schedule in bold capital letters on a chalkboard over her head. "Ever stop to think that 'family's' been holding you back all these years? It's like a diseased tree limb. You don't hack it off it overtakes the whole tree. You love these men, you got to cut them loose. Straight, no chaser."

Rory watched her smile flicker then disappear. "Stop mocking us."

"Now, if I was managing you, you'd have a real contract and a pot to piss in."

"Oh yeah? You know how many times I've heard that?"

270

Divinity got up and tapped the performance schedule. "Booked solid for the next few months. We could do this clear across the country. Hit every Black neighborhood church and some of the white ones too. Ofays coming along for the ride'll gobble it down like it's apple pie ala mode spiked with bourbon. You know how desperate they are for Negro product from when you was over in Europe. Shit, we're a multi-billion dollar empire. Should be on the New York Stock Exchange for all the generations of white parasites that's gorged on us. If things heat up here we could take it overseas and make a killing. You and Card playing tight rhythm and lead together unfiltered will make 'em want to slap their grandmas. Y'all got a legacy to uphold."

"I'll decide what my legacy is, and it ain't gospel," she leaned forward across the desk. "They're playing me again on the radio. Every AM station from here to Louisiana. You know it, just like you know what Daddy Simmons did with that bill of sale for the church land."

Divinity winced, swiveling around to look at the ravine, the advancing darkness. She closed the blinds, flicking dust from the slats. "You're a strong woman, Rory, and I respect you. But I never wanted you to misinterpret my intentions."

"What intentions?"

"Whatever you think Pastor was guilty of on God's green earth… he had his judgment day. I can't set right whatever you're going through in your head."

"Don't give me that shit—"

"Gospel ain't gonna bury you. Might even set you free, be a springboard to a real revival in your life. Redemption is sizzling hot right now. The white girl couldn't do it for you. Your so-called representation couldn't do it. Dragging around those little boys for a decade like nursery school was in session sure as hell didn't do it for you."

"Redemption? You want to pimp us out on the New York Stock Exchange! What I got to be redeemed for?"

"Someone's got to tell you the truth, Rory, not spoon feed vanilla pudding up your crack."

"So, you've appointed yourself as truth teller… That's real rich. I don't have the money to sue your ass for stealing—"

"I didn't steal shit and I wasn't hiding out gutless in nobody's glass house like you. Stayed here to face it. Didn't rip and run. Got back at those motherfuckers by building this church and daring to get this center off the ground. Now I'm rubbing their noses in it."

"Right, and you turned into one of them. You did just like every no talent Black man does, run into the ministry and use Negresses too scared to break away from the Jesus crap as a shield."

"Looks like I was talented enough to get you here, employ you and that Motown basket case of yours."

The evening shift callers had already begun firing up their pitches in a gum snapping cacophony. They rang a bell installed on the door when a big Jesus pledge came in, oohing, aahing, pretending to be over the moon for the lucky recipient. The hallmarks of Monday, the need to push the droning work week faster, to keep up a mock sorority in Divinity's presence. A fate worse than death to Rory.

Divinity listened to the bustle and smiled. "Golden."

"You like collecting people," Rory said. "That's why you wanted me here in the first place."

"I don't collect, I provide opportunity. Everybody up in that room wants to be there. Know why? Waitressing, working cash registers, cooking food, bagging groceries, taking care of somebody's babies in some fire trap with no insurance, no business plan, no way to grow beyond the four walls? They ain't going nowhere with that. This opens up doors to a whole new world."

"That what Sprat, Ronald Reagan, and the developers are doing for you?"

Divinity crossed her legs, mock dainty, amused, smug over the clanging bell in the other room, the thrill of fresh wriggling bait. "So now you want to be all up in community affairs so late in life. What did I say about glass houses? Can't even pay the bills and still got a mouth on you. That's some cheek." She picked up a marker from her desk and took a whiff. "If you still want the apartment I'll have the keys by tomorrow."

Rory looked past her, to the scribbled set list on the wall. "'Course I do. For now."

Divinity got up and stood over her, a tiny ripple of concern lighting up her failed poker face. She inhaled the marker again, snapping the cap back on with a loud click. "Take something to calm yourself. Patton's got Valiums, some of that herbal stuff. Practically a walking medicine cabinet for our girls. Pep 'em up, keep 'em going when they get rundown. See what she can set you up with. I need you and Cardinal to be at the top of your game for the next several shows. Donors will be there taking notes."

Patton stuck her head in the door.

"We've got a visitor."

"Yes?"

"The Justis woman, some shriveled up little men packing guns bigger than them patrolling her car, and another white girl creeping up behind her like a Cocker Spaniel"

"Shit's better than a carnival. They packing? White boys need some leashes. Them things better be holstered."

Patton sighed. "Girl ain't got no home training. She can't just roll up in here without an appointment."

"She has one."

"What??"

"Always keep back channels open. Send her in."

A Stranger in This World

THEY GOT UP FROM their call station desks to investigate the commotion outside the window, agitated, pressing into the pane, fingers hot and stiff as dynamite sticks from four solid hours of dialing for dollars. Zinnia led the inquisition. Could barely keep her eyes open after having worked her second job at a strip club the night before. The sight of the monstrosity skipping up the lawn jolted her back to life.

Would you look at that. That's her. The white lady they play 24-7, one always trying to sound blacker than us.

Trying to sound? Bitch outright steals.

Ain't nothing halfway about it.

Ears bleeding, girl.

Radio blowing up.

Every time that so-called new song of hers comes on, I'm like, where the fuck's my 38 Special?

I'd like to scoop out them dj's brains with a butter knife my damn self.

Girl looks smaller, raggedier, and paler in real life.

Rich as sin. See all the bodyguards she brought with her, and that tricked out car? You read what they said about her so-called 'net worth' in Billboard magazine?

Ain't nobody read that crap but you.

Bet she never worked a hard day in her life and look where she is. Making millions off of buck dancing.

Must be real nice.

Don't matter that she butt ugly. All you gotta do is be white and wet behind the ears. That's the gold-plated ticket. They still making movies and shit about Marilyn Monroe and her no-acting flat ass been dead as a doorknob forever. What they ever done on Ethel Waters, Pearl Bailey or Lena Horne?

Difference with them is they black and still breathing. Lena is the highest of high yellow and still ain't got no respect. Nothing better than a dead bleach-blond white girl.

Whole industry built on it. The young ones think they shit gold, the old ones wanna be more holy than Jesus. Talked to a white woman today who wanted me to come pray with her on the plantation. Defaulted on her mortgage and her kids done flown the coop. Hag is struck dumb that none of the neighborhood Negroes would drop every damn thing to go wait on her.

Should've taken the money and run. Seventy-five percent for you and twenty-five percent for boss lady.

Hold on, here she comes.

Patton strode in wearing a new hat, a bowler tipped cautiously over her brow, her eyes flashed insomniac red after a night of poring over Accounts Receivable ledgers. "How's the numbers coming girls?"

"Just fine."

"Today's top recruiter gets a front row seat at the revival concert with Miss Tharpe."

"Oh gee."

"Don't be ungrateful."

"We wouldn't dream of it."

"What's that white lady here for?"

"Don't worry about her. Take your break and give me a solid three hours then you can be nosy."

The women grumbled and settled back into their seats. Zinnia remained standing, winding a salt and pepper strand of freshly pressed hair around her finger.

"I can't do three hours."

"Sure you can."

"I got to pick up my babies at six. Plus, I got my sister's kid to take care of."

"You said that last time, Zinnia. We found out you went to the track instead."

"Naw, she was stripping."

"You too long in the tooth for that, baby girl," one woman said.

"Black don't crack, sweetheart," Zinnia retorted.

"'Cept if it's your ass cheeks."

The women guffawed. "We know they was running some good horses at the strip joint," one said, ribaldly stressing her words. "And if you got to choose between babies and live stallions—"

"Can't do three hours," Zinnia said to Patton. "I already went out for the training the other night and I'm still waiting for my commission." She turned to the women. "And what I do off the clock ain't none of y'alls business."

"Calm down," Patton said, the vein on her forehead starting to throb. "Nobody here has the right to sit in judgment of you."

Zinnia looked Patton in the eye. "What's the white lady here for?"

"Business."

"What kind of business?"

"That's not your concern."

"You can't tell us what's our concern. We work up in here day in day out nine, ten hours a pop and y'all keeping secrets about who's really running this joint, this church."

"There aren't any secrets about who's running the church, Zinnia. It's all part of the public record. And maybe you're forgetting that you get a regular paycheck from this 'joint'—"

"That don't mean that you own me, or nobody else in here."

"Who gave you the idea—"

"You, with the way you talk down to us."

A phone rang in the back row. The women leaned in, waiting for a response. They squashed their grins behind their hands, biting back anticipation of a bare-knuckled brawl.

"Can you get that please?" Patton said quietly.

A woman in the back row picked up the phone. She cleared her throat with fanfare and began her spiel, keeping her gaze on Patton.

"Now," Patton said, easing onto the table at the head of the room. She took in the women one by one, lingering on the more hardened faces, coaxing with pregnant pause. "Our numbers are up, but we still need a push to meet our monthly target of one hundred sanctified subscribers who'd be willing to take that extra step and dig a little bit deeper into their purses before the year is out—"

The woman on the phone stopped her conversation. "I don't think you heard her, ma'am."

"In addition to the glory from God, they can count anything they donate as a tax write-off."

Zinnia picked up her purse and moved toward the door. "I said, who's propping y'all up?"

"Stop talking nonsense—"

"I go way back with the good Rev," Zinnia snapped. "All the way back to Sunday School, when a whole shitload of folks took off, escaped to Chicago. Even though she makes like she don't remember me. The guitar dyke y'all brought back was part of our church. Was big shit back then, playing when she was little. Now you got that skanky white woman don't know her head from a hole in the ground when it comes to music turning tricks for these church revivals while we're busting our butts with no benefits, retirement or overtime."

Patton stood up, the life going out of the room. "You want to make this into a career with benefits then step up and get serious. You want to talk about busting butts? The Pastor and I are here at hours you didn't even know existed, keeping the light, heat and water on so you have a place to work, bring your babies if you need to."

"Found out this morning that the property management company at my place is trying to jack up our rent and evict us. Sprat owns them. What you know about that?"

"I just gave you more hours and if you want to make it regular—"

"Ain't doing straight time if I go over my shift hours. Get another sucker for that. And I guess since you didn't answer my question, it's true your boy is behind this eviction mess."

"He's not our boy."

"May as well be. If you want folks to work more hours, then pay 'em overtime."

"We will. When we get more capital. Remember, ladies, we're family," Patton said.

"Right, and you the daddy."

"If I need to be. Whatever I'm called to do to make sure we stay afloat."

"Ain't that a blip. Growing yourself a pair just like the other pecker-wood crooks funding you."

A trembling voice piped up from the back. "Hers are bigger."

A few of the women cackled, then fell silent, turning quickly to their phones in synchronized clatter.

"Clever," Patton said. "What did God say to Lazarus?" She picked up a phone receiver, playing with the twisted chord. "I got a paid day off for anyone who knows."

"Can you give us a hint, Miss Lady?"

"Give you a hint about what?"

Divinity swept into the room with Jude, her freshly dry-cleaned minister's robe on, towering over the white woman blinking wide-eyed at the neat rows of rotary phones, hold buttons flashing like fangs in a maw.

"Miss Lady here is quizzing us about Bible knowledge," Zinnia said.

"I'm sorry but I didn't know you had a new name," Divinity said.

"I don't, Pastor, she's just forgetting—"

"My place? Some of us were wondering where y'all are getting the money to run this thing."

"Speak for yourself, girl, we just wanna get paid."

Jude smiled, giddy as a kid strolling through the aisles of a candy store. Divinity clapped her hands. "Some of y'all may know Jude here, Jude Justis, the singer. Well, she's interested in learning more about what we do. Wants to give to a needy family. Get involved with our program of redemptive education."

"Just show me the way," Jude blurted out. "Like I said, I've been a longtime admirer of your radio show on that televangelist network thing. My folks got it on all the time whenever I call, which granted ain't often. It's better than any of that other Good Ol' Boy guilt trip shit, I mean stuff, they got on there. Sorry, ladies. I'm always a tad uncouth before dinnertime."

"Like a zoo animal," Divinity said. "We don't have any red meat here."

"You got me on that one. Looks like you running a pretty tight operation."

"You're lucky. Not many folks get a guided tour of our offices."

"Then I feel very blessed to spend time with you lovely ladies."

Patton grunted. "Excuse us," she said, motioning for Divinity to go into the hallway. She closed the door behind them. "How much is she writing the check for?"

"Undisclosed. At least five figures."

"Her ass can give more than that."

"Slow down, baby. Never heard you get vulgar like that before."

"What's she doing here, Divinity? The girls are already riled up."

"Why?"

"A few of them think you're a front for Sprat."

"They'll have a field day with Jude then."

"Careful. This isn't a game. They see signs about Sprat's relocation deal plastered all over the neighborhoods. They know you're getting funding from him…"

Divinity reached over, plucking invisible lint from Patton's lapel. "I'm depending on you to keep the ship together."

"Right, I just need to know what your intentions are with this woman."

"She's got money, influence, and she's a seeker. No mystery."

"What's this about her looking for a family to sponsor?"

"She ain't no spring chicken. Filthy rich, no kids. Feds, lawyers are all circling for the kill and she wants to play benefactor before the industry drops her like a hot brick. Thinks country Negroes are a good investment opportunity to assuage her white guilt, so why shouldn't we capitalize on it before some other enterprising fuck does."

A drowning kitten caterwaul went up from behind the door. Jude was singing, urging the women to join her, butchering another spiritual in a raspy incantation. Divinity ignored the sound, turning her attention to a ringing phone in her office.

"I have an appointment with the deacon board. Keep the white girl occupied until I'm through."

"Occupied with what?"

"You're a mind reader. I never need to tell you anything."

Divinity took a step back, giving Patton's pinstripe blazer an approving onceover. Patton drank in her curdled perfume, the familiar stench filling the hallway. The dark, teasing outline of an estrogen deficit mustache played on her lip. The years they'd been together knotted around them invisibly, burnt vines in a forest crumbling to ashes.

279

Who would die first?

"I always liked pinstripes on you," Divinity said. "Gives you that landed gentry look. By the way, I thought I heard you offering the girls a day off if they could answer a question about Lazarus."

"You did."

"Told you, you were a mind reader. My Sunday sermon will be about resurrections. Second acts. What we get in exchange for faith. All the shit hours we've put into praying, hoping, wishing, groveling on our knees. Speaking of resurrections, I've invited the white girl to sing with Rory and the choir at the revival tomorrow night, shake her pancake ass, rake in the dough. Sprat will have a team film it. It'll go over like gangbusters with all the Ofays who claim they love them some gospel. Burnish her street cred. Make us a national name. We'll get first distribution rights in North America and overseas. Instant revenue stream."

Patton pulled away from Divinity, her face whittled down to a rusted nub of suspicion. "She shouldn't be here, Divinity."

Divinity paused. "Don't call me by my first name when we're here."

"Are you serious?" Patton asked.

"If anyone overheard, it would sound like you're disrespecting me."

"Who is anyone? You didn't hear them. They were practically at my throat before you came in. Now you throw Jude into the mix. The treachery of a white woman is ten times worse than a white man for some of them."

"Then we'll use it to our advantage," Divinity said. "Which one of them doesn't want to see Jude get her ass whupped... figuratively that is."

"You know it ain't figurative."

"Before I was ordained, the head pastor of this church used to take me to cockfights on the low. Used to love to see the birds dance before they ripped the shit out of each other. Said it was training before I graduated to bigger animals. We'll give 'em a little training tomorrow night."

Zinnia paced at the bus stop in front of the call center. The Buick had been on the blink since the visit to Hepburn's; no money for a diagnostic, or even gas. She'd gotten Sid enrolled in school for the next week. All she needed were TB and chicken pox shots. In limbo, bored, and restless, the girl spent her time reading the funnies, playing the cassette recorder, singing Rory and Funkadelic songs under her breath when she thought Zinnia wasn't listening.

The big car from the call center drove up to her. Jude leaned her head out.

"Can I talk to you?"

"What for?"

"You need a ride?"

"Course I need a ride. Ain't standing out here for my health."

A group of men slammed by in a pickup, gawking at her legs. Zinnia hitched her bag up onto her shoulder and went to the car.

"Ok. Drop me off at Ventner and Seventh. Few miles from here."

She got in the back with Jude.

Jude took a joint from behind her ear. "Want a hit?"

"Naw."

"Thought you might, after all that back there. Seems pretty intense."

"What you know about it?"

"Nothing, obviously."

They rode in silence for a few blocks.

"How long you been working there?"

"Eight months."

"Ball and chain?"

"It's a job. Quite sure you never worked a real one."

"Putting caps on tubes in a toothpaste factory for ten hours straight. Real as a heart attack."

Zinnia snorted. "Lucky you."

"Lasted a year. No union, nothing. Same as you. Bosses were pigs, forever trying to stay in our panties."

"What else is new? Male, female, shit's the same."

"What's your name?"

"Zinnia."

"Pretty."

She stared straight ahead, then asked, "Can you stop at this store? I have an item I need to get."

Jude nodded for the driver to stop. Zinnia bounded from the car. She came out five minutes later with a paper bag.

"What's that?"

"Hot tamales candy. Only thing that'll keep me awake tonight. Have to be at work in three hours."

"Back at the call center?"

"You sure asking a lot of questions."

"Sorry."

"No, you ain't."

They pulled up to a train crossing. The warning alarm rang as the semaphore lit up, and the arms of the gate began descending.

"Fuck me," the driver said.

Jude settled back into her seat and lit the joint.

Zinnia popped a handful of candy into her mouth. "Mighty white of you," she said, crunching.

"Try some, might relax you."

"I don't need that to relax me. Police see me smoking I can get killed over that shit. You ever thought of that?"

Jude puffed, exhaling.

"You steal our shit and act like you ain't got a brain in your head."

"What exactly am I stealing? Can't steal emotion, can't tell me that I'm not feeling what I'm feeling when I sing."

"Use your own people's music to express it then."

"What people would that be?"

"Honkies."

"Motherfuckers rejected me right out the gate."

"You sitting up in a big ass Lincoln and talking about they rejected you?"

The train continued to lumber past, a hundred cars crawling around the bend into infinity. The driver pounded on the steering wheel. Zinnia met his eyes in the rearview mirror, shifty, familiar. He'd been at the strip club the night before, in the front row, nursing a Michelob. One of a handful of 5 o'clock shadow white boys who watched, waited, and didn't tip.

"Sitting up in this big ass Lincoln with a skinflint pervert talking about being rejected."

"Huh?"

"Your driver gets his rocks off on black titties but won't pay."

"What are you talking about?"

"You don't pay him enough to give a decent tip for when he rolls into a club? Or do he think we're still back in slave times?"

Jude rummaged in her pocket. "How much you need?"

"Six hundred bucks."

She took another drag on the joint. "I got it back at the hotel in the safe."

"Six hundred for a sneak peek?" the driver said.

"Shut your dirty mouth," Jude snapped. She turned to Zinnia, voice softening. "That your rent money?"

"What's it to you whether it's rent money, play money or milk money. It's peanuts next to what you raking in from the record company."

The train horn blasted as the final car came around the bend.

"The record company ain't what it looks like from the outside."

"I got three kids, two jobs, rent they're trying to jack up in a rattle trap they gonna kick us out of and that pastor motherfucker is probably behind the motherfuckers who want to evict us. You gonna claim you're broke?"

"Why do you think she's behind the evictions?"

"Why are you changing the subject?"

"You-you brought up that—"

"I'll go with you to the hotel for the cash."

"You got a call with the bookers for the London show when we get back, Jude," the man in the passenger seat next to the driver said.

"They can wait, Leonard."

"That's a hundred grand on the table."

"Must be nice," Zinnia said. She took the joint out of Jude's fingers and threw it out of the window. "Focus."

Jude scratched at her arms, jittery. "Why the fuck did you do that? That was primo shit."

"I said, focus."

Jude tapped the back of the driver's seat. "Go back to the hotel... naw... wait... take her home."

"Figures. You got a hundred grand on the table, gotta turn another trick to clinch it."

"How old are your kids?"

"Young. Why?"

"I uh, I want to be a sponsor for one of them."

"Sponsor? What does that mean? They ain't no basketball team."

"That's not what I meant. I was thinking like, like a long-term kind of thing. For your future."

The driver raised his eyebrows in the rear mirror.

"I don't know how much longer I have on God's earth," Jude started.

"Sounds like a personal problem," Zinnia said.

"You're right, but, I—I want to leave something behind."

Zinnia sized her up. "Spit it out."

"I need an heir."

"An heir?"

Leonard screwed his head around, jabbing a scaly finger in the air. "Do you know how bat shit crazy you sound?"

"I want to do right by everybody—"

"Everybody you done wronged," Zinnia said mockingly. "We can't be bought."

"You hear that?" Leonard cracked.

The train caboose went by and the gates lifted. "So where am I going, JJ?" the driver asked.

Leonard settled back into his seat. "You're dumping this lady off at home so we can get back to the hotel."

"I'd still like you to consider my offer," Jude said to Zinnia.

"What's in it for you?"

"She doesn't want to get shit on when she dies," Leonard said.

They were almost to Zinnia's building. She considered having the driver drop her off around the corner. Biting back shame over the greasy alley her apartment stared down onto, the listless shadows of the men, clustered, playing the dozens, timed for her arrival as usual. It didn't matter whether it was hot as Hades or subzero. Rain, sleet, or snow they could be depended on to be there.

The men perked up as the Lincoln pulled in front of them. "You sure is riding in style today," a man with a bowler hat yelled.

"Get a job," Zinnia said, hauling her bag out of the car.

"Baby, this is my job. Seeing as how I can't get one at the call center since the Pastor Lady don't like niggers scaring the white church ladies she's trying to put her hooks in."

Jude squeezed her crotch. "I gotta pee, can I come in?"

"Oh, hey now," another man said, pointing at the Lincoln. "Got some high rolling honky friends tonight. That bitch is famous. I seen her on something."

Jude edged out of the car, face twisted, holding it in, pleading to Zinnia. "Please."

Zinnia started up the walkway. "Ok, be quick about it. I got to get ready for work."

The man snapped his fingers. "I know, it was one of them variety shows. Can I get your autograph?"

"That's the one's gonna be singing at the church."

Zinnia walked up to the door of her apartment. A piece of paper stamped "eviction" flapped from the peephole. The second one that week. She snatched it off, Jude teetering behind her.

"Motherfuckers."

"I'm sorry," Jude said.

Zinnia doubled back out onto the walkway, waving the notice at the men. "Did one of y'all do this?"

"Naw. Some Mexicans came by and put that on. White boy was at the wheel."

Zinnia crumpled it up and unlocked the door. "Bathroom's back there," she gestured to Jude. "Got some socks in the sink, just dump them in the tub before you wash your hands."

Jude rammed past the card table and four chairs stationed in the middle of the sundrenched room. Zinnia put her purse down, taking off her shoes and the dingy knee highs she wore to the office every day, glad not to give a fuck about how she looked in the anonymous drear and drone of the call center. She shoved the eviction notice into her purse, staring blankly at the nicks and scars on the table marking years of hunger, of just getting by on less than minimum wage while cleaning gas station bathrooms. A rickety hunk of junk of a table where she'd meandered month after month, wanting, waiting for something big and wondrous to happen to her. She had a talent for reading people, analyzing the news, forecasting the future. How could she channel it into something real? Sitting there, in the dream time she drifted to before her children detonated all of it with their squawking demands and omnipresence; the spitting image of their fathers, the spitting image of her; their bodies, gestures, smells, tiny eruptions, contrariness a rebuke and tribute rolled into a smoking gun.

A muffled guitar sound filched through from the bedroom on the other side of the wall where Sid was playing her cassette again. Zinnia rubbed her feet. Her sister had been a motherfucker. Selfish, sniveling. Baby of their disjointed family. A vaporous presence in life; a nuisance in death. She listened, tired of the music, of the silence between her and Sid.

The men's voices rang out from downstairs, catcalling a girl, playing the dozens. A wave of nausea came over her, pulling her back to the church, to the little girl waiting outside the pastor's door with the others. Instead of her face, it was Sid's, a half-moon of fear trying to will herself into the future, to the soft nothingness before birth and after death, before the dog-eat-dog scrounging for survival.

Jude came out of the bathroom, wiping her hands on her pants. She stopped short at the sound of the recording. Sid sang along behind the closed door.

"Why, what's that precious sound?"

"It's a tape," Zinnia said.

"Mind if I take a closer listen?" She leaned into the door. "That your kid? Some kind of live footage?" Jude knocked on the door, cracking it open. "Hello? Hi, sweetie, that sounds right divine."

Sid turned the volume down, staring up at the messy white woman from the floor where she sat. She blinked, recognizing her from her mother's 45s back in Texas, one of the Top 40 radio voices she'd tried to bust out with her hammer a lifetime ago.

Jude tilted her head down, straining to hear. "That's Rory Tharpe. I covered that song a few times. Where'd you get that?"

The horn of the Town car sounded downstairs. "Alright, alright, I'm coming. Assholes," She crouched down next to Sid. "You got perfect pitch, little lady."

"I'm not a lady."

Jude smiled. "Touché. I hated being called that too, when I was your age... How'd you come across that tape, sweetie?"

"Found it."

The horn blasted again. "Jude, get your ass down here!"

Zinnia came up behind her, looking at her watch. "You best be going."

"Can I borrow that tape?"

"Hell no… It's hers, what you want it for?"

"Record company might want to take a listen. If it's a bootleg, or a basement tape, as they say, it could be valuable."

Zinnia's face hardened. "You best be going."

"I made it in Idaho," Sid blurted out.

The two women stared at her. "Idaho?"

"What were you doing out there?" Zinnia asked.

Sid gathered the cassette recorder up in her arms. "I made it for Rory. I'm going to give it back to her."

Downstairs, a beer commercial blared out of the Town car's windows. The sound faded, shifting to a disco horn intro and a woman's voice singing, hoarse, crackling, as the deejay breathlessly announced the arrival of Jude Justis' new rising hit single, "Motherless Child".

"I am the resurrection and the life. He who believes in me will live, even though he dies; and whoever lives and believes in me will never die."

Mama Katy had Jesus' message to Lazarus taped up on every wall of the house she lived in. Carried it with her whenever she traveled. Put it over the mirrors in the cramped, running toilet disasters they dumped her in because there were no dressing rooms for middling talent. Taped it inside the waist of her high society Cotton Club sequined dress, the mauve one Rory had cut tiny little pieces out of in warning, in insurrection.

Rory had heard that certain cloth particles could accumulate in the lungs over time and shut down the respiratory system. While she was learning the pentatonic backwards, forwards, pulverizing the fret board, keeping Crudup and House and Patton in the back of her mind, she bided her time, monitoring Katy's every bedside cough and sniffle, half hopeful, half terrified that she'd croak in her sleep. Robbing Rory of the last word.

God would strike you down.

Careful, shush, the first cut said, the sight of the triangle shaped snippet in Rory's hand oddly liberating. *Careful, shush*, the fifteenth cut said, joining all the other pieces in a raging pocket tornado. It was seasoning fit for a feast that she drizzled into her mother's pork chop gravy the morning after Katy beat her with a meticulously chosen switch from a birch tree. She was mad at the plunky, un-tunable organ that management had stuck her with. Mad at the baby cancer cells making her spit up blood between sets. Mad at the singer fucking up the time signatures they'd rehearsed. She imagined management tittering about her age when it came time to book third string acts after the crème de la crème players had given them the shaft. She'd never made it to any of the well-paying top tier New York clubs on her own. Had always been an afterthought, a tease, a rearview mirror attraction at the Negro dives, where they diluted the booze with tap water to keep it flowing longer, cranking out shots to the obsessed, the desperate needing a warm roof over their heads until after last call.

When Rory had a hit in 1955 with a Muddy Waters cover, the big venues all wanted her. They circled around, dogs in heat, pumping her with compliments about how she was doing good for a dark-skinned woman with a gap between her teeth and an expiring contract and a trifling husband riding her tit into the sunset. She and Katy crisscrossed the South Atlantic, playing the Jim Crow clubs, listening to reports of Emmett Till's lynching and the uprising of Black women on the buses in Montgomery, Alabama. She'd struggled to write a song with a bridge that went somewhere, fighting the buzz of stolen melodies in her head. Had the delusion that more money coming in would make it easier. Still woke up every morning cataloguing the work of other singers, comparing, handwringing. Ella, Dinah, Mahalia. It was in the shadow of Till's mass funeral that the bottle started dragging her under when she got blocked, nipping at her as she tinkered on Katy's organ for chords that hadn't been invented. Coming up short with disobedient noise.

How was it, mama, that Lazarus could die and still come back to life? She'd asked, running Katy's bathwater after the beating, watching her loll in the kitchen tub, famished, spent from a gig, smudged with midnight conversations from the half-empty train back to their tenement apartment in Brooklyn. Her pocketknife had been sharpened to a point, scrubbed of some subway station lout's dried blood, then tucked in her sleeve for easy access.

Hell if I know, you're too curious, Katy said.

She sank down into the water and disappeared, body morphing into the dark ridges of a bedtime story serpent, a fantastical creature caged between the covers of the dog-eared hand-me-down white kids' books Katy brought back from the houses she cleaned.

Mama? Rory called out softly. The surface of the water grew still, dreamy, an abandoned lake longing for a boat to anchor on it.

Mama? She called out again, her hand wavering on the edge of the tub that smelled of jasmine bath salts scraped from the drugstore bargain bins.

She waited. The outline of her mother's body settled at the bottom, dimly visible beyond the murk.

The wall clock struck five, then Rory got up, sleepwalked to the bathroom door, went through the kitchen, to the bedroom they shared, a lamb on an invisible leash. Ticking off the neighbors' questions in her head, rehearsing the panic she'd have to feign to get change for the hallway phone, to call for help, to describe the drowning to the listless white operator. It would be an eternity until the ambulance would come. The body peeled off the floor of the tub by listless white hands in butcher gloves.

She sat, sipping the quiet.

It was an accident, she told the invisible hands, whispering the exact words in the broken cadence of the freshly bereaved. There would be no notoriety attached to two Negresses in a ten-dollar-a-month tenement. No fuss or landlord liability, no lingering interrogation. No eyes of God to judge.

All throughout the building, she could hear sounds she'd never been able to hear. An underworld of hearts beating, spinal fluid dripping, pillow drool pooling, gastric juices splashing, all with a finite number, marked in a universal ledger somewhere down to the last second of expiration.

If I never, ever see you anymore. I'll meet you on that other shore.

The floorboards creaked. She looked up and saw her mother treading spitefully toward her, amniotic wet, naked as the day she was born.

"Put the rice on the stove and get to practicing," she ordered. "How else you think we gonna stay in this hole and not get evicted?"

Lazarus

AND ON THE SEVENTH day, God rested. He said the shit was real good, then kicked back and went to sleep for the rest of infinity.

You gonna say that in your sermon?

Naw…

Divinity watched the white woman yawn, struggle up from the cranberry satin sheets of her king size bed. White hair cascaded down her rusty freckled shoulders.

And on the eighth day he let all the sinners prosper and the Blacks fend for themselves.

Eighth day? What you talkin' about, lady? The white woman laughed.

She'd invited Jude to discuss the concert deal at her house that night, quivering at the prospect of being the kingmaker between herself and Rory. The white woman would be dutiful and eager to please, she could smell it all over her. Earlier that evening, they'd driven around Little Rock looking at the new church complex, the state capitol, the properties Sprat had promised her.

In her room, Divinity's big new Zenith TV was set to the New Hampshire primary. The early race where white folks would tip the scale toward the presidential candidate.

"How'd I get here again?" the white woman asked.

"A quart of Jim Beam."

"Did we do it?"

"Naw. On lockdown."

"For da Lawd."

"Don't talk that way. Makes you sound like a damn fool."

"I like it when you discipline me," the white woman said. "Takes me back to all them old blue-haired Texas schoolmarms I had that slapped me on the knuckles with a ruler and took my milk money to buy beer."

Jude dangled her legs over the side of the bed, calves riddled with injection marks. Divinity studied her neck, freckled, limp, snappable as a dry twig. The disembodied voice on the radio wilted in front of her; another fucked up mortal seeking absolution. She stared at the ceiling, then back at Jude, letting herself wonder for a second what the exalted country of white ladyhood must be like, hating the envy, disgust, and desire washing over her.

"I don't do white girls," she said.

"Why?"

"Taste I haven't acquired."

"You're special then, real special. All your life, the man tried to beat that taste into you."

"They didn't try to beat nothing into me. I ain't from slaves. Shake my family tree. Ain't none in it."

"You ashamed of slaves?"

Divinity waved her hand, interrupting her. "I have no frame of reference for what you're calling 'slaves'. Family tree is mostly freeborn Blacks that came down from enslaved Africans. Some were involved in the Back to Africa movement started right here in Arkansas." She took an envelope of money from her nightstand drawer. "I got a grand as a down payment for you to do five revival concerts with Rory."

Jude sat up, dumfounded. "Five? I don't know about—"

"It's a down payment. We're a struggling church. You want to help us out, let's do this deal under the table, with none of your boys snooping around for a cut."

Jude laughed. "Under the table. I haven't heard that term in years. What makes you think that's going to fly?"

"You're going to make it fly. You want access, bill it as your annual charity bid. A pro bono jam session featuring duets with the legendary Rory Tharpe that we can market as a gospel blues album extravaganza. Proceeds go to the Revivals, Inc development fund, our new health, wellness and housing complex, and foster kids in the greater Little Rock area."

Thunder crackled outside, the sky turning a smoke purple. A police helicopter swooped out from coiled spring clouds, circling over the houses.

"Goddamn, do they always do that?"

"In Negro neighborhoods, yeah. Better get used to it."

"Sounds like 'Nam."

"What you know about any 'Nam besides what you've seen on TV?"

"TV's enough. I know the government made it into hell on earth... Five gigs is a lot. I don't think management's gonna go for that and it's not as if this is a prime market."

"Who's running things in your shop? Them, or you?"

Jude hesitated. "It's complicated."

"Don't have to be. Stop acting like a fucking puppet. You want me to help you pick an 'heir' then you got to put up."

"Yeah, yeah, I know... I been trying to leave them—"

"Ain't interested in the shit show you got going with them. We can be useful to each other. Have that girl you stringing along run some pieces about the gigs in the papers. I want white butts in seats. Hillbillies, politicians, postmen, teachers, society dames, anybody in your target audience who can drop ducats in our woe-is-us-Negroes collection plates. Make 'em feel like they're saving the ghetto for a night and it's all tax deductible."

"I—I love it. It's just that I, I could be in breach of contract."

Divinity sat down next to her. She took out a one-hundred-dollar bill and sniffed it. "Crying me rivers of turkey gravy for the suffering you have to endure. It's unconscionable."

"Stop it."

She put the hundred in front of Jude's face. "Know how many meals this buys in the liquor store down the street?"

"You can buy meals at a liquor store?"

"Two-course feast. Pork rinds, potato chips or peppermint sticks. That's my point. Once the complex opens, it'll serve hot, healthy meals for fifty families a night. You want your heir to be fortified, don't you?"

"Yeah. Maybe we'll make enough from the concert to help build a real grocery store."

Divinity put the money back in the envelope and got up. "We'll?"

"Sorry, I meant you. Did—did you hear about what I did with Bessie Smith's grave?"

"Yup. God told me all about it through a little birdie. He identified you as just the right candidate for this mission."

Jude looked down at the marks on her legs, covering them up with the sheet. "You have a woman who works for you named Zinnia?"

"What about her?"

"Gave her a ride home yesterday. She's got a real talented kid. Perfect pitch. Darndest thing. Was singing along to some kind of bootleg recording—"

The doorbell rang. Normally Divinity could hear footsteps from her bedroom. She'd arranged it so no one could approach the front door without being detected. The walkway echoed with the slightest noise, invaders repelled by the sharp military hedges and cartoon gargoyles guarding the gate. She'd accidentally left it open the night before while messing around with Jude. A shiver of panic went through her as she pictured Jude half-dressed, lurching down the stairs, out of control and blabbing about their imagined rendezvous.

The doorbell rang again, followed by a brisk knock. She slipped on her flats and went downstairs, peering out of the window at the baton of a cop. He was a weather beaten, mid-career fixture in the neighborhood, low on the totem pole, Black mother, Mexican father.

She opened the door and saw Card standing behind him, his bass guitar strapped around his chest.

"Morning, Pastor," the cop said. "Sorry to disturb you. You know this man?"

"Yes."

"He was hanging around outside your house."

"Wasn't hanging."

"Lucky I didn't take his ass in. I guess he called himself serenading the air."

"Practicing, not serenading. I make my living doing this, Jack. What you know about earning a decent living?"

The cop ignored Card, turning to Divinity. "I figured he was one of your people. Like I said, lucky I didn't take his ass in. Peckerwoods on the force wouldn't have time for no polite conversation."

"Thanks, Officer Coronado for keeping your eyes and ears open," Divinity said.

"Sure thing. I can tell this brother ain't from around here, otherwise he'd know the code."

"I ain't your brother."

"I'm gonna give you a pass this time because of the good Pastor. She does a lot for the community."

"Appreciate the compliment," Divinity said. "Make sure your rank and file boys know to come on time to the revival concerts. Already notified the captain."

"Will do, Pastor. Time and a half pay gonna make 'em real punctual."

He tapped his baton in parting and walked to the squad car, giving them a backward glance as he put on his hat.

Card glared at him, turning to Divinity. "Cozying up with the pigs, now?"

"What can I do for you, Cardinal?"

"Can I come in?"

"What do you want?"

"Now that ain't no way to treat a lost soul wandering in the wilderness... Can I come in?"

"For a few minutes. I have a board meeting in an hour."

He stepped into the entryway, noting the pristine walls festooned with family portraits and drab watercolors of landscapes.

"So, this is where you crash at night," he said.

"What can I do for you, Cardinal?" she repeated.

"I need an advance."

"You haven't even done the work for the first advance and you're asking for a second?"

"Must've got me mixed up with those trifling niggas in your choir. I earn my keep. I don't know what lies Rory has been spreading about me."

"Actually, she's never said anything about you to me. Don't think you score so high in her hall of fame."

"She always been more partial to the white boys."

"I said I had sixty minutes. You already burned five of them. I might have to dock your little advance."

He gestured to the pictures. "These your real family or did you hire them too?"

"They're family. Most of them are estranged, out of state and/or dead, thankfully."

"Convenient."

"Which don't mean they ain't still in my pocket."

"Well from the looks of it you sure didn't take no poverty vow. Plenty to go around."

A car drove up into the driveway. Divinity went to the window. It was Jude's bodyguards and another man she didn't recognize.

"Shit."

"Folks crashing the party? Mind if I sit down? My feet are killing me."

"I do mind."

Card sat down anyway, putting his feet up on the empty coffee table. "Pacing around out there in the cold all night gets real tiring."

"What do you mean?"

He laughed. "I'm just playing with you. I have better things to do with my time, like trying to figure out how it is a small pond fish like you got all this backing to develop million dollar projects."

Divinity watched the car for movement. The men seemed in no hurry to exit. They met her gaze and looked away.

Card thumped on the bass. "What are you looking at out there? You hear me talking to you, Pastor?"

"You ain't saying nothing, and that's six minutes now."

"Aww. That's harsh."

"You've spent half your life feeling sorry for yourself. Trying to drag Rory and anybody that's within a five-foot radius down with you."

"How about we go down together, then. You'd like that, huh? Administering to a poor old, trifling sinner. Ain't that supposed to be your calling?"

He settled back into the chair, spreading his feet wide.

Divinity's face fell. "Look, I'll give you the money. Just need you to get up and get out of here—"

"I could never afford a place like this. Not even when I was almost making bank at Motown. Credit was too fucked up. Nothing but a slave system, just like sharecropping was. Any delusional woman looked at me then thought I was hot shit with a Swiss bank account, but I couldn't own shit because of bad credit."

"Told you I'd give you the advance."

"This ain't about no advance. Don't get distracted by them white boys outside."

The hallway upstairs creaked. Card looked up, frowning. "We got company?"

Divinity dropped the blinds and faced him. She sat down on the coffee table in front of him, raising her voice so Jude could hear. "If you were anybody else, you'd have been out on the street by now. But I've always admired you."

He smiled bitterly, dropping his gaze. "The one and only, legend in his own mind, Card Jefferson."

"In a lot of other minds."

"Patronizing me again."

"Naw. Never."

She put her hand on his leg, grasping the bone, the curve of his knee, his thigh. She could feel Jude straining to listen in the hallway. A slap-happy maggot in crap.

"It's a travesty what they did to you. I'd be the first to say it during the revival. No reason we got to step over each other to earn a living. It's what I teach my girls in the call center."

"Your girls. You just like all the rest of the Toms. All about ownership and overseeing. Seeing how many scared niggers you can collect and serve up for the minstrel show."

"I said, it's a travesty—."

"I can't eat out on that for the next twenty years."

"Then start fighting."

"What do you think I've been doing?"

She picked up his left hand. "Sandpaper fingertips. Rory's is like that."

"It's called four decades of having guitar strings welded to them… You been holding her hand lately too?"

"No."

"But you'd like to, right? That why you brought her all the way the fuck out here? If you can't be her, then you can fuck her and put her on a leash."

Card yanked his hand away from her. "We… my family, got stranded out here in Little Rock once on Halloween night looking for a place to sleep. Five of us stuffed in the car, no money even for the little Negro rooming house listed in the Green Book. I was seven. Big for my age. Got puberty early. Always hungry, always eating. Car broke down by this big plantation kind of house and there was a basket out on the front porch. My brother double-dared me to snatch it while our granddaddy was asleep. He had me stealing that basket just to one up him. I took it and saw it was full of kid's drawers and candy canes. Soiled shit somebody was probably too fucking lazy to wash. White lady booked out on my heels and was ready to chop my balls off."

"You were Black and trespassing. Lucky to be alive."

"I was seven and she wanted a plaything."

Divinity stiffened.

He took her hand and put it up to his cold cheek. "Feels like it was yesterday."

His skin was soft, moist. He sat unmoving, wanting to snatch his words back. The first time he'd ever spoken what happened into the world beyond the lilac-choked parlor and the wraith of his old seven-year-old self, waving from the porch as his grandparents' car drove away from the house.

Divinity leaned in, taking him into her arms in spite of herself, battling the urge to go upstairs to block Jude. He flinched, putting his hands up to his face.

"I'm sorry," she whispered.

"Stop with all that shit. I don't need it. What's that gonna do for me now?"

"Nothing. Except, if you stay here in Little Rock for a while, I could set you up with something."

The stairs creaked. Jude staggered down the steps, holding the banister tightly. "Well, ain't that sweet," she said, nodding at them. "Top o' the morning, Card."

Card gripped his chair, startled. "What's she doing here?"

"I spent the night. Up there getting saved. And what kind of greeting is that?"

Divinity got up from the table, adjusting her coat. "She was drunk. I let her crash here."

Jude slid down to the bottom step. "Oh, yeah, she gave me real shelter from the storm. Was stone sober though."

"Your boys are waiting outside for you."

"Let 'em wait. You tell Card we going to be battling for God's army on the same bill tonight?"

"If you're on that stage I won't be."

"Yes, you will," Divinity said. "We have an agreement, remember."

He stood up. "If she's on that stage, then it's off."

"Why?"

"We did her shit in Nashville and didn't get a damn thing but stolen from after all her promises and showing her ass."

Jude chortled, tightening her grip on the bannister. "You got to come up with something better than that. I don't owe you nothing. Fact is, Rory brought you on as an act of charity."

"Dizzy ass junkie drunk." Card picked up the bass, fiddling with the tuning knobs. "This guitar here makes more sense than you. Must be nice like that. Crapping left and right and the whole world is whispering in your ear, telling you it's worth a mint." He nodded at Divinity. "Ok, you got a deal. But I'm gonna need combat pay."

"I'm late for my meeting. Let Rory know what you're going to do."

Car doors slammed outside, followed by footsteps and a heavy knock. "Jude in there?" a man's voice yelled.

Divinity opened the door. "Good morning, can I help you boys with something?"

"Ma'am, Reverend, is Jude in there?"

"Yes."

"'Scuze us." They pushed past her into the living room, scowling at the sight of Jude on the staircase. "Game's up, JJ, the label wants you back in New York now."

Card put down the bass. "You people got no home training—"

The men ignored him. "Let's go, Jude."

"Get out," she said.

"You want to be in court for the rest of your fucking life? Come on." They grabbed her arm, dragging her off the stairs.

"Let me go! You got no right—"

"The hell we do, you're on the label's dime now. According to their calculations you're burning up one hundred dollars a minute."

"Like a prize cut of beef," Card said, sitting back, a smirk dawning on his face. "Got to get all the value out of it before it rots."

Divinity stood in front of the door. "Let go of her, or I'm calling the cops."

"Call 'em. We don't have no issue with you, Rev. She's in violation of her contract and we have instructions to retrieve her."

"Like I said, prize cut of beef and you only got so long before something younger, whiter, and more cocksucking and desperate comes along to show you up with the overseers at the label."

"I got free will, you don't run me! They ain't gonna run me—"

Leonard jerked Jude's arm behind her back, dragging her to the door. "That's enough out of you, ungrateful little fuck! Earn your keep and do what you're told for once in your life. Think your shit's royal? Like he said, there's a hundred more waiting in the wings at the label who got lower overhead and less mess than you and don't swing both ways for blow—"

Jude wrestled free of him, spitting in his face. "You're fired!"

Leonard's eyes widened. "Fine, you ain't coming? Then we'll file a missing persons' report and tell the cops you been kidnapped. These crackers'll come after the Rev and her whole church, tear the town up looking for a dumb white bitch who got herself tangled up with some, what do they call you down here? Porch monkeys? I know you want to see that, right? See this lady's shit get fucked up because of you acting dumb?"

Divinity was already on the phone, calling Officer Coronado. "You come in acting like savages in my house, calling me out of my name. She and I have a verbal agreement about her performing at my church revival for at least a week."

"Verbal?"

"The officer's on the way."

"She's got five dates already scheduled by contract for the Big Apple, so verbal ain't gonna cut it."

"Get out of my house."

"Not leaving without her."

"You heard the lady," Card said, not rising from his seat. "Get the fuck out."

"So now you want to be chivalrous," Jude spat from behind a curtain of hair.

"Naw, truth be told I don't care if they run you out of here on a rail, in fact, it would be top flight entertainment."

He stood up. Leonard nodded his head resignedly at Jude, flashing a brass knuckle from his pocket. "We'll be outside until the cops get here. Better for you if you decide to come out on your own."

Divinity followed them to the door and slammed it behind them. Card slung his guitar over his shoulder. "I'll take the stage with her ass, but I need a little more insurance I won't be dumped after she's gone back to the high life."

Divinity took out her checkbook from a cabinet by the stairs. "How much you think you're worth?"

"You serious?"

"As a heart attack."

"Better strike while the iron is hot," Jude said.

"How much?" She wrote out a figure, signing the check with a flourish. "You lowball yourself I'll tear it up and come down to your price."

"Ain't playing that game."

"You said you wanted insurance."

"I said I wanted job security."

Sirens sounded outside. Two police cars pulled up, doors slamming as two white officers and Coronado jumped out, pausing by Leonard and Stimson who were leaning into their car hood, smoking.

"Y'all got business in there?" one of the white officers asked, bullfrog voice cracking in the haze of cigarette smoke.

"We work for NCA Records. Here to collect Jude Justis for a gig she got in New York."

"Why she need to be collected?"

"Just doing our jobs, officer. Girl's gone bat shit crazy, acting like she ain't got to make good on her obligations."

The officer strode to the door, giving them a slack-jawed, backward glance. "Don't she got a blow problem anyway? Don't all of 'em got something wrong with 'em so they can't function like regular people doing real work?"

Divinity met them at the door. "Can you escort these men off my property?"

"Rev, this is the second time we had to be up here. Now, we were alerted to a kidnapping underway. What you know about that?"

"That's some bullshit," Card said.

"Who are you?"

"Cardinal Jefferson."

"Didn't your mama teach you not to speak unless you're spoken to?"

"Didn't have a mama."

"Oh, it's the coppers," Jude said, swishing up behind Divinity. "Is this display of manpower all for little ol' me? I'm not going with them. Should file assault and battery charges against them, the way they tried to fuck me up."

The white officer looked Jude up and down, radiating disgust, torn between addressing Card and Jude at the same time. "Jefferson. Name sounds familiar." He nodded to Coronado. "Look this boy up for us, see if he got any priors."

"Already checked. He don't, but she does."

"We ain't trying to get in your business, ma'am, but why don't you want to go with those boys out there?"

"You're right, it ain't none of your business. They roughhoused me. You should be harassing them, not Card."

The police radio sputtered with a call. The white officer went to the car to check it, walked back, agitated, swagger newly stoked. "We got to roll out of here." He turned to Divinity, pointing at Card. "This boy been here with you all morning?"

Card thrust his body toward the officer. "I ain't no boy."

Divinity put her hand up, drilling a bullet glance of warning into the officer's pinched, rodent-in-a-steel-trap eyes. "Revivals gave quite generously to the police protective league and winter ball last year."

"Yeah? What's that got to do with the price of tea in China, lady?"

"Pastor."

"Don't get smart with me. I don't care if you got the pope on a rope. You just make sure this boy stays his ass up in here with you."

Divinity remained between Card and the officer. She held Card's arm, steadying him to make sure he wouldn't jump the white man, his breath hot on their faces. Coronado stood stock still behind him, avoiding Divinity's eyes. The radio squawked another All Points Bulletin.

"Go on, jump, Nee-gro," Card growled at Coronado. "You know that sound makes your dick hard."

Coronado lunged at him, breaking Divinity's hold. He grabbed Card by the scruff of his neck. The white officers stepped back, mocking. "Oh my," the first one said, mud brown mustache glistening as he wiped his runny nose, rubbing reflexively at his holster for moral support.

"C'mon now, boys, break it up, that ain't ladylike."

The second officer pulled them apart, kneeing Card until he sprawled on the floor, gasping. "Should know better than to use that kind of terminology with an Afro American policeman, boy. It's like waving a red flag in front of a bull."

He picked up Card's bass, dangling it low over his crotch as he strummed it. "Always wanted to play one of these. Too dirt poor for lessons. The Blacks used to call us mayonnaise sandwich crackers. That was a motherfucking hoot 'cause I aspired to be Chuck Berry not Elvis. He could play honky tonk better than any white man living or dead."

"Mayonnaise sandwich cracker," Jude laughed. She sat slumped in a heap at the bottom of the stairs. "You know that's a bass guitar, bright boy?"

He took off the guitar and laid it on her lap, sweeping the stray hairs off her face. She slapped his hand away. "Bitches cracking wise. The scourge and the salt of the earth," he said.

"You got a call to answer," Divinity said. "You best attend to it."

"Or what? You going to stop donating your nickels to the league? They sold us out on pay raise negotiations so we don't owe them jack."

Divinity opened the door, waiting for the three of them to step out of it.

"I invited the chief to next week's concerts," she said. "I know he'll be interested to hear all about this morning's adventures."

The white officer swiveled his hips, taking his time to leave. Jude's men perked up as they stepped outside. "Just because you're laying up under Sprat, taking his money, don't mean you got a get-out-of-Negro-free card."

She slammed the door behind them.

"Was what he said true?" Card asked. "Are you doing that fat fuck?"

Divinity picked up her briefcase, stuffing project files from the cabinet into it.

Jude bit her lip, fidgeting. "Can I stay here another night until—"

"Shit no, this ain't Tara."

It was either very early or very late. The sky always had a way of doing that to her. Making her confused, unsure of whether it wanted to be dawn or midnight. She watched for the sunrise in the east for a clue. For the first betraying rays. It was said that God could change the sun's direction in the blink of an eye, but he had not deigned to make Katy go back to the dead.

She was due in Arkadelphia at three o'clock. The concert would begin at six. She would rest up that night, put another call in to the lawyers in the morning, face the long, winding, perilously blank page of the song she'd been scratching out in her head, make plans to go West.

She didn't remember how she'd gotten to the church. The world had gone white. She'd been driving in a car as if blindfolded, going against traffic, an audience of dogs sitting upright in a flatbed truck in front of her, eyes plucked from their faces. Every time she opened her mouth to sing, nonsense words tumbled out, a sitcom laugh track ringing in her ears.

Divinity had given her a dressing room all to herself. Rory began the automaton ritual of combing her wig, putting on lipstick, patting powder on her cheeks, plucking rogue hairs from her lip. She took off the wig, vowing for a moment to go natural, then slid it back on, inserting a pearl accent comb on the side, second-guessing herself, still. Tonight, she would ignore the tingle in her fingers and the cramp in her back, the lines gouging her face, the years of doubt, travel, insomnia, regret roaring back at her in the mirror.

The peals of a rehearsal echoed from down the hall, pierced by a familiar, atonal shriek.

In her dream the night before, she'd driven the tour bus onto a beach. Through the sand, past white swimmers rolling on sun-kissed picnic blankets, pink legs intertwined. Past a colony of sand crabs plowing through the dunes as they had for a million years before despoiling humans came. Past gutted castles built by children cheating adulthood. Past the smoldering remains of bonfires, plastic wrappers, condoms, TV dinner boxes, and headlong into the white waves, free and clear. The bus floated for a minute then began its downward spiral, stealthy as the nose of a missile, the water closing over her head, a torn stage curtain letting the crabs peekaboo.

Maybe it was because Butch and Thurston were leaving for the airport the next morning, but she'd tossed and turned that night, dankly semi-conscious, half dreading, half savoring their departure. Thurston headed to San Antonio, chasing a drumming job with five other candidates. Butch was off to Seattle, pissing and moaning about having to see what was left of his family again. They'd cleared out their equipment from the bus overnight, tossing dirty stage clothes, unearthing weed bags hidden under the seat cushions, cassette tapes from a decade's worth of gigs that Butch had fantasized about turning into an album and selling in Hamburg, Germany where Rory was a big draw. He hadn't said goodbye to her. After they left, she sat in the back of the bus, replaying the motel fight, willing herself to be calm, to keep Katy away for good.

In Butch and Thurston's absence, every crevice of the bus conspired against her. She felt Katy's fingers on her neck, standing behind her in the mirror, wearing her Sunday morning biscuit-burning apron, holding a toy coffin.

No one will ever love you like I do, she said, opening the lid.

There was a knock on the dressing room door. Mick rushed in, thrusting a manila envelope at Rory.

"The motherfucker's suing you."

"What?"

"Thurston. Six years of back pay, insurance expenses and 'pain and suffering'. A messenger served it to me as your so-called manager."

He dropped the envelope on the table.

"My manager? And you accepted it? How come you didn't try to find me?"

"My name's on it too. Traitorous, limp dick motherfucker. All the breaks you gave him and this is how he repays you. To think that I ever had any kind of attraction to him."

Card walked in, gray stubble fresh on his chin. "Good you never made a move on him, then, right, daddio?" He looked at Rory. "Can I talk to you?"

Mick frowned. "Do you mind?"

"Yeah, I do."

"We've got a crisis we're trying to deal with."

"Table that shit until I'm done." He pushed past Mick and into the dressing room, closing the door on him.

She put her earrings on. Faded handbills from revivals past curled on the wall above the closet. "Nice of you to surface. We go on in an hour."

"Those choir scores are rinky-dink. They could put Curious George up there playing that mess. It's just a big show for the white boys."

"I heard you spent the night with Divinity."

"Yeah, I was at Divinity's. Crashed there for a minute after the police tried to frame me. You tailing me?"

"I don't care what you two do on your own time, you just need to be where you say you're going to be when we have to rehearse."

"You don't give a shit about no rehearsal and you're not paying me to be nowhere anyway, she is. You was too high and mighty to be a duo, so what you got your nose out of joint for."

"I wasn't being high and mighty. And I vouched for you on this job."

"So, I gotta bow down and kiss your ring again?" He paced the floor, picking at the stubble on his face. "Soon as we done with this, I'm out, Rory."

"Going back to chase Motown?"

"Haven't decided yet. Always have to keep a pecking order with brothers on the very bottom and the white boys a few rungs up, don't you? I see why limp dick is suing you though. Sold him and Butch out too. Probably got royalty checks stashed on that bus just to spite us."

"You're out of your mind."

He stopped pacing, putting his foot up on the empty chair beside her. "Barbecue rib tips. Had some last night, one of her many admirers dropped some off." He held out his fingers, dangling them in her face. "Want a taste?"

"Stop it."

"Don't know what you're missing."

An organ sound echoed in the distance. He smiled wide. "So, this time I got a better offer than those crumbs preacher lady was throwing. When I'm through, Motown's gonna be chasing me."

Rory stood up, checking her outfit, perfuming out the smoke from her sequined jacket. "I don't care, Card."

"Yes, you do."

"We're on in fifteen minutes."

He backed up, blocking the door. "Jude's gonna hire *me* to be her band director. While you dick around and play hard to get, my black ass is taking the money and running. Means I get royalties on any song I so much as pluck a chord for. Fuck free rides for record companies and publishing companies, that shit's officially over. We go out on world tour to New Zealand right after this dump."

"Congratulations."

"Her shit's raggedy but it's more than you or preacher lady ever offered me."

"True. But I ain't a white woman vulture. You two deserve each other."

"That moral high ground mess ain't gonna work anymore."

"Move out of the way."

He rested against the door, folding his arms. "That all you got to say."

"Your tunings were off last time. And I hope you're going to clean up before you go out there."

He took her comb out of her hair and raked it through his. "Clean enough for you?"

She took it away from him. He grabbed her hand, holding it in his. "Look, I—I know, I know you ain't got no feelings for nobody but yourself and preacher lady."

"Let go of me."

"I see how you look at her."

"You're fucked up in the head."

"I'm not fucked up enough to be ignorant of how you've been stealing everybody blind for years."

She snatched her hand away. "I gave you a lifeline when nobody else wanted you—"

"Tell me what you see in her," he said quietly. "I got all the time in the world."

Mick pounded on the door. "Rory!"

Card smiled. "White knight always on cue." He kicked at the door. "I said, I got all the time in the world to hear what you see in her."

"Get out of the way, sick bastard."

"I'm no sicker than you, baby girl."

He peered down at her, eyes fearful, squirming like a pocketful of earthworms studded with summer dirt.

"We ain't through in here," he growled to the doorknob at Mick.

"Yes, we are," she said. "Get up."

"I can't."

"Don't do this."

He shrank back into the door, cradling his knees. "Can you get me something? A drink, I—I don't care what it is… Just something."

"You don't need any of that crap. Just pull it together for another hour."

"I can't."

She started to walk past him. He grabbed her ankles, stroking them.

"I asked you a simple question. Ain't gonna kill you to answer for once."

She took the comb out of her hair. "If you don't want this engraved in your face, back the fuck off."

He clapped his hands. "Finally got a rise out of you. Ladies and gents, there's blood running in those veins after all."

A scuffling sound rose up from the hallway, the music volume increasing in a caged roar of choir voices, drums, and belching organ for the first bars of Clara Ward's version of "How I Got Over".

Card sang with the choir. "I believed all that 'Jesus setting us free' garbage once. Long time ago, back in never-never land. Then, this white lady… She." His eyes clouded over. "Did you believe it, Rory? Believe all that whoopin' and hollerin' and carryin' on was about something real?"

"Yeah. Of course. That ain't got nothing to do with now, though."

He stood, indignant. "The hell it does—"

"I can't sit up here philosophizing with you when we got to deliver for all those people out there—"

"You mean *you* got to deliver! I been hustling all my life making other people rich and ain't got a damn thing to hold onto or show for it. G-man and his accountants fucked me out of every thin dime I ever earned. All those years, all those sessions, every hook I created, niggas sopped it up like bacon grease, licked their fingers and gave me the middle one while they was making worldwide bank twenty times over. Those handkerchief heads out there up on stage whoopin' and hollerin' about heaven? Preacher lady's playing them good just as lowdown as the G-man. If those white shits got something for me, I'm gonna ride it into the goddamn sunset."

"Then more power to you. Move, so I can go to work."

He grabbed her shoulders. "That all you got to say? You such a bottom line bitch that that's all you can muster up?"

She wriggled out of his grasp, pushing him into the door as she took the comb out of her hair and held it up to his throat. "Stop wallowing. Get on with it."

He smacked the comb from her hand. "I ain't going out there to be up under you. Can't do it again." She opened the door. He pushed it shut, pleading. "Look, I… You got to give me a sign, Rory. Just—just give me something. Not trying to play house or nothing like that. I just—"

"You don't want me. You want a nurse. A groupie to give you your meds, stroke you, prop you up, rub you to a shine and whisper sweet nothings in your ear! That ain't never going to be me, you hear? I gave you and all the rest of them a chance while I was drowning… while I was fighting for my goddamn life on that stage, on the road, trying to stay out of the motherfucking ditch where they threw my mama and every scratching and clawing Black woman practically started out six feet under when they was born—"

He shook his head. "Aww yes, praise be and hallelujah to the scratching and clawing Negresses… wake up, baby, they all cut out on you! I'm the only one standing. And that white boy camped outside the door don't give a rusty fuck about you—"

"It's noise, Card! You been blowing noise out your ass the entire time you been with the band and you wonder why we ain't skipping off into the sunset? Like I said, I ain't your mama or your nursemaid. Get straight and go out there, blow the church up with your bass, after that you can get the fuck out of my sight, go to Jude, drag your ass back to Motown, I don't care."

He picked up the comb from the floor, tried to put it in her hair, fumbling for a spot in her scalp, cursing under his breath at his blunder.

"I'm sorry," he whispered, still blocking the door, an army beating to get in, pounding at the walls with a battering ram. He shrank back, sputtering sorry again, trying to hide both of them from the army, teleport them out like he'd read in a comic book once but he couldn't think fast enough to where they might go. His mind slogged through the memory of the white woman's fingers testing him, cornering him in the drafty room, a scratched 78 playing "I'm So Glad" by Skip James. Seven years old and it was the first time he'd noticed that guitar picking style, losing himself in the majesty of James tearing up the strings before the darkness closed in over him.

Nobody's gonna believe you, little nigger. The gremlin in his head said, growing bigger and stronger every year. You ain't no girl and you ain't no sissy.

Nobody's gonna believe you, he thought he heard Rory say, in the tongue of the gremlin. He strangled it, drawing it up in a slugger's grip to silence it forever.

Light from the hallway flooded into the dressing room as men from the choir barged in, pulling him off of her. "You alright, ma'am?"

"Yes. I don't need ya'll to rescue me," she said. "I'm not an invalid."

Card sat crumpled against the makeup chair, his knees pulled up to his chest. The comb lay on the floor. She stepped on it and walked out the door.

High Infidelity

There was a moment in the Boise recording when she thought she heard it. An announcer clearing his throat to give the details of her death in super slo-mo; regaling the audience with the time, weather, circumstance; the glittering backdrop of American pop hits that were all the rage overseas. She'd unpacked that night in the bar a thousand times, stripped it naked to the bone, fantasizing, amidst the smoke, roar, and stink of the white voyeurs lip synching to Blondie on the jukebox, that Rory would dedicate the first song of the band's set to her, Sid, in commemoration of the almost-dead girl.

She replayed it again in her head, sitting in the VIP section of the sweltering Arkadelphia church with aunt Zinnia, under the gaze of a bloody, anorexic stained-glass Jesus, resplendent in his crown of thorns. Stiff in the secondhand dress Zinnia had fought with her to wear. Careful not to sit wide-legged like a boy. The radio announcer on the Revivals show that morning said a lucky child had won a mystery prize. Made a big fanfare about it after the campaign commercial for the Baptist church peanut man who was sho nuff gonna lose to the warmonger Ron Ray-gun in November. We need y'all's votes and we need y'all's prayers, he burbled. Then, Pastor Divinity came on and plugged that evening's concert with the legendary Rory Tharpe, fish fry to follow, best cornmeal batter in ten counties.

One minute to curtain, and Rory's scalp was smoking under the wig. She ducked into the bathroom and took it off, raking her fingers through her Afro, tossing the wig to the shitting bricks choir assistant who stood gaping at her in the wings. Mick handed her her Gibson guitar. She kissed it and kept moving. Damn Divinity's set list.

The sold-out concert was a sensation in all of Clark County.

TV cameras scraped over the crowd, devouring the pomp of fantabulous hats, dresses, pinstripes, feathers, vests, ascots, patent leather pumps shined to blinding.

The ushers stood at attention in the back of the church, on loan from Revivals, sneering at the Ofays sprinkled in the crowd, counting down to the collection plate loot, the fish fry, the sanctified sounds that infested their childhoods.

The reverend of Holy Mount had lent his pulpit to Pastor Divinity, grudgingly declaring a cease fire to their five-year feud over a purloined donor list she'd used for the call center.

There she is, the ushers buzzed when Rory descended onto the stage. Girl's going straight up back to the roots in an Afro. Girl messed herself up down there in Memphis fooling with those strikers. Girl got a habit and can eat a linebacker under the table. They tittered in mock appreciation as the choir massed around her, dulcet voices harmonizing over the first guitar peals burning through a distortion-laced 6/8 time rendition of Bob Dylan's "Dear Landlord".

And, now, Rory stalked the stage, shredding, daring her strings to give out on her, ignoring the choir director's feverish attempts to restore order and calm. The organist and the church band started and stopped three intros, lush, pillowy, melt in your mouth chords. She rammed through them, giving no quarter to the meticulously prepared sheets of hallowed-be-his-name songs fluttering on their music stands as a soft voice rose up in a familiar trill:

"Fly up on the horizon. Where the black moon floats and stalls. Beat your wings a little faster. Might be there to catch you when you fall."

It was Katy, double timing on the organ to an old duet she'd written, locking eyes with Rory in quiet reverie, as she carried her over the finish line.

"We're honored to have a very special guest with us tonight," Divinity announced, grasping the pulpit. She moistened her lips, patting at her face with a silk handkerchief, wilting in the slither of anxious faces in front of her. Rory had played two solo numbers, trashing the set list as Divinity paced in the wings, weighing whether to stop her. A few members of the band gamely backed her up. A drummer and a keyboard player, newly hired, defiant, cunning. She resolved to deal with their betrayal later.

"Here at Revivals, we're honored to always be on the cutting edge of gospel music," she declared with emphasis. "Put your hands together, family, to welcome Ms. Jude Justis, all the way from the East Coast."

A ripple went through the white folks in the audience, followed by uproarious applause. Jude breezed onstage, sporting a prairie dog brown buckskin coat with fringe. She shook Divinity's hand then fell in alongside the choir, swaying her hips in time to the chirping organ, eyes closed in rapture.

The choir riffed on the line "Pharaoh's army drowned in the Red Sea" from the song "Mary Don't You Weep". Sid had always been scared by that image, listening to Aretha's recording at the End Times church. Picturing a monster tide closing in on toy soldiers falling from horse drawn chariots, screaming for rescue in tiny toy voices.

She shivered as Divinity ordered the congregation to rise. The whole room stood, shaking and singing. A fat white man that Sid had seen on TV selling insurance dabbed his forehead with a napkin embroidered with the church's logo, coaxing the Pastor on. Sid had never seen so many whites in one place. Whites pretending to get the Holy Ghost. Whites sweating and rooting around in the flow of the music like pigs. Whites closing in on her, surfing the Pharaoh's Red Sea. Divinity announced the near completion of the new sanctuary, a gym, a daycare, a community center. After ten years of planning, deliverance was nigh.

"God finds a way," she said quietly. "When you think He's forsaken you, when you think He's out for the count. He finds a way."

Sid thought about the drive out to California with her uncle. The accident that had nearly cut their truck in half. The butterfly that had suddenly, inexplicably, flown into his face and blinded him as his free hand roamed over her body again. Was that God or Satan's doing? Was it the circle of evil or good? Which force would account for the steady hum of death in her head at the ripe old age of twelve? She looked around at the adults, nodding, clapping, mugging for the church photographer and the televangelist newscast cameras. She flinched as Zinnia stooped to pull the hem of Sid's dress over her knee, reeking of the blowtorch cologne she used to mask the alcohol stench from the strip club's midnight brawl.

"Our Little Rock cathedral will be the envy of the nation and the cream of the city," Divinity continued. "It wouldn't have been possible without the generous assistance of several prominent donors who would like to remain anonymous until the unveiling."

"Almost anonymous," the white man offered under his breath.

"And we've been honored to have Sister Rory Tharpe lend her talents to our fundraisers. Because of her and Jude Justis, we'll be well over the quarter of a million mark for these concerts. God is great, family. God is great."

"God?" Rory struck up another chord of "Mary", stepping center stage. "We're going to review the story of two sisters," she sang. "Mary and Martha. They had a brother named Lazarus."

Divinity raised her eyebrows. The choir shifted, exchanging puzzled glances, robes aflutter, distortion and amp fuzz filling the air.

"God? Don't make me fucking laugh," Rory sang. "Jesus resurrected 'ol Lazarus, but it was nothing but a grinning skull, a glorified bag of bones. You put your faith in God, Jesus, and the Holy Ghost, that shit will swallow you whole."

Divinity drew herself up, fighting to get her face under control, bursting from the seams of her pickaxe sharp burgundy suit in rage. "Get out," she whispered into the mic. "Get the hell out of this church!"

"*My* church," Rory sang. "One small detail, remember, how your people stole my mother's half. The payment she made to your grandfather, Daddy Simmons. Now what would he say if Jesus raised him from the dead, baby girl?"

Sid stood up from her seat. "Sit down," Zinnia hissed.

Card lurched out of the wings with his bass guitar strapped around his shoulders. He barreled onstage to gasps from the audience, grabbing Divinity's mic.

"That's right, all you dumb as dirt niggers! You been bamboozled, hoodwinked by this Judas and her pimps. Ain't shit about to open up here. All they gonna do is put in more call centers paying ya'll punk asses minimum wage across the whole South, then run a Ponzi scheme with broke old folks doing it."

Security guards rushed onstage as members of the choir surrounded him, pushing him down, snatching the mic from his hand. Two guards dragged him away, a third taking Rory by the arm. She shook him off, clutching the Gibson to her body, the audience on their feet, in an uproar, milling in the aisles, some booing, some hissing, some chanting for her to stay.

Sid yelled out and jumped up again, breaking from Zinnia, pushing past the bejeweled and bewigged parishioners gawking in indignation as she beat on butterfly wings toward the stage and saw the guard and the choir director grab both of Rory's arms and lead her off stage, distortion splitting through the air in a giant one-minute ear bleed rocking the congregation from pillar to post.

"Leave her alone!" Sid screamed, throwing herself between Rory and the men. She took the knife out of her pocket, pointing it at them, lowering it to their crotches like the butterfly had shown her.

Rory squinted, staggering back as though a flashbulb had exploded in her face. "Sid?"

"Leave her alone," Sid repeated in a voice of steel.

"C'mon, sweetheart, put that thing down," the choir director said. "We don't want nobody to get hurt."

"My name's Sid, not sweetheart, not girl. Let her go and none of y'all get hurt."

The guard put his hand on his radio. "Nobody's playin' with you, you little bitch, better stop this cuttin' up or—"

"Back off, fucker or this guitar's going down your throat! Sid, it's ok... I'm—"

Peals of "How I Got Over" rose up from the stage as Divinity took the mic, her voice trained in the direction of the cameras, soothing the rising dark of turbulence in the aisles. "Yes, Lord, my soul sits back in wonder at how I got over... Family, at Revivals we don't believe in throwing sick folks, needy folks, or even those who don't walk by faith, out without lending a helping hand from God. Even, and most especially when we get tested. That's why our call centers offer intervention support, twenty-four-hour prayer circles and temporary rent assistance to anyone who needs it... That's why we've entered into a special partnership with Ms. Jude Justis, a good Christian and a new friend to our philanthropic community. As a force in the music industry, having sold several million records across the globe, Ms. Justis has pledged a special scholarship to one of our neighborhood children. Sidra Hastings, please come up on stage."

Sid froze, looking around for a place to bolt, cursing the stiff clownish dress. The guard seized the moment, twisting the knife from her hand, pricking his thumb. Blood from the wound dripped onto her jacket. He lunged at her. Rory shoved him, gathering Sid up in her arms, shielding her from both men as Zinnia appeared backstage, heaving past the crowd to Sid.

"Get away from her you dirty predator!" she screamed, grabbing Sid's arm. "C'mon, get out there girl!"

Scattered, tentative applause echoed through the church. "… In addition, Ms. Justis has graciously offered to be the child's sponsor until she turns twenty-one. Then, all her holdings will be in her custody."

"Holy shit," the guard said, cradling his thumb. "Brat's gonna be filthy rich."

Zinnia cocked her head, dazed. "Sponsor? Nobody talked to me," she said as she turned back to Sid. "Get your tail out there."

Sid yanked away from her. A cassette tape fell out of her pocket. Rory picked it up, turning it over to read the label. "What's this?"

"You, in Boise. Recording you asked me to make. White lady out there said it was worth a lot of money… That's what she really wants."

"… Custody of the Justis estate," Divinity continued. "Royalties, publishing, licensing. Overseen by an appointed legal team, of course."

Jude beamed at her side, rocking back and forth, wondering if the cameras had caught her good side as Zinnia dragged Sid from the wings, foul-mouthed, bloody.

There it was, thumping large. They heard it before they rolled up to the police station to get Card after he'd been arrested for disorderly conduct. The backbeat bass blasted from a speaker outside the laundromat next door.

"*Dum, da dum da dum da, dum, da dum da dum da…*"

Somebody had put a Temptation's song on an eternity loop. A boll weevil drilling into every active brain within a half-mile radius. Rory had always hated the song for David Ruffin's cloying. Hated crooners ever since she was little and learning to play the open position on guitar. She'd been told she should stick to singing about love, loss, begging to stay up under some man, enfolded in his teeny tiny universe of fear and rage.

Jude gave Rory most of Card's bail money. Asked her to keep it quiet. Sauntered through the clutch of white girls who'd come to see her at the revival concert for an evening of cheap thrills after beer, blow, and McDonald's French fry dinners. Rory took the money and walked away before Jude could start grandstanding. She kicked in twenty bucks for the balance, telling herself it was the last time in life she'd rescue any man, even as she convinced Mick to go with her to the station. Be the white man buffer if things got dicey with the police.

"I could care less what they do with him," Mick said. "Let his ass rot in there."

"Like the rest of the ghetto?"

"You know I didn't mean it that way."

"No, I don't know."

"I'm talking about the way he acted towards you. You got amnesia? It's insane you're even devoting a speck of your time bailing him out, and Jude's an even bigger fool for throwing her money around, angling for sainthood."

"She's afraid of death. Now she's got Zinnia believing they've been delivered by God with a free lunch—"

"Jude's trying to outrun it. Like you."

He put his hand on hers. They sat still, listening to the Temptations blare. Counting down who would move first. Outside, women led little children into the station, waited for the payphone, secured care packages, exchanged bail bonds cards; consoling, pacing, sharing green Tic Tacs from their purses.

"If that cowboy fuckface gets elected next year, all this is going to get worse," Rory said.

"Think it'll be martial law?"

"Just as bad."

"We can always go to Canada."

"That ain't no real escape hatch."

"I can dream for both of us."

She put her hand on the door handle. "Let's get this over with."

"Wait. Listen. Don't take him back."

"I'm not taking him back. He got a love hate thing with Jude. He's her problem now."

"And you're just doing her bidding."

"You and him are just alike. Ain't happy if you're not shit starting."

"You don't listen to me anyhow. What have I got to lose?"

"I said, let's get this over with."

The police had strip searched Card, ransacked his clothes until they conjured up a quarter kilo of weed in his shirt pocket, then dumped him in a packed holding cell with five other men screaming for the county's only public defender.

He was practicing scales on his leg when Rory came in. Face puffy and creased from being bounced by the police. Her presence barely registered when they led him out after she paid his bail.

They walked out silently. The clerk had returned his belongings and discharge papers in a dirty laundry bag. The music began another loop as it started to drizzle. The kids waiting outside squealed with delight, mouths open to the sky.

"Well, fuck me," he said as he got in the car and saw Mick.

Mick cut his eyes at him in the rearview mirror. "Consider yourself lucky you got sprung."

Card threw his stuff onto the backseat. "Where'd you get the dough?" he asked Rory.

"Where you want us to take you?" she replied.

"Can't do Venus, Saturn or Neptune, then Greyhound will suffice. I said, where'd you get the dough?"

"From the collection plate."

"No shit. Robbing from the poor to give to the poor."

They drove past the shell of Divinity's new cathedral. "We'll take you to Greyhound."

"That's mighty white of y'all."

"You still got stuff on my bus, what you want me to do with it?"

"Burn it, sell it. I don't give a fuck. I'm going to get what I'm due from the G-man."

Mick turned the corner, eyeing the envelope on the seat next to Card. "How're you going to do that? Don't you have a notice to appear?"

"Pulaski County's valentine. Can't wait to wipe my ass with it."

"Real smart strategy. They issue a warrant for your arrest you'll be in jail longer than you were before. This time, nobody in their right mind will hire you."

Panhandlers thronged in front of the Greyhound station, jockeying for position, offering to schlep suitcases, trunks, duffel bags for a few dimes. Men kicked back on benches, jumping up to rush the taxis that came in the parking lot, pulling their jackets up over their heads to shield against the thickening rain. A game of craps had begun on the side of the building by the exit. A saxophone busker dipped and swayed to a lilting ballad, eyeing every new arrival hopefully, shivering in his red satin pajamas.

Rory watched the men haggle. "Look, what you did, what you tried to do back at the church—"

"Just spit it out, I failed. What's that old saying... you can lead a horse to water..." He put his hand out of the window, feeling the rain. "I'm going to get back to my kids."

"Teach 'em to play like you, maybe?" she said. "Train 'em to be one of the greats."

"That would be more of a curse than a blessing."

She lowered her eyes. "Card, look—"

"Save it, hear?"

He grabbed his stuff and opened the door, stepping into the soupy grayness of the afternoon.

"What about your fare?" Rory asked.

He pointed at his face. "Gonna hitch a ride with my looks. All these motherfuckers are in the presence of royalty and they don't even know it."

They watched him walk to the station door. The saxophonist nodded, turning to serenade him. He threw the envelope into his instrument case and disappeared inside.

318

Limitless and Free

THE *LITTLE ROCK POST COURIER* headline in the Sunday Business section screamed that the merger would go down in forty-eight hours. NCA Records and all its subsidiaries. Its back catalogues, doo-woppers, honky tonkers, glam rockers, disco spinners, and vanilla punk malcontent wana-bees stuffed down the gullet of entertainment giant Empyrean Global, which had recently been acquired by an East Coast nuclear arms manufacturer. Below the NCA headline, in smaller print, was an announcement about Divinity's cathedral. A black and white picture of Jude mugging next to Sid and Zinnia floated under it, the choir huddling in a blur behind them.

Divinity folded the newspaper and put it on the pillow next to her, skimming it as she listened to the white girl bump around in her en-suite bathroom.

Empyrean dominated the stock market as Reagan's candidacy surged. On the campaign trail, Reagan talked peace, stability, solidarity while Empyrean execs routed their campaign checks to him through underground political action committees. Untraceable, stealthy as a virus.

She had grown to like the smell of the white girl's hair. Grown to tolerate it at least; quivered to the unnatural, clinical damp of it, the feral lost-in-a-foxhole mess of it, how it was everywhere, all the time.

After the service, the white girl had entertained Sid and Zinnia in her hotel suite, then wound up on Divinity's doorstep, claiming she needed sanctuary from her howling entourage. Divinity had reluctantly let Jude in, or so she told herself, worn out from the drama of the day, bracing for the clamor of donors, creditors, the pressure of another big insurance payment looming that month. Later, she and Patton would settle down to their dreaded weekly ritual of counting the collection plate proceeds, rolling through the dance of pain and pleasure they'd been doing for seven years, deciding how much would go into payroll, marketing, building maintenance, childcare. Divinity would recommend another five hundred bucks for Sprat's retainer. He'd go to bat for Revivals in the city council planning committee meeting, renew their commitment to jobs and rehab treatment services in exchange for the easing of environmental restrictions on air pollution.

Divinity turned on the TV. Reagan appeared again. Holding forth at the Republican National Convention. He never went off now. Every station in the country broadcasted his malevolence.

Jude took her sweet time coming out of the bathroom. Divinity thought she might have to force her out, shoot a poison-tipped arrow through the wall.

"You lied to me," Jude said, slinking out of the door, stuffed into Divinity's velour robe, reeking of reefer and Dial soap. "Said you could never get it up for a white girl and now here we are, turtle dove. There's this experimental surgery I've been researching. Cost $20,000 dollars for a total brain transfer. They attach all the synapses like an erector set. Neat as a pin."

"When are you going to cut us a check?"

"Record company hasn't given me this month's royalties yet, so I'm floating everybody."

"If I don't make a payment on the cathedral, we're getting foreclosed on and my credit rating, the church corporation's rating, will be fucked up."

"I'll see what I can do tomorrow."

"Need you to do it today, not tomorrow. Did you understand what I said? Do you know anything about the way credit works for Black folks?"

"'Course not, teach me."

"Take my robe off."

"You do it."

"Acting like a bitch."

"You wouldn't have it any other way."

Divinity snatched at the belt of the robe. Jude flinched, pulling the robe tightly around her chest. She backed into the closet mirror, making the sign of the cross with her grubby fingers.

"C'mon, you know you want some and you just can't fucking stand it. God's going to ground you right down to hell for your sinful, invert urges—"

"Take it off."

"Naw. I'll keep this in exchange for the check. It'll be a nice souvenir from the time we spent together. When you get world-famous I'll be able to say I fucked a holy woman of the cloth. Ooh, no pun intended."

Divinity grabbed Jude's hair, twisting it into a knot around her knuckles, whipping Jude's head back, her face melting into the grainy pink of raw hamburger meat as she squawked in pain, then laughed, her body arcing downwards.

"I don't bruise easily," she said.

"My intent wasn't to bruise."

"Or scare. Besides, this body isn't long for this world."

"All the money in the world isn't going to transfer your brain to that girl's body."

"If God can produce miracles—"

"You don't believe in God."

"Neither do you."

Divinity wrapped Jude's hair tighter around her fist, guiding Jude to the bed, sitting her down.

"I've been at this my entire life. Grandfather built this right after Emancipation. All over the country they were burning Negroes out of churches, running them off their own property, stealing their businesses, sucking them dry like a wishbone while your people was worrying about debutante balls and clearing the pimples off their faces—"

"We didn't have no debs in my family—"

"Shut up." Divinity let go of Jude's hair, arranging it prissily around her shoulders, wondering if she could wait another minute before ripping it from the roots.

Jude slumped onto the bed, staring up at the ceiling, past the darkening sky outside, a conspiracy of exoplanets drawing them together in a roil of misery and desire.

Divinity held Jude down. She relaxed, wrapping her legs around Divinity. "I believe in God and divine providence for cracker white girls."

"Do tell," Jude said. "Cracker white's redundant. Sounds like a good title for an album though."

"You steal it, you owe me," Divinity laughed. "On top of what I'm already due."

They kissed, tentative then long, sloppy, time killing. Jude rubbed up hungrily against her, opening her eyes; grey marbles that popped out at Divinity, the near-death stare of a mackerel wriggling on a hook. A mechanical click jolted them back to the present, as the room came back into mundane focus.

"Going to be the last time for that."

Rory stood in the doorway, a Polaroid camera in her hand.

They blinked at her and stood up, startled. Divinity staggered toward her.

"How did you get in?"

"A four-star general gave me the key. Named after an ol' white boy." She tapped the camera, keeping her gaze on the two of them. "I guess you thought nobody was going to know about your little collaboration. I ain't never hid who I was, who I loved. And I fucking paid for it... Now, according to you, 'God' sees everything, judges everything, including the church you stole right out from my mama."

"You're drunk. Come to the call center tomorrow, we can get you into rehab."

"I'm stone cold sober."

Rory took a picture out of the camera and fanned it, blowing on it to let it dry. The developing image of Divinity and Jude intertwined flashed out at them. "These are gonna be mighty fine collectibles."

Divinity went to the closet and pulled out a new pair of boots, price tag still on. "You don't want to do that."

Rory tapped the picture, the image deepening now in vivid color. "Memorabilia," she said to Jude. "Like the so-called 'bootleg' tape of mine you were scheming on giving to the House."

Jude chortled. "What they need that for? The House's got vaults and vaults of that kind of unfiltered stuff. They can package it up, sell it to Mercedes Benz and make a million bucks before you even unzip to shit." She twirled a lock around her finger, an edge to her voice. "Look, we were just horsing around here. No need to string us up."

Rory turned to Divinity. "I want all the church records."

Divinity sat down on the bed and put her boots on. "Chile you startin' to sound redundant."

The rain was coming down harder. The house vibrated. The women stopped to listen for a second, awed, tight as coiled springs. Divinity needed to deposit Jude's check in the bank to cover loan payments she'd made for the buildings. If the loan checks bounced, the account would be closed. Then she'd be swallowed up in late fees, cancellation fees, monster interest, the cathedral opening delayed another six months to a year. Her credibility trashed. She'd be the Negress who had butter fingers with money, like all the others. The Negress who needed a white man to front. Craved it. Cried out for it. Stalked it, like all her life she'd been lusting after the trash motherfucker smirking right now on her bed, in the Polaroid photo, a deer tick in her eardrum.

Rory held the picture up to the light. "I don't generally like courthouses. Too much like auction houses. Like how this place smells. Think we need a little air freshener." She walked to the door and pushed it open wide. Patton stepped in with the call center clipboard pressed to her chest. She held out a piece of paper to Divinity. "Speaking of memorabilia."

"What's this supposed to be?"

"A promissory note that Daddy Simmons wrote to Katy."

Divinity's nostrils flared at the faded piece of paper. "Where'd you get that?"

"From the Sunday school Bible you wield like a weapon when it's convenient. If you'd cracked it open more than a few times for God's wisdom maybe you would've found it first."

"Maybe. But you're going to have to do better than conjure up some crusty, old forged piece of garbage if you're aiming for world domination. Both of y'all get the fuck out of my house, I have real work to do."

Jude sniffled, looking from Divinity to Patton to Rory as she wrapped the robe more tightly around her body. "Look, c-can you at least give us the pictures?"

"Now why would I do that, Cinderella?"

"Please."

"Unless, of course, you had something that I wanted."

"Spit it out."

"The money you've been dangling in front of Divinity. I want it in cash, today."

"I—"

"Don't even fix your lips to say you can't. My price just went up."

Jude dug her hands into her hair. "Like I told her, I—"

"Those amps have fried your hearing, right?"

Jude kept her eyes on the pictures, as if the hardness of her stare would make them go up in smoke. While she was angling Divinity had gotten dressed with her usual brisk efficiency; burgundy suit coat straight, pleated slacks crisp, boots pointed forward in tight formation to meet the world. She lingered, waiting for Rory to make the next move, a flash of morbid curiosity flickering across her face.

"You can use the phone in the living room if you need more privacy," Divinity told Jude.

Rory put the pictures in her bag, patting it for safekeeping. "Naw, let her talk here. That's why you have that fancy phone right by your night-stand. You never let the quarry out of earshot or out of view."

Jude picked up the phone and dialed. A gravelly voice answered. She cleared her throat, then began her negotiations, going back and forth on figures, talking over the voice as it became more agitated. "Who earned the shit, Mitch," she snapped. "They're my royalties over ten years… What back taxes? Nobody ever told me about that crap… Can you wire me twenty thousand to start? Do whatever you have to do with the accounting to free it up. I'm good for it… no, it ain't going up my nose."

She slammed down the phone. "It'll be here first thing tomorrow. Now, can I have the pictures and the camera please?"

Rory shook her head, keeping her eyes on Divinity. "We might be crazy but we ain't dumb."

The Rover

THE CADILLAC'S FINS shimmered in the afternoon light. Part fish, part prairie schooner. Glancing out the window of the bus, Rory could just make out the driver and the passenger. A woman sat behind the wheel, remote and erect in dark shades. Divinity lounged in the passenger's seat, fumbling through her briefcase, sucking a coke bottle. After the revival fiasco, Rory had moved the bus to a trailer park and started living in it again, waiting on the three day hold for Jude's money transfer to clear. The park was tucked behind a drab knot of apartment complexes facing a power plant. The manager took her twenty dollars for the first two weeks' rent, squinting at her with his good eye as he polished off a fried egg sandwich.

"Play me slide guitar like you did on "Jesus Make Up My Dying Bed" and I'll deduct a buck. I saw you open at the Starlight Club in '59," he chuckled. "Blew you a kiss from the second row. Not that it was too crowded then, or nothing. You sounded real nice. I could see the head-liner was a little jealous of how fine you could play. Had you and the song in my head the whole entire week."

He gave her a spot right at the end of the park. The power plant generators buzzing in lullaby all night long. Mick took up residence in the back of the bus. A sheet acted as a makeshift wall, a partition of doom between them. They had an unspoken agreement to leave each other in peace until a game plan shook out. In the mornings, he went to the unemployment office, applying for security guard gigs, light carpentry, office janitorial, playing up his back injury from years of roadie lifting and hauling to get on general relief for a spell. In the mornings, she futzed around with the chorus to a new song, then trudged to the payphone, leaving messages at the call center for Zinnia and Sid.

Some of the residents came out to watch as the Cadillac pulled into the trailer park. Children out of school threw gravel at the roaring fins. Fenced dogs reared up, growling and hissing. Adults between shifts muted their soaps, eyewitness news and game shows, coughing at the exhaust, relaxing their hard stares of suspicion a little when they saw it was Pastor Divinity.

Mick had already taken off for an interview. He was old, lived in; but still white, still first in the pecking order, still last hired, last fired. Rory sat in the second row of the bus, wrapped in a blanket, suspended between masturbating and writing out a schedule for the day. She zipped up her pants and straightened her clothes, ripe from forty-eight hours without a shower, not giving a fuck.

Divinity climbed out of the car. "So, this is where you've been hiding." She took a swig of the coke and waited for Rory to come out.

"I'm not hiding."

"Renting a space in a trailer park sure looks like you don't want to be found."

"What do you want, Divinity?"

"I have a peace offering."

The driver got out of the car. It was Zinnia.

Rory took a step back. "This the peace offering? Gave Patton the boot? Last conversation Ms. Z and I had I was a dirty predator."

Divinity smirked. "Patton's gonna collect a nice fat unemployment check because of me."

Rory turned to Zinnia. "H-how's Sid?"

Zinnia curled her lip and handed Rory an envelope. Rory tore it open, blinking at a check for five thousand dollars, signed by Divinity as chairwoman of the board of the Revivals, Inc. nonprofit development corporation.

"Why?"

"Reparations," Zinnia said.

"Fancy term for a simple concept," Divinity said.

"What's the simple concept?"

"Getting you up and running as a functional human being."

"The first parcel of land Revivals church was built on was your mother's," Zinnia said. "This is payment for what the Pastor's grandfather stole."

"This the best y'all can do on the interest over fifty years? Tryin' to shit on me and call it chocolate cake?"

"Best we can do until our source ponies up," Divinity said.

"I'm not going to be bought off to soothe your conscience or keep this out of court."

"And what exactly would taking me to court achieve in the long run? That promissory note won't hold up. Seems to me you going to be swimming in a lot of nasty litigation and debt between taking on a respected Christian pastor and getting your publishing rights from them parasites in the industry. Not to mention keeping your last white man standing on the payroll."

The kids sidled up, pointing, giggling. "Can we ride in y'all's hooptie?"

Divinity shrugged, mock quizzical. "Hooptie? Sure, we can take you for a spin. What church your mama and daddy go to?"

The kids leaned into the car, sniffing the seats, turning their noses up at the funk of the purple tree air freshener hanging from the rearview mirror.

"Who's the source?" Rory asked.

"Jude."

"How'd you manage that?"

"Obviously we have a mutual interest in getting those pictures back."

Rory went inside the bus and came back out with the pictures. She handed the check and the pictures to Divinity. "Here. Take them."

Divinity stuffed them into her pocket. "Good start. Still want you to have the money though."

"It ain't about the money."

"It's always about the money."

Rory pointed at the check. "Then use that to raise your people's salaries so your girl here don't have to bust her ass working a second job at a strip club."

"Come on away from there and get out of grown folks' business!" A woman hanging wet socks on a clothesline yelled to the kids from the trailer next door. "Pastor, I listen to you on the radio. Keep doing God's work."

"Thank you, ma'am. You a subscriber?"

"No."

Divinity walked over to the woman and handed her a card. A junked bathtub on the dime-sized lawn sprouted withered tomato plants. Brown water trickled from a hose down the cracked driveway, past an obstacle course of Pork n' Beans cans the kids had lined up for a game. Divinity picked up a can, shaking her head in disgust at the ingredients; the salt, fat and unpronounceable sludge she'd once slurped down with gusto at their age. Might as well open up their veins and pump gasoline in. Leave them to live and die young in the cesspit of MSG and the power plant's kill rays. The new cathedral could deliver them all. Lift them up, cleanse, heal, purify in one fell swoop if everything she'd dreamed of came to pass. God working through her, God working against her, God absent, strung out, jerking off. What did she know anymore?

The woman squinted doubtfully at the card, then at Divinity. "You ain't Jesus, you know."

A nub of a white man from the Water and Power department made his way through the courtyard, stopping behind each trailer to read the meters.

"Speak the gospel," Rory said to the woman.

"I don't claim to be Jesus, ma'am," Divinity said.

Rory turned back to Zinnia. "Asked you how Sid was… I'd like to see her some time—"

"She's real busy with her studies, catching up with school after all the time she lost."

"That's good. She's whip smart."

"Yep, that she is."

"Maybe I could come by some time, teach her how to play guitar…"

Zinnia cut her eyes at her. "I don't think so. That child done been through enough."

"I made some mistakes and I want to own up to them."

Zinnia watched the kids scamper in and out of the car. "Join the club. Fortunately, she's twelve, not a hundred and twelve. Got a bright future ahead of her."

Divinity strode back over to Rory. Business cards fluttered from her hand onto the ground. "You're not better than me, hear? If the House wanted your shit again you'd sell yourself in a second. And if the white lady ponies up more money, you'll be crawling right back to us."

"Not likely. I'll see all of y'all in court."

Rory went back inside the bus. She heard the kids squeal as Divinity started up the engine, battle-axe belching all the way to the next county.

Four a.m., and a clock radio alarm cut on playing "Moon River" then "Boogie Fever", like two station signals had mated, spat out a mutant baby, took a branding iron to the sleeping trailer park, waking everyone up. More than twenty families had had their power shut off by Water and Power for nonpayment after the meter reader left. No TVs, no radios, no lights, no heat.

"Motherless Child" came on the radio. The GOP had adopted the song as their campaign anthem to stick it to Carter and the Democrats, accusing them of running the country into the ground, treating the hinterlands, the small towns, Main Streets, and burbs like orphans in the march to Commie enslavement. After Jude sang it at the revival, it blazed to number one on the pop charts, going to platinum in seventeen different countries, giving her another skinny dip in the fountain of youth. The news of her contribution to a little Black girl reverberated through the music industry. She was a beacon of humanitarianism. A pork rind and whiskey inhaling Mother Teresa. A guiding light for all the sagging, dragging, sperm pumping white boy rockers frantic for a career boost and global cred. Awards flowed, dignitaries called, and Lavender stepped up to head her new foundation, Womyn's Roar Infinity, grooming her for a second act as an elder stateswoman scrubbed of disreputableness, ready for the wild ride of the eighties.

After Rory had gone to bed, she'd gotten two messages from the manager's office. A producer from Los Angeles. A girl who wouldn't give her name but left a number. She called the second number at noon the next day on an empty, Tums bloated stomach. It rang a hundred times until someone picked up. Car horns blasted in the distance, then the phone went dead.

Half of the park basked in shadow. Blotted out by the generators towering omnisciently overhead. A group of teens prowled around a rusted TV on the office porch, watching Gomer Pyle reruns. When Rory walked by them in the morning to pay her rent, they snickered, writing her off as the weird old bitch with no job fucking the fat honky as a hustle to keep out of bankruptcy court. They had fun selling wolf tickets speculating about what went on in the bus, making a soap opera out of her backstory. When the beer commercial of her band broke, the disdain turned to muted awe. It was ten seconds of Rory and the boys riffing in the background to a white couple dry humping a bar stool. Listen to that old lady get her Geritol swigging groove on.

The bank would call when the money cleared. Then she'd be on the first thing smoking out of Arkansas. Finalize a spot with the Los Angeles producer. Cut a new record. Hook up with an attorney. Live on a California beach for a little while. Stowaway in a sandcastle. Surf the carcass of Brian Wilson. Locate the bomb in her head.

She tried the phone number again. A person answered on the third ring. Traffic rustled through the receiver, the din of a dive night club, instrument tunings, her voice slurring the high notes of "Swallow You Whole" when it was still chicken scratch on the back of a napkin.

"Sid?"

The generators murmured under the roar of the audience, clapping, catcalling, chanting her name.

Folks always made California out to be some sort of paradise, Katy said on the other end of the line.

Rory slammed the phone down and ran back to the bus. She rummaged in the glove compartment for chips, crackers, any old shit to take the edge off her hunger.

California didn't do us no better than anywhere else, though, Katy continued.

—It'd be a new start. Got a producer out there who wants to work with me.

—Pipe dream.

—No, it ain't.

—Just gotta make sure they don't scrape your ass right off the beach with the high tide.

—If my record sold, I could invest in some cheap real estate. Maybe start my own label.

—Cheap and Los Angeles is like oil and water.

—I've been reading up on real estate deals.

—Cheap and Los Angeles is a bunch of snake oil.

—Saw it with my own eyes in the newspaper.

—Seem to recall you playing Central Avenue in '63. Little Jack Horner pipsqueak guitarist trying to upstage you didn't know his head from a hole in the ground. That was a real good show, baby.

She stretched her arms out to Rory, drawing her close, onto her lap.

The shadows had gotten longer. Rory rose up from Katy's lap and walked off the bus, going to the back to turn on the mobile generator she kept for power outages. The space where she kept it was empty. She stuck her head through the door, panting with rage over the stolen machine.

She went to the bathroom to look for a lighter. Butch had kept some for his bongs under the sink. She tested a few until she found a good one, the dim sliver of fire dancing through the aisle, catching Katy's eyes as she swiveled around toward Rory. The same gouged out unrecognizable eyes that had tracked her at birth and would hunt her down in the afterlife.

A car drove into the driveway of the trailer park. Rory heard it stop at the office by the pay phone. It made its way slowly down, tires crunching on gravel as she held the lighter in front of her and walked down the aisle of the bus toward the grinning skull peeking through the hollowed-out mask of what had once been her mother's face.

Rory flinched at the sight, tripping, the sizzle of the generators rising to a white drone as the lighter fell onto the seat and caught fire, flames licking, leaping to the next row.

—Go on, now! Katy hissed, handing Rory the Gibson.

She strapped it on. A minor, to E minor, to G, ricocheting through her head like the time when she was first starting to stretch her fingers across the frets and they'd come up bruised, strings of barbed wire on the tips.

—*Teach me how to play*, a voice said from the fire, bursting into orange butterflies, pieces of black highway, busted radio guts from the Cadillac outside where Sid sat behind the wheel.

Rory tripped down the stairs of the bus, gulping smoke and darkness, clawing sky and stars.

The child watched for a moment, listening to the music of the flames pop and hiss. She pressed the record button on the cassette player on her lap and opened the door.

"Get in."

Acknowledgments

I'd like to express appreciation to my loved ones for their long-time, unqualified support of my writing and artistic work: My family Stephen Kelley, Jasmine Hutchinson Kelley, Earl Ofari Hutchinson, Yvonne Divans Hutchinson, Fanon Hutchinson, and Barbara Bramwell and dear friends Heather Aubry, Kamela Heyward-Rotimi, Von Hurt, and Sumitra Mukerji have all been an invaluable and treasured part of this journey.

Made in the USA
Columbia, SC
16 May 2021